P9-CEQ-889

SUMMER ISLAND

Also by Kristin Hannah

Angel Falls

On Mystic Lake

KRISTIN

HANNAH

Summer Island

A Novel

CROWN PUBLISHERS

NEW YORK

Published by Crown Publishers, New York, New York.
Member of the Crown Publishing Group.

Random House, Inc. New York, Toronto, London, Sydney, Auckland
www.randomhouse.com

CROWN is a trademark and the Crown colophon is a registered trademark of
Random House, Inc.

Printed in the United States of America

Library of Congress Cataloging-in-Publication Data
Hannah, Kristin.
　Summer Island / by Kristin Hannah.
　1. Women Comedians—Fiction.　2. Mothers and daughters—Fiction.　3. Los Angeles
(Calif.)—Fiction.　4. Washington (State)—Fiction.　5. Biographers—Fiction.
6. Extortion—Fiction.　I. Title.

PS3558.A4763 S86 2001
813'.54—dc21　　　　　　　　　　　　　　　　　　　　　　　　　00-047325

ISBN 0-609-60737-5

10 9 8 7 6 5 4 3 2 1

First Edition

In memory of my mother,

Sharon Goodno John

Acknowledgments

Thanks to Gina Centrello, Shauna Summers, George Fisher, and the whole Ballantine team for making 2000 so memorable.

Thanks to Chip Gibson, Steve Ross, Andrew Martin, Joan De Mayo, Barbara Marks, Whitney Cookman, Alison Gross, and everyone at Crown Publishers.

Thanks to Kim Fisk for keeping me (as much as possible) on track.

Thanks to Ann Patty and Megan Chance again, for everything.

Last but not least, thanks to my family. I was blessed to be born into a great clan. So, here's to Kent and Laura and Dad. We're lucky to be friends as well as family.

And to the "Canadian contingent"—Uncle Frank, Aunt Toni, Leslie, Jacqui, Dana, and, of course, to Johnsie, the first storyteller.

And most important, to Tucker and Benjamin, who teach me a little more about love every day.

PART ONE

"There is only the fight to recover what has been lost
And found and lost again and again: and now under conditions
That seem unpropitious. But perhaps neither gain nor loss.
For us, there is only the trying. The rest is not our business."

T. S. ELIOT, FROM "EAST COKER"

Chapter One

An early evening rain had fallen. In the encroaching darkness, the streets of Seattle lay like mirrored strips between the glittering gray high-rises.

The dot-com revolution had changed this once quiet city, and even after the sun had set, the clattering, hammering sounds of construction beat a constant rhythm. Buildings sprouted overnight, it seemed, reaching higher and higher into the soggy sky. Purple-haired kids with nose rings and ragged clothes zipped through downtown in brand-new, bright-red Ferraris.

On a corner lot in the newly fashionable neighborhood of Belltown, there was a squat, wooden-sided structure that used to sit alone. It had been built almost one hundred years earlier, when few people had wanted to live so far from the heart of the city.

The owners of radio station KJZZ didn't care that they no longer fit in this trendy area. For fifty years they had broadcast from this lot. They had grown from a scrappy local station to Washington's largest.

Part of the reason for their current wave of success was Nora Bridge, the newest sensation in talk radio.

Although her show, *Spiritual Healing with Nora,* had been in syndication for less than a year, it was already a bona fide hit. Advertisers and affiliates couldn't write checks fast enough, and her weekly newspaper advice column, "Nora Knows Best," had never been more popular. It appeared in more than 2,600 papers nationwide.

Nora had started her career as a household hints adviser for a small-town newspaper, but hard work and a strong vision had moved her up the food chain. The women of Seattle had been the first to discover her unique blend of passion and morality; the rest of the country had soon followed.

Reviewers claimed that she could see a way through any emotional conflict; more often than not, they mentioned the purity of her heart.

But they were wrong. It was the *impurity* in her heart that made her successful. She was an ordinary woman who'd made extraordinary mistakes. She understood every nuance of need and loss.

There was never a time in her life, barely even a moment, when she didn't remember what she'd lost. What she'd thrown away. Each night she brought her own regrets to the microphone, and from that wellspring of sorrow, she found compassion.

She had managed her career with laserlike focus, carefully feeding the press a palatable past. Even the previous week when *People* magazine had featured her on the cover, there had been no investigative story on her life. She had covered her tracks well. Her fans knew she'd been divorced and that she had grown daughters. The hows and whys of her family's destruction remained—thankfully—private.

Tonight, Nora was on the air. She scooted her wheeled chair closer to the microphone and adjusted her headphones. A computer screen showed her the list of callers on hold. She pushed line two, which read: *Marge/mother–daughter probs.*

"Hello and welcome, Marge, you're on the air with Nora Bridge. What's on your mind this evening?"

"Hello . . . Nora?" The caller sounded hesitant, a little startled at actually hearing her voice on the air after waiting on hold for nearly an hour.

Nora smiled, although only her producer could see it. Her fans, she'd learned, were often anxious. She lowered her voice, gentled it. "How can I help you, my friend?"

"I'm having a little trouble with my daughter, Suki." The caller's flattened vowels identified her as a midwesterner.

"How old is Suki, Marge?"

"Sixty-seven this November."

Nora laughed. "I guess some things never change, eh, Marge?"

"Not between mothers and daughters. Suki gave me my first gray hair when I was thirty years old. Now I look like Colonel Sanders."

Nora's laugh was quieter this time. At forty-nine, she no longer found gray hair a laughing matter. "So, Marge, what's the problem with Suki?"

"Well." Marge made a snorting sound. "Last week she went on one of those singles cruises—you know the ones, where they all wear Hawaiian shirts and drink purple cocktails? Anyway, today, she told me she's getting married again to a man she met on the boat. At *her* age." She snorted again, then paused. "I know she wanted me to be happy for her, but how could I? Suki's a flibbertigibbet. My Tommy and I were married for seventy years."

Nora considered how to answer. Obviously, Marge knew that she and Suki weren't young anymore, and that time had a way of pulverizing your best intentions. There was no point in being maudlin and mentioning it. Instead, she asked gently, "Do you love your daughter?"

"I've always loved her." Marge's voice caught on a little sob. "You can't know what it's like, Nora, to love your daughter so much . . . and watch her stop needing you. What if she marries this man and forgets all about me?"

Nora closed her eyes and cleared her mind. She'd learned that skill long ago; callers were constantly saying things that struck at the heart of her own pain. She'd had to learn to let it go. "Every mother is afraid of that, Marge. The only way to really hold on to our children is to let them go. Let Suki take your love with her, let it be like a light that's always on in the house where she grew up. If she has that for strength, she'll never be too far away."

Marge wept softly. "Maybe I could call her . . . ask her to bring her boyfriend around for supper."

"That would be a wonderful start. Good luck to you, Marge, and be sure and let us know how it all works out." She cleared her throat and disconnected the call. "Come on, everybody," she said into the microphone, "let's help Marge out. I know there are plenty of you who have mended families. Call in. Marge and I want to be reminded that love isn't as fragile as it sometimes feels."

She leaned back in the chair, watching as the phone lines lit up. Parenting issues were always a popular topic—especially mother-daughter problems. On the monitor by her elbow, she saw the words: *line four/trouble with stepdaughter/Ginny.*

She picked up line four. "Hello and welcome, Ginny. You're on the air with Nora Bridge."

"Uh. Hi. I love your show."

"Thanks, Ginny. How are things in your family?"

For the next two hours and thirteen minutes, Nora gave her heart and soul to her listeners. She never pretended to have all the answers, or to be a substitute for doctors or family therapy. Instead, she tried to give her friendship to these troubled, ordinary people she'd never met.

As was her custom, when the show was finally over, she returned to her office. There, she took the time to write personal thank-you notes to any of those callers who'd been willing to leave an address with the show's producer. She always did this herself; no secretary ever copied Nora's signature. It was a little thing, but Nora firmly believed in it. Anyone who'd been courageous enough to publicly ask for advice from Nora deserved a private thank-you.

By the time she finished, she was running late.

She grabbed her Fendi briefcase and hurried to her car. Fortunately, it was only a few miles to the hospital. She parked in the underground lot and emerged into the lobby's artificial brightness.

It was past visiting hours, but this was a small, privately run hospital, and Nora had become such a regular visitor—every Saturday and Tuesday for the past month—that certain rules had been bent to accommodate her busy schedule. It didn't hurt that she was a local celebrity, or that the nurses loved her radio show.

She smiled and waved to the familiar faces as she walked down the corridor toward Eric's room. Outside his closed door, she paused, collecting herself.

Although she saw him often, it was never easy. Eric Sloan was as close to a son as she would ever have, and watching him battle cancer was unbearable. But Nora was all he had. His mother and father had written Eric off long ago, unable to accept his life's choices, and his beloved younger brother, Dean, rarely made time to visit.

She pushed open the door to his room and saw that he was sleeping. He lay in bed, with his head turned toward the window. A multicolored afghan, knitted by Nora's own hands, was wrapped around his too-thin body.

With his hair almost gone and his cheeks hollowed and his mouth open, he looked as old and beaten as a man could be. And he hadn't yet celebrated his thirty-first birthday.

For a moment, it was as if she hadn't seen him before. As if . . . although she'd watched his daily deterioration, she hadn't actually *seen* it, and now it had sneaked up on her, stolen her friend's face while she was foolishly pretending that everything would be all right.

But it wouldn't be. Just now, this second, she understood what he'd been trying to tell her, and the grieving—which she'd managed to box into tiny, consumable squares—threatened to overwhelm her. In that one quiet heartbeat of time, she went from hopeful to . . . not. And if it hurt her this terribly, the lack of hope, how could he bear it?

She went to him, gently caressed the bare top of his head. The few thin strands of his hair, delicate as spiderwebs, brushed across her knuckles.

He blinked up at her sleepily, trying for a boyish grin and almost succeeding. "I have good news and bad news," he said.

She touched his shoulder, and felt how fragile he was. So unlike the tall, strapping black-haired boy who'd carried her groceries into the house . . .

There was a tiny catch in her voice as she said cheerfully, "What's the good news?"

"No more treatments."

She clutched his shoulder too hard; his bones shifted, birdlike, and immediately she let go. "And the bad news?"

His gaze was steady. "No more treatments." He paused. "It was Dr. Calomel's idea."

She nodded dully, wishing she could think of something profound to say, but everything had already been said between them in the eleven months since his diagnosis. They'd spent dozens of nights talking about and around this moment. She'd even thought she was ready for it—this beginning of the end—but now she saw her naïveté. There was no "ready" for death, especially not when it came for a young man you loved.

And yet, she understood. She'd seen lately that the cancer was taking him away.

He closed his eyes, and she wondered if he was remembering the healthy, vibrant man he'd once been, the boy with the booming laugh . . . the teacher so beloved by his students . . . or if he was recalling the time, a few years before, when his partner, Charlie, had been in a hospital bed like this one, fighting a losing battle with AIDS . . .

Finally, he looked up at her; his attempt at a smile brought tears to her eyes. In that second, she saw pieces from the whole of his life. She pictured him at eight, sitting at her kitchen table, eating Lucky Charms, a shaggy-haired, freckle-faced boy with banged-up knees and soup-ladle ears.

"I'm going home," he said quietly. "Hospice will help out . . ."

"That's great," she said thickly, smiling too brightly, trying to pretend they were talking about where he was going to live . . . instead of where he'd chosen to die. "I'm way ahead on my newspaper columns. I'll take the week off, visit you during the day. I'll still have to work the show at night, but—"

"I mean the island. I'm going *home*."

"Are you finally going to call your family?" She hated his decision to handle his cancer privately, but he'd been adamant. He'd forbidden Nora to tell anyone, and as much as she'd disagreed, she'd had no choice but to honor his wishes.

"Oh, yeah. They've been so supportive in the past."

"This is different than coming out of the closet, and you know it. It's time to call Dean. And your parents."

The look he gave her was so hopeless that she wanted to turn away. "What if I told my mother I was dying and she still wouldn't come to see me?"

Nora understood. Even a thin blade of that hope could cut him to pieces now. "At least call your brother. Give him the chance."

"I'll think about it."

"That's all I ask." She forced a smile. "If you can wait until Tuesday, I'll drive you—"

He touched her hand gently. "I haven't got much time. I've arranged to be flown up. Lottie's already up at the house, getting it ready."

Haven't got much time. It was infinitely worse, somehow, to hear the words spoken aloud. She swallowed hard. "I don't think you should be alone."

"Enough." His voice was soft, his gaze even softer, but she heard the barest echo of his former strength. He was reminding her, as he sometimes had to, that he was an adult, a grown man. "Now," he said, clapping his hands together, "we sound like a goddamn Ibsen play. Let's talk about something else. I listened to your show tonight. Mothers and daughters. That's always tough on you."

Just like that, he put them back on solid ground. As always, she was amazed by his resilience. When life seemed too big to swallow, she knew he made it through by cutting it into bites. Normal things . . . ordinary conversations were his salvation.

She pulled up a chair and sat down. "I never really know what to say, and when I do offer advice, I feel like the biggest hypocrite on the planet. How would Marge feel if she knew I hadn't spoken to my own daughter in eleven years?"

Eric didn't answer the rhetorical question. It was one of the things she loved best about him. He never tried to comfort her with lies. But it helped her that someone recognized how painful it was for Nora to think about her younger daughter. "I wonder what she's doing now."

It was a common question between them, one they speculated about endlessly.

Eric managed a laugh. "With Ruby it could be anything from having lunch with Steven Spielberg to piercing her tongue."

"The last time I talked to Caroline, she said that Ruby had dyed her hair blue." Nora laughed, then fell abruptly silent. It wasn't funny. "Ruby always had such pretty hair . . ."

Eric leaned forward. There was a sudden earnestness in his eyes. "She's not dead, Nora."

She nodded. "I know. I try to squeeze hope from that thought all the time."

He grinned. "Now, get out the backgammon board. I feel like whooping your ass."

It was only the second week of June, and already the temperature hovered around one hundred degrees. A freak heat wave they called it on the local news, the kind of weather that usually came to southern California later in the year.

The heat made people crazy. They woke from their damp bed-sheets and went in search of a glass of water, surprised to find that when their vision cleared, they were holding instead the gun they kept hidden in the bookcase. Children cried out in their sleep, and even doses of liquid Tylenol couldn't cool their fevered skin. All over town, birds fell from phone wires and landed in pathetic, crumpled heaps on the thirsty lawns.

No one could sleep in weather like this, and Ruby Bridge was no exception. She lay sprawled in her bed, the sheets shoved down to the floor, a cold-pack pressed across her forehead.

The minutes ticked by, each one a moaning sound caught in the window air-conditioning unit, a *whoosh-ping* that did little but stir the hot air around.

She was lonely. Only a few days earlier, her boyfriend, Max, had left her. After five years of living together, he'd simply walked out of her life like a plumber who'd finished an unpleasant job.

All he'd left behind was a few pieces of crappy furniture and a note.

Dear Ruby:
I never meant to fall out of love with you (or into love with Angie)
but shit happens. You know how it is. I need to be free. Hell, we both
know you never really loved me anyway.
Be cool.
Max.

The funny thing was (and it definitely wasn't ha-ha funny), she hardly missed him. In fact, she didn't miss *him* at all. She missed the idea of him. She missed a second plate at the dinner table, another body in this bed that seemed to have enlarged in his absence. Mostly, she missed the pretense that she was in love.

Max had been . . . hope. A physical embodiment of the belief that she could love, and be loved in return.

At seven A.M., the alarm clock sounded. Ruby slid out of bed on a sluglike trail of perspiration. The wobbly pressboard headboard banged against the wall. Her bra and panties stuck to her damp body. She reached for the glass of water by the bed, pressed it to the valley between her breasts, and went to the bathroom, where she took a lukewarm shower.

She was sweating again before she was finished drying off. With a tired sigh, she headed into the kitchen and made a pot of coffee. She poured herself a cup, then added a generous splash of cream. White chunks immediately floated to the surface and formed a cross.

Another woman might have thought simply that the cream had gone bad, but Ruby knew better: it was a sign.

As if she needed magic to tell her that she was stuck in the spin cycle of her life.

She tossed the mess down the sink and headed back into her bedroom, grabbing the grease-stained black polyester pants and white cotton blouse that lay tangled on the floor. Sweating, headachy, and in desperate need of caffeine, she got dressed and went out into the stifling heat.

She walked downstairs to her battered 1970 Volkswagen Bug. After a few tries, the engine turned over, and Ruby drove toward Irma's Hash House, the trendy Venice Beach diner where she'd worked for almost three years.

She'd never meant to *stay* a waitress; the job was supposed to be temporary, something to pay the bills until she got on her feet, caused a sensation at one of the local comedy clubs, did a guest spot on Leno, and—finally—was offered her own sitcom, aptly titled *Ruby!* She always pictured it with an exclamation mark, like one of those Vegas revues her grandmother had loved.

But at twenty-seven, she wasn't young anymore. After almost a decade spent trying to break into comedy, she was brushing up against "too old." Everyone knew that if you didn't make it by thirty, you were toast. And Ruby was beginning to think that she should start collecting jam.

Finally, she maneuvered between the old station wagons and Volkswagen buses that filled the 1950s-style diner's crowded parking lot. Surfboards were lashed to every surface; most of the cars had more bumper stickers than paint. The sun-bleached "hey dude" set came from miles away for Irma's famous six-egg omelette. She parked alongside a bus that could have come from *Fast Times at Ridgemont High*.

She forced a smile onto her face and headed for the diner. When she opened the front door, the bell tinkled gaily overhead.

Irma bustled toward her, her three-story beehive hairdo leading the way. As always, she moved fast, keeled forward like the prow of a sinking ship, then came to an abrupt halt in front of Ruby. Her heavily mascaraed eyes narrowed, and Ruby wondered—again—if human beings could be carbon-dated by makeup. "You were scheduled for last night."

Ruby winced. "Oh, shit."

Irma crossed her bony arms. "I'm letting you go. We can't count on you. Debbie had to work a double shift last night. Your final paycheck is at the register. I'll expect the uniform back tomorrow. Cleaned."

Ruby's lips trembled mutinously. The thought of pleading for this shitty job made her sick. "Come on, Irma, I *need* this job."

"I'm sorry, Ruby. Really." Irma turned and walked away.

Ruby stood there a minute, breathing in the familiar mixture of maple syrup and grease, then she snagged her paycheck from the counter and walked out of the restaurant.

She got in her car and drove away aimlessly, up one street and down the other. Finally, when it felt as if her face were melting off her skull, she parked alongside the street in a shopping district. In the trendy, air-conditioned boutiques, she saw dozens of beautiful things she couldn't afford, sold by girls who were half her age. She realized she was close to hitting rock bottom when a HELP WANTED sign on a pet-store window actually caught her attention.

No way. It was bad enough serving beef sludge to the Butt family. She'd be damned if she'd sell them a ferret, too.

She got back into her car and drove away, this time speeding recklessly toward her destination. When she reached Wilshire Boulevard, she pulled up in front of a high-rise building and parked.

Before she had time to talk herself out of it, she went to the elevator and rode it up to the top floor. When the doors opened, sweet, cooled air greeted her, drying the sweat on her cheeks.

She walked briskly down the hallway toward her agent's office and pushed through the frosted-glass double doors.

The receptionist, Maudeen Wachsmith, had her nose buried in a romance novel. Barely looking up, she smiled. "Hi, Ruby," she said. "He's busy today. You'll have to make an appointment."

Ruby rushed past Maudeen and yanked the door open.

Her agent, Valentine Lightner, was there, seated behind the glassy expanse of his desk. He looked up. When he saw Ruby, his smile faded into a frown. "Ruby . . . I wasn't expecting you . . . was I?"

Maudeen rushed in behind Ruby. "I'm sorry, Mr. Lightner . . ."

He raised a slim hand. "Don't worry about it, Maudeen." He leaned back in his chair. "So, Ruby, what's going on?"

She waited for Maudeen to leave, then moved toward the desk. She was humiliatingly aware that she was still wearing her uniform, and that her underarms were outlined in perspiration. "Is that cruise ship job still available?" She'd laughed at it three months before—cruise ships were floating morgues for talent—but now it didn't seem beneath her. Hell, it seemed above her.

"I've *tried* for you, Ruby. You write funny stuff, but the truth is, your delivery sucks. And that's no ordinary chip on your shoulder, it's a section of the Hoover Dam. You've burned too many bridges in this business. No one wants to hire you."

"Someone—"

"No one. Remember the job I got you on that sitcom? You slowed down the first week's production and made everyone insane with rewrites."

"My character was an idiot. She didn't have one funny line."

Val looked at her, his ice-blue eyes narrowed slowly. "Shall I remind you that the show's still on the air and another—less talented—comedian is making thirty thousand dollars an episode saying what she's told to say?"

"It's a shitty show." Ruby collapsed into the plush leather chair in front of his desk. It took her a moment to squeeze her ego into a tiny box. "I'm broke. Irma fired me from the diner."

"Why don't you call your mother?"

She closed her eyes for a second, drawing in a deep breath. "Don't go there, Val," she said quietly.

"I know, I know, she's the bitch from hell. But come on, Ruby, I saw that article in *People*. She's rich and famous. Maybe she could help you."

"You're rich and famous and you can't help me. Besides, she's *helped* me enough. Any more motherly attention and I could end up strapped to a table in Ward B singing 'I Gotta Be Me.'" Ruby got to her feet. It took a supreme effort, considering that she wanted to curl into a ball and sleep. "Well, thanks for nothing, Val."

"It's that sparkling personality that makes helping you so damned easy." He sighed. "I'll try Asia. They love U.S. comedians overseas. Maybe you can do the nightclub circuit."

It made her feel sick, just thinking about it. "Telling jokes to a translator." She winced, imagining herself in one of those men's bars, with naked women writhing up and down polished silver poles behind her. She'd already put in her time in joints like that. Her whole youth had been spent in the shadows behind another performer's light. "Maybe it's time for me to give up. Cash in. Throw in the towel."

Val looked at her. "What would you do?"

Not, *don't do that, Ruby; you're too talented to give up*. That's what he'd said six years earlier.

"I've got half an English lit degree from UCLA. Maybe it would get me a supervisor spot at Burger King."

"You certainly have the right personality for serving the public."

She couldn't help laughing. She'd been with Val a long time, since her first days at the Comedy Store. Val had always been her champion, her biggest fan, but in the past few years, she'd disappointed him, and somehow that was worse than disappointing herself. She'd become hard to work with, temperamental, difficult to place, and, worst of all, unfunny. Val could overcome anything except that. She didn't know what was wrong with her, either. Except that she seemed to be angry all the time. She should be standing on a ledge somewhere. "I appreciate everything you've done for me, Val. Really, I know it's hard to get work for a prima donna with no talent."

The moment the words were out, Ruby heard what lay beneath them. Hesitant, afraid, but there nonetheless. A good-bye. And the worst part was that she knew Val heard the same thing, and he didn't say *no, don't do that, we're a long way from over.*

Instead, he said, "You have as much raw talent as anyone I've ever seen. You light up a goddamn room with your smile, and your wit is as sharp as a blade." He leaned toward her. "Let me ask you a question. When did you stop smiling, Ruby?"

She knew the answer, of course. It had happened in her junior year of high school, but she wouldn't think about that time—not even to give Val an answer.

Objects in a mirror are closer than they appear. That was true of memories as well; it was best not to look.

"I don't know." She spoke softly, refusing to meet his gaze. She wished she could let Val see how frightened she was, how alone she felt. She thought that if she could do that, if she could for once show a friend her vulnerability, she would perhaps be saved.

But she couldn't do it. No matter how hard she tried, Ruby couldn't let down her guard. Her emotions were packed tightly inside her, hermetically sealed so that every wound and memory stayed fresh.

"Well," she said at last, straightening her shoulders, puffing out her unimpressive chest. She had the fleeting sense that she looked absurd, a wounded sparrow trying to impress a peregrine falcon. "I guess I'd better go. I'll need to pick up some fishnet hose and a can of Mace if I'm going to start hooking."

Val smiled wanly. "I'll make the calls about Asia. We'll talk in a few days."

"I'm grateful." She would have added more, maybe even groveled a little, but her throat seemed swollen shut.

Val came around the desk and closed the distance between them. She saw the sadness in his eyes, and the regret. "You lost yourself," he said quietly.

"I know."

"Listen to me, Ruby. I know about getting lost. You need to start over."

She swallowed hard. This sort of honesty was more at home in other parts of the country, where time was measured in seasons or tides. Here in L.A., time elapsed in thirty-second spots; true emotion didn't thrive under that kind of pressure. "Don't worry about me, Val. I'm a survivor. Now, I'm going to go home and learn to speak Japanese."

He squeezed her shoulder. "That's my girl."

"Sayonara." She wiggled her fingers in an oh-so-California-darling wave and did her best to sashay out of the office. It was tough to pull off, sashaying in a sweat-stained waitress uniform, and the minute she was out of his office, she let go of her fake smile. She walked dully into the elevator and rode it down to the lobby, then headed for her car. The Volkswagen looked like a half-dead june bug, huddled alongside the parking meter. When she got inside, she immediately winced. The seat was scorchingly hot.

There was a parking ticket on her windshield.

She rolled down her window and reached out, yanking the paper from beneath the rusted windshield wiper. She wadded it into a ball and tossed it out the window. To her mind, ticketing this rattrap and expecting to get paid was like leaving a bill on the pillow at a homeless shelter.

Before the ticket even hit the street, she'd started the engine and pulled out onto Wilshire Boulevard, where she was immediately swallowed into the stream of traffic.

In Studio City, the streets were quieter. A few neighborhood kids played lethargically in their small front yards. With the risk of fire so high, there was no wasting water for things like slip-n-slides or sprinklers.

Ruby maneuvered past a big, drooling Saint Bernard who lay sleeping in the middle of the street, and pulled up to the curb in front of her apartment complex.

Sopping her forehead, she headed up the stairs. No one came out to say hello; it was too damned hot. Her neighbors were probably huddled in family pods around the window-unit air conditioners in their apartments—the modern L.A. equivalent of cavemen camped around the marvel of fire.

By the time she reached her floor, Ruby was wheezing so badly she sounded like Shelley Winters after her swim in *The Poseidon Adventure,* and she was practically that wet. Sweat slid down her forehead and caught on her eyelashes, blurring everything.

It took her a moment to open her door; it always did. The shag carpeting had pulled up along the threshold. She finally crammed the door open and stumbled through the opening.

She stood there, breathing hard, staring at the wretched furniture in her dismal little apartment, and felt the hot sting of tears.

Absurdly, she thought: If only it would rain.

Her whole day might have been different if the damned weather had changed.

Chapter Two

June was a hard month in Seattle. It was in this season, when the school bells rang for the last time and the peonies and delphiniums bloomed, that the locals began to complain that they'd been cheated. The rains had started in October (invariably Seattleites swore it had come early this year); by the last week in May, even the meteorically challenged denizens of Seattle had had enough. They watched the news religiously, seeing the first tantalizing shots of people swimming in the warm waters farther south. Relatives began to call, talking on cell phones as they stood outside to barbecue. Summer had come to every other corner of America.

The locals saw it as a matter of fairness. They *deserved* summer. They'd put up with nine solid months of dismal weather and it was past time for the sun to deliver.

So, it was hardly surprising that it rained on the day Nora Bridge celebrated her fiftieth birthday. She didn't take the weather as an omen or a portent of bad luck.

In retrospect, she should have.

Instead, she simply thought: Rain. Of course. It almost always rained on her birthday.

She stood at the window in her office, sipping her favorite drink—Mumm's champagne with a slice of fresh peach—and stared out at the traffic on Broad Street. It was four-thirty. Rush hour in a city that had outgrown its highway system ten years ago.

On her windowsill, dozens of birthday cards fanned along the gleaming strip of bird's-eye maple.

She'd received cards and gifts from everyone who worked on her radio show. Each one was appropriate and lovely, but the most treasured card had come from her elder daughter, Caroline.

Of course, the joy of that card was tempered by the fact that, again this year, there had been no card from Ruby.

"You'll be fine tomorrow," she spoke softly to her own reflection, captured in the rainy window.

She gave herself a little time to wallow in regret—ache for the card that wasn't there—and then she rallied. Fifteen years of therapy had granted her this skill; she could compartmentalize.

In the past few years, she'd finally gotten a grip on her tumultuous emotions. The breakdowns and depressions that had once plagued her life were now a distant, painful memory.

She turned away from the window and glanced at the crystal clock on her desk. It was four-thirty-eight.

They were down in the conference room now, setting out food, bottles of champagne, plates filled with peach slices. Assistants, publicists, staff writers, producers, they were all preparing to spend an hour of their valuable personal time to put together a "surprise" party for the newest star of talk radio.

She set her champagne flute down on her desk and opened one of her drawers, pulling out a small black Chanel makeup case. She touched up her face, then headed out of the office.

The hallways were unusually quiet. Probably everyone was helping out with the party. At precisely four forty-five, Nora walked into the conference room.

It was empty.

The long table was bare; no food was spread out, no tiny bits of colored confetti lay scattered on the floor. A happy-birthday banner hung from the overhead lights. It looked as if someone had started to decorate for a party and then suddenly stopped.

It was a moment before she noticed the two men standing to her left: Bob Wharton, the station's owner and manager, and Jason Close, the lead in-house attorney.

Nora smiled warmly. "Hello, Bob. Jason," she said, moving toward them. "It's good to see you."

The men exchanged a quick glance.

She felt a prickling of unease. "Bob?"

Bob's fleshy face, aged by two-martini lunches and twenty-cigarette days, creased into a frown. "We have some bad news."

"Bad news?"

Jason eased past Bob and came up to Nora. His steel-gray hair was perfectly combed. A black Armani suit made him look like a forty-year-old mafia don. "Earlier today, Bob took a call from a man named Vince Corell."

Nora felt as if she'd been smacked in the face. The air rushed out of her lungs.

"He claimed he'd had an affair with you while you were married. He wanted us to pay him to keep quiet."

"Jesus, Nora," Bob sputtered angrily. "A goddamn *affair*. While your kids were at home. You should have told us."

She'd told her readers and listeners a thousand times to be strong. *Never let them see you're afraid. Believe in yourself and people will believe in you.* But now that she needed that strength, it was gone. "I could say he was lying," she said, wincing when she heard the breathy, desperate tone of her voice.

Jason opened his briefcase and pulled out a manila envelope. "Here."

Nora's hands were shaking as she took the envelope and opened it.

There were black-and-white photographs inside. She pulled out the top sheet. It wasn't more than halfway out when she saw what it was.

"Oh, God," she whispered. She reached out for the chair nearest her and clutched the metal back. Only pure willpower kept her from sinking to her knees. She crammed the pictures back into the envelope.

"There must be a way to stop this." She looked at Jason. "An injunction. Those are private photographs."

"Yes, they are. His. It's obvious that you . . . knew the camera was there. You're posing. He's probably been waiting all this time for you to become famous. That piece in *People* must have done it."

She drew in a deep breath and looked at them. "How much does he want?"

There was a pregnant pause, after which Jason stepped closer. "A half million dollars."

"I can get that amount—"

"Money never kills this kind of thing, Nora. You know that. Sooner or later it'll come out."

She understood immediately. "You told him no," she said woodenly. "And now he's going to the tabloids."

Jason nodded. "I'm sorry, Nora."

"I can explain this to my fans," she said. "Bob? They'll underst—"

"You give *moral* advice, Nora." Bob shook his head. "This is going to be a hell of a scandal. Jesus, we've been promoting you as a modern version of Mother Teresa. Now it turns out you're Debbie Does Dallas."

Nora flinched. "Not fair, Bob."

"Believe us," Jason said. "The trailer-park set in Small-town U.S.A. will *not* understand that their idol just had to be free."

Bob nodded. "When these photos hit the air, we'll lose advertisers instantly."

Nora clasped her trembling hands and tried to appear calm. She knew it wasn't working. "What do we do?"

A pause. A look. Then Jason said, "We want you to take some time off."

It was all coming at her too fast. She couldn't think straight. All she knew was that she couldn't give up. This career was all she had. "I can't—"

Jason moved closer, touched her shoulder gently. "You've spent the better part of the past decade telling people to honor their commitments and put their families first. How long do you think it will take the press to uncover that you haven't spoken to your own daughter since the divorce? Your advice is going to ring a little hollow after that."

Bob nodded. "The press is going to rip you limb from limb, Nora. Not because you deserve it, but because they can. The tabloids love a celebrity in trouble . . . and with sexy pictures. Hell, they'll be jumpin' up and down over this."

And just like that, Nora's life slipped beyond her grasp.

"It'll blow over," she whispered, knowing in her heart that it wasn't true, or if it was true, it wouldn't matter, not in the end. Some winds were hurricane force and they demolished everything in their path. "I'll take a few weeks off. See what happens. Spend some time coming up with a statement."

"For the record," Jason said, "this is a scheduled vacation. We won't admit that it has anything to do with the scandal."

"Thank you."

"I hope you make it through this," Jason said. "We all do."

Jason and Bob both spoke at once, then an awkward silence descended. Nora heard them walk past her. The door clicked shut behind them.

She stood there, alone now, her gaze blurred by tears she couldn't hold back anymore. After eleven years of working seventy-hour weeks, it was over.

Poof. Her life was gone, blown apart by a few naked photographs taken a lifetime ago. The world would see her hypocrisy, and so too—oh, God—would her daughters.

They would know at last, without question, that their mother had had an affair—and that she'd lied to all of them when she walked out of her marriage.

Ruby had a pounding headache. She'd slept on and off all day.

Finally, she stumbled into the kitchen and went to the fridge. When she opened it, the fluorescent lighting stabbed her aching eyes. Squinting, she grabbed the quart of orange juice and drank it from the container. Liquid trickled down her chin. She backhanded it away.

In the living room—what a joke; if you were living in this empty room, you were either dying or too stupid to keep breathing—she leaned against the rough wall and slid down to a sit, stretching her legs out. She knew she needed to walk down to Chang's Mini-Mart and pick up a newspaper, but the thought of turning to the want ads was more than she could bear. The job at Irma's hadn't been much—had been godawful, in fact—but at least it had been hers. She hadn't had to stand in a hot line, begging for a chance, saying *I'm really a comedian* again. As if she were special, instead of just another loser in the string of men and women who came to Hollywood with a cheap one-way ticket and a dream of someday.

The phone rang.

Ruby didn't want to answer. It could hardly be good news. At best, it would be Caroline, her *über*-yuppie, Junior League sister who had two perfect kids and a hunk of a husband.

It was *possible* that Dad had finally remembered her, but Ruby doubted it. Since he'd remarried and started a second family, her father was more interested in midnight baby feedings than in the goings-on of his adult daughter's life. Frankly, she couldn't even remember the last time he'd called.

The ringing went on and on.

Finally, she crawled across the shag carpet and answered on the fourth ring. "Hello?" She heard the snarl in her voice, but who gave a shit? She was in a bad mood and she didn't care who knew it.

"Whoa, don't bite my head off."

Ruby couldn't believe it. "Val?"

"It's me, darlin', your favorite agent."

She frowned. "You sound pretty goddamn happy, considering that my career is circling the hole in the toilet bowl."

"I am happy. Here's the scoop. Yesterday I called everyone I could think of to hire you. And baby, I hate to say it, but no one wanted you. The only nibble was from that shit-ass, low-rent cruise line. They said they'd take you for the summer if you promised no foul language . . . and agreed to wear an orange sequined miniskirt so you could help out the magician after your set."

Ruby's head throbbed harder. She rubbed her temples. "Let me guess, you're calling to tell me there's a man named Big Dick who has a night job for me on Hollywood and Vine."

Val laughed. It was a great, booming sound, with none of the strained undertones she was used to hearing. A client got to know the subtle shades of enthusiasm—it was a skill that came with being at rock bottom on the earning-potential food chain. "You won't believe it. Hell, *I* don't believe it, and I took the call. I'm going to make you guess who called me today."

"Heidi Fleiss."

There was a palpable pause; in it, Ruby heard Val's exhalation of breath—he was smoking. "Joe Cochran."

"From *Uproar*? Don't screw with me, Val. I'm a little—"

"Joe Cochran called me. No shit. He had a sudden cancellation. He wants to book you for tomorrow's show."

How could a world spin around so quickly? Yesterday, Ruby had been pond scum; today, Joe Cochran wanted her. The host of the hottest, hippest talk show in the country. It had been patterned after *Politically Incorrect,* but because *Uproar* was broadcast on cable, the show explored racier issues—and foul language was encouraged. It was a young comedian's dream gig. Even if she wasn't so young anymore.

"He's giving you two minutes to do stand-up. So, kiddo, this is it. You'd better spend the time between then and now practicing. I'll send a car around to pick you up at eleven tomorrow morning."

"Thanks, Val."

"I didn't do anything, darlin'. Really. This is all you. Good luck."

Before she hung up, Ruby remembered to ask, "Hey, what's the topic of the show?"

"Oh, yeah." She heard the rustle of papers. "It's called 'Crime and Punishment: Are Mommy and Daddy to Blame for Everything?'"

Ruby should have known. "They want me because I'm *her* daughter."

"Do you care why?"

"No." It was true. She didn't care why Joe Cochran had called her. This was her shot. Finally, after years of crappy play dates in smoke-infested barrooms in towns whose names she couldn't remember, she was getting national exposure.

She thanked Val again, then hung up the phone. Her heart was racing so hard she felt dizzy. Even the empty room looked better. She wouldn't be here much longer, anyway. She would be brilliant on the show, a shining star.

She ran to her bedroom and flung open the louvered doors of her closet. Everything she owned was black.

She couldn't afford anything new . . .

Then she remembered the black cashmere sweater. It had come from her mother, disguised in a box from Caroline two Christmases earlier. Although Ruby routinely sent back her mother's guilty gifts unopened, this one had seduced her. Once she'd touched that beautiful fabric, she couldn't mail it back.

She grabbed the black V-necked sweater off its hanger and tossed it on the bed.

Tomorrow she'd jazz it up with necklaces and wear it over a black leather miniskirt with black tights. Very Janeane Garofalo.

When Ruby had picked out her clothes, she kicked the bedroom door shut. A thin full-length mirror on the back of the door caught her image, framed it in strips of gold plastic.

It was hard to take herself seriously, dressed as she was in her dad's old football jersey and a pair of fuzzy red knee socks. Her short black hair had been molded by last night's sweatfest into a perfect imitation of Johnny Rotten. Pink sleep wrinkles still creased her pale face. Remnants of last night's makeup circled her eyes.

"I'm Ruby Bridge," she said, grabbing a hairbrush off the dresser to use as a mike. "And yes, you're right if you recognize the last name. I'm *her* daughter, Nora Bridge's, spiritual guru to Middle America." She flung her hip out, picturing herself as she would look tomorrow—hair tipped in temporary blue dye, a dozen tacky neck-laces, tight black clothes, and heavy black makeup. "Look at me. Should that woman be telling you how to raise kids? It's like those commercials on television where celebrities come on and tell you to be a mentor to a kid. And who does Hollywood pick to give out advice?

"A bunch of anorexics, alcoholics, drug addicts, and serial marri-ers. People who haven't spent ten minutes with a kid in years. And *they're* telling you how to parent. It's like—"

The phone rang.

"Damn." Ruby raced into the living room and yanked the cord out of the wall. She couldn't be bothered for the next twenty-four hours. Nothing mattered except getting ready for the show.

Like all big cities, San Francisco looked beautiful at night. Multi-colored lights glittered throughout downtown, creating a neon sculpture garden tucked along the black bay.

Dean Sloan glanced at the wall of windows that framed the pan-oramic view. Unfortunately, he couldn't leave his seat. He was—as always—trapped by the flypaper of good manners.

Scattered through the ornately gilded ballroom of this Russian Hill mansion were a dozen or so tables, each one draped in shimmer-ing gold fabric and topped by a layer of opalescent silk. The china at each place setting was white with platinum trim. Four or five couples sat at each table, making idle conversation. The women were expen-sively, beautifully gowned and the men wore tuxedos. The party's hostess, a local socialite, had hand-chosen the guest list from among the wealthiest of San Francisco's families. Tonight's charity was the opera, and it would benefit mightily, although Dean wondered how many of the guests actually cared about music. What they really cared about was being seen, and even more important, being seen doing the *right* thing.

His date, a pale, exquisite woman named Sarah Brightman-Edgington, slid a hand along his thigh, and Dean knew that he'd been silent too long. With practiced ease, he turned to her, giving her the smile so well documented by the local society media.

"That was a lovely sentiment, don't you think?" she said softly, taking a small sip of champagne.

Dean had no idea what she was talking about, but a quick look around the room enlightened him. An elderly, well-preserved woman in a deceptively simple blue dress was standing alongside the ebony Steinway. No doubt she'd been waxing poetic about the opera and thanking her guests in advance for their unselfish contributions. There was nothing the wealthy liked quite so much as pretending to be generous.

It was, he knew, the official beginning of the end of the evening. There would be dancing yet, some serious schmoozing and even more serious gossiping, but soon it would be polite to leave.

There was a smattering of quiet applause, then the sound of chairs being scooted back.

Dean took hold of Sarah's hand. Together they slipped into the whispering crowd. The band was playing something soft and romantic, a song that was almost familiar.

On the dance floor, he pulled Sarah close, slid his hand down the bare expanse of her back, felt her shiver at his touch.

The crowd eddied and swirled around them. Overhead, thousands of tiny lights twinkled like stars. There was a faint, sweet smell of roses in the air.

Or maybe that was the scent of money . . .

He gazed down at Sarah's upturned face, noticing for the first time how lovely her gray eyes were. Without thinking about it, he bent slightly and kissed her, tasting the champagne she'd drunk. He could tell by this kiss where the night could go. She would want him. If he cared to, he could take her hand, lead her out of this crush, and take her to his bed. She would offer no objections. After that, he would call her, and they would probably sleep together a few times. Then, somehow, he would forget her. Last year, a local magazine had named him San Francisco's most *ineligible* bachelor because of his reputation for nanosecond affairs. It was true; he'd certainly slept with dozens of the cities' most gorgeous women.

But what the reporter hadn't known, hadn't even imagined, was how tired Dean was of it all. He wasn't even twenty-nine years old and already he felt aged. Money. Power. Disposable women who seemed to hear his family name and become as malleable as wet clay. For more than a year now, Dean had felt that something was wrong with his life. Missing.

At first, he'd assumed it was a business problem, and he'd rededicated himself to work, logging upwards of eighty hours a week at Harcourt and Sons. But all he'd managed to do was make more money, and the ache in his gut had steadily sharpened.

He'd tried to speak to his father about it. As usual, that had proven pointless. Edward Sloan was now—and always had been—a charming, frivolous playboy who jumped at his wife's every command. It was Mother who held all of the ambition, and she'd never been one to care overly about things like fulfillment or satisfaction. Her comment had been as he'd expected: *I ran this company for thirty years; now it's your turn. No whining will be allowed.*

He supposed that she'd earned that right. Under his mother's iron fist, the family business, begun by her grandfather and expanded by her father, had become a hundred-million-dollar enterprise. That had always been enough for her. All she ever wanted. But that same success felt vaguely hollow to Dean.

He'd even tried to talk to his friends about it, and though they'd wanted to help, it was clear that none of them understood his feelings.

It wasn't so surprising, after all. Although they were all from the same background, Dean had grown up in a slightly different world than his peers.

Lopez Island. Summer Island.

He'd spent ten perfect years in the San Juan Islands. There, he and his brother, Eric, had been—for a short time—ordinary boys. Those remote islands had formed and defined Dean somehow, provided a place where he felt whole.

Of course, Ruby had been there. And before she went crazy and ruined everything, she'd taught him how love felt.

Then she'd shown him how easily it was broken.

Dean sighed, wishing he hadn't thought about Ruby now, when he had a beautiful, willing woman in his arms . . .

Suddenly he was tired. He simply didn't have the energy to spend tonight with another woman he didn't care about.

"I'm not feeling well," he said, wondering briefly whether it was a lie, or not quite one.

She smiled up at him, revealing a set of perfect white teeth. Her hand moved up his arm, curled possessively around the back of his neck. They were always possessive, he thought tiredly. Or perhaps that was merely his sense of it.

"Me, too," she purred. "My place is just around the corner."

He reached up and took her hand, kissing the back of her knuckles gently. "No, I'm *really* not feeling well, and I've got a crack-of-dawn conference call coming from Tokyo. I think I'll take you home, if you don't mind."

She pouted prettily, and he wondered if that was one of the things they taught wealthy young girls at schools like Miss Porter's. If not, it had been passed down from one generation to another as carefully as the secret of fire.

"I'll call you tomorrow," he said, although he didn't mean it. There were only two choices available to a man at a time like this: hurt her by not saying it, or hurt her by not doing it. One—lying now—was easier.

Once he'd made his decision, Dean couldn't get out of the room fast enough. He maneuvered through the crowd like a Tour-de-France cyclist, saying good night to the few people who really mattered, getting Sarah's wrap (fur in June???), and hurried out to stand beneath the portico.

Sarah made idle chitchat as they stood there together, and he listened politely, answered at what he assumed were the appropriate places. Finally, he heard his car drive up. The black Aston-Martin roared up the driveway and screeched to a halt. A uniformed valet jumped out of the driver's seat and rushed around to open Sarah's door, then helped her into her seat.

Dean nodded at the man as he walked past. "Thanks, Ramon," he said, getting into his car. He slammed the door shut and drove off, hitting the gas too hard.

It was a full minute before Sarah asked, "How did you know his name was Ramon?"

"I asked him when we arrived."

"Oh."

Dean glanced at her, saw her perfect profile cameoed against the blackened window glass. "What? Is there something wrong with knowing his name?"

A frown darted across her face. She lifted a hand, pointed idly. "Here's my house."

Dean pulled up the circular driveway and parked beneath an antique street lamp.

She turned to him, frowning slightly. "You're not what I expected. The girls . . . they talk about you."

He ran a hand through his too-long blond hair. "I hope it's a good thing, not being what you expected."

"It is," she said quietly. "I won't see you again, will I?"

"Sarah, I—"

"*Will* I?" she interrupted forcibly.

Dean took a deep breath, released it. "It's not you. It's me. I'm restless lately. It doesn't make for good company."

She laughed; it was a practiced, silvery sound that only held traces of mirth. "You're young and rich and sheltered. Of course you're restless. Poor people are driven and hungry. Rich people are restless and bored. I've been bored since grade school, for God's sake."

It was such a sad thing to say. Dean didn't know how to respond. He got out of the car and went around to her door, helping her out. Slipping a hand along the small of her back, he walked her to the door of her father's hilltop mansion. Quietly, he said, "You're too beautiful to be bored."

She looked sadly up at him. "So are you."

Dean kissed her good night, then returned to his car and raced home.

In less than fifteen minutes, he was standing in his living room, staring out at the night-clad city, sipping warmed brandy from a bowl-size snifter. On the walls all around him were framed photographs—his hobby. Once, the sight of them had pleased him. Now, all he saw when he looked at his photographs was how wrong his life had gone.

Behind him, the phone rang. He waited a few rings for Hester, his housekeeper, to answer it. Then he remembered that Hester had gone to see her kids tonight. He strode to the *latte*-colored suede sofa, collapsed onto the down-filled cushion, and answered the phone. "Dean Sloan." It was, he knew, an impersonal greeting, but he didn't care.

"Dino? Is that you?"

"Uh . . . Eric? How in the hell are you?" Dean was stunned. He hadn't heard from his brother in what . . . a year? Eighteen months?

"Are you sitting down?"

"That doesn't sound good."

"It isn't. I'm dying."

Dean felt as if he'd been punched in the gut. A cold chill moved through him. "AIDS?" he whispered.

Eric laughed. "We *do* get other diseases, you know. My personal favorite is cancer."

"We'll get you the best treatment. I can make some calls right now. Mark Foster is still on the board at—"

"I've *had* the best treatments. I've seen the best specialists, and they," Eric said softly, "have seen me." He took a deep breath. "I don't have much time left."

Dean couldn't seem to draw a decent breath. "You're thirty years old," he said helplessly, as if *age* were relevant.

"I should have told you when I was first diagnosed, but . . . I kept thinking I'd tell you when it was over, and we'd laugh about it . . ."

"Is there *any* chance we'll someday laugh about it?"

It took Eric a moment to answer. "No."

"What can I do?"

"I'm going back to the island. Lottie's already there, waiting for me."

"The island," Dean repeated slowly. A strange sense of inevitability drifted into the room. It was as if Dean had always known that someday they'd end up back there, where everything had begun. Where everything had gone so wrong. Maybe a part of him had even been waiting for it.

"Will you come up?"

"Of course."

"I want us to be brothers again."

"We've always been brothers," Dean answered uncomfortably.

"No," Eric said softly, "we've been members of the same family. We haven't been brothers in years."

Chapter Three

The scandal broke with gale force. Those humiliating photographs were everywhere, and the newspapers and television stations that didn't own the pictures described them in excruciating detail.

Nora sat huddled in her own living room, refusing to go anywhere. The thought of being seen terrified her.

Her assistant, Dee Langhor, had shown up bright and early in the morning—*I came the minute I heard*—and Nora had felt pathetically grateful. Now Dee was in Nora's home office, fielding phone calls.

With everything on Nora's mind, one thing kept rising to the surface; she should have called Caroline the day before, to warn her about the coming media storm.

But how did you tell your child something like this? *Oh, honey, and don't mind about the pictures of your naked mother that are front-page news?*

In the end, Nora had chosen to handle the impending disaster as she handled all difficult things: she'd taken two sleeping pills and turned off her phone. In the morning, she'd had a short respite . . . then she'd turned on the television. The story had been picked up by every morning show.

Now she had no choice. She had to call.

She reached for the phone, accessed the second line, and pushed number one on the speed-dial list. Her heart was pounding so hard she couldn't hear the ringing on the other end.

"Hello?"

It took Nora a moment to respond—God, she wanted to hang up the phone. "Caro? It's me. Mom."

There was a pause that seemed to strip away a layer of Nora's tender flesh. "Well. Well. I hope you're going to tell me you were kidnapped yesterday and the FBI just freed you from your prison in the back of some psycho fan's trunk."

"I wasn't kidnapped."

"I found out this morning when I dropped Jenny off at preschool." She laughed sharply. "Mona Carlson asked me how it felt to see pictures of my mother like that. How it *felt*."

Nora didn't know how to respond. Defending herself was pointless; worse, it was offensive. "I'm sorry. I couldn't . . . call."

"Of course you couldn't." Caroline was quiet for a moment, then she said, "I can't believe I let it hurt my feelings, either. I should have known better. It's just that in the last few years . . . I thought . . . oh, hell, forget it."

"I know. We've been getting closer . . ."

"No. Apparently *I've* been getting closer. You, obviously, haven't changed at all. You've been like some Stepford mom, pretending, saying the right things, but never really feeling connected to me at all. I don't know when I got stupid enough to expect honesty from you. And I'm not even going to get into the content of those photographs, what they mean to our family."

"Please," Nora pleaded, "I know I screwed up. Don't shut me out of your life again . . ."

"You're priceless. You really don't get it, do you? I'm not the one who shuts people out, not in this family. Maybe Ruby was the smart one—she hasn't let you hurt her in years. Now, I've got to go."

"I love you, Caroline," Nora said in a rush, desperate to say the words before it was too late.

"You know what's sad about that?" Caroline's voice broke. A little sob sounded in her throat. "I believe you." She hung up.

The dial tone buzzed in Nora's ears.

Dee rushed into the living room, her eyes wide. "Mr. Adams is on the phone."

"Oh, God—"

"I told him you weren't here, but he screamed at me. He said to tell you to pick up the *f*-ing phone or he was going to call his lawyers."

Nora sighed. Of course. Tom Adams hadn't become a newspaper mogul by playing nice. He was a good ole boy who had fought his way to the top by never giving an inch to anyone.

She rubbed her suddenly throbbing temples. "Put him through."

"Thanks," Dee said. Turning, she hurried out of the living room and went back into Nora's office.

Nora answered the phone. "Hello, Tom."

"Jee-zuz Kee-riste, Nora, what in the Sam Hill were you thinking? I heard about this godawful mess when I was on the crapper this A.M. If I hadn't had the television on, I don't know when I'da found out. My little woman said to me, 'Gee, Tommy, your little gal has herself in a pickle, don't she?'"

Nora winced. "Sorry, Tom. I was caught off guard by the whole thing myself."

"Well, you're on guard now, little lady. Tamara tells me that you haven't gotten any letters yet, but you will. My guess is they'll start comin' in tomorrow."

"You've got two months' worth of columns from me on file. That'll give me some time to figure out how I want to handle this."

He made a barking sound. "I pay you a wagonload of money to answer readers' letters, and now that they finally got something interesting to ask about, you sure as hell aren't going to play possum. Scandals sell newspapers and I mean to cash in on your heartache. Sorry, Nora—and I do mean that; I've always liked you—but business is business. Your agent sure understood business when he bled me for that million-dollar contract."

Nora felt sick to her stomach. "The radio station is giving me some time off—"

"Don't you confuse me with those tie-wearin' pantywaists. I

haven't backed down from a fight in my life, and my people aren't going to, either."

The headache blossomed into a full-blown migraine. "Okay, Tom," she said softly. She'd say anything to end this conversation. "Give me a few days. Use what you have for now, and then I'll start to answer the hate mail."

He chuckled. "I knew you'd see the light, Nora. Bye now."

She hung up. The silence that came after all that yelling was strangely heavy.

Tom actually expected her to sit down and read angry, disappointed letters from the very people who used to love her.

Impossible.

Ruby stood in her steam-clouded bathroom, staring through the mist at her watery reflection. The lines beneath her puffy eyes looked like they'd been stitched in place by an industrial sewing machine.

It wouldn't do to look this old, not in Hollywood. She wanted people to think of her as young and hip and defiant, not as a woman who'd wasted her youth in nightclubs and had nothing to show for it except early-onset wrinkles.

She used makeup to take off the years. Enough "heroin-chic" black eyeliner and people would assume she was young and stupid. Sort of the way gorgeous celebrities wore godawful hairdos to the Academy Awards; their message had to be *looks don't matter to me.*

As if.

Only a beautiful woman would even consider making that ridiculous statement.

Ruby dressed carefully—V-necked cashmere sweater, black leather miniskirt, and black tights. She hadn't had time to run to the store for temporary hair dye, but a lot of gel had made her hair poke out everywhere instead. She layered fourteen cheap plastic Mardi Gras necklaces around her neck and painted her stubby, bitten-off fingernails a glittery shade of midnight blue. Finally, she put on a pair of clunky black sunglasses—Rite Aid knockoffs of the newest designer fashion.

Then she took a deep breath, grabbed her handbag, and headed outside.

The sleek black limousine was already parked at the curb. Ruby couldn't help wishing that Max were here right now. She'd just love to shove past him and drive away.

A uniformed driver stood beside the car. "Miss Bridge?"

She grinned. No one ever called her that. "That's me. I'm going to—"

"I know, miss. The Paramount lot. I'll be waiting to take you home after the taping."

The driver came around and opened the door for her. Ruby peered into the dark interior and saw a dozen white roses in a sheath of opalescent tissue paper lying on the backseat. An ice bucket held a bottle of chilled Dom Pérignon.

Ruby slid into the seat, heard the satisfying thud of the closing door, and plucked the card from the flowers.

People as talented as you don't need luck. They need a chance, and this is yours. Love, Val.

God, it felt good. As if those tarnished dreams of hers were finally coming true.

She had never meant to need it all so much. It had begun as a lark—something she did well without a lot of effort. Ruby the class clown, always making people laugh. But after her mother abandoned them, everything had changed. *Ruby* had changed. From that moment on, nothing and no one had been quite enough for her. She'd come to need the unconditional acceptance that only fame could provide.

She scooted closer to the window, grinning as the limo pulled up to the security booth at the entrance to Paramount. The twin white arches, trimmed in golden metallic scrollwork, announced to the world that through these gates was a special world, open only to a lucky few.

Ruby hit the button to lower the privacy shield just in time to hear the driver say, "I have Miss Bridge for *Uproar*."

The guard stepped back into his booth, consulted a clipboard, then waved them through. Ruby plastered herself close to the window, looking for celebrities, but all she saw were regular people milling about. The closest she came to seeing a movie star was a red sportscar parked in a stall marked JULIA ROBERTS.

At the visitors' lot, the driver parked the car and came around, opening Ruby's door. "There's your ride," he said, pointing to a vehicle that looked like a stretched-out golf cart. A man in tan-colored shorts and a matching polo shirt was standing beside it. "They'll zip you up to the studio. I'll be right here whenever you get back."

Ruby tried to look blasé, as if she did this all the time. To tell the truth, if her blood pressure bumped up another notch, she was probably going to stroke out.

She took a deep breath and headed toward the cart. Once she got in, the driver settled behind the wheel and started the soundless engine. The cart moved jerkily between the huge soundstages. There were people everywhere, walking, riding bicycles. They passed a battalion of aliens—was that Patrick Stewart?—and veered around a gathering of cowboys. Finally, they pulled up to soundstage nine, a hulking, flesh-colored building. Above the door was a neon sign that read UPROAR! A NEW KIND OF TALK SHOW WITH JOE COCHRAN.

Ruby jumped off the cart and crossed the street. She paused a minute, then opened the door. Inside was a kaleidoscope of colored lights, darkened seating, and people. That's what she noticed most of all—there were people everywhere, scurrying around like ants with clipboards, checking and rechecking, nodding and cursing and laughing.

"You're Ruby Bridge?"

Ruby jumped. She hadn't even noticed the small, platinum blonde who now stood beside her, peering up at Ruby through the ugliest pair of brown-framed glasses she'd ever seen. "I'm Ruby."

"Good." The woman grabbed Ruby's arm and led her through the swarming people, down a quieter hallway and into a small waiting room. On the table beside a brown sofa were a bowl of fruit and a bottle of Perrier on ice. "Do you need makeup?"

Ruby laughed. "Are you thinking of an intervention?"

The woman frowned, cocked her head, birdlike. "Excuse me?"

Ruby nodded stiffly. "My makeup's fine. Thanks."

"Good. Sit here. Someone will come and get you when it's time to go on." The woman consulted her papers. "You get two minutes up front. You were a last-minute guest, so there's no time for an interview; we'll just have to make do. Be fast and be funny." With a quick sniff, the woman was gone.

Ruby collapsed on the sofa. Suddenly she was more than nervous. She was terrified. *Be funny.*

What had she been thinking? She wasn't funny. Her material might be funny, but *she* wasn't. It usually took her three minutes into a routine before she calmed down enough to make people laugh.

So, a minute after she was finished, she'd be a riot.

She shot to her feet. Her heart was pounding so hard she thought for a second that someone was at the door.

"Calm down, Ruby," she said, forcing her fingers to uncurl. She focused on her breathing. In and out, in and out. "You are funny. You are."

There was a knock at the door. "They're ready for you, Miss Bridge."

"Oh, my God." Ruby glanced at the wall clock. She'd been standing here, hyperventilating, for thirty minutes, and now she couldn't remember one goddamn line of material.

The door swung open.

Bird lady stood there, pointy face tilted to the left. "Miss Bridge?"

Ruby exhaled slowly, slowly. "I'm ready," she said, and though she was facing the woman, she was really talking to herself. She *was* ready; she'd been ready all her life.

She followed the woman toward the stage. As she got closer, she could hear the familiar strains of the opening music. Then came Joe's voice; the audience laughed in response to something he said.

"Remember," the woman said in a stage whisper, "we want *opinions,* the more outrageous and controversial the better."

Ruby nodded in understanding, although truthfully, she didn't think she had an opinion on anything right now except her own shortcomings. And as an added bonus, she was sweating like a geyser. Mascara was probably running down her cheeks.

She'd look like something out of *Alien* by the time—

"Ruby Bridge!" Her name roared through the sound system, chased by the sound of applause.

Ruby pushed through the curtains, smiling to the best of her ability. She forced herself not to squint, although the lights were so bright she couldn't see anything. She just hoped she didn't walk off the end of the stage.

She went to the microphone. It made a fuzzy, crackling sound as she pulled it off its stand. "Well," she said with a bright smile, "it's nice to know I'm not the only person who can come to a talk show in the middle of the day. Of course, it's easy for me. I was fired yesterday. *Fired,* from a trendy, shit-ass restaurant that I won't name— but it sounds like Irma's Hash House. I won't even *tell* you what I thought we'd be selling . . ."

A smattering of laughter.

"Actually, if they were going to fire me, I'm glad it happened on Thursday. Friday is all-you-can-eat night. And trust me, people take that literally. Irma's is the only restaurant in L.A. where they have defibrillators on the table. Ketchup? Mustard? Restart your heart?" She let silence have a beat of her time. "I mean, this is the new millennium. I kept saying to people, for the love of God, *eat fruit.*"

More laughter, deeper this time. It gave her confidence.

She grinned, then launched into the rest of her routine, saving the best jokes—about her mother—for last.

At the end of her abbreviated routine, Ruby stepped back from the mike. Amid the beautiful sound of applause, Joe Cochran crossed the stage toward her. He was smiling, which was definitely a good sign.

He placed a hand warmly on her shoulder and turned to face the crowd. "You've all met the very funny Ruby Bridge. Now, let's meet the rest of our players for tonight. There's family therapist Elsa Pine, author of the bestselling book *Poisonous Parents,* and the honorable Sanford Tyrell, congressman from Alabama."

Elsa and Sanford walked onstage, looking like a pencil and a softball. They were careful not to make eye contact with each other.

Joe clapped his hands together. "Let's get started."

The three guests followed Joe to the artfully arranged leather chairs on the stage. Joe sat down in the center seat, then looked up at the audience and smiled. "I don't know about you all, but I'm sick and tired of the way our judicial system handles criminals. Every time I open the paper, I read about some psychopath who killed a little girl and got off because the jury felt sorry for him. I mean, sorry for *him.* Who's looking out for the victims here?"

"Now, Joe." Elsa leaned forward, her eyes narrowed and hard beneath the sensible, round glasses. She was so thin, Ruby wondered how her lungs could fill with air without knocking her over. "Criminals aren't born, they're made. It makes perfect sense to understand that some people have been so abused by their parents that they no longer know right from wrong."

"Little lady," the good congressman said, his florid face creasing into a good-ole-boy grin, "that's about as wrong-headed as a filly can be."

Ruby frowned at the audience. "Did he call her a filly? Tell me I heard wrong . . ."

Laughter.

Elsa ignored it. "You heard right. Congressman—"

"Call me Sanford." He pulled almost four syllables out of his name.

"The measure of a society is its compassion."

"What about compassion for the victim's family," Joe said, "or do you bleeding-heart liberals just want us to be compassionate toward the murderer?" He looked at Ruby. "You know something about toxic parents, Ruby. Is everything wrong in your life your mother's fault?"

Elsa nodded. "Yes, Ruby, you of all people should understand how deeply a parent can wound a child. I mean, your mother is a huge proponent of marriage. She positively waxes poetic about the sanctity of the vows—"

Ruby laughed. "So does Bill Clinton."

Elsa wouldn't be sidetracked by the audience's laughter. "You were probably the only person in America who wasn't surprised by the *Tattler* today."

"I don't read the tabloids," Ruby answered.

A whisper moved through the audience, chairs squeaked. Joe's enthusiastic smile dimmed. He shot a quick look at bird woman, who was standing just offstage. Then he leaned forward. "You haven't read today's *Tattler*?"

Ruby's frown deepened. "Is that a crime now?"

Joe reached down, and for the first time Ruby noticed the

newspaper folded beneath his chair. He picked it up, handed it to her. "I'm sorry. You were supposed to have known."

Ruby felt a sudden tension in the room, the kind of hush that fell just before a bar fight started. She took the newspaper from him, opened it. At first, all she noticed was the headline: RAISING MORE THAN SPIRITS. It made her smile. How did they come up with this stuff?

Then she saw the photograph.

It was a blurry, grainy shot of two naked people entwined. The editors had carefully placed black "privacy strips" across the pertinent body parts, but there was no denying what was going on. Or who the woman was.

Ruby looked helplessly at the faces around her. Joe appeared focused, a dog poised on the scent. The therapist frowned thoughtfully. They were imagining her pain.

She tossed the newspaper down in disgust. It landed on the floor with a muffled thwack. "There's a lesson to women everywhere in this. When your lover says, 'One little photo, honey, just for us,' you better cover your naked ass and run."

Elsa leaned forward. "How does it make you feel to see—"

Joe raised his hands. "We're getting off the topic here. The question is, how much of our screw ups are our fault? Does a bad parent give someone a free ride to commit crime?"

"This country's gone excuse crazy," the congressman said, not meeting Ruby's gaze. "Every time some loony bin goes crazy, we put his mother on trial. It ain't right."

"Exactly!" Joe said. "Too damn bad if you were abused. If you do the crime, you do the time."

Ruby sat perfectly still. There was no reason for her to speak, and truthfully, she couldn't think of a thing to say. She knew she'd given *Uproar* what it had wanted—a reaction. Her surprise was icing on the cake. By tomorrow, she knew her blank-eyed, dim-witted reaction to the scandal would lead every report. She'd look like an idiot from coast to coast.

She should have known it would be like this . . . her big break. What a joke. How could she have been so naive?

Finally, she heard Joe wrapping up. She blinked, trying to look normal.

"That's all the time we have for today, folks. Tune in next week, when our subject will be communicating with the dead—possible? Or just plain fraud? Thank you."

The applause sign lit up and the audience responded immediately, clapping thunderously.

Ruby rose from her chair and moved blindly across the stage. People were talking to her, but she couldn't hear anything they were saying.

Someone touched her shoulder. She jumped and spun around.

"Ruby?" It was Joe. He was standing beside her, his handsome face drawn into a tight frown. "I'm really sorry about ambushing you. The story broke yesterday. It never occurred to us that you'd miss it. Every station covered it, and since so much of your material is about your relationship with your mother . . ." He let the explanation founder.

"I turned off my phone and television," she answered, then added, "I was getting ready for the show."

He sighed. "You thought this was your big break. And it turned out—"

"Not to be." She cut him off. The pity in his eyes was more than she could bear. She knew he used to be a stand-up comic himself; he knew exactly what had happened. She didn't want her disappointment cemented into words she'd remember forever.

"You know, Ruby," he said, "I've seen your act a few times. The Comedy Store, I think. Your material's good."

"Thanks."

"Maybe you should think about writing, like for a sitcom. They could use your talent at the networks."

Ruby stood there with a fake smile pasted on her face. He was telling her to give up. Try something else.

It felt to Ruby as if she were fading away, but like the Cheshire cat, she'd smile to the end. "Thanks, Joe. I have to go now."

She ran back to her chair and grabbed her handbag. At the last second, she plucked up the *Tattler* and crammed it under her armpit. Without glancing at anyone, she raced out of the studio.

In her apartment, Ruby closed all the blinds and turned off the lights.

She slumped onto her worn sofa and thumped her feet onto the cheap, wood-grain coffee table. A half-full water glass rattled at the movement. The tabloid lay beside her, barely seen in the darkness.

Mommie Dearest had an affair, after all.

It didn't surprise her, that realization, not truly. Any woman who would leave her children to go in search of fame and fortune wouldn't think twice about having an affair. What surprised Ruby was how much it still hurt.

Her fingers shook as she reached for the phone and dialed her sister's number. It was rare that Ruby called Caroline—too expensive—but it wasn't every day you saw naked pictures of your mother having sex with a stranger.

Caroline answered on the second ring. "Hello?"

"Hey, sis," Ruby said, feeling a sudden tide of loneliness.

"So, you finally plugged your phone in. I've been going crazy trying to reach you."

"Sorry," she said softly. Her throat felt embarrassingly tight. "I saw the pictures."

"Yeah. You and everyone else in America. I was always afraid something like this would happen."

Ruby was stunned. She had *never* imagined it. "Did you know about the affair?"

"I suspected."

"Why didn't you ever tell me?"

"Come on, Rube. You've never once mentioned her name to me, not in all these years. You didn't want to know anything about her."

Ruby hated it when Caroline acted like she knew everything. "I suppose you've already forgiven her, Caroline-the-saint."

"No," Caro said softly. "I'm having a hard time with this one. It's so . . . public."

"Ah. Appearances. I forgot about that."

"Don't make me sound so shallow. There's more to it than that and you know it."

Ruby was instantly contrite. She hated how easy it was for her to say hurtful things—even to the people she loved. When Mom had left them, Caroline had been the one who held the family together, even though she'd been no more than a teenager herself. She'd stepped up and been everything Ruby needed. Without Caroline, Ruby honestly believed she wouldn't have made it through that awful year. "I'm sorry. You know how goodness brings out the worst in me."

"I'm not so good. Yesterday, I said some really nasty things to her. I couldn't seem to help myself. I was so mad."

"You talked to her? What did she say?"

"She's sorry. She loves me."

Ruby snorted. "Yeah, just imagine if she hated us."

Caroline laughed. "I'm going to call her when I calm down. Maybe we can finally talk about some of the things . . . you know, the stuff that matters."

"Nothing she has to say matters, Caro. I've been telling you that for years."

"You're wrong about that, Rube. Someday you'll see that, but for now, all I know is that this thing is going to get a heck of a lot worse before it gets better."

"Only for you, Glenda. I'm not the one who keeps trying to forgive her."

Before Caroline could respond, the doorbell rang. It played a stanza of *I just met a girl named Maria* . . .

Ruby made a mental note to change the damned bell. Max had thought it was funny; Ruby disagreed. "I gotta run, Caroline. There's someone here to see me. With my luck, it's probably the landlord, looking for my rent check."

"Take care of yourself."

"You, too. And kiss my niece and nephew for me." She hung up, then decided not to answer the door anyway. It probably *was* the landlord.

She went into the kitchen. Flipping through the mostly empty cabinets, she found a half-full fifth of gin and a bottle of vermouth, both of which Max had obviously forgotten. She made herself a martini in a Rubbermaid container, then poured the drink into a plastic tumbler.

By the third repeat of "Maria," she gave up. Taking a quick sip of the martini, she padded across the shag carpeting and peered through the peephole.

It was Val, standing beside a woman so thin she looked like a windshield wiper.

"Oh, *perfect*."

She wrenched the door open. Val grinned at her. He looked acutely out of place in the dim, ugly corridor.

Val leaned forward and kissed Ruby's cheek. "How's my newest star?"

"Fuck you," she whispered, smiling brightly at the strange woman. "I never saw it coming."

Val drew back, frowning. "I tried to call you. I even sent a messenger over. You didn't answer the door."

Ruby would have said more, but the way the lady was watching them made her uncomfortable. She turned to her, noticing the woman's severe haircut and expensive black dress. An unlit cigarette dangled from her bony fingers.

New Yorker. Definitely. Maybe a mortician.

"I'm Ruby Bridge," she said, extending her hand.

The woman shook her hand. Firm grip. Clammy skin. "Joan Pinon."

"Come on in." Ruby backed away from the door, made a sweeping gesture with her hand. She tried not to see the apartment through their eyes, but it was impossible. Tacky furniture, dusty shag carpeting, garage-sale decor.

Val went right to Max's old velour Barcalounger and sat down. Joan perched birdlike on the end of the sofa.

Ruby flopped down on the sofa's other cushion. She took a sip of her drink. A big gulp, actually. "I know it's early for drinks, but it's not every day you see nude pictures of your mother *and* lose your career. I'll probably get hit by a bus later today."

Val leaned forward. "Joan is an editor from New York."

"Really?"

"She's here because of your mother."

Ruby took a long, stinging swallow. "Of course she is." She wished she had an olive to nibble on; she needed something to do with her hands. She turned to Joan. "What do you want?"

"I work for *Caché* magazine. We'd like you to write an exposé on your mother." Joan smiled, showing a mouthful of smoker's teeth. "We could hire a ghostwriter if you'd like, but Val tells me you're a first-rate writer."

A compliment. That felt good. Ruby settled back in her seat, eyeing Joan. "You want a daughter's betrayal."

"Who betrayed whom?" Joan said. "Your mother has been telling America to honor commitments and put their children first. These photographs prove that she's a liar and a hypocrite, plain and simple. We checked the records. Nora was married to your father when those pictures were taken. People have a right to know who they're taking advice from."

"Ah, the people's right," Ruby said, taking another sip of her martini.

"It's just an article, Ruby, not a book. No more than fifteen thousand words, and . . ." Val said, "it could make you famous."

"*Rich* and famous," Joan added.

Now *that* got Ruby's attention. She set the glass down and looked at Joan. "How rich?"

"Fifty thousand dollars. I'm prepared to pay you half of that amount right now, and the other half when you deliver the article. The only catch is: you can't do any interviews until we publish."

"Fifty thousand *dollars?*" Ruby reached for her drink again, but she was too wound up to take a sip. For a few measly words . . .

And all she had to do was serve up her mother's life for public consumption.

She set her drink down. This wasn't something to take lightly. She wished she had someone to ask about it, but Ruby had always had problems trusting people, and that made close friendships impossible. There was her dad, but he was so busy with his new family that he and Ruby weren't as close as they'd once been. And her sister had spent the past decade trying to forgive their mother; there was no doubt she'd tell Ruby to turn down the deal. Caro would despise the idea of airing their family's dirty laundry in public.

"I don't know my mother that well," she said slowly, trying to think through it. "The last time I saw her was at my sister's wedding nine years ago. We didn't speak."

That wasn't entirely true. Ruby had spoken to her mother. She'd said, "And I thought the worst part of this day would be wearing pink polyester." Then she'd walked away.

"We don't want cold facts and figures. We want your opinions, your thoughts on what kind of a person she is . . . what kind of a mother she was."

"That's easy. She'd step on your grandmother's throat to get ahead. Nothing—and no one—matters to her, except herself."

"You see?" Joan said, eyes shining. "That's exactly the perspective we want. Now, I'm sure you'll understand that we need to go to press fast. While the scandal's still hot. I brought the contract with me—Val has already had a literary agent look it over—and a check for twenty-five thousand dollars." She reached into her black snakeskin (appropriate, Ruby thought) briefcase and pulled out a stack of papers and a check. She slapped the papers down on the table, with the check on top.

Ruby stared down at all those zeros and swallowed hard. She'd never had that much money at one time. Hell, it was more than her salary for all of last year.

Joan smiled, a shark's grin. "Let me ask you this, Ruby. Would your mother turn down this offer if *you* were the subject of the article?"

The answer to that question came easily. Her mother had once had to make a choice like this. She could have chosen her husband and her daughters . . . or her career. Without a backward glance, Nora Bridge had chosen herself.

"This is your chance, Ruby," Val said. "Think of the exposure. The networks will be fighting over you."

She felt flushed. There was this strange sensation that she was removed from her body, watching the scene unfurl from a distance. Slowly, she heard herself answer, "I'm a good writer . . ." That was one thing she'd always believed. Now she knew that Val believed it, too. She bit her lower lip, worrying it. If the article made her famous, maybe she could parlay notoriety into a sitcom. "I certainly know the beginning of her career—who she may have fucked to get to the top and who she just plain screwed."

Joan was smiling now. "We've tentatively booked you on *The Sarah Purcell Show* for a week from now . . . to promote the article."

The Sarah Purcell Show . . .

Ruby closed her eyes, wanting it so much her head hurt. She'd clawed and scratched through life for so long, been a nobody, a nothing . . .

She thought of all the reasons she should say no—the moral, ethical reasons—but none of them found a place to stick. Instead, she thought about those damned photos . . .

And all of her mother's lies.

She took a deep breath, then exhaled. Slowly, she reached down for the check and picked it up. The numbers swam before her eyes. "Okay," she said. "I'll do it."

Chapter Four

Ruby cranked the Volkswagen's radio to full blast. A raucous Metallica song blared through the small black speakers. Her whole body was moving to the beat.

Fifty thousand dollars.

She wanted so badly to share this day with someone. If only she had Max's new number; she'd call him and tell him what he'd missed out on. She would have spent a lot of this money on him . . . on them . . .

The thought brought a quick thrust of sadness, and the feeling pissed her off. Max didn't deserve one cent of this fortune.

She drove into Beverly Hills. Usually, she didn't even drive past this area; it was too depressing to see all the luxuries she couldn't afford. But today, she was flying high. She felt invincible.

When she saw an open spot on Rodeo Drive, she pulled over and parked. Grabbing her purse (with the yellow deposit slip for twenty-five thousand dollars inside), she got out of the car and slammed the door shut behind her. For once, she didn't bother locking the car; if someone was desperate enough for transportation to steal *this* one, they were welcome to it.

She strolled around for a while, passing pods of women dressed in expensive, beautiful clothing. No one made eye contact with her. In this part of the world, a twenty-seven-year-old woman dressed in what could only be called "grunge" simply didn't exist. And fifty thousand dollars wasn't nearly enough to get these women's attention.

Then she looked into a store window and saw a sheer, beaded, silvery blue dress with a plunging V neckline and a split in the side that came up to midthigh. It was the most perfect dress she'd ever seen, the kind of thing she'd never imagined she could own.

She held her handbag close and pushed through the glass doors. A bell tinkled over her head.

Over in the corner, across an ocean of white marble flooring and chrome-topped rounders of clothing, a woman looked up. "I'll be right with you, dear," she said in one of those cultured, sorority-girl voices.

Ruby felt uncomfortable. She wished she could tape the deposit slip to her forehead.

Finally the saleswoman came over. She was tall and reed-thin, dressed in black from head to foot. Not a hair was out of place. She gave a little sniff when she saw Ruby, but her voice was kind. "May I help you?"

Ruby pointed helplessly toward the window. "I saw a blue dress in the window."

"You have excellent taste. Would you like to try it on?"

She nodded.

"Wonderful."

The woman led Ruby to a dressing room that was bigger than the average bedroom. "Would you like a glass of champagne?"

Ruby laughed. Now, *this* was shopping. "I'd love some."

The saleswoman raised her hand; just that, and within a minute, a man in a black tuxedo was handing Ruby a sparkling glass of champagne.

"Thanks," she said, collapsing onto the cushy seat in the dressing room. The champagne's bubbles seemed to float through her blood, making her instantly giddy. For the first time in years, she felt like somebody.

Someone knocked at the door.

"Come in."

The saleslady peeked her head in. "Here you go. I'm Demona. Just holler if you need me."

Ruby trailed her fingers down the beaded, sheer-as-tissue fabric, then quickly undressed and slipped into the dress.

It was like stepping into another personality . . . a different life. Self-consciously, she peeked out of the dressing room. The coast was clear. She walked over to the wall-size mirrors in the corner.

Her breath caught. Even with her hair too short and her makeup too heavy, and her feet wedged into scuffed old Reeboks, she looked . . . beautiful. The plunging neckline accentuated her small breasts; her waist appeared tiny, and the slit slimmed her fleshy thighs.

This was the woman she had hoped someday to become. How had she veered so far off the path?

"Oh, my," Demona said wistfully, "it's perfect. And you don't need a stitch of alterations. I've never seen anything fit so well right off the rack."

"I'll take it," Ruby said in a thick voice.

At least she could have this moment, she thought, this memory of a perfect day. The dress would hang in her closet forever, a pristine reminder of the woman Ruby wanted to be.

She wrote a check—almost thirty-five hundred dollars, including the tax and shoes—and hung the dress carefully in the backseat of the Volkswagen.

Then, cranking the music back up—Steppenwolf this time—she sped toward the freeway. She was almost home when she passed the Porsche dealer.

Ruby laughed and slammed on the brakes.

Nora lay curled on the elegant sofa in her darkened living room. Hours ago, she'd sent Dee home and disconnected the phones.

Then she'd watched the news.

Big mistake. Huge.

Every station had the story; they played and replayed the same footage, showed the lurid blacked-out photographs again and again, usually followed with sound bites of Nora expounding on the importance of fidelity and the sanctity of the marriage vows. What hurt the most were the "man in the street" interviews. Her fans had turned on her; some women even cried at the betrayal they felt. "I trusted her" was the most common refrain.

She was finished. Never again would someone write her a letter and ask for advice; never again would people stand in line in the pouring rain outside the station for a chance to meet her in person.

She knew, too, what was happening in the lobby downstairs. She'd called her doorman several times today, and the report was always the same. The press was outside, cameras at the ready. One sighting of Nora Bridge and they would spring on her like wild dogs. Her doorman claimed that the garage was safe—they weren't allowed in there—but she was afraid to chance it.

She sat up. Huge glass windows reflected the town's bright lights, turned them into a smear of color. The Space Needle hung suspended in the misty sky, an alien ship hovering above the city.

She walked toward the window. Her reflection, caught in the glass, looked bleary and small.

Small.

That's how she felt. It was a familiar feeling, one that had defined her life long ago. It was this sense of being . . . nothing . . . that had set her on the path to ruin in the first place, and she didn't miss the irony that she was here again.

If her father were alive, he'd be laughing. *Not so big a star now, are you, missy?*

She walked into the kitchen and stood in front of the makeshift "bar" she kept for company. Nora hadn't taken a drink in more years than she could count.

But now she needed *something* to help her out of this hole. She felt as if she were drowning . . .

She poured herself a tumbler full of gin. It tasted awful at first—like isopropyl alcohol—but after a few gulps, her tongue went dead and the booze slid down easily, pooling firelike in her cold stomach.

On her way back into the living room, she paused at the grand piano, her attention arrested by the collection of gilt-framed photographs on the gleaming ebony surface. She almost never looked at them, not closely. It was like closing her hand around a shard of broken glass.

Still, one caught her eye. It was a picture of her and her ex-husband, Rand, and their two daughters. They'd been standing in front of the family beach house, their arms entwined, their smiles honest and bright.

She tipped the glass back and finished the drink, then went back for another. By the time she finished that one, she could barely walk straight; there seemed to be a sheet of wax paper between her and the world.

That was fine. She didn't want to think too clearly right now. When her mind was clear, she knew that she'd been on the run for all of her life, and—at last—she'd hit a brick wall. The world knew the truth about her now, and so did her children.

She swayed drunkenly, staring at the photographs. On one side of the piano were family pictures—Christmas mornings, little girls in pink tutus at dance recitals, family vacations taken in that old tent trailer they'd hauled around behind the station wagon.

On the other side were photographs of a woman who was always alone, even in the biggest of crowds. She looked beautiful—makeup artists and hairdressers and personal trainers saw to that. She was flawlessly dressed in expensive clothes, often surrounded by fans and employees.

Adored by strangers.

She stumbled away from the piano and plugged the phone into the wall. Bleary-eyed, she dialed her psychiatrist.

A moment later, a woman answered. "Dr. Allbright's office."

"Hi, Midge. It's Nora Bridge." She hoped she wasn't slurring her words. "Is the doctor in?"

A sniff. That was the only sound, but Nora knew. "He's not in, Ms. Bridge. Shall I take a message?"

Ms. Bridge. Only days ago it had been Nora.

"Is he at home?"

"No, he's unreachable, but I can put you through to his service. Or he left Dr. Hornby's number for emergency referrals . . ."

Nora struggled to remain steady. Call waiting beeped. "Thanks, Midge. There's no need for that." She waited an endless second for Midge to respond, and when the silence began to ache, Nora hung up. Then she ripped the cord out of the wall again.

In some distant part of her mind, she knew that she was sinking into a pool of self-pity, and that she could drown in it, but she didn't know how to crawl out.

Eric.

He would be on the island by now. If she hurried, maybe she could still make the last ferry . . .

She grabbed her car keys off the kitchen counter and staggered into her bedroom. After cramming a blond wig over her cropped auburn hair, she put on a pair of Jackie O sunglasses. On the bedside table, she found her sleeping pills. Of course it would be bad— wrong—to take one now; even in her drunken state, she knew she couldn't mix booze and pills. But she wanted to.

God, she wanted to . . .

She tossed the brown plastic bottle in her purse.

The only thing she took from her condominium was an old photograph of their family, one taken at Disneyland when the girls were small. She shoved it in her handbag and left without bothering to check the lock.

She banged along the wall, using it as a guardrail as she tottered toward the elevator. Once inside, she clung to the slick wooden handrail, praying there wouldn't be a stop in the lobby. She got lucky; the mirrored elevator went all the way down to the parking garage, where it stopped with a clang.

The doors opened.

She peered out; the garage was empty. She careened unsteadily toward her car, collapsing against the jet-black side of her Mercedes. It took her several tries to get the key in the lock, but she finally managed.

She slid awkwardly into the soft leather seat. The engine started easily, a roar of sound in the darkness. The radio came on instantly. Bette Midler singing about the wind beneath her wings.

Nora caught sight of herself in the rearview mirror. Her face was pale, her cheeks tear-streaked. She'd chewed at her lower lip until it was misshapen.

"What are you doing?" she asked the woman in the sunglasses. She heard the slurring, drunken sound of her voice, and it made her cry. Hot tears blurred her vision.

"Please, God," she whispered, "let Eric still be there."

She slammed the car into reverse and backed out of the spot. Then she headed forward and hit the gas. Tires squealed as she rounded the corner and hurtled up the ramp. She didn't even glance left for traffic as she sped out onto Second Avenue.

Dean stood on the slatted wooden dock. The seaplane taxied across the choppy blue waves and lifted skyward, its engine chattering as it banked left and headed back to Seattle.

He'd forgotten how beautiful this place was, how peaceful.

The tide was out now, and this stretch of beach, as familiar to him once as his own hand, smelled of sand that had baked in the hot sun, of kelp that was slowly curling into leathery strips. He knew that if he jumped down onto that sand, it would swallow his expensive loafers and reclaim him, turn him into a child again.

It was the smell that pulled him back in time, that and the slapping sound of the waves against barnacled pilings. A dozen memories came at him, gift-wrapped in the scent of his parents' beach at low tide.

Here, he and Eric had built their forts and buried treasures made of foil-wrapped poker chips; they'd gone from rock to rock, squatting down, scraping their knees on driftwood in search of the tiny black crabs that lived beneath the slick gray stones.

They had been the best of friends in those days, inseparable brothers who seemed so often to think with a single mind.

Of the two of them, Eric had been the strong one, the golden boy who did everything well and fought for his heart's desires. At seven, Eric had demanded to be taken to Granddad's island house on Lopez, the one they'd seen pictures of. And it was Eric who'd first convinced Mother to let them stay.

Dean could still remember the arguments. They were hushed, of course, as all Sloan disagreements were required to be, full of sibilant sounds and pregnant pauses. He remembered sitting at the top of the stairs, his scrawny body pressed so tightly against the railing that he'd worn the marks later on his flesh, listening to his older brother plead for the chance to go to the island school.

Absurd, Mother had declared at first, but Eric had worked on her relentlessly, wearing her down. As a child, Eric had been every bit as formidable as their mother, and in the end, he'd won. At the time, it had seemed a monumental victory; with age came wisdom, however. The truth was, Mother was so busy running Harcourt and Sons that she didn't care where her children were. Oh, occasionally she tried to do the "right" thing, as she called it—make them transfer to Choate—but in the end, she simply let them be.

Dean closed his eyes, then opened them quickly, startled by the sound of laughter.

But it was only an echo in his mind, an auditory memory. He hated what had brought him home at last, hated that it had taken a disease to bring him back to his brother. Even more, he hated the way he felt about Eric now; they'd grown so far apart. And all of it was Dean's fault. He saw that, knew it, hated it, and couldn't seem to change it.

It had happened on a seemingly ordinary Sunday. Dean had moved off of the island by then, gone to prep school; he'd been a senior, nursing a heart so broken that sometimes he'd forgotten to breathe. Eric had been at Princeton. They were still brothers then, separated only by miles, and they'd spoken on the phone every Sunday. One phone call had changed everything.

I've fallen in love, little bro . . . get ready for a shock . . . his name is Charlie and he's . . .

Dean had never been able to remember more than that. Somehow, in that weird, disorienting moment, his mind had shut down. He'd felt suddenly betrayed, as if the brother he'd known and loved was a stranger.

Dean had said all the right things to Eric. Even in his shocked confusion, he'd known what was expected of him, and he'd complied. But they'd both heard the lie beneath the words. Dean didn't know how to be honest, what words he could mold into an acceptable truth. He'd felt—ridiculously—as if he'd lost his brother that day.

If they'd gotten together back then, talked it through, they might have been okay. But they'd been young men, both of them, poised at the start of their lives, each one faced in a different direction. It had been easy to drift apart. By the time Dean graduated from Stanford and went to work for the family business, too much time had passed to start again. Eric had moved to Seattle and begun teaching high-school English. He'd lived with Charlie for a long time; only a few years before, Dean had received a note from Eric about Charlie's lost battle with AIDS.

Dean had sent flowers and a nice little card. He'd meant to pick up the phone, but every time he reached for it, he wondered what in the world he could say.

He turned away from the water and walked down the dock, then climbed the split-log stairs set into the sandy cliff. He was out of breath when he finally emerged on top of the bluff.

The sprawling Victorian house was exactly as he remembered it— salmony pink siding, steeply pitched roof, elegant white cutwork trim. Clematis vines curled around the porch rails and hung in frothy loops from along the eaves. The lawn was still as flat and green as a patch of Christmas felt. Roses bloomed riotously, perfectly trimmed and fertilized from year to year.

It was something his mother never forgot: home maintenance fees. Every house she owned was precisely cared for, but this one more than most. She knew—or imagined, which to her was the same as certainty—that Eric occasionally visited the summer house with *that man*. She didn't want to hear any complaints from them about the property.

Dean headed toward the house, ducking beneath the outstretched branches of an old madrona tree. As he bent, a glint of silver caught his eye. He turned, realizing a moment too late what he'd seen.

The swing set, rusted now and forgotten. A whispery breeze tapped one of the red seats, made the chains jangle. The sight of it dragged out an unwelcome memory . . .

Ruby. She'd been right there, leaning against the slanted metal support pole, with her arms crossed.

It was the moment—the exact second—he'd realized his best friend was a *girl.*

He'd moved toward her.

What? she'd said, laughing. *Am I drooling or something?*

All at once, he'd realized that he loved her. He'd wanted to say the words to her, but it was the year his voice betrayed him. He'd been so afraid of sounding like a girl when he spoke, and so he'd kissed her.

It had been the first kiss for both of them, and to this day, when Dean kissed a woman, he longed for the smell of the sea.

He spun away from the swing set and strode purposefully toward the house. At the front door, he paused, gathering courage and molding it into a smile. Then he knocked on the door.

From inside came the pattering sound of footsteps.

The door burst open and Lottie was there. His old nanny flung open her pudgy arms. "Dean!"

He stepped over the threshold and walked into the arms that had held him in his youth. He breathed in her familiar scent—Ivory soap and lemons.

He drew back, smiling. "Hey, Lottie. It's good to see you."

She gave him "the look"—one thick gray eyebrow arched. "I'm surprised you could still find your way here."

Though he hadn't seen her in more than a decade, she had barely aged. Oh, her hair was grayer, but she still wore it drawn back into a cookie-size bun at the base of her skull. Her ruddy skin was still amazingly wrinkle-free, and her bright green eyes were those of a woman who'd enjoyed her life.

He realized suddenly how much he'd missed her. Lottie had come into their family as a cook for the summer and gradually had become their full-time nanny. She'd never had any children of her own, and Eric and Dean had become her surrogate sons. She'd raised them for the ten years they'd lived on Lopez.

"I wish I were here for an ordinary visit," he said.

She blinked up at him. "It seems like only yesterday I was wiping chocolate off his little-boy face. I can't believe it. Just can't believe it." She stepped back into the well-lit entryway, wringing her hands.

Dean followed her into the living room, where a fire crackled in the huge hearth. The furniture he remembered from childhood still cluttered the big space. Cream-colored sofas on carved wooden legs faced each other. A large, oval-shaped rosewood coffee table stood between them, a beautiful Lalique bowl on its gleaming surface.

The room was gorgeously decorated in a timeless style. Not a thing was trendy or cheaply made. Every item reflected his mother's impeccable taste and boundless bank account.

The only thing missing from the room was life. No child had ever been allowed to sit on those perfect sofas, no drink had ever been spilled on that Aubusson carpet.

Dean glanced toward the stairway. "How is he?"

Lottie's green eyes filled with sadness. "Not so good, I'm sorry to say. The trip up here was hard on him. The hospice nurse was here today. She says that the new medication—something called a pain cocktail—will help him feel better."

Pain.

That was something Dean hadn't thought about, although he should have. "Jesus," he said softly, running a hand through his hair. He'd thought he was ready. He'd been mentally preparing himself, and yet now that he was here, he saw what an idiot he'd been. You couldn't prepare to watch your brother die. "Did Eric call our parents?"

"He did. They're in Greece. Athens."

"I know. Did he speak to Mother?"

Lottie glanced down at her hands; he braced himself. "Your mother's assistant spoke to him. It seems your mother was shopping when he called."

Dean's voice was purposely soft. He was afraid that if he raised it, even a bit, he'd be yelling. "Did Eric tell her about the cancer?"

"Of course. He wanted to tell your mother himself, but . . . he decided he'd better just leave a message."

"And has she returned his call?"

"No."

Dean released his breath in a tired sigh.

Lottie moved toward him. "I remember how you boys used to be. You'd walk through fire for one another."

"Yeah. I'm here for him now."

"Go on up." She smiled gently. "He's a bit the worse for wear, but he's still our boy."

Dean nodded stiffly, resettled the garment bag over his shoulder, and headed upstairs. The oak steps creaked beneath his feet. His hand slid up the oak banister, polished to sleek perfection by the comings and goings of three generations.

At the top of the stairs, the landing forked into two separate hallways. On the right was his parents' old wing; his-and-hers bedrooms that hadn't been occupied in more than fourteen years.

To the left were two doors, one closed, one partially open. The closed door led to Dean's old room. He didn't need to enter the room to picture it clearly: blue wool carpeting, maple bed with a plaid flannel bedspread, a dusty poster of Farrah Fawcett in her famous red bathing suit. He'd dreamed a million dreams in that room, imagined his unfolding life in a thousand ways . . . and none had presaged a moment like this.

Tired suddenly, he rounded the corner, passed his old bedroom, and came to Eric's door.

There he paused and drew in a deep breath, as if more air in his lungs would somehow make things better.

Then he walked into his brother's room.

The first thing he noticed was the hospital bed. It had replaced the bunk bed that once had hugged the wall. The new bed—big and metal-railed and tilted up like a lounging chair—dominated the small room. Lottie had positioned it to look out the window.

Eric was asleep.

Dean seemed to see everything at once—the way Eric's black hair had thinned to show patches of skin . . . the yellowed pallor of his sunken cheeks . . . the smudged black circles beneath his eyes . . . the veiny thinness of the arm that lay atop the stark white sheets. His lips were pale and slack, a colorless imitation of the mouth that had once smiled almost continually. Only the palest shadow of his brother lay here . . .

Dean grabbed the bed rail for support; the metal rattled beneath his grasp.

Eric's eyes slowly opened.

And there he was. The boy he'd known and loved. "Eric," he said, wishing his voice weren't so thick. He struggled to find a smile.

"Don't bother, baby brother. Not for me."

"Don't bother what?"

"Pretending not to be shocked at the way I look." Eric reached for the small pink plastic cup on his bedside tray. His long, thin fingers trembled as he guided the straw to his mouth. He sipped slowly, swallowed. When he looked up at Dean, his rheumy eyes were filled with a terrible, harrowing honesty. "I didn't think you'd come."

"Of course I came. You should have told me . . . before."

"Like when I told you I was gay? Believe me, I learned a long time ago that my family didn't handle bad news well."

Dean fought to hold back tears, and then gave up. They were the kind of tears that hurt deep in your heart. He felt a stinging sense of shame.

Remorse, regret, boredom, anticipation, ambition . . . these were the emotions that had taken Dean through life. Those, he knew how to handle, how to manipulate and compensate for. But this new emotion . . . this feeling in the pit of his stomach that he'd been a bad person, that he'd hurt his brother deeply and known it and never bothered to make it right . . .

Eric smiled weakly. "You're here now. That's enough."

"No. You've been sick for a long time . . . by yourself."

"It doesn't matter."

Dean wanted to smooth the thin strands of hair from Eric's damp forehead, to offer a comforting touch, but when he reached out, his hands were trembling, and he drew back.

It had been years since he'd comforted another human being; he didn't remember how.

"It matters," he said, hearing the thickness in his voice. He would give anything right now to erase the past, to be able to go back to that Sunday afternoon, listen to that same confession of love from his brother, and simply be happy.

But how did you do that? How did two people move backward through time and untie a knot that had tangled through every moment of their lives?

"Just talk to me," Eric said sleepily, smiling again. "Just talk, little brother. Like we used to."

Chapter Five

The phone rang in the middle of the night. Ruby groaned and glanced bleary-eyed at the bedside clock. One-fifteen.

"Shit," she mumbled. It had to be one of those idiot reporters.

She reached across Max's empty half of the bed and yanked the phone off the hook. Rolling onto her back, she brought it to her ear. "Bite me."

"I gave that up in kindergarten."

Ruby laughed sleepily. "Caro? Oh, sorry. I thought you were one of those bottom feeders from the *Tattler*."

"They aren't calling me. Of course, I haven't made a career out of dissing Mom."

"It isn't much of a career." Ruby scooted backward and leaned against the rough stucco wall. Through the phone lines, she could hear a baby crying. It was a high-pitched wailing sound, one only dogs should be able to hear. "Jesus, Caro, you must be chewing Excedrin. Does the baby Jesus always wail like that?"

"Mom's been in a car accident."

Ruby gasped. "What happened?"

"I don't know. All I know is that she's at Bayview. Apparently she'd been drinking."

"She never drinks . . . I mean, she never used to." Ruby threw back the covers and stood up. She wasn't sure why she did it, except that she had a sudden need to be moving. She held the cordless phone to her ear, walking toward the darkened kitchen. There, she stared out the slit in the tattered curtains at the black street below. The pink neon vacancy sign flickered and buzzed. She ran a hand through her sweaty hair. "How bad is it?"

"I don't know. I'm going to drop the kids off with Jere's mom first thing in the morning and go to the hospital. But I don't want to do this alone. Will you come?"

"I don't know, Car—"

"She could be dying. Think of someone besides yourself for a change," Caroline said sharply.

Ruby sighed heavily. "Okay, I'll come."

"I'll call Alaska Airlines and put a ticket on my card. There's a flight at five forty-five. You can pick it up at the counter."

"Uh . . . you don't have to do that. I have money now."

"*You?* Oh . . . well, that's great."

"I'll be there by noon." Ruby hung up the phone. Crossing her arms tightly, she paced her apartment, back and forth, back and forth, unable to stop.

She had been angry at her so-called mother forever. She couldn't really remember *not* hating her . . . and the past few days had only added fuel to the fire.

But now . . . an accident. Horrible images slammed through her mind. Paralysis . . . brain damage . . . death.

She closed her eyes. (It took her a moment to realize that she was praying.) "Take care of her," she whispered, then added a single, unfamiliar word, "Please?"

When Nora woke up the next morning, she had a moment of pure, heart-pumping fear. She was in a strange bed, in an austere room she didn't recognize.

Then she remembered.

She'd been in a car accident. She recalled the ambulance ride . . .

the flashing red lights . . . the metallic taste of her own blood . . . the surprise on the young paramedic's face when he'd realized who he was treating.

And the doctors. The orthopedist who'd spoken to her just before and after the X rays. *A severe break above the ankle; another, small fracture below the knee . . . a sprained wrist.* He'd said she was lucky.

When he'd said that, she'd cried.

Now, her leg was in a cast. She couldn't see it beneath the blankets, but she could feel it. The flesh tingled and itched and her bone ached.

She sighed, feeling sorry for herself and deeply ashamed. Drinking and driving.

As if the *Tattler*'s photographs weren't enough to ruin her career, she'd added a crime to the list.

It wouldn't be long before the media picked up her scent. Someone would figure out that there was a buck to be made in telling the world that Nora Bridge was in Bayview. The accident report was probably worth thousands.

There was a knock at the door, short and sharp, and then Caroline swept into the room. Her back was ramrod straight, her pale hands clasped at her waist. She wore a pair of camel-colored cashmere pants and a matching sweater set. Her silvery blond hair was cut in a perfect bob, one side tucked discreetly behind her ear. Huge diamond studs glittered in her earlobes. "Hello, Mother."

"Hi, honey. It's nice of you to come." Nora recognized instantly how distant she sounded, and it shamed her. She and Caroline had worked hard in the past few years, trying to come back together in an honest way. Nora had treated her elder daughter with infinite care, always letting Caro make the first move. Now, all that progress had been blown to hell; she could see how far apart they'd fallen again. There was a coldness in Caroline's eyes that Nora hadn't seen in years.

Caroline glanced at her quickly, smiled—or winced. She looked vulnerable suddenly.

Nora couldn't stand the awkward silence that fell between them. She said the first thing that popped into her mind. "The doctors say I'll need to be in a wheelchair for a few days—just until my wrist gets strong enough to make crutches possible."

"Who is going to take care of you?"

"Oh . . . I hadn't thought about that. I guess I'll hire someone. Shouldn't be difficult." She kept talking—anything was better than that silence. "The big question is, *where* will I go? I can't go back to my condo. The press has the place staked out. But I need to stay close to my doctors."

Caroline took a step toward the bed. "You could use the summer house. Jere and I never find time to make it up there, and Ruby won't set foot on the island. The old house is just sitting there . . ."

The house on Summer Island. A stone's throw from Eric. It would be perfect. Nora looked up at her daughter. "You'd do that for me?"

Caroline gave her a look of infinite sadness. "I wish you knew me."

Nora sagged back into the pillows. She'd said the wrong thing again. "I'm sorry."

"God, I've heard that from you so often, I feel like its tattooed on my forehead. Quit saying you're sorry and start acting like it. Start acting like my mother." She reached into her purse and fished out a set of keys. Pulling a single key from the ring, she set it down on the bedside table.

Nora could see that her daughter was close to breaking. "Caro—"

"Call me when you've settled in." Caroline stepped back, putting distance between them.

Nora didn't know what to say. Caroline was right; Nora hadn't had the courage to act like a mother in years.

"I have to go now."

Nora nodded stiffly, trying to smile. "Of course. Thanks for coming." She wanted to reach out for Caroline, hold her daughter's hand, and never let go.

"Good-bye, Mom."

And she was gone.

Ruby stepped out of the main terminal at SeaTac International Airport. Rain thumped on the skybridge and studded the street, creating a pewter curtain between the terminal and the multilayered parking garage across the street.

The early morning air smelled of evergreen trees and fertile black earth. Like a dash of spice in a complex recipe, there was the barest tang of the sea; a scent only a local would recognize.

As she stood beneath this bloated gray sky, smelling the moist, pine-scented air, she realized that memories were more than misty recollections. They stayed rooted in the soil in which they'd grown. There were places up north, in the San Juan Island archipelago, where bits and pieces of Ruby's life had been left scattered about like seashells on the shore. Somewhere up there sat the shadow of a thin, bold-eyed girl on a pebbly beach, tearing the petals off a daisy, chanting *He loves me; he loves me not.* She knew that if she looked hard enough, she would be able to find the invisible trail she'd left behind, the pieces of her that led from the present back to the past.

She wasn't surprised at how fresh the memories were. Nothing could ever dry up and turn to dust in the moist Seattle air. Everything thrived.

Ruby hailed a cab and climbed into the backseat, tossing her carry-on bag in beside her. She glanced at the cabbie's registration (a habit she'd formed during visits to New York) and saw that his name was Avi Avivivi.

There was a joke in that, but she was too tired to go digging around for it. "Bayview," she said, thumping back into the smelly brown velour seat.

Avi hit the gas and rocketed into the next lane.

Ruby closed her eyes, trying not to think of anything at all. It seemed like only a few minutes later, Avi was tapping her on the shoulder.

"Mrs.? Ma'am? You are well, yes?"

Ruby jerked awake, rubbing her eyes. "I'm fine, thanks." Fishing thirty rumpled dollars out of her pocket, she handed Avi the fare and tip. Then she grabbed her purse and bag, slung both straps over her shoulder, and headed toward the hospital's double glass doors, where a few people were milling about.

Ruby was almost in their midst when she realized they were reporters.

"It's her daughter!"

The reporters turned to her all at once, yelling above one another, elbowing for position.

"Ruby, look here!"

"Was your mother drunk at the time of—"

"What did you think of the photographs—"

Ruby heard every shutter click, every picture frame advance. She noticed the strand of hair that was stuck to her lower lip, the tiny paper cut on her index finger.

It was as if she were standing miles apart from the crowd, even though she could have reached out and touched the woman from CNN.

"Ruby! Ruby! Ruby!"

For a dizzying moment, she let herself pretend that this was for her, that she had earned this attention.

"Did you know about your mother's affair?"

At that, Ruby turned. She locked eyes with a small, beak-nosed man wearing a KOMO 4 hat. "No." She flashed a bright, fake smile. "I'd make a joke about it, but it's not very funny."

She pushed through the crowd, holding her head up, looking straight ahead. Their questions followed her, rocks thrown at her back, some hitting hard.

She strode through the pneumatic doors. They whooshed shut behind her.

Inside, it was quiet. The air smelled of disinfectant. Boldly patterned chairs dotted the vast white lobby. There were cheery, generic paintings on the walls, placed awkwardly between gilt-framed portraits of sour-looking men and women who'd obviously donated millions to the hospital.

"Ruby!"

Caroline rushed forward. Her hug almost knocked Ruby off her feet. As she held her sister, Ruby could feel how thin Caro had become, could feel the tremble in her sister's body.

At last, Caro drew back. Her mascara had run, ruining the impossible perfection of her face. "I'm sorry," she said, snapping her purse open, fishing for a lace handkerchief, which she found and dabbed at her eyes. Ruby could sense that Caroline was embarrassed by her uncharacteristic display of emotion. If old patterns ran true, Caro would pull back now, distance herself while she whittled her feelings down to an acceptable size.

Caroline closed her eyes for a moment. When she reopened them, she looked at Ruby with a kind of quiet desperation. Ruby recognized that look. Her sister was wondering why everything in life couldn't be easier, why they all couldn't simply love each other.

Silence fell between them, soft and cold as an early morning rain. In that quiet, Ruby heard the echo of a broken family; they were individual pieces, now separate, wanting a wholeness that had been shattered.

"So, how is Nora?" Ruby asked at last.

Caroline gave her a sharp look. "She still hates it when we call her Nora."

"Really? I'd forgotten that."

"I'll bet you did. Anyway, she drove her car into a tree. Her leg is broken; her wrist is sprained. She'll be in a wheelchair for a few days.

That makes it pretty tough to do the ordinary bits and pieces of life. She'll need help."

"I pity the poor nurse who takes *that* job."

Caroline looked at her. "Would *you* want to be cared for by a stranger?"

It took Ruby a minute to get her sister's drift. When she did, she burst out laughing. "You're delusional."

"This isn't funny. You saw the reporters out front. They're ready to tear Mom apart, and she's always been fragile."

"Yeah, in that pit-bull kind of way."

"Ruby," Caroline said in her we're-a-team-and-you're-not-playing-fair voice. "A stranger could sell her out to the tabloids. She needs someone she can trust."

"Then you'd better do it. She can't trust me."

"I have kids. A husband."

A life. The implication was clear, and the truth of it stung. "Doesn't she have any friends?"

"It should be you, Ruby." Caroline looked disgusted. "Jesus. You're going to be thirty in a few years. Mom's fifty. When are you going to get to know her?"

"Who says I'm *ever* going to?"

Caro moved closer. "Tell me you didn't think about it last night."

Ruby couldn't swallow. Her sister was so close . . . she smelled of expensive perfume, gardenias, maybe. "About what?"

"Losing her."

The words hit dangerously near their mark. Ruby stared down at the speckled linoleum floor. There was no doubt in her mind what she should do—go out those front doors and fly home. But it wasn't quite so easy this time, especially with the *Caché* article out there to write. A little time with Nora Bridge would certainly make the piece better. A *lot* better.

She took a deep breath, then turned to face her sister. "One week," she said evenly. "I'll stay with her for one week."

Caroline pulled Ruby into a fierce hug. "I knew you'd do the right thing."

Ruby felt like a fraud. She couldn't meet her sister's gaze. Weakly, she said, "A week with Nora. You'd better start a defense fund."

Caroline laughed. "Go tell her. She's in six twelve west. I'll wait for you here."

"Coward." Ruby flashed her a nervous smile, then headed for the elevators. On the sixth floor, she began a room-to-room search until she found 612.

The door was ajar.

She took another deep breath and stepped inside.

Her mother was asleep.

Ruby exhaled in relief. The tension in her shoulders eased a little, she unclenched her fists.

She stared down at her mother's pale, beautiful face and felt an unexpected tug of longing. She had to forcibly remind herself that this lovely, red-haired woman who looked like Susan Sarandon wasn't really her mother. Ruby's mother—the woman who'd played Scrabble and made chocolate-chip pancakes every Sunday morning—had died eleven years ago. This was the woman who'd killed her.

Nora opened her eyes.

Ruby felt an almost overwhelming urge to run away.

Nora gasped and scooted up to a sit, self-consciously smoothing the tangled hair from her face. "You came," she said softly, a note of wonder in her voice.

Ruby forced her hands to stay bolted to her sides. It was an old stand-up rule. No fidgeting. The audience could smell a set of nerves. "How are you?"

Stupid question, but Ruby was off-balance, afraid of pitching headfirst.

"I'm fine." Nora smiled, but it was an odd, uncertain smile.

Ruby crossed her arms—another antifidget technique. "So, I guess you've lost your good-driver discount."

"That's my Ruby. Quick with a joke."

"I wouldn't say 'your' Ruby."

Nora's smile faded. "I'm sure you wouldn't." She closed her eyes and rubbed the bridge of her nose, exhaling softly. "I see you still think you know everything . . . and you still don't take any prisoners."

Ruby could feel the shale of old habits sliding beneath her feet. A few more well-chosen words and there would be a full-scale war going on between them.

"I don't know everything," Ruby said evenly. "I don't think I ever knew my mother."

Nora laughed, a fluttery, tired sound. "That makes two of us."

They stared at each other. Ruby felt a mounting urge to escape; she knew it was a survival instinct. Already she knew she couldn't spend a week with this woman and feel nothing . . . the anger was so sharp right now it overwhelmed her.

But she had no choice.

"I thought . . . I'd stay with you for a while. Help you get settled."

Nora's surprise was almost comical. "Why?"

Ruby shrugged. There were so many answers to that question. "You could have died. Maybe I thought of what it would be like to lose you." She smiled woodenly. "Or maybe this is your darkest hour, the loss of everything you left your family for, and I don't want to miss a minute of your misery. Or maybe I got a contract to write a magazine article about you and I need to be close to get the inside scoop. Or maybe I—"

"I get it. Who cares why. I need help and you obviously have nothing better to do."

"How do you do it—slam me in the middle of a thank-you? Jesus, it's a gift."

"I didn't mean to slam you."

"No, you just thought you'd point out that I have no life. It wouldn't occur to you that I've rearranged my life to spend some time with you, would it?"

"Let's not start, okay?"

"You started it."

Nora's hand moved to the bed rail, her fingers slid close to touch Ruby. She looked up. "You know I'm going to the summer house, right?"

Ruby couldn't have heard right. *"What?"*

"Reporters are camped outside my condo. I can't face them." Nora's gaze lowered, and Ruby saw how hard it was for her mother to face *her,* too. The past was between them again, a sticky web that caught old hurts and held them. "Your sister offered me use of the summer house. If you want to change your mind, I'll understand."

Ruby went to the window and stared out at the gray, rainy streets of Capitol Hill.

It had seemed doable a few moments ago; go to this woman's house—Nora's house, not really her mother at all—sit with her for a few days, make a few meals, look through a few old photo albums, ask a few questions. Get enough information to write the "where Nora Bridge came from" section of the article.

But . . . at the summer house.

It was where so many of the memories were buried, both good and bad. She would rather see Nora in some glass-walled high-rise that success had purchased. Not in the clapboard farmhouse where Ruby would remember gardening and painting and the sound of laughter that had long since faded.

Fifty thousand dollars.

That's what she had to think about. She could handle a week at the summer house.

"I guess it doesn't matter where we are . . ."

"You mean it?" There was a disturbing wistfulness in her mother's voice.

Finally, Ruby turned. She meant to close the distance between them, but her feet wouldn't move. "Sure. Why not?"

Nora was looking at her thoughtfully. She said, "You'll need to rent me a wheelchair—just until my wrist is strong enough for crutches. And I'll need a few things from my apartment."

"I can do that."

"I'll talk to my doctor and get checked out of here. We'll have to leave quietly, through the back way, maybe. We don't want to be followed."

"I'll rent a car and pick you up in—what—three hours?"

"Okay. My purse is in the closet. Get my credit cards. Use the platinum Visa for anything you need. I'll draw you a map to my apartment and call Ken—he's the doorman. He'll let you in. And Ruby . . . get a nice car, okay?"

Ruby tried to smile. This was going to be bad. Her mother was already making demands—and judgments. "Only the best for you, Nora." She went to the closet, saw the expensive black handbag, and grabbed it. The wide strap settled comfortably on her shoulder. Without a backward glance, she headed out.

Her mother's voice stopped her. "Ruby? Thank you."

Ruby shut the door behind her.

Chapter Six

Ruby walked into her mother's penthouse condominium and closed the door behind her. The place was eerily silent and smelled faintly of flowers.

She dropped her jacket onto the gleaming marble floor, beside an ornate wrought-iron and stone table that held a huge urn full of roses.

She turned the corner and literally had to catch her breath. It was the most incredible room she'd ever seen.

A wall of floor-to-ceiling windows wrapped around the whole apartment, showcasing a panoramic view of Elliot Bay.

The floors were polished marble, a color somewhere between white and gold, with twisting black and green threads running through each square. Brocade-covered furniture, perched on gilded legs, sat in a cluster in the living room around a beautiful gold and glass coffee table. In one corner stood an ebony Steinway, its lacquered top cluttered with photographs in gilt-edged frames.

A dimly lit hallway led past several more rooms—formal dining room, gourmet kitchen, home office—and ended at the master bedroom. Here, the windows were dressed in steel-gray silk curtains that matched the woven cashmere bedspread. There were two huge walk-in closets. She opened the first one, and a light came on automatically, revealing two rows of clothes, organized by color.

Ruby's fingers drifted through the clothing. Silks, cashmeres, expensive woolens. She saw the labels: St. John, Armani, Donna Karan, Escada.

She released her breath in an envious sigh. The thought *This is what she left us for* winged through her mind, hurting more than she would have expected.

She pulled the list out of her pocket.

> Hairdryer
> Curling iron
> Shorts
> Sundresses
> Socks

They were ordinary items, but nothing in this closet cost less than three hundred dollars.

She backed out, closing the door behind her. At the rosewood, gilt-trimmed bombé chest, she opened the top drawer. Little piles of perfectly folded lingerie lay there. She picked out a few pieces, then gathered up some shorts and cap-sleeved tops from the second drawer. She set the pile on the bed and moved to the second closet.

Again, the light came on automatically, but the clothing in this closet looked as if it belonged to another woman. Worn gray sweatpants; baggy, stained sweatshirts; jeans so old they were out of date. A few brightly colored sundresses.

Her mother had expensive designer clothes, and lie-around-the-house clothes, but nothing in between. No clothes for going out to lunch with a friend or stopping by to catch a matinee.

No clothes for a real life.

Weird . . .

She reached for a sundress. As she pulled it toward her, the lacy hem caught on something. Ruby gently pushed the other clothes out of the way and saw what had snagged the dress.

It was the upraised flap of a cardboard box. On the beige side, written in red ink, was the word *Ruby.*

Her heart skipped a beat. She had a quick, almost desperate urge to back out of the closet and slam it shut. Whatever was in that box, whatever her mother had saved and marked with Ruby's name, couldn't matter . . .

But she couldn't seem to make herself move. She dropped the dress, let it clatter to the floor, hanger and all, and fell to her knees. Scooting forward, she dragged the box toward her. Her fingers were trembling as she opened it.

Inside, there were dozens of tiny wrapped packages, some in the reds and greens of Christmas, some in bright silvery paper with balloons and candles.

Birthdays and Christmases.

She counted the packages. Twenty-one. Two each year for the eleven Nora had been gone from them, less the black cashmere sweater that Caroline had sneaked past Ruby's guard.

These were the gifts that Nora had bought every year and sent to Ruby, the same ones Ruby had ruthlessly returned, unopened.

"Oh, man." She let out her breath in a sigh and reached for one of the boxes. It was small, like many of the others, the size of a credit card and about a half inch deep. The one she'd chosen was wrapped in birthday paper.

The paper felt slick in her hands and as she lifted it toward her, she heard a tiny clinking from inside, and the sound filled her with a terrible longing. It made her angry, this welling up of useless emotion, but she couldn't make it go away.

Carefully, she peeled the paper away and was left with a small white box imprinted with a jewelry store logo. She lifted the lid.

Inside, on a bed of opalescent tissue, lay a silver charm. It was a birthday cake, complete with candles.

Ruby knew she shouldn't pick up the charm, but she couldn't help herself. She reached down and picked it up, feeling the steady weight of it in her palm, then turned it over. On the back, it was inscribed.

HAPPY 21ST. LOVE, MOM.

The silver charm blurred.

She refused to open any more; she didn't need to. She knew that somewhere in these boxes were a bracelet and more carefully chosen charms—many representing the years they'd been apart.

She could imagine her mother, dressed perfectly, makeup flawless, going from store to store for the ideal gift. She would be chatting pleasantly with the salespeople, saying things like, *My daughter is twenty-one today. I need something extra special.*

Pretending that everything was normal . . . that she hadn't abandoned her children when they needed her most.

At that, Ruby felt a rush of cold anger, and control returned. A few trinkets didn't mean anything.

What mattered was not what Nora had tried to *give* Ruby, but rather what she'd taken away.

There had been no seventeenth birthday party for Ruby. On that day, there had only been more silence. No family had gathered around a big kitchen table strewn with gifts. Those times . . . those precious moments had died when their family died.

A few nicely wrapped gifts found stuffed in a cardboard box in a closet couldn't change that.

Ruby wouldn't let it.

As Ruby neared her mother's hospital room, she slowed. A man was standing by the door. He was tall and effete, a man who dressed for women—gray slacks, pink shirt, and vibrant navy blue suspenders. His hair was snowy white and thinning. She noticed that he kept running his hand through it, as if to assure himself that it was still there.

At her approach, he looked up. Narrowed, penetrating black eyes fixed on her. "Are you Ruby Bridge?"

She came to a stop. She'd misjudged the distance, and taken one step too close to him. He exuded a sweet, musky scent. Expensive cologne, used too liberally. She could see that he was disturbed by her invasion of his personal space.

He took a step backward and cleared his throat—a gentle reminder that he'd asked if she was Ruby Bridge.

"Who wants to know?"

Smiling—as if that was precisely what he would have expected Ruby Bridge to say—he extended his hand. "I'm Dr. Leonard Allbright, your mother's doctor."

"Where's your white coat?"

"I'm her psychiatrist."

That surprised Ruby. She couldn't imagine her mother spilling her guts to anyone. "Really?"

"I've just spoken to her, and she told me all about your . . . arrangement." He said the final word as if it tasted bitter. "I'm aware of your past history, so I thought I'd caution you to keep in mind that your mother is fragile."

"Uh-huh. Are you married, Dr. Allbright?"

A pained expression slipped into the grooves of his face. "No. Why do you ask?"

"My mother collects men who believe she's fragile. She's a real Tennessee Williams kind of gal."

Dr. Allbright did not look pleased by that observation. "Why have you offered to care for her?"

"Look, Doc, when it's all over, you can ask Nora all the questions you want. She'll pay you a huge fee to listen to her moan about the bitch daughter who betrayed her. But *I'm* not going to talk to you."

"'Betrayed' is an interesting word choice."

Ruby flinched. "If that's all . . ."

He reached into his pocket and withdrew a slim silver case with the initials LOA etched in gold. Inside lay a neat stack of expensive business cards. He handed her one. "I don't know if it is a good idea for you to take care of Nora. Especially not in her current state of mind."

Ruby took the card, tucked it into the elastic waistband of her leggings. "Yeah? Why not?"

He studied her, and she could see by the deepening frown that he wasn't pleased. "You haven't seen or spoken to your mother in years, and you're obviously very angry at her. Considering . . . what happened to her, it could be a bad mix. Maybe even dangerous."

"Dangerous how?"

"You don't know her. And as I said, she's fragile now—"

"I lived with her for sixteen years, Doc. You've talked to her once a week for . . . what, a year or two?"

"Fifteen years."

Ruby's chin snapped up. "*Fifteen* years? But everything was fine back then."

"Was it?"

His question threw her into confusion. Fifteen years ago, Ruby had been barely out of braces, singing along to Madonna and wearing a dozen crucifixes and imagining that her future would follow the course of her childhood, that her family would always be together.

"Your mother keeps a lot to herself," Dr. Allbright went on, "and as I said, she's fragile. I believe she always has been. You obviously disagree." He took a step toward her. This time it was Ruby who felt encroached upon. She steeled herself to stand her ground. "Your mother was doing almost seventy miles per hour when she hit that tree. And on the same day she lost her career. Pretty coincidental."

Ruby couldn't believe she hadn't made that connection. A chill moved through her. "Are you telling me she tried to kill herself?"

"I'm saying it's coincidental. Dangerously so."

Ruby released a heavy breath. Suddenly, it didn't seem like a good idea to be responsible for her mother, not even for a few days. No one emotionally unstable should be entrusted to Ruby—hell, *goldfish* couldn't survive her care.

"You don't know your mother. Remember that."

That observation put Ruby back on solid ground. "And who's fault is that? I'm not the one who walked out."

He stared down at her, gave her the kind of look she'd seen time and time again in her life.

Oh, good, she thought, *now I'm disappointing total strangers.*

"No, you're not," he said evenly, "and you're not sixteen anymore, either."

Ruby should have rented a bigger car. Like maybe a Hummer or a Winnebago.

This minivan was too small for her and Nora. They were trapped in side-by-side front seats. With the windows rolled up, there seemed to be no air left to breathe, and nothing to do but talk.

Ruby cranked up the radio.

Celine Dion's pure, vibrant voice filled the car, something about love coming to those who believed.

"Do you think you could turn that down?" Nora said. "I'm getting a headache."

Ruby's gaze flicked sideways. Nora looked tired; her skin, normally pale, now appeared to have the translucence of bone china. Tiny blue veins webbed the sunken flesh at her temples. She turned to Ruby and attempted a smile, but in truth, her mouth barely trembled before she closed her eyes and leaned against the window.

Fragile.

Ruby couldn't wrap her arms around that thought. It was too alien from her own experience. Her mother had always been made of steel. Even as a young girl, Ruby had known her mother's strength. The other kids in her class were afraid of their fathers when report cards came out. Not the Bridge girls. They lived in fear of disappointing their mother.

Not that she ever punished them particularly, or yelled or screamed. No, it was worse than that.

I'm disappointed in you, Ruby Elizabeth . . . life isn't kind to women who take the easy road.

Ruby had never known what the easy road was, exactly, or where it led, but she knew it was a bad thing. Almost as bad as "fooling yourself"—another thing Nora wouldn't abide.

The truth doesn't go away just because you shut your eyes had been another of her mother's favorite sayings.

Of course, those had been the "before" days. Afterward, no one in the family cared much about disappointing Nora Bridge. In fact, Ruby had gone out of her way to do just that.

"Ruby? The music?"

Ruby snapped the radio off. The metronomic *whoosh-thump, whoosh-thump* of the windshield wipers filled the sudden silence.

Only a few miles from downtown Seattle, the gray city gave way to a sprawling collection of squat, flat-topped strip malls. A few miles more and they were in farming land. Rolling, tree-shrouded hills and lush green pastures fanned out on either side of the freeway. The white ice-cream dome of Mount Baker sat on a layer of fog above the flat farmland.

Ruby actually sped up as they drove through the sleepy town of Mount Vernon; she was afraid her mother would say something intimate, like *Remember how we used to bicycle through the tulip fields at festival time?*

But when she glanced sideways, she saw that Nora was asleep.

Ruby breathed a sigh of relief and eased off the accelerator. It felt good to drive the rest of the way without wondering if she was being watched.

At Anacortes, the tiny seaside town perched at the water's edge, she bought a one-way ferry ticket and pulled into line. It was still early in the tourist season; two weeks from now the wait for this ferry could well be five hours.

Less than a half hour later, a ferry docked, sounded its mournful horn, and unloaded its cargo of cars and bikes and walk-on passengers.

Then, an orange-vested attendant directed Ruby's car to the bow, where she parked and set the emergency brake. First car in lane two, a primo spot. The gaping, oval mouth of the ferry was a giant, glass-less window that framed the view.

The Sound was rainy-day flat, studded by the ceaseless rain into a sheet of hammered tin. Watery gray skies melted into the sea, the line between them a smudge of charcoal, thin as eyeliner. Puppy-faced gray seals crawled over one another to find a comfortable perch on the swaying red harbor buoy.

Ruby got out of the car and went upstairs. After buying a latte at the lunch counter, she walked out onto the deck.

No one was out here now. The rain had diminished to little more than a heavy mist. Moisture beaded the handrails and slickened the decks.

A long, single blast of the boat's horn announced their departure.

Ruby slid her fingers along the wet handrail, holding on, shivering at a sudden burst of cold. A few brave seagulls hung in the air in front of her, wings outstretched, motionless, riding a current of air. They cawed loudly, begging for scraps.

Lush green islands dotted the tinfoil sea, their carved granite coast-lines a stark contrast to the flat silver water. Polished red madrona trees slanted out from the shore, their roots clinging tenaciously to a thin layer of topsoil. Houses were scattered here and there but, for the most part, the islands looked empty.

She closed her eyes, breathing in the salty, familiar sea air. In eighth grade, she'd started taking the ferry to school at Friday Harbor on San Juan Island; memories of high school were inextricably linked with this boat . . .

She and Dean had always stood together at just this spot, right at the bow, even when it was raining.

Dean.

It was strange that she hadn't thought of him right away.

Well, perhaps not so strange. It had been more than a decade since she'd seen him, and still it hurt to remember him.

After her mother had left, Ruby hadn't thought it was possible to hurt more. Dean had taught her that the human heart always made room for pain.

She still thought of him now and then. Sometimes, when she woke in the middle of a hot, lonely night and found that her cheeks were slicked and wet, she knew she'd been dreaming of him. She knew from Caroline (who knew from Nora) that he'd followed in his mother's footsteps after all, that he was running the empire now. Ruby had always known that he would.

At last, the ferry turned toward Summer Island. The horn sounded, and the captain came on the loudspeaker, urging passengers to return to their vehicles.

Ruby raced downstairs and jumped into the minivan.

The captain cut the engine and the boat drifted toward the rickety black dock. A weatherbeaten sign—it had been old when Ruby was a child—hung at a cockeyed angle from the nearest piling. It read SUMMER ISLAND WELCOMES YOU.

A woman walked out of the closet-size terminal building and stood watching the ferry float toward her. She was wearing a floor-length brown dress with neither collar nor cuffs. An ornate silver crucifix hung from a thick chain around her neck. Waving at the few walk-on passengers clustered at the bow's railing, she dragged a tattered, wrist-thick length of rope across the dock and tied the boat down.

"Oh, Lord," Nora said, blinking awake, "is that Sister Helen?"

Ruby couldn't believe it herself. The nuns had always run the ferry traffic on Summer Island, but it was still a shock to see that nothing had changed. "Amazing, isn't it?"

Nora sighed. It was a tired sound, as if maybe she wondered if changelessness were a good thing. Or maybe, like Ruby, she had just realized how it would *feel* to be here again, at the site of so much heartache.

Ruby drove off the ferry, past the post office and general store. What struck her first was the total lack of meaningful change. She felt as if she'd just taken a boat ride back in time. Here, on Summer Island, it was still 1985. If she turned on the radio, it would probably be Cyndi Lauper or Rick Springfield . . .

This was why she'd stayed away.

The road turned, climbed up a short hill, then flowed down into a rolling green valley.

To her left, the land was a Monet painting, all golden grass and green trees and washed-out silvery skies. To her right lay Bottleneck Bay, and beyond that was the forested green hump of Shaw Island. Weathered gray fishing boats sat keeled on the pebbly beach, forgotten by their owners more than a generation ago. A few sleek sailboats—mostly owned by the few Californians brave enough to purchase a summer home on this too-quiet island where drinking water was never guaranteed and power came and went with the wind—bobbed idly in the gently swelling sea.

There were only a few farmhouses visible from the road. The island boasted five thousand acres, but only one hundred year-round residents. Even in the summer, when mainlanders swarmed to their island vacation homes, Summer Island had fewer than three hundred residents.

It was as different from California as a place could be. Here, hip-hop was the way a rabbit moved, and a drive-by meant stopping to say hello to your neighbor on your way to town.

Nora looked out the rain-dappled window. Her head made a thumping sound as she rested it against the glass. The lines around her mouth were deeply etched, heavy enough to weigh her lips into a frown. "When I first came here . . . no, that doesn't matter now . . ."

Ruby approached the beach road. Instead of turning, she eased her foot off the gas and coasted to a stop. Her mother's half sentence had implied . . . secrets . . . things unspoken, and Ruby didn't like it.

Fifteen years, Dr. Allbright had said. He'd been treating Nora for fifteen years . . . yet none of them had known it.

"What were you going to say?"

Nora's laughter was a fluttery thing, a bit of spun sugar. "Nothing."

Ruby rolled her eyes. Why had she even bothered? "Whatever."

She eased her foot back onto the accelerator, flicked the signal on, and turned toward the beach. The narrow, one-lane road wound snakelike through the towering trees. Though it was afternoon, you wouldn't have known it. The tree limbs were heavy with rain; their drooping branches darkened the road. Here and there, small turnouts, overgrown with weeds, made space for parking when another car was coming from the opposite direction.

At last, they came to the driveway. A pair of dogwood trees stood guard on either side of the needle-strewn lane. Any gravel that had once been dumped here had long ago burrowed into the dirt.

Ruby turned down the driveway. The knee-high grass that grew in a wild strip down the center of the road thumped and scraped the undercarriage.

At the end of the tree-lined road, Ruby hit the brakes.

And stared through the rain-beaded windshield at her childhood.

The farmhouse was layered in thick white clapboards with red trim around the casement windows. One side jutted out like an old woman's bad hip—that was the addition her grandparents had built for their grandchildren. A porch wrapped around three sides of the house. It sat in the midst of a pie-shaped clearing that jutted toward the sea. In this, the middle of June, the lawn was lush and lime green; in the dog days of summer, Ruby knew it would grow tall and take on the rich hue of burnished gold. Madrona trees marked the perimeter.

"Oh, God," she whispered, soaking it all in.

A white picket fence created a nicely squared yard around the farmhouse. Inside it, the garden was in full, riotous bloom.

Obviously Caroline had paid a gardener to keep the place up. It looked as if the Bridge family had been gone a season instead of more than a decade.

With a tired sigh, Ruby got out of the car.

The tide made a low, snoring sound. Birds chattered overhead, surprised and dismayed by their unexpected guests. But no city sounds lived this far north, no horns or squealing tires or jets flying overhead.

There was now, as there had always been, a quiet otherworldliness to Summer Island, and as much as she hated to admit it, Ruby felt the island's familiar welcome. Time here was measured in eons, not lifetimes. In how long it took the sea to smooth the rough edges off a bit of broken glass, in how long it took the tide to shape and reshape the shoreline.

She went around to the back of the van and pulled out the wheelchair, then wheeled it around to the passenger side and helped Nora into the seat.

Taking hold of the rubber-coated grips, she cautiously pushed her mother down the path. At the gate, Ruby stopped and walked ahead, unlatching it. The metal piece clanked, the gate swung creakily open.

When Ruby turned back around, she noticed how pale her mother was. Nora touched the fence's sagging slat. A heart-shaped patch of paint fell away at the contact, lay in the grass like a bit of confetti.

Nora looked up, her eyes shiny and moist. "Remember the summer you and Caro painted every slat a different color? You guys looked like a pair of rainbow Popsicles when you were finished."

"I don't remember that," Ruby said, but for a split second, when she looked down, her tennis shoes were Keds, speckled with a dozen different colors of paint. It pissed her off, how easy it was to remember things in this place, to *feel* them. Nothing seemed to have changed here except Ruby, and the new Ruby sure as hell didn't belong in this fairy-tale house.

She walked back up the slope and took her place behind the wheelchair. She cautiously moved down the rutted path, guiding the chair in front of her. They had just reached the edge of the porch when her mother suddenly spoke.

"Let me sit here for a minute, will you? Go on in." Nora fished the key out of her pocket and handed it to Ruby. "You can come back and tell me how it looks."

"You'd rather sit in the rain than go into the house?"

"That pretty much sums up my feelings right now."

Ruby stepped around her and walked onto the porch. The wide-planked floor wobbled beneath her feet like piano keys, releasing a melody of creaks and groans.

At the front door, she slipped the key into the lock.

Click.

"Wait!" her mother cried out.

Ruby turned. Nora was smiling, but it was grim, that smile. More like gritted teeth.

"I . . . think we should go in together."

"Jesus, let's not make an opera out of it. We're going into an old house. That's all." Ruby shoved the door open, caught a fleeting glimpse of shadows stacked on top of each other, then she went back for Nora.

She maneuvered the wheelchair up onto the porch, bumped it over the wooden threshold, and wheeled her mother inside.

The furniture huddled ghostlike in the middle of the room, draped in old sheets. Ruby could remember spreading those sheets every autumn, snapping them in the air above furniture. It had been a family ritual, closing up this house for winter.

The house may not have been lived in in a while, but it had been well cared for. There couldn't have been more than a few weeks' worth of dust on those white sheets.

"Caroline has taken good care of the place . . . I'm surprised she left everything exactly as it was." There was a note of wonder in Nora's voice, and maybe a touch of regret. As if, like Ruby, she'd hoped that Caroline had painted over the past.

"You know Caro," Ruby said, "she likes to keep everything pretty on the surface."

"That's not fair. Caro—"

Ruby spun around. "*Tell* me you aren't going to explain my sister to me."

Nora's mouth snapped shut. Then she sneezed. And again. Her eyes were watering as she said, "I'm allergic to dust. I know there's not much, but I'm really sensitive. You'll need to dust right away."

Ruby looked at her. "Your leg's broken; not your hand."

"I can't handle it. Allergies."

It was the best reason for not cleaning Ruby had ever heard. "Fine. I'll dust."

"And vacuum—remember, there's dust in the carpets."

"Oh, really? That comes as a complete surprise to me."

Nora had the grace to blush. "I'm sorry. I forgot for a minute that you're not . . . never mind."

Ruby gazed down at her. "I'm not a kid anymore, and dusting was one of the many things Caroline and I had to learn to do after you left us." She saw the pain move into Nora's green eyes; it made her look old suddenly, and fragile.

That word again. It was not something Ruby particularly wanted to see. She grabbed the wheelchair and pushed her mother into the center of the room, where the ancient Oriental carpet sucked up the metallic thump of the chair's wheels and plunged them into silence again.

"I guess I'll have to sleep in your old room. There's no way we can get me upstairs."

Ruby dutifully wheeled Nora into the downstairs bedroom, where two twin beds lay beneath a layer of sheeting. Between them was a gingham-curtained window. A painted wooden toy box held most of Ruby's childhood.

The wallpaper was still the pale pink cabbage roses that she and Caroline had picked out when they were children.

Ruby refused to feel anything. She yanked the sheets away. A fine layer of dust billowed into the air. She heard her mother coughing behind her, so Ruby leaned forward and wrenched the window open, letting in the sound of the waves slapping on the shore.

"I think I'll lie down for a minute," Nora said when the dust had settled. "I'm still fighting a headache."

Ruby nodded. "Can you get out of the chair by yourself?"

"I guess I'd better learn."

"I guess so." Ruby turned for the door.

She was almost free when her mother's voice hooked her back again. "Thanks. I really appreciate this."

Ruby knew she should say something nice, but she couldn't think of anything. She was too damned tired, and the memories in this room were like gnats, buzzing around her head. She nodded and kept walking, slamming the door shut behind her.

Chapter Seven

Dean tossed his garment bag on the floor of his old bedroom and sat down on the end of the bed.

Everything was exactly as he'd left it. Dusty baseball and soccer trophies cluttered the bureau's top; posters covered the cream-colored walls, their edges yellowed and curled. If he opened the toy chest, he'd find all the mementos of his past—G.I. Joe with the kung-fu grip, Rock 'Em–Sock 'Em Robots, maybe even his old Erector set. An autographed GO SEAHAWKS pennant hung above the desk, a reminder of the year Jim Zorn had visited the grade school.

Dean hadn't taken anything with him when he left here, not even a photograph of Ruby. *Especially* not a picture of her. He got to his feet and crossed the room. At the bureau, he bent down and pulled at the bottom drawer; it screeched and wobbled, then slid open.

And there they were, still stacked and scattered exactly as he'd left them: reminders of Ruby. There were framed pictures and unframed ones, shells they'd collected together on the beach, and a couple of dried boutonnieres. He reached randomly inside, drawing out a small strip of black-and-white pictures—a series that had been taken in one of those booths at the Island County Fair. In them, she was sitting on Dean's lap, with her arms curled tightly around him and her head angled against his. She was smiling, then frowning, then sticking her tongue out at the unseen camera. In the last frame, they were kissing.

It was bad enough to remember Ruby in the abstract; to follow this photographic trail of their childhood would be like swallowing glass bits. They'd started together as kids, he and Ruby, kindergarten best friends. Then they'd fallen into the sweet, aching pool of first love, and ultimately washed up on that emotion's rocky, isolated shore. He remembered the ending, and that was enough.

He dropped the photos back into the drawer and kicked it shut.

Someone knocked at the door, and Dean opened it.

Lottie stood there, clutching her big vinyl purse. "I'm off to the store," she said. "The fridge isn't making ice; we need a bag."

"I'll go—"

"Of course you won't. You'll be needing time with Eric." Smiling, she thrust a champagne glass at him. Inside was a thick pink liquid. "This is your brother's medicine. He needs it now. Bye."

She left him standing there, a grown man in a boy's room, holding pain medication in a fluted champagne glass.

He walked slowly to Eric's bedroom. The door was closed.

Dean stared at it for a long time, remembering the days when these doors had never been closed. They'd always come bursting into each other's room whenever they wanted.

He turned the knob and went inside. The room felt stuffy and too warm. The curtains were drawn.

Eric was asleep.

Dean moved quietly toward the bedside table and set down the glass, then he started to leave.

"I *hope* that's my Viagra," Eric said sleepily. In a second, the bed whirred to life, eased him to a near sitting position.

"Actually, it's a double shot of Cuervo Gold. I added the Pepto-Bismol to save you time."

Eric laughed. "You'll never let me forget MaryAnne's going-away party."

"A night that will live in infamy." Dean opened the windows and flung back the curtains. The windows boxed a gray and rainy day and let a little watery light into the room.

"Thanks. Bless Lottie, but she thinks I need peace and quiet. I haven't the nerve to tell her that I'm getting a little scared of the dark. Too damn coffinlike for me." He grinned. "I'll be there soon enough."

Dean turned to him. "Don't talk about that."

"Death? Why not? I *am* dying, and I'm not afraid of it. Hell, another week like this one and I'll be looking forward to it." He gave Dean a gentle look. "What am I supposed to talk about—the Mariners' next season? The next Olympic Games? Or maybe we could discuss the long-term effects of global warming." Eric eased back into the pillows with a heavy sigh. "We used to be so close," he said quietly.

"I know," Dean answered, moving toward the bed. He saw Eric move, try to turn slightly to look up at him; he saw, too, when the sudden pain sucked the color from his brother's cheeks. "Here," Dean said quickly.

Eric's hands were shaking as he reached for the glass and brought it back to his colorless lips. Wincing, he swallowed the whole amount, then wiped his mouth with the back of his bony wrist.

Eric tried to smile. "I'd kill for a margarita from Ray's Boathouse right about now . . . and a platter of Penn Cove mussels . . ."

"Tequila and shellfish—with your tolerance for booze? Sorry, pal, but I'll have to pass on that little fantasy."

"I'm not seventeen anymore," Eric said. "I don't slam alcohol until I puke."

There it was, the sharpened reminder of how they'd drifted apart. They'd known each other as boys; the men were strangers to each other.

"Will that medication help?" Dean asked.

"Sure. In ten minutes I'll be able to leap tall buildings in a single bound." Eric frowned. "What is a single bound, exactly? And why have I never wondered about that before?"

"Whatever it is, it's better than flying. Even first class has gone to hell. My flight up here was godawful."

Eric smiled. "Even first class is bad? You're talking to a high-school English teacher who was disinherited, remember?"

"Sorry. I was just trying to make conversation."

"Don't. I'm dying. I don't need time-filler. Jesus, Dean, you and I have spent our whole adulthood talking around anything that mattered. I know it's genetic, but I don't have time for it anymore."

"If you remind me that you're dying again, I swear to God, I'll kill you myself. It's not like I'm going to *forget*."

Eric laughed. "Praise Jesus! That's the first hint of my brother I've seen in a decade. I'm glad to know he survived."

Dean relaxed a little. "It's good to hear you laugh. It's been a long time." He moved idly to the chest of drawers beside the bed, where a collection of pictures sat clustered together. Most of them were photographs of Dean and Eric as boys.

But there was one—a shot of the brothers and another boy from the football team—all standing with their arms around one another, grinning.

It looked ordinary enough, but when he turned back to Eric, Dean couldn't help wondering. Had it been there all along, the difference between him and his brother? Had Dean simply *missed* the obvious?

"I wish I'd never told you I was gay," Eric said.

It was as if Eric had read his mind. Slowly, Dean turned. He wasn't ready for this conversation yet, but he had no choice. Eric had thrown him into cold water, now he had to swim. "It's kind of hard to keep a secret like that when you're living with a man."

"People do it all the time, keep that secret, I mean. I was so naive, I *wanted* to tell you." Eric lifted his head off the pillows and stared at Dean. "I knew our folks wouldn't accept it. But you . . ." His voice cracked a little. "You, I didn't expect. You broke my heart."

"I never meant to."

"You stopped calling me."

Dean sighed, wondering how to say it all. "You were away at college, so you didn't know what it was like back here. The technicolor meltdown of the Bridge family. It was front-burner news. And then . . . Ruby and I broke up."

"I always wondered what happened between you two. I thought—"

"It was fucking awful," Dean said quickly, unwilling to delve into that particular heartache. "I called Mother and demanded to be transferred to Choate—where, I might add, I met a bunch of snotty elitist rich kids. I hated it there. I couldn't seem to make friends. But every Sunday night, my brother called, and that one hour made the rest of the week bearable. You weren't just my best friend, you were my only friend. Then one Sunday, you forgot to call." Dean remembered how he'd waited by the phone that day, and the next Sunday and the next. "When you finally did call again, you told me about Charlie."

"You felt abandoned," Eric said softly.

"More than that. I felt like I didn't know you at all, like everything you'd ever said to me was a lie. And then all you wanted to talk about was Charlie." Dean shrugged. "I was seventeen years old and nursing a broken heart. I didn't want to hear about your love life. And yeah, the fact that it was with another man was hard for me to handle."

Eric leaned deeper into the pillows. "When you stopped returning my calls, I assumed it was because you hated me. Then you went to work for the family biz, and I wrote you off. I never thought about what it was like for you. I'm sorry."

"Yeah. I'm sorry, too."

"Where do these apologies take us?"

"Who the hell knows? I'm here. Isn't that enough?"

"No."

Suddenly Dean understood what Eric wanted. "You want me to remember who we used to be, to remember *you,* and then . . . watch you die. It doesn't sound like a real kick-ass plan from where I'm standing."

Eric reached up, placed a cold, trembling hand on top of Dean's. "I want *someone* in my family to love me while I'm alive. Is that so much to ask?" He closed his eyes, as if the conversation had exhausted him. "Ah, hell . . . I'm going too fast. I need *time* damn it. Just stay here until I fall asleep—can you do that for me?"

Dean's throat felt tight. "Sure."

He stayed at his brother's bedside until long after Eric's breathing had become regular and his mouth had slipped open. And still he didn't know what to say.

He would have given his fortune—hell, he'd have given everything he had or owned or could borrow—in exchange for the one thing he'd always taken for granted. The one thing Eric needed.

Time.

By the time Nora hopped to the bathroom and back into the bedroom, she was dizzy and out of breath. She shifted onto the bed and leaned back against the wobbly wooden headboard.

She knew she needed to handle Ruby with kid gloves, to treat her daughter's pain (which Nora never forgot that *she* had caused) respectfully, to let Ruby make all the first moves toward a reconciliation. No matter how much it hurt, how deeply the ache went, Nora didn't want to bulldoze the situation.

But Ruby had always brought out the worst in her. Even in the good times, her younger daughter had had a way of saying things that rubbed Nora the wrong way. More often than not, they both ended up saying something they regretted.

And Ruby knew that every coldly spoken "Nora" would break her heart just a little. It was, she knew, Ruby's way of reminding Nora that they were strangers.

You have to keep your cool.

And for God's sake, don't tell her what to do . . . or pretend you know her.

If they'd gone somewhere else, maybe this would have been easier, but nothing new could grow here, not in this soil contaminated by the past.

It was in this house that Nora had made her biggest mistake—and given the life she'd led, that was saying a lot. This was where she'd come when she left Rand. She had meant for it to be temporary. At the time she'd simply thought: *Space; if I don't get some space I'll start screaming and never stop.*

All she'd wanted was a little room, some time to herself. She'd been overwhelmed by her life. A twenty-minute ferry ride had seemed perfect. She hadn't known that two miles could stretch into more than a decade.

She remembered that whole summer, and the bad years that had preceded it, in excruciating detail.

She remembered how it had felt and tasted, that slowly descending depression, like a thick glass jar that closed around you, sucking away the air you needed to breathe, creating a barrier between you and the world. The hell of it was that she'd been able to see all that she was missing, but when she'd reached out, all she touched was cold, hard glass.

It had started with a few dark days, a few nightmares, but as the winter had turned into spring, and then into summer, she had simply . . . fallen. All these years later, she'd never found a better word for it. She'd felt then—as she did now—as brittle as a winter leaf. It had always taken so damned little to break her.

If she hadn't left Rand then, she believed she would have died. Her pain had been that great. Still . . .

She'd thought she could come home again, that women were granted the same latitude in marriage that men were. How naive she had been.

She reached for the bedside phone and picked it up, thankful to find a dial tone. She wouldn't have expected any less from Caroline.

She dialed Eric's number, but no one answered. He was probably exhausted from the trip. He tired so easily these days.

She didn't want to think about that now, about how the cancer was erasing him. If she thought about that now she'd fall apart, and with Ruby on the other side of that door, Nora didn't dare fall apart.

She dialed another number. Dr. Allbright answered on the second ring. There was a moment of silence at the other end, the sound of a match flaring. "Hello?"

"Hi, Leo. It's me, Nora."

He inhaled, blew the smoke from his cigarette into the phone. It came through in a whooshing sound. "How are you?"

"I'm fine," she said, wondering if he could *hear* the lies in the same way that he could see them on her face. "You asked me to call when we arrived, so . . ."

"You don't sound fine."

"Well . . . Ruby and I are crowded in with a lot of old ghosts." She tried to laugh. "This house . . ."

"I don't think you should be there. We talked about this. With all that's happening, you should be in the city."

It was nice to have someone care about her—even if she paid him to do so. "And let the vultures pick at me?" She smiled ruefully. "Of course, it appears to be open season on Nora Bridge wherever I go."

"Ruby," he said.

"I knew it wouldn't be easy." That much was true, at least. She'd known how much it would hurt to see her daughter's bitterness in such sharp, close detail; and it did.

"We talked about this, Nora. If she hates you, it's because she was too young to understand."

"I'm fifty, Leo, and I don't understand it all."

"You owe it to yourself—and to Ruby—to tell her the truth."

She sighed wearily. The thought of opening herself like a rotting flower to her beloved daughter was more than she could bear. "I just want to see her smile at me. That's all. Just once and I could carry that image forever. I don't expect her to like me . . . let alone love me."

"Ah, Nora," he said, and she heard the familiar disappointment in his tone.

"You ask too much of me, Leo."

"And you ask too little, Nora. You're so afraid of your past that—"

"Tell me something useful, Leo. You're a parent, give me some advice."

"Talk to her."

"About what? How do we get past what happened eleven years ago?"

"One step at a time, that's how. Try this: tell her one personal thing about you every day. Just one, and try to find out one thing about her. That would be a start."

"One personal thing." Nora considered it.

Yes, she could do that. She'd just have to find a way to share one honest moment a day with her daughter. It wasn't much, and it wouldn't change everything, but it felt . . . possible. For now, that was all she could hope for.

Ruby strode through the house, going from window to window, yanking the gingham cotton curtains open, letting what little sunlight was possible into every room. By now it was nearly three o'clock. Soon there would be no daylight through the clouds at all. She wanted to catch what she could.

She was desperately tired all of a sudden. The middle-of-the-night phone call, the predawn flight, the drive to the islands . . . suddenly it all caught up with her and sapped her strength. If she wasn't careful, she could lose a fight with her own emotions and start crying at the sight of this old house.

At last, she found herself in the kitchen/dining room.

Nothing had changed.

A round maple table sat tucked beneath the kitchen window, its four ladder-back chairs pulled in close. A centerpiece of dirty pink plastic dahlias was flanked by a set of porcelain salt and pepper shakers shaped like tiny lighthouses. A cookbook was in its rack on the kitchen counter, its pages open to a recipe for lemon squares. Four hand-embroidered dishcloths hung in a row across the front of the oven.

She passed beneath the archway that separated the kitchen from the living room, noticing the brass mariner's clock that hung in the center of the arch's plaster curl. That clock was silent now, its chimes—two quick *ding-dings* every half hour—had been a constant punctuation to their family's noisy soundtrack. But it had probably been years since anyone had remembered to change the batteries.

In the living room, an overstuffed sofa and two leather chairs faced a big, river-rock fireplace. On the back wall were bookcases filled with two generations' worth of Reader's Digest editions, and an RCA stereo. A red plastic milk box held all of the family's favorite albums. From here, Ruby could see the upper half of the top album: "Venus" by Bananarama.

That one was hers.

Next, the photographs on the mantel caught her eye. They were different frames than she remembered. Frowning, she walked toward the fireplace.

All the pictures were of Caroline's children.

There was not a single shot of Ruby. Not even one of Ruby and Caroline.

"Nice, Caro," she said, turning away. She headed for the stairs, but as she walked up the creaking, narrow steps to the second floor, she felt . . . forgotten.

Her fingers trailed through the dust on the oak banister, leaving two squiggly lines. The second floor was small, barely big enough for a full-size bedroom. The bathroom—added by Grandpa Bridge in the early 1970s—had once been a closet. It was barely big enough to bend over at the sink to brush your teeth. Ugly, avocado-green shag carpeting covered every inch of the floor.

She pushed the door open to her parents' old bedroom and flicked the light switch.

A big brass bed filled the room, flanked by two French Provincial end tables. The bedside lamps were yellow, their green shades draped in golden plastic beads.

A touch of Las Vegas class, her grandmother had often said, and with that unexpected memory, Ruby remembered her grandma, sitting in that corner rocker, her veiny hands making knitting needles work like pistons. *You can never have too many afghans,* she'd said every time she started a new one. There had always been an Elvis album playing on the turntable when Grandma knitted . . .

It had been a long time since she'd had so clear a memory of her Nana.

Maybe all she'd needed to remember the good times was to see this place again. The room was exactly as Nana had made it; Nora had never bothered to redecorate. When Nana and Pop had died, Dad had moved their family into the bigger house on Lopez Island, and left this house for summer use.

Ruby crossed the room and went to the French doors, opening them wide. Sweet, rain-scented air made the lacy curtains tremble and dance. The bloated gray sky and steel-blue water were perfectly framed by twin Douglas firs, as thin and straight as pipe cleaners.

She stepped out onto the tiny second-floor balcony. A pair of white deck chairs sat on either side of her, their slatted backs beaded with rain.

For a split second, she couldn't imagine that she'd ever lived in a valley so hot and airless that boiling water sometimes squirted out of ordinary green garden hoses.

She backed off the balcony and turned into the room. Out of the corner of her eye, she noticed the new photographs on the bedside table.

"God *damn* it," she muttered, looking through them.

Caroline had done it again. They were all pictures of Caroline's new life. It was as if her sister were trying to exorcise Ruby from the family.

Frowning, she marched back downstairs and went outside. She grabbed their two suitcases from the car and carried them inside, dropping her mother's in front of the closed bedroom door.

Upstairs, she opened the closet's louvered doors, then yanked down on the beaded light chain. A bare lightbulb in the ceiling came on in the empty closet.

She tossed her suitcase inside. It hit a cardboard box, rattling it.

She knelt onto the dusty shag carpet and pulled the box toward her. In bold, black marker pen, someone had written BEFORE across the top flap.

Ruby opened the box . . . and found herself.

Photographs. Dozens of them. These were the pictures that used to sit on every flat surface in this house—tables, mantels, windowsills. Pictures of two littles girls in matching pink dresses . . . of Dean and Eric in Little League uniforms . . . of Dad waving from the stern of the *Captain Hook*. And one of Nora.

She slowly withdrew that one.

This was the mother she'd forgotten, the woman she'd grieved for. A tall, thin woman, with auburn hair cut in the layered Farrah Fawcett style, wearing crisp white walking shorts and a celery-green T-shirt. The photograph was old and creased, but even the maplike fissures couldn't dim her mother's smile. In the background was the peaked white tip of the Matterhorn.

Their trip to Disneyland.

In a bittersweet rush, Ruby remembered all of that day; the screams of older kids on scarier rides, the sudden, plunging darkness of Mr. Toad's Wild Ride, the rollicking music of Country Bear Jamboree, the sugary residue of churros, eaten while you walked, the magic of the Electrical Light Parade. Ruby had watched it from the best seat in the house—on her daddy's shoulders.

And she understood what Caroline had done. Caro, who couldn't stand conflict or confrontation . . . Caro, who just wanted everything to be *normal*.

It had hurt her sister to look back on these years.

Better to simply . . . go on. Start over. Pretend that there had never been happy summers spent on these shores, in these rooms.

Ruby released her breath in a heavy sigh and boxed the photographs back up. Her sister was right. It was too damned hard to see the past in Kodachrome.

God . . . she'd already lost her equilibrium in this house, and it had only been a day. Suddenly she was wound tightly, full of nervous energy. She had to get back on track. Remember why she was here.

The magazine article. *That* would keep her focused.

She unzipped the side pocket of her suitcase and withdrew a yellow legal pad and a blue pen. Then she crawled up onto the dusty bed, drew her knees in . . .

. . . and stared down at all those blue lines.

We want your thoughts, your memories, what kind of mother you thought she was.

"Okay, Ruby," she said aloud. "Just start. You can always change the beginning later."

It was the first rule of comedy writing; it should work here, too.

She took a deep breath, released it slowly, and wrote the first thing that came to mind.

In the interest of full disclosure, I must tell you (she decided to talk directly to the *Caché* readers) *that I was paid to write this article. Paid* handsomely, as they say in the kind of restaurants where a person like me can't afford to order a dinner salad. Enough so that I could trade in my beat-up Volkswagen Bug for a slightly less beat-up Porsche.

I should also tell you that I dislike my mother. No, that's not true. I dislike the snotty salesclerk who works the night shift at my local video store.

I hate my mother.

That seems like a pretty harsh statement, I know. We're taught in childhood not to use the word "hate" because it represents a blight on our own soul, perhaps even a karmic misalignment. But silencing a word doesn't eliminate its meaning.

It's not like I hate her for no reason, or even for a stupid, petty reason. She's earned my contempt. To explain, I have to open the door to my mother's and my life, and welcome you in as friends.

The story of us starts eleven years ago, in a place few of you have ever seen: the San Juan Islands up in Washington State. I grew up in a small farmhouse on a patch of land that had been homesteaded by my great-grandfather. The island . . . the town . . . my house . . . they all belong on Hallmark cards. I went to school with the same kids for thirteen years; the only crime I can recall happened in 1979, when Jimmy Smithson broke into the local pharmacy, ripped open all the condom packages, and wrote "Peggy Jean likes sex" in Dial soap on the front window.

And then there was my family.

My dad was—is—a commercial fisherman who repairs boat engines in the winter months to make ends meet. He was born and raised on Lopez Island; he is as fixed in that place as one of the ancient trees that line the main road.

Although my mother was born off-island, she was a local by the time I came along. She volunteered for every town charity event and was a fixture around school.

In other words, we were a perfect family in a quiet little town where nothing ever happened. In all my growing-up years, I never heard my parents argue.

Then, in the summer before my seventeenth birthday, everything changed.

My mother left us. Walked out the door, got into her car, and drove away. She didn't call or write all that summer, she just . . . vanished.

I can't remember now how long I waited for her to return, but I know that somewhere along the way, in the pool of a thousand tears, she became my Mother, and then, finally, Nora. My mom was gone. I accepted the fact that whatever she wanted out of life, it wasn't me.

I could describe what it was like, the waiting, but I won't. Not even for the money. The worst of it was my father. For my last two years of high school, I watched him . . . disintegrate. He drank, he sat in his darkened bedroom, he wept.

And so, when Caché came to me, asking for my story, I said yes. Hell yes.

I figured it was time that America knew who they were listening to, who was giving them moral advice.

Like the rest of you, I heard her message stream over the airwaves: Commit to your family and make it work. Be honest. Hold fast to the vows you made before God.

This from a woman who walked out on her marriage and abandoned her children, and——

"Ruby!"

She tossed down the pen and paper and went to the doorway, poking her head out. "Yeah?"

"Can you breathe okay, with all this dust?"

Ruby rolled her eyes. As always, her mother was as subtle as an exclamation mark. "I see you found enough air in your lungs to scream at me," she muttered, hurrying downstairs.

As she passed her mother's bedroom, she heard a sneeze.

Ruby smiled; she couldn't help it.

In the kitchen, she knelt in front of the cabinet beneath the sink and opened the doors. Everything she needed to clean the house, and in quantities large enough to clean *any* house, stood in four straight rows. When she realized that the supplies were organized in alphabetical order, she burst out laughing.

"Poor Caro," she whispered, realizing how badly her sister wanted everything to be tidy. "You were *definitely* born into the wrong family."

Then, as tired as she was, she started to clean.

Chapter Eight

Nora tried not to watch her daughter clean the house. It was simply too irritating.

Ruby dusted without moving anything, and she clearly thought a dry rag would do the job. Oh, she'd brought out the industrial-size can of Pledge, but she'd left it sitting on the tile counter in the kitchen. When she started mopping the floor with soapless water, Nora couldn't help herself.

"Aren't you going to sweep first?" she asked from her wheelchair, tucked into the open doorway of her bedroom.

Ruby slowly turned around. Her face was flushed—from what exertion, Nora couldn't imagine. "Excuse me?"

Nora wished she'd kept silent, but now there was nowhere to go except forward. "You need to sweep the floor before you mop . . . and soap in the water is a big help."

Ruby let go of the mop. The wooden handle clattered to the floor. "You're criticizing my cleaning technique?"

"I wouldn't call it a technique. It's just common sense to—"

"So, I have no common sense, either."

Nora sighed. "Come on, Ruby. You know better than that. I taught you—"

Ruby was in front of Nora before she could finish the sentence. "*You* do not want to bring up the things you taught me. Because if I do as I've been *taught,* I'll walk out that door, climb into the mini-van, and drive away. I won't even bother to wave good-bye."

Nora's irritation vanished; regret swooped in to take its place. She sagged like a rag doll in her chair. "I'm sorry."

Ruby took a step back. "According to Caro, those are your favorite words. Maybe you should think about what it really means to apologize before you bother." She stomped back to the kitchen sink, grabbed some liquid soap, and squirted a stream into the white plastic bucket. Then she began mopping again; her strokes were positively vicious.

Nora sat there, watching. The *thwop-squish-clack* of the mop moving across the floor (streaking clumps of dirt, Nora noticed but obviously didn't mention) was the only sound in the room.

Finally, Nora wound up the nerve for a different approach. "Maybe I could help?"

Ruby didn't look at her. "I stripped the bed upstairs. The sheets are piled on the washing machine. You could take care of your bed and start a load of laundry."

Nora nodded. It took her almost an hour of maneuvering in her chair to strip the sheets off her bed, roll into the cubicle-size laundry room, and start the first load. By the time she finished, she was wheezing like a dying crow.

She rolled back into the kitchen and found that the room was sparkling clean. Ruby had even replaced the horrid plastic flowers on the table with a fragrant bouquet of roses.

"Oh," Nora said, taking her first decent breath since coming into the house. "It looks beautiful. Just like—"

"Thanks."

Nora understood that Ruby didn't want the past mentioned. It didn't surprise Nora, that reaction. Ruby had always been an expert at denial. Even as a child, she'd had the ability to compartmentalize and forget. She could box up whatever she didn't want to face and store it away. It had been this very trait that had allowed her to shut Nora out of her life so completely.

Out of sight for Ruby had always meant out of mind.

Nora decided not to let it be so easy this time. "I thought I'd help you make dinner."

Ruby turned to look at her. There was a look of genuine horror on her face.

Nora smiled. "You look like John Hurt, just before the alien popped out of his chest. Close your mouth."

"There's no food. We—I—have to go shopping."

"We both know Caroline better than that. In these cupboards, I guarantee you, are the makings for several emergency dinners. Probably labeled as such. All we have to do is look around."

"You don't need my help, then. I'll just run upstairs—"

"Not so fast. I can't reach everything. We'll need to work together."

Ruby looked like she'd just bitten down on a lemon. "I don't know how to cook."

Nora wasn't surprised. "You were never too interested in it."

"I got interested in it when I was seventeen. Not that you would know this."

Direct hit. "I could teach you now."

"Lucky me."

Nora refused to be hurt by that comment. She wheeled into the kitchen. With her back to Ruby, she scavenged through the cupboards, finding several cans of tomatoes, a bag of angel-hair pasta, an unopened bottle of olive oil, jars of marinated artichoke hearts and capers, and a container of dried Parmesan cheese. She pulled out everything she needed and set the supplies beside the stove. Then she waited patiently.

Her patience didn't last as long as she would have liked. "Ruby?" she said at last.

Ruby walked over to the stove. "Okay, what do you want me to do?"

"See that big frying pan hanging on the rack—no, the bigger one. Yes. Take that and put it on the front burner."

It hit with a clang.

Nora winced. "Now put about a tablespoon of olive oil in it and turn on the gas."

Ruby opened the oil and poured in at least a half cup.

Nora could practically *feel* her hips expanding, but she bit back a comment as she reached for the can opener. She was proud of herself for saying simply, "The measuring spoons are in the top drawer, to your left." Then she opened the canned tomatoes. "Here, add these. And turn the flame to low."

When Ruby had done that, Nora went on. "Cut up the marinated artichoke hearts and add them. Maybe a half cup of that canned chicken broth would be good, too."

Ruby went to the counter, turned her back to Nora, and began chopping.

"Ow. *Shit!*"

Nora spun the wheelchair toward her daughter. "Are you okay?"

Ruby stepped back. Blood was dripping in a steady red stream from her index finger; it plopped onto the tile counter.

Nora yanked a clean towel off the oven door. "Come here, honey. Get on your knees in front of me. Keep your hand up."

Ruby dropped to her knees. She seemed unable to look away from her finger. Her face was pale.

Nora gently took hold of her daughter's hand. Seeing that blood—her child's—made Nora's own hand throb. Just like old times; Nora had always experienced a phantom pain whenever one of her kids was hurt. She carefully coiled the towel around the wound, and without thinking, wrapped her own hands around Ruby's.

When she looked up, Nora saw the emotion on Ruby's face, and knew that her daughter remembered this simple routine. The only thing missing was a kiss to make it all better. She saw the longing flash through Ruby's eyes. It was only there for an instant, but Nora had waited so long to see it . . .

Ruby yanked her hand back. "It's just a cut, for God's sake. We don't have to go looking for my finger on the floor or anything."

That gap yawned between them again, and Nora wondered suddenly if she'd imagined the longing in her daughter's eyes. If she'd seen only what she wanted so desperately to see.

Her voice was shaky when she said, "Put the artichoke hearts and two tablespoons of capers into the sauce." She turned quickly to the spice drawer, yanking it open. But when she stared down into the drawer, all she saw was Ruby's face as it had been for that one second, that instant that had somehow been both then and now.

Nora grabbed the herbs she needed and wheeled back around, adding them to the sauce. "Put a big pot of water on to boil, won't you?"

For the next thirty minutes, Ruby did as she was told without uttering a word. She was vigilant in her refusal to make eye contact.

But finally, the meal was ready, and they were seated across from each other at the round wooden kitchen table. Ruby picked up her fork and rammed it into the pasta, twirling it.

"Don't you want to say grace?" Nora asked.

Ruby looked up. "No."

"But we—"

"There is no *we*. Dinnertime prayers are one of those family traditions that went the way of our family. God and I have an understanding. When He stopped listening, I stopped talking."

Nora sighed. "Oh, Ruby . . ."

"Don't give me that wounded-deer look." Ruby turned her attention back to the plate and started eating. "This is good."

"Thanks." Nora closed her eyes. "Thank you, God," she said softly, her voice barely loud enough for Ruby to hear. "For this food . . . and this time that Ruby and I have together."

Ruby kept eating.

Nora tried to eat, but the silence tore at her nerves. It was hard enough to be estranged from your child when thousands of miles separated you . . . but estrangement at the same table was brutal.

One personal thing.

Leo's advice came back to her. It had seemed easy enough when she was on the phone with her doctor; now, sitting beneath this cone of silence, it felt like a herculean undertaking.

She was still trolling for an icebreaker when Ruby said, "Excuse me," got up from the table, and went across the kitchen. She started filling the sink with water.

Nora hadn't realized that eating was a timed event. Fortunately, she kept this observation to herself. She cleared the table, stacked the dishes on the counter at Ruby's elbow. In an unnerving silence, Ruby washed and Nora dried. When they were finished, Nora wheeled herself into the living room.

She mentally prepared for round two.

Ruby swept past her—practically running—and headed for the stairs.

Nora had to think fast. "Why don't you make us a fire? June nights are always chilly."

Ruby stumbled to a halt. Without answering, she went to the hearth and knelt down to build a fire.

She did it exactly as she'd been taught by Grandpa Bridge.

"I guess some things you never forget," Nora said.

Ruby sat back on her heels and held her hands out toward the fire. It was a full minute before she turned to Nora and said, "Except how it feels to have a mother."

Nora sucked in a sharp breath. "That's not fair. I was with you every day until . . ."

"Until the day you weren't."

Nora clasped her hands together and slid them between her legs. She didn't want Ruby to see how badly she was trembling. "You and Caroline were my whole world."

Ruby laughed drily and got to her feet, moving toward Nora.

"We weren't your whole world the summer I was sixteen; that *was* the year you walked into the living room, dropped your suitcase on the floor, and announced that you were leaving, wasn't it? And what was it you said to us—'Who wants to come with me?' Yes, that was it. 'Who wants to come with me?' As if Caroline and I would set down our forks, clear the table, and move away from our dad and our home just because you decided you didn't want to be here."

"I didn't decide . . . I left because—"

"I don't care *why* you left. That's what you care about."

Nora longed to make Ruby understand, even if it was only the merest bit. Just enough so that they could simply talk. "You don't know everything about me."

Ruby looked down at her. Nora thought she saw a war going on inside her daughter, as if Ruby wanted both to keep fighting and to stop. It surprised Nora. She understood why her daughter would want to keep distance between them. What she couldn't imagine was why Ruby was still standing here. It was, in truth, a little disconcerting. She got the unsettling feeling that Ruby—honest-to-a-fault Ruby—was hiding something.

"Tell me something about you, then," Ruby said at last.

This was Nora's chance. She knew she needed to tread carefully. "Okay, let's go sit on the porch—like we used to, remember? We'll each share one piece of information about ourselves."

Ruby laughed. "I asked you to tell me about *you*. I didn't offer to reciprocate."

Nora stood her ground. "I need to know about you, too. Besides, if we're both talking, we can pretend it's a conversation."

Ruby wasn't laughing now. "Very *Silence of the Lambs* of you, Nora. Quid pro quo. For every secret you tell me, I tell you one."

"I suppose I'm Hannibal Lecter in your little comparison. A cannibal . . . and a psychopath, how lovely."

Ruby studied her a minute longer. "This should be interesting. I'm twenty-seven; you were fifty . . . when, the day before yesterday? I guess it's time we talked. Come on."

She watched her daughter walk through the kitchen and disappear onto the porch. The screen door banged shut behind her. Nora finally allowed herself to smile.

Ruby had remembered her birthday.

Finally, she wheeled out onto the porch, thankful to see that the rain had stopped. Cool night air breezed across her cheeks, carrying with it the smells of a life gone by—the sea, the sand, the roses climbing along the railings. They had bloomed early this year, as they always did after a mild winter. In another two weeks there would be saucer-size blossoms crawling up the trellises and along the picket fence.

Shadows crept along the ground like slowly seeping India ink, moved up the sides of the house, and slipped through the slats on the picket fence. Sunset tinted the sky purple and pink.

The porch light cast Ruby's back in an orangey glow. She looked young and vulnerable, with her black hair so poorly cut, and her clothes all tattered and torn. The urge to reach out, to brush the hair off Ruby's face, and say softly—

"Don't say it, Nora."

Nora frowned. "Say what?"

"'Ah, Ruby, you could be so beautiful if you'd just try a little.'"

It startled Nora, that bit of mind reading. Sure, she'd said that often to Ruby, had thought in fact to say it a second ago, but it meant nothing. To Nora, the comment had simply been grains of sand in the desert of a mother's advice. Obviously, Ruby had felt otherwise, and she'd carried the words with her into womanhood.

Nora saw how heavy they had become, and she was ashamed. "I'm sorry, Ruby. What I should have said is: you're beautiful, just the way you are."

Ruby turned, stared down at her.

Silence settled between them, broken only by the sounds of the sea and the occasional caw of a lone crow hidden in the trees.

"Okay, Nora," Ruby said, crossing her arms, leaning with feigned nonchalance against the porch rail. "Tell me something I don't know."

Nora gazed up at her daughter, saw the wary expectation in those dark eyes, and took a deep breath. "You think I don't understand you," she began softly, "but I know how it feels to turn your back on a parent."

Ruby pulled away from the railing. Frowning, she sat down on the white wicker chair beside Nora. "You loved your parents. You told us all about them."

"The stories I told you girls were true," she answered slowly, "and they were lies. I was never good at making stuff up, so my bedtime stories were always bits and pieces of my life . . . cleaned up. I wanted you and Caro to have a sense of where you'd come from."

"What do you mean, cleaned up?"

Nora's gaze was steady. "No matter how dark a place is, there are always moments of light. That's what I passed on to you and Caroline, my moments of light." She took a deep breath. "On the day I graduated from high school, I left home, and I never went back again."

"Did you run away?"

"From my father, yes. I loved my mother."

"How long was it before you saw them again?"

Nora couldn't help it; she closed her eyes. "I saw my father once—at my mother's funeral. Before you and Caroline were born."

"And never again?"

"Never again." Nora wished those two little words didn't hurt. The emotion was so old it ought to have decomposed by now. She leaned toward Ruby. "I never saw him again, didn't even attend his funeral, and all my life I've had to live with that decision. It's not regret I feel so much, but more of . . . a sad longing. I wish he had been a different man. Most of all, I wish I could have loved him."

"Did you *ever* love him?"

"Perhaps . . . when I was young. If so, I don't remember it."

Ruby got up, walked to the railing, and stared out at the sea. Without turning around, she said, "I read the *People* magazine article about you. It said—and I quote: 'The cornerstones of Nora Bridge's message are forgiveness and commitment.'" Ruby turned around at last. "Did you try to forgive him?"

Nora wanted to lie. It was easy to see that Ruby was asking as much about *their* relationship as she was about Nora and her father's. But there was little enough chance for Nora and Ruby; with deception, there would be none at all. "Years later, after I'd had my own children—and lost their love—I began to regret how I'd treated him. As a young woman, I didn't—couldn't—understand how hard life can be. I think that's how he felt. It's no excuse, but it gives me a way to see him that turns the hatred into pity. Of course, that understanding came too late. He was already gone."

"So, I should forgive you now, while I still have the time. Is that your none-too-subtle message?"

Nora looked up sharply. "Not everything is about you, Ruby. I told you something painful about me tonight, painful and private. I expect you to handle my life with respect, if you can't manage care."

Ruby looked abashed. "I'm sorry."

"Apology accepted. Now, tell me something about you."

Ruby stared at Nora through unreadable eyes.

Nora steeled herself. This was going to be bad . . .

"That summer—you remember it, that time you left—I thought you'd come back."

"That's no secret."

"I waited and waited. By the next June, Caroline had left, and it was just Dad and me at home. One night I just . . . snapped." She swallowed hard and looked away for a moment, then collected herself and began again. "I drove down to Seattle and went to that dance club, the Monastery, all by myself. I picked up some kid—I can't even remember his name. He had blue hair and pierced ears and dead eyes. I went back to his apartment and let him fuck me." She paused for effect. "It was my first time."

It hurt as much as Ruby had intended. Nora thought: *There it is. My legacy.* She didn't dare to say she was sorry. Ruby would only toss those ridiculously inadequate words right back at her.

"I did it to hurt you. I thought you'd come home eventually and then I'd tell you. I used to imagine the look on your face when I described it."

"You wanted to see me cry."

"At the very least."

Nora sighed. "I would have, if that makes you feel better."

"It's too late for any of us to be feeling better." She sighed. "Dean didn't take it very well, either."

Dean. For a moment Nora hurt so much she couldn't breathe evenly.

That's how the grief hit her lately. Like a rogue wave rising from a flat sea, it came out of nowhere and hit with hurricane force. Sometimes she went whole hours without thinking about Eric, and then she would suddenly remember.

Now, it had been Dean's name that reminded her, but it could have been anything—the sound of a school bell ringing, a man's laughter coming from another room. Anything.

She knew she should say something—the pain in Ruby's eyes when she said Dean's name was unmistakable—but Nora's throat was blocked too tightly to speak.

"That's enough quid pro quo for one night," Ruby said sharply. "I'm going to go upstairs and take a bath."

Nora watched her daughter leave. Then, quietly, she said, "Good night, Ruby."

Wheeling back into her bedroom, Nora elbowed the door shut behind her and crawled up onto the bed. Then she reached for the phone and dialed Eric's number.

He answered on the third ring, and she could tell that he was heavily medicated. "Hullo?"

"Hey, Eric," she said, leaning back against the headboard. "You sound like you've been shooting heroin."

"Thass how I feel." It seemed to take a long time for him to speak, and the words came out mangled and elongated.

"Are you okay?" she asked softly.

"Ssshure. Jesst a little doped up. New meds . . ."

Nora had seen him go through this before. It was always hell to get the pain prescription just right. She knew it wasn't a good time for them to speak. "I'll let you sleep now, okay? I'll call back tomorrow."

"Ssleep," he murmured. "Yeah. Morrow."

"Good night, Eric."

"Goo' night."

Nora listened to the dial tone so long the recording came on, then, finally, she hung up.

Ruby went upstairs, where she grabbed her yellow legal pad and crawled up onto the bed.

This place, Summer Island, is killing me. When I left Los Angeles, I was strong and funny—not successful, perhaps, but at least I was me. Here, things are different. I smell the roses my grandmother planted and dry my hands on towels she embroidered . . . I sit at the table where I grew up, remembering when I couldn't reach the floor with my feet. I stare at the beach, and in the movement of the waves, I hear my sister's laughter.

And then there is my mother.

We have battles to fight; there is no doubt about it, but I'm afraid to ask the questions, and she, I can tell, is afraid to answer them. So we dance out of time to different pieces of music.

Quid pro quo. My secret for one of yours; this is the game we have begun to play. With it, I know I won't be able to stand on the edge of intimacy. Sooner or later, I will have to dive into those cold, deep waters, and there is no end to the ripples my entrance will make.

I will learn things about my mother that I don't want to know. Hell, I already have. I know, for instance, that she ran away from home right after high school and never spoke to her father again.

Even yesterday, I wouldn't have been surprised by that. I would have said, "Of course. Running away is what Nora Bridge does best."

But I watched her eyes as she spoke of her father. I saw the pain . . .

It hurt her to run away. Part of me wishes I hadn't seen that because, as I stood there, listening to my mother's heartache, I wondered for the first time if it hurt her to leave her children.

Chapter Nine

Dean sat cross-legged on the end of the dock, watching the sun rise.

The Sound was rough now at the changing of the tides. Waves slapped against the old sailboat that bobbed alongside the dock. The lines creaked and moaned.

He heard the sound of motors in the distance, and he smiled.

The fishing boats were going out. They were too far away to see clearly—they were, as always, hugging the coast of Shaw Island on their way to Haro Strait—but Dean had seen it all a thousand times, the battered, rattrap boats, made of painted wood or aluminum, setting out for the day. How many times had he and Ruby stood on a dock somewhere, watching Rand's boat chug out to sea? She'd always squeezed Dean's hand at the last moment, when the *Captain Hook* rounded the point and disappeared. He had known, without her ever having to tell him, that she lived with a tiny bit of fear that one day her father wouldn't return.

Dean had taken his watch off when he arrived on Lopez Island, so he wasn't sure how long he sat there. All he knew was that by the time the sun gained strength and heated his cheeks, he'd been there long enough.

Tiredly, he got to his feet and turned around. To his right, the old family sailboat bobbed wearily in the tide.

The mast—once a bright white—had been discolored by the endless rain and pitted by the wind. Red sides had been scraped down to bare wood in a dozen places, and the deck around the big metal steering wheel was hidden beneath a layer of blackened, slimy leaves and green-gray mold.

Of course, that was when he heard her voice: *Let's take out the Wind Lass, Dino, come on!*

He closed his eyes, remembering Ruby. In the beginning, he'd flinched at every memory, held his breath, and waited for the images to pass, but then the memories had started to fade, and he'd gone in search of them, reaching out like a blind man.

Now he understood how precious were his memories of first love, and he treasured both their pleasure and their pain.

He grabbed the line and pulled the boat closer to the dock, then stepped aboard. The boat undulated unsteadily, as if surprised to be boarded after so many lonely years.

He had always felt free on this boat. The flapping sound of sails catching wind had buoyed his spirits like nothing else. He and Eric had spent so much of their youth on the *Wind Lass*. On these teak decks, they'd spun dreams for a future that stretched out years and years. Though neither of them had ever said it aloud, they'd both imagined growing old on this boat, bringing wives and children and grandchildren aboard.

Dean loved to sail, and yet he'd walked away from it, let sailing be part of the life he'd left behind . . .

Obviously Eric had done the same. The *Wind Lass* could have been docked in Seattle, a stone's throw from Eric's house, and yet here she sat, untended and untouched.

And suddenly Dean knew what he needed to do.

He would restore the *Wind Lass*. Scrape the old paint away, strip the wood and re-oil it, scrub its every inch. He'd take this forgotten, once-loved boat and return it to its past glory.

If he could get Eric out here for an afternoon—just that, a single afternoon—maybe the wind and the sea could take them back in time . . .

Ruby woke to the smell of frying bacon and brewing coffee. Snagging yesterday's leggings off the floor, she pulled them on under-

neath her long nightshirt and hurried through her morning bathroom routine, then padded downstairs.

Nora was in the kitchen, maneuvering the wheelchair like General Patton along the front. There were two cast-iron skillets on the
stove, one with steam climbing out. A yellow crockery mixing bowl
sat by the empty skillet; a metal-handled spoon rested against its side.
She smiled up at Ruby. "Good morning. Did you sleep well?"

"Fine." She stumbled past the wheelchair and poured herself a
cup of coffee, adding sugar and cream.

After a sip, she felt more human. Leaning back against the cupboards, she saw that her mother had made bacon and pancakes. "I
haven't eaten a breakfast like this since you left us."

It was obviously an effort for her mother to keep smiling. "Do you
want me to put an M-and-M face on your pancakes like I used to?"

"No, thanks. I try to avoid carbohydrates layered with chocolate."
Ruby set the table, then dished up two plates and sat down.

Nora sat down across from her. "Did you sleep well last night?"
she asked, pouring syrup in a tiny puddle by her pancakes.

Ruby had forgotten that her mother dipped each bite of pancake
into syrup. The quirk reminded her of all the bits and pieces of their
common life; the things that inextricably bound a mother and
daughter, whether Ruby wanted those ties or not. "You already asked
me that."

Nora's fork clanged on the plate edge. "Tomorrow I'll remember
to wear a Kevlar vest under my nightgown."

"What am I supposed to do? Be like Caroline—pretend
everything is fine between us?"

"My relationship with Caroline is not for you to judge," Nora said
sharply, looking up at her. "You've always thought you knew
everything. I used to think it was a good trait for a girl to have, but
there's a dark side to all that certainty, Ruby. You . . . hurt people."
Ruby saw her mother swell up with anger, and then as quickly fade
into a tired thinness. "But I suppose it's not entirely your fault."

"Not *entirely*? How about not at all my fault?"

"I left Caroline, too. It didn't make her cold and hard and unable to love people."

Now *that* pissed Ruby off. "Who said I couldn't love people? I lived with Max for five years."

"And where is he now?"

Ruby pushed back from the table and stood up. Suddenly she wanted distance between them.

Nora looked up. There was a gentle understanding in her gaze that didn't sit well with Ruby. "Sit down. We won't talk about anything that matters. I'll comment on the weather, if you like."

Ruby felt like a fool standing there, breathing too hard, showing exactly how deeply she'd been wounded by her mother's remark.

"Ruby Elizabeth, sit down and eat your breakfast." Her mother spoke in one of those voices that immediately turned a grown woman into a child. Ruby did as she was told.

Nora took a bite of bacon. Her chewing was a loud *crunch-crunch-crunch*. "We need to go grocery shopping."

"Fine."

"How about this morning?"

Ruby nodded. Finishing her last bite, she stood up and began cleaning the table. "I'll do the dishes. We'll leave in about thirty minutes?"

"Make it an hour. I have to figure out how in the hell to do a sponge bath."

"I could lasso your leg and lower you into the bath like an anchor."

Nora laughed. "No, thanks. I don't want to drown naked with my leg stuck up in the air. The tabloids would have a field day with that."

The remark took a moment to sink in. When it did, Ruby turned back to the table. "I wouldn't let you drown."

"I know. But would you rescue me?" Without waiting for an answer, Nora spun around and rolled into her bedroom, shutting the door behind her.

Ruby stood there, staring at the closed door.

Would you rescue me?

The Benevolent Order of the Sisters of St. Francis had first come to Summer Island during World War One. A generous donor (who had no doubt lived a life that imperiled his immortal soul) had granted them more than one hundred waterfront acres. The sisters, who were equally high-minded in spiritual and business matters, had opened a general store next to the dock that would become the ferry terminal. On the rolling acreage behind the store, they'd built a sanctuary that tourists never saw. They raised cattle and owned the most profitable apple orchard on the island. They wove their own cloth, dyed it with extracts from their own gardens, and hand-stitched it into brown robes. Their sanctuary was open to any of their order, as well as to any woman who sought refuge from an unhappy life. Such women were welcomed into the fold and given that precious commodity so missing from the hectic, violent outside world: time. Here, they could don the clothing of their grandmothers, do the simple chores required of subsistence living, and commune with the God they felt they'd lost.

On Sundays, the sisters opened their small wooden chapel to their friends and neighbors. A priest from the monastery on a nearby island conducted quiet services in Latin. It was a humble church, where no one minded the cries of bored babies or the emptiness of a collection plate when times turned hard.

Theirs was still the only store on the island. Ruby pulled the minivan into the gravel parking lot behind the "He Will Provide" grocery store and parked beside a rusty pickup truck.

She helped Nora into the chair. Together they made their way down the rickety wooden boardwalk that connected the town's three buildings. Wisteria grew along the posts that supported the roof's overhang and festooned the upper timbers with fragrant white flowers. Here and there along the boardwalk were benches, handmade by the sisters. Later in the tourist season, those seats would be filled by people waiting for a ferry.

Ruby came to the store's screen door and pulled it open. A bell tinkled gaily overhead as they wheeled inside. The murky store was long and narrow, built like a shoe box.

Light pushed through the twin windows and illuminated a small desk with a cash register on it. Beyond that, layered wooden bookcases held carefully arranged dried goods. A small freezer offered all manner of island-raised meat—beef, chicken, pork, lamb—and a refrigerated case held vegetables grown on the sisters' own land.

The nun at the cash register looked up at their entrance.

"Nora Bridge? Ruby? I don't believe it!" Sister Helen waddled around the desk, her skirt hiked up to reveal heavy white calves sheathed in nubby woolen socks. Her green rubber clogs thumped with every step. Her fleshy face was scrunched into a welcoming grin that turned her bespectacled eyes into slits. She looked—as always— like a sprightly old gnome. "Praise God," Sister said. Her thick German accent turned the words into *prais Gott.* "It has been so long . . ." She turned to Ruby. "And how is the funny one?"

Ruby smiled. "I'm still a stitch, Sister. How 'bout you—got any good Heaven jokes for me?"

"I will think on it, that is for sure. It is *wunderbar* to see you both." She elbowed Ruby. "Mother Ruth still talks about the day your rabbit ran through services, *ja*? She will be happy to see you again."

Ruby stepped away from the wheelchair. "I . . . uh . . . haven't been to services in a while. I'm only on the island a week, anyway."

Helen gave her "the look"—every Catholic recognized it. "There is a Sunday in every week, *ja*?"

"Uh . . . maybe."

Nora smiled up at the nun. "Some things never change."

Helen nodded. Her habit slipped down on her forehead and she gave it a quick shove back. "Most things never change. That is what I have learned in seventy-three years of life." She leaned back on her heels and crossed her beefy arms. "It is good to see you two together again, that much is for sure. You have stayed away from this island for too long." She turned to Ruby. "You have babies, *ja*, like your sister?"

"No babies—and before you ask, no husband. I'm either foot-loose and fancy free or lonely and unlovable. Take your pick."

Helen laughed. "Always you were this way, Ruby. Making a joke out of everything. However—just for the record—my guess would be . . . fancy free and lonely." She clapped her hands together. "Anyway, the store is set up as it always was. Get what you need. Shall I begin a new account for you?"

"No," Ruby answered.

"Yes," Nora said at the same time, shooting her a dark look. "*I* may be here a while."

Ruby grabbed one of the small red baskets stacked by the desk and handed it to Nora. "Let's get started."

They moved past the tourist supply section—postcards, pens with ferries on them, little brown and white candlesticks made from Mount Saint Helens ash, Christmas ornaments. Ruby went on ahead; Nora rolled slowly behind her.

They came to the cereal first. Ruby grabbed a box of Cap'n Crunch and tossed it into the basket in her mother's lap.

"There's nothing good for you in that cereal."

Ruby turned, saw her mother's frown. "Should I get the kind with crunchberries? It adds fruit."

"Very funny. Will you grab one of those granolas for me—the sisters make it, if I remember correctly."

Ruby reached for the beribboned bag of cereal and plopped it into the basket. If *she* remembered correctly, it tasted like carpet fibers.

"We'll need several cans of tomatoes," Nora said. "No, not those; the ones in the green cans."

Ruby put back the unacceptable canned tomatoes and chose the "right" brand.

"Spaghetti and penne, please. God, no, not that cheap brand; get the good stuff . . . from Italy."

Like it was actually made in Italy. Ruby gritted her teeth and kept moving, but with every word her mother spoke, she felt her anger rise. When Ruby reached for the Twinkies, her mother practically shrieked.

"You cannot eat that."

That was it. Very slowly, Ruby turned around. "I'm sorry, do you *hear* me asking for dietary advice?"

"No, but—"

"That's the point. It's *my* butt that's going to swell to the size of Nebraska, not yours. So please . . . shut . . . up."

Nora snapped her teeth together. "Fine."

Ruby could hear Sister Helen chuckling.

Miraculously, she and her mother made it all the way to the end of the aisle without another argument.

Apparently, Nora was saving her strength for the battle over vegetables.

"That ear of corn is gross. Get one of the white ones . . . not *that* onion, for God's sake, get a Walla Walla Sweet . . . come on, Ruby, that broccoli is half dead. What on earth do you eat in California?"

Ruby dropped the broccoli into the basket and walked away. It was safer that way. She poked her head around the end of the aisle and called out to Sister Helen, "Where are the aspirin?"

Sister Helen chuckled. "Along the back wall, honey, by the Pepto-Bismol . . . which you might want to consider, too."

Ruby snagged an industrial-size container of Excedrin and tossed it into the basket. It hit a tomato with a juicy *thwack!*

"Lovely," Nora said, wiping her cheek. Then she glanced toward the left corner, where the nuns offered a few T-shirts and shorts for sale. "I could get you some clothes, if you'd like—"

"That's it. We're done." Ruby grabbed the handles on the wheelchair and spun it around, then strode up to the cash register. She stopped so suddenly her mother was thrown forward like a rag doll.

Sister Helen was doing her level best not to smile. "It's just like old times, seeing you two together."

Nora gave her a tight smile. "Yes, Sister, we've always enjoyed these mother–daughter outings."

Ruby nodded. "Just remember what she was like to shop with . . . when the police come to question you."

Sister Helen laughed at that and started ringing up the groceries. She chattered nonstop about this and that—who was running for mayor come autumn, whose horse had recently foundered, whose well had gone dry—as her fingers flew across the keys.

Ruby left the store and stared at the cars in line for the next ferry. She was just about to turn around when the row of newspaper machines caught her eye.

She glanced back into the store, then hurried down to the box that held *USA Today.*

And there, in the upper-right-hand corner, was a picture of her mother beneath the headline: WHERE IS NORA BRIDGE HIDING?

Ruby dug into her fanny pack, found two quarters, and slipped them into the machine.

"Ruby, honey?" came her mother's voice from inside the store.

Ruby yanked the paper out, rolled it up, and shoved it into her waistband, pulling her shirt down in front of it. "Just a second," she hollered, running past the store. At the minivan, she opened the back door and shoved the paper in underneath the backseat. By the time she got back into the store, she was breathless.

Nora was staring up at her. "The bags are on the counter. I can carry two of them if you can manage the third."

Ruby was certain that the patented mother's X-ray vision had somehow seen what she'd bought.

"Sure. Bye, Sister Helen." She snatched the bag off the counter, settled it under one arm, and wheeled her mother toward the car.

As soon as they got home, Ruby helped her mother into the house, carried the groceries in, and put them away. Then she turned to Nora, who was watching her closely.

"I . . . uh . . . I'm going to walk on the beach. It's such a nice day." Flashing a fake smile, Ruby went back outside. At the minivan, she retrieved her paper and tucked it under her shirt—just in case—then walked down to the beach.

She sat down on a flat granite rock and pulled out the lifestyle section, using a big chunk of silvery driftwood to pin the rest of the paper into the sand. The wind flapped at the edges of the paper and tried to rip it from her hands.

WHERE IS NORA BRIDGE HIDING?

In the wake of an ugly scandal, Nora Bridge has disappeared. Executives at KJZZ, which broadcasts her popular talk show, "Spiritual Healing with Nora," are closing ranks, saying only that Ms. Bridge is on a previously scheduled vacation.

Tom Adams, the controversial and outspoken owner of Adams News Organization, reports that nothing has changed with Ms. Bridge's daily advice column, "Nora Knows Best."

Yesterday, Adams talked to Katie Couric. He encouraged viewers to write to Nora, promising that "she wants to hear from her faithful readers and she will answer their questions. Even the tough ones."

Sources close to Ms. Bridge, however, seem unconvinced that she will return. As one employee, who asked to have her name withheld, put it, "I guess she was a big talker. All that advice about the sanctity of marriage . . . well, it's a real disappointment to find out what a liar she is."

There was obviously a full-scale media frenzy going on out there—*Today* . . . *Larry King Live*. Reporters were probably scouring the country, talking to anyone and everyone who ever knew Nora Bridge; they'd tear her apart if they could.

And Ruby's article would make it worse . . .

Ruby sat on the bed in her parents' old bedroom, with her knees drawn up and her yellow pad in her lap. The *USA Today* lay beside her; that grainy, unflattering photograph of her mother stared up at her.

My mother is being destroyed in the press. It's only fitting, I suppose. She ruined her family in pursuit of a career, and now that career is detonating.

It's what I wanted to happen. I'm sure it's part of what made me accept the money for an article. A need for some kind of . . . if not vengeance, then fairness.

And yet . . . something about it doesn't sit well with me—

"Ruby! Come help me make dinner."

For a weird, disorienting second, Ruby was fourteen again, hiding in her bedroom, reading *The Lord of the Rings* when she was supposed to be doing homework. Shaking her head to clear it, she rolled over on her stomach and yanked open the top drawer in her mother's nightstand. Pens and junk clattered forward. As she started to put her pad away, she saw a brown prescription bottle.

She picked it up and read the label. VALIUM. NORA BRIDGE. 1985. The doctor listed was Allbright.

Ruby frowned. Her mother was on Valium in 1985?

Chapter Ten

Valium.

That discovery opened a door, hinted at a woman Ruby had never known, never even imagined.

In 1985, everything had been fine. Great.

Or so Ruby had thought.

She wished she hadn't found the bottle. It was the sort of thing she didn't want to know. Like accidentally finding your mother's vibrator. Some things were supposed to remain hidden.

Finally, Ruby couldn't stand being in the bedroom anymore. She went downstairs and found Nora already in the kitchen.

"We're going to make chicken divan. How does that sound?"

Ruby groaned. "Cooking together."

"I want you to chop that broccoli. The cutting board is right there."

Ruby did as she was told.

"Smaller, please. Each piece needs to fit in a human mouth."

Ruby took a deep breath and started over.

For the next half hour, they worked side by side. Ruby boiled and cut up the chicken—in human-size bites—while Nora did everything else. Finally, the casserole was in the oven.

"I have a surprise for you," Nora said, putting the cutting board away. "There's a big cardboard box in my closet. Will you get it?"

Ruby shook her head. "I don't think so." A surprise from her mother just couldn't be a good thing.

Nora gave her "the look," and Ruby caved. Some things were bigger than willpower, and a mother's raised eyebrow was one of them. She went into the bedroom, opened the closet's louvered doors, and found the box. As she hefted it into her arms, it made a rattling, clanking sound like auto parts crammed together.

She took it into the living room and set it down on the glossy wormwood coffee table. It hit with a clatter.

Nora had followed her into the living room. "Open it."

Ruby pulled the cardboard flaps apart and peered inside the box. "Oh, *shit*."

It was their sixteen-millimeter movie projector and a reel of film. She turned to her mother.

"Home movies," Nora said with a forced smile.

"Don't tell me you want us to bond over old times?"

"*I* want to watch them, that's all. You can join me . . . or you can set it up and leave me . . . alone."

Ruby was trapped. Whether she watched the movies or not, she'd know that the film was here, in the house, waiting like a monster beneath a child's bed. She reached deeper into the box and found a folded white sheet and a set of thumbtacks. Their old "screen."

She set up the projector on a table in the living room, clicked the reel into place, and plugged the cord in. Then she tacked the sheet onto the wall.

She refused to dwell upon how big a deal it used to be to watch family movies. Every Christmas Eve, they'd sat together in their pajamas, with their unopened gifts glittering seductively beneath the tree, and watched the highlights of their year. It was an essential tradition in a family that had only a few.

Ruby turned off the lights. With a dull, clacking sound, the film started as a gray and black square in the center of the sheet.

Ruby lowered herself to the sofa's arm.

The words LOPEZ ISLAND TALENT REVUE stuttered understood across the makeshift screen. There was a buzz of people talking, then her mother's voice, clear as day, *There! Rand; she's coming.*

Ruby couldn't have been more than five years old, a scrawny, puffy-cheeked kindergartner dressed in a ragged pink tutu. She twirled and swirled drunkenly across the stage, her toothpick arms finding all kinds of awkward angles.

—Oh, Rand, she's perfect—

—Hush, I'm trying to concentrate—

Onstage, Ruby executed an uneven spin and sank into a curtsy. Applause thundered.

The picture went dark, then stuttered back to life. This time they were down at the beach. Caroline, in a skirted one-piece bathing suit, was splashing in the ankle-deep water, laughing. Ruby was wearing a bikini; her belly poked out above banged-up stick legs. Her mother was sitting in the sand, looking through a plastic bucket full of shells and rocks. Ruby ran over to her and stamped a foot down beside the bucket. Mom leaned over and fixed a strap on her saltwater sandals, then pulled a wiggly, laughing Ruby into her arms for a kiss.

Mom . . .

There she was.

Ruby slid off the arm of the sofa and landed on the soft, thread-bare cushion. Her whole childhood played out in front of her in staccato, black-and-white images accompanied by the sounds of children laughing.

How was it she'd forgotten how much they'd laughed . . . or how regularly her mother had hugged and kissed her? She'd remembered the feel of riding on her dad's strong shoulders, of seeing the world from way up high, but not the gentle pressure of her mother's kiss.

But she remembered it now. She was *seeing* it.

There was no way to keep her distance from this.

There was Dad, twirling Ruby around and around in a circle . . . and Mom, teaching Ruby how to tie her shoe . . . a rainy Halloween with two princesses skipping hand in hand up to the Smithsons' front door, carrying pumpkin-headed flashlights . . . the snowy Christmas morning when Ruby had gotten a guinea pig from

Santa . . . Mom and Dad, dancing in the living room of this very house, the picture blurry and bouncing from a camera held in a child's hands . . .

By the time the final bit of film flapped out of the reel and the screen went blank, Ruby felt as if she'd run a ten-mile race. She was unsteady as she turned off the camera and hit the lights.

Her mother (*Nora,* she reminded herself) sat hunched in her wheelchair, hands drawn into a tight-fisted ball in her lap. Tears glistened on her cheeks and lashes. She caught Ruby's gaze and tried to smile.

At the sight of her mother's tears, Ruby felt something inside of her break away. "You and Dad looked so happy together."

Nora smiled unevenly. "We were happy for a lot of years. And then . . . we weren't."

"You mean *you* weren't. I saw what it did to him when you walked out. Believe me, he loved you."

"Rand would have stayed with me forever; you're right about that. Just as he'd vowed to do."

Ruby frowned. "He would have stayed because he loved you, not just because he'd promised to."

"Ah, Ruby . . . there's so much you don't know. Your dad and I have a . . . history that's ours alone. No child can judge her parents' marriage."

"You mean you won't tell me why you left him."

"Beyond saying that we were unhappy? No, I won't."

Ruby wanted to be angry, but in truth, she was too battered. The movies had hurt so much she couldn't think straight. For the first time in years, she'd seen *Mom.*

"I had forgotten you," Ruby said softly, closing her eyes. "I've never dreamt of you or had a single childhood memory with you in it." When Ruby opened her eyes, she saw that her mother was crying, and it made Ruby uncomfortable, as if she'd done something wrong. It was crazy to feel that way, but there it was. Strangely, she didn't want to make her mother cry. "But tonight I remembered the locket you gave me on my eleventh birthday. The silver oval that opened up. I kept a picture of you on one side and Dad and Caro on the other side."

Nora wiped her eyes and nodded. "Do you still have it?"

Ruby got up, went to the fireplace. She stared at the pictures of Caroline's family. When she reached up and touched her own bare throat, she felt the phantom locket. She'd been sixteen the last day she'd worn it.

It had been a hot, humid day in the second week of August. Ruby and Caroline had refused to go school shopping. It had been the rock-bottom basement of their faith, the thing they'd said to each other for weeks: *Mom would be home in time for school . . .*

But she wasn't, and August had bled into September, and their lives couldn't be kept on hold anymore.

In that season, when all their friends and neighbors had been gathered together for picnics and barbecues and parties at Trout Lake, the Bridge family had stayed huddled in their too-quiet house. Ruby and Caro had learned to move soundlessly that summer. They did their best to disappear. Girls who were invisible didn't have to answer people's questions or make painful explanations.

It had been easy to do. Dad had seen to that. He'd started drinking and smoking when Nora left in June. By August, he never came out of his room. The *Captain Hook* sat idle all summer, and by the fall, Dad had had to sell off another chunk of land to pay their bills.

Finally, on the first day of school, Ruby had taken the locket off and thrown it to the ground . . .

"Ruby? I asked about the locket."

She turned and looked at her mother. "I threw it away."

"I see."

"No, you don't. I didn't throw it away because I hated you." She drew in a deep breath. For a split second, she almost lost her nerve;

she had to force the confession out. "I threw it because it hurt too much to remember you."

"Oh, Ruby . . ."

In the kitchen, the oven's timer went off.

Ruby lurched to her feet. "Thank God. Let's eat."

Nora wrestled through a long and sleepless night. Finally, around dawn, she gave up and went out onto the porch to watch the sunrise. As soon as the sun was up, she called Eric, but there was no answer, and somehow, that made her feel even lonelier. She wheeled herself back out to the porch.

It was low tide now. The shy water had drawn back, revealing a wide swatch of glistening, pebbled shoreline.

She remembered so many times on that beach, gathering oysters, clams, and geoducks with Rand's father for a Sunday barbecue.

I had forgotten you.

Nora had known that Ruby blamed her, hated her. But to have *forgotten* her?

Nora didn't know how to combat that.

Do you want me to be like Caroline? Ruby had asked. *Pretend that everything is fine between us?*

Nora leaned back in her chair, sighing tiredly. Ruby was right. Ruby, with her fire, her anger, her chipped shoulder . . . at least she was honest. All or nothing. Black or white. She couldn't live in the shades of gray that comforted her sister.

"I miss you, Ruby," she whispered, daring to say the words to this silent world; words she couldn't imagine being able to say to her younger daughter. Sadness welled up inside her. Instead of pushing it away or pretending it didn't exist, she allowed herself to wallow in it. *I miss you, baby girl . . .*

She thought of all the years that had passed her by—Ruby leaving for college . . . quitting college . . . moving to Los Angeles (had she taken Rand's ratty old Volkswagen or had she found a way to buy a new car?) . . . renting her first apartment . . .

So much time gone.

"Enough," she said at last. Straightening her spine, she opened her eyes.

What she needed was a plan. She needed to attack the problem with Ruby aggressively—there was no other way to deal with her.

There would be no second chance; she knew that. Nora had one week—six days, now—to crack through the hard shell of the past.

But how?

"Okay," she counseled herself. "Pretend this is a reader letter."

> *Dear Nora:*
>
> *Years ago, I walked out on my marriage and left my children. My younger daughter has never forgiven me. Now she tells me that she's forgotten all memories of me. How do I make amends?*

She took a deep breath, thinking it through. If Nora had received a letter like this, she would have taken the woman to task for her unpardonable behavior, would have told her it was no surprise that her daughter hated her.

"Hypocrite," she hissed. No wonder she'd lost her career.

Anyway, after moralizing for a few sentences, she would have said . . .

Force her to remember you.

The answer came easily when offered to a stranger.

Nora smiled. If she forced Ruby to remember the past, they could possibly find their way into the present . . . maybe even peek at a different future.

It wouldn't be easy, she knew. Or particularly pleasant.

Probably excruciating, in fact.

But it was the only way. Right now, it was easy for Ruby to hate Nora—she only remembered the horrible choices made that summer. Would it be so easy if Ruby remembered the good times?

Behind her, the screen door squeaked open. "Nora?"

Nora wheeled around, smiling brightly. "Hi, honey."

Ruby frowned. "You're awfully chipper for eight in the morning. Do you want a cup of coffee?"

"No, thanks. I've got some. Why don't you get a cup and join me out here? It's beautiful."

Ruby ran a hand through her spiky, sleep-molded hair and nodded. Wordlessly, she went back inside, then came out a few minutes later and sat down in the rocker.

Nora stared down at the beach. The silence between them was strangely companionable, not unlike a thousand other mornings, long ago, when they'd sat together out here.

She took a sip of her coffee and glanced out at the point. "Remember the Fourth of July barbecues we used to have out here? Your dad was always gone fishing and the three of us girls would load up on firecrackers."

Ruby smiled. "Sparklers were my favorite. I couldn't wait for it to get dark."

"We wrote things in the light, remember?" Nora said, watching Ruby. "I always wrote: I love my girls."

Ruby curled her hands around her coffee cup, as if she needed a sudden infusion of warmth. "Caroline always scrawled the name of whatever boy she was in love with at the time. Remember when it was Alexander Jorgenson? It took two sparklers to spell his whole name—she was in a panic."

Nora smiled. She pictured Eric and Dean, standing around the grill, laughing. They'd had impeccable timing, those boys. They never missed a meal. There was a sudden lump in her throat, and so her voice was soft when she said, "You only wrote Dean's name. Year after year."

Ruby sighed. "Yeah . . . He and Eric always showed up right when you put the salmon on the barbecue—remember?" She looked up. "Caroline tells me you've stayed in touch with Eric. How is he?"

Nora had known this moment was coming; she'd thought she was prepared for it, but she wasn't. She released her breath in a slow sigh. There was no way to honor Eric's wish for privacy, not with Nora unable to drive. Sooner or later, she would have to elicit Ruby's help, and when she did, Ruby would learn about Eric. But how did you tell your daughter that one of her best childhood friends was dying?

"Mom?"

Nora casually wiped her eyes and met Ruby's expectant gaze. "Eric has cancer."

Ruby paled. "Oh, my God . . ."

Nora watched the memories move through Ruby's eyes. She knew her daughter was thinking back to lazy summer days spent down at the lake with Dean and Eric. It was a long time before Ruby found her voice. "How bad is it?"

"Bad."

"Is he going to die?"

It hurt to answer. "Yes, honey, he is."

Ruby slumped forward, burying her head in her hands. "I should have stayed in contact with him. God . . ." She fell silent, shaking her head, and Nora knew her daughter was crying. "It seems like yesterday we were all together. I can't imagine him . . . sick."

"I know. I keep thinking about those Fourth of July barbecues. I used to watch you and Dean on the beach. You'd hold hands and duel with your sparklers. I could hear your laughter all the way up here, and when you got older, and started whispering . . . then I worried."

Ruby looked up. Tears spiked her eyelashes, made her look about ten years old. "I never knew that."

"Motherhood is full of secret worries." Nora realized a second too late that she'd made herself vulnerable. She should never have used the word *secret*. But, thankfully, Ruby had bigger things on her mind.

"Can we visit Eric?"

"Of course. He's staying at the old house on Lopez. I know he'd love to see you." Nora leaned back in her chair and stared out at the

Sound. "Sometimes, when I close my eyes, I can picture all of us. You, me, Caroline . . . Eric and Dean. What I remember most are days out on the *Wind Lass*. Dino and Eric loved that boat . . ."

"I know what you're doing," Ruby said after a long pause; her voice was thick and low. "You want me to remember."

"Yes."

"Remembering stuff like that hurts."

"I know, honey. But—"

Inside the house, the phone rang. Ruby got slowly to her feet and went inside. The screen door banged shut behind her. "Hello?"

Nora could hear Ruby's half of the conversation.

"Who is this? Oh, I'm her daughter, Ruby . . . Yes, she is . . . just a minute, I'll get her. Nora?" Ruby yelled. "It's your personal assistant, Dee."

"Tell her I'm not here."

Ruby opened the screen door and poked her head out. "I already told her you were here. Come on. She's waiting."

Nora wheeled into the kitchen and took the phone. "Hello, Dee."

"Oh, Nora, thank God. A box of letters just landed on your desk. There was nothing I could do about it. Tom Adams called—he threatened to get me fired if I didn't forward them to you. Today." Dee made a sniffling sound. "I *need* this job, Nora. I know you'd never fire me, but what if . . . you know . . ."

"I lose my job." Nora sighed. "I understand completely. Go ahead and mail the stuff to me at the address I gave you."

"Tom wants me to send Lake Union Air up for today's delivery."

Of course. With Tom, everything had to happen instantly. "Did you read the letters, Dee?"

"Uh . . . a few."

Nora's stomach turned sour. "How bad is it?"

"It's ugly, Nora. People around here are starting to talk to the tabloids . . . they're not saying nice things . . . and some lady in Iowa went on television last night and said she was going to file a lawsuit against you. Fraudulent advice or some stupid thing."

Nora glanced over at Ruby, who was shamelessly eavesdropping. "Okay, Dee. Send me the letters."

"I thought I'd send your 'best of' file, too. In case you wanted to sneak some old letters in. Tom wouldn't know."

"Good thinking."

Dee sighed heavily. "I *knew* you were going to do the column. People are saying—"

"I'll make sure that you're taken care of. Don't you worry about that. Thanks for everything, Dee. Really. Good-bye." She leaned forward and hung up the phone. She wanted to make a joke for Ruby's benefit, but she hadn't the strength.

"Nora?"

Slowly, she lifted her head.

Ruby stood by the refrigerator, her arms crossed. Her cup of coffee sat on the counter, forgotten. "What was that all about?"

"My boss at the newspaper expects me to answer some . . . rather unflattering letters from my readers."

"Well, it *is* your job."

Nora didn't bother answering. Ruby couldn't possibly understand. She didn't know how it felt to *need* acceptance; and how, without it, you could feel invisible. Worse than invisible.

Some lady in Iowa . . . a lawsuit . . . fraudulent advice . . .

She closed her eyes and rubbed the bridge of her nose. "David Letterman is probably having a field day with this . . ."

For two days, she'd been able to forget that her life was unraveling, that she was a national scandal. No more.

She heard Ruby run upstairs.

Thank God.

But in a minute, Ruby was back, tapping her on the shoulder. "Nora?"

Nora opened her eyes.

Ruby was standing beside her, holding a section of newspaper. "I bought this yesterday at the store. Maybe you should . . . read what they're writing about you."

Nora stared at the newspaper. She could see a big, grainy picture of herself.

It had been taken at the Emmys last year—God, she hated that shot. It made her look all puffy-cheeked and squinty-eyed.

She took the paper from Ruby and glanced through the article. "It's over," she said dully, letting the newspaper fall to the floor.

Ruby frowned. "Don't be stupid. You'll get through this. Look at Monica Lewinsky—she's selling expensive handbags now. She went to the Oscars last year. And that idiot who married the millionaire got a fortune from *Playboy*."

"Thank you for those comforting comparisons."

"I just meant—"

"You're too young to understand, Ruby. My career is over. I have no intention of answering a single letter. I'm going to hide out until this . . . shit . . . is over. Another story will come along and they'll forget about me. Then I'll just fade away."

"You're kidding me, right?"

"No."

"But you're *famous*."

"I'm infamous. Believe me, there's a difference."

"With the right spin, you can—"

"You don't understand my career, Ruby. I've never put a wall between me and my readers. Everything I think and feel and believe is found in my words to strangers. That's why they believed in me, they sensed my honesty."

Ruby's eyebrow arched upward. "According to the press, your columns said you believed in marriage. Is that the kind of honesty they got from you?"

"I *do* believe in marriage. And love, and family, and commitments. I just . . . failed at it."

Ruby looked surprised by that answer. "That's an interesting word choice. Failed."

"I don't suppose either one of us would characterize my wife-and-motherhood as successful."

"No. But I wouldn't have expected you to see it that way. As a failure, I mean."

They were finally circling something that mattered. Nora's voice was gentle. "How did you imagine I'd feel?"

Ruby frowned. "I would have thought you'd see leaving us as . . . a success. You did it so well. Like leaving a job you hate. You might miss the income, but you're proud of yourself for finding the guts to quit."

"I wasn't proud of myself."

"Why?" Ruby asked the question in a whispered voice. "Why did you do it? Couldn't you have a career *and* raise children?"

Nora sighed. There were so many ways to answer that, and she was too damned depressed to pick the right one. So, she said the first thing that came to mind. "What happened to us isn't some event, like the sinking of the *Titanic*. It's little things, strung together over decades. To really understand it all, you'd have to grow up and see the way things really were in our family, but you don't want to do that, Ruby. You want to forget I ever existed . . . forget *we* ever existed."

"It's easier that way," Ruby said quietly.

"Yes. And it's easier for me to walk away from my career. I can't fight these charges . . . not with the life I've led and the choices I've made. The press will uncover what I did to my children . . . to you, Ruby . . . and it'll get even worse."

"I never saw you as a quitter."

Nora gave her a sad, knowing smile. "Ah, Ruby . . . you, of all people . . . you should have."

Chapter Eleven

It was early afternoon, the peak of a surprisingly hot June day. The sea and sky were a solid sheet of sparkling blue. Sunlight glinted along the surface of the water. At the edge of the property, just before it dipped down to meet the sand, trees reached out to one another, their leaves whispering in the wind. Starlings banked and dove along the eaves, chirping loudly, flying low above the grass.

Ruby sat in the white Adirondack chair on the second-floor balcony. She couldn't seem to stop crying.

She kept thinking about Eric, about all the times they'd spent together, how he'd been the big brother she'd never had—and the thought of losing him was unbearable . . . but no worse than the realization that she'd lost him years earlier, thoughtlessly, by walking away and never bothering to call.

Never bothering to call.

It was the story of her life. Ruby the half-wit girl who exits stage right.

She had loved Eric. Not in the searing, heartbreaking way she'd loved his brother, but in a solid, dependable way. For all the years of her youth, he'd been there. It was Eric who'd taught her to set up a pup tent when the Girl Scout jamboree was coming . . . Eric who'd shown her how to stand on the bow pulpit of the *Wind Lass* on a windy day.

And yet she'd walked away, let him become a faded snapshot in the drawer of her life.

"I'm sorry," she whispered aloud, hearing the pathetic edge to her voice. It wasn't good enough, her apology into thin air. She acknowledged that. But the thought of *seeing* him terrified her. How could she stand by his bed and talk to him . . . smile as if they'd stayed friends . . . and say good-bye?

How could she watch him die?

Closing her eyes, she leaned back into the chair. In the bedroom behind her, the phone rang, but when she picked it up, there was no answer.

When the *briiiiing* sounded again, she realized it was her cellular phone. She dove over the bed and reached for the phone on the floor. She'd plugged it in less than an hour earlier.

"Hello?"

"Jesus, Rube, I've been trying this number endlessly. How's life in the outback?"

It was Val. She could hear his exhalation of cigarette smoke into the receiver. "It's Summer Island, Val, not Siberia. And things are fine."

"I thought you might need to be airlifted out."

Ruby laughed. "No, just keep that alibi handy in case I need it."

"How's the article coming?"

"Okay, I think. Maybe even good."

"Excellent news. I talked to Joan this morning. Things are really heating up on this story. The press is crucifying your mother."

Ruby was caught off guard by her reaction to that. It made her mad. "She doesn't care. She's walking away from her career. Quitting."

"No shit?"

"Amazing, huh? Anyway, I'm working hard."

"Joan'll be glad to hear that. Remember, you're booked on *Sarah Purcell* for next week. See you then, babe."

Babe. Ruby couldn't help rolling her eyes. He'd never called her that before; it must be a term reserved for clients who actually made him money. "Okay, Val. Talk to you soon."

After she hung up, she retrieved her paper and pen, then went back out onto the balcony and sat in the oversize chair her grandfather had made by hand.

She forced herself to stop thinking about Eric. For now, she needed to work on the article.

She looked down at her yellow pad, then slowly picked up her pen and began to write.

I have spent most of my adult life pretending I was motherless. At first, it took effort. When a memory of my mother came to me, I ruthlessly squelched it and forced other images into my mind—a slamming door; the sound of tires sputtering through gravel; my father, sitting on the edge of his bed, weeping into his hands.

In time, I taught myself to forget, and in that state of suspended amnesia, things were easy. Time moved on.

But last night, my mother and I watched some old home movies. There, in a darkened living room, the doors I'd tried to keep closed slowly opened.

Now I am left with a disturbing and disorienting question: In forgetting my mother, how much have I forgotten about myself?

It seems I don't know either one of us. My mother tells me now that she is going to walk away from her career. I don't know what to make of that. She traded our family for fame and fortune; how could it mean so little to her?

Ruby set the pen and pad down on the rusty, frosted glass table beside her chair, unable to think of anything to add.

She couldn't forget her mother's face when she'd said, *I'll just fade away.*

Her mother had looked . . . broken, resigned, and more than a little afraid. Just like another time.

I'm leaving. Who wants to come with me?

For eleven years, Ruby had remembered only the words, the harsh, ugly sound of them in the silence of that morning.

Now, she remembered the rest.

Her mother's eyes had been filled with that same agonizing pain, and when she spoke, her voice had been strained . . . not her voice at all.

Then, Ruby had heard nothing beyond the good-bye. She'd understood that her mother was leaving . . . but what if Nora had been running away?

I never saw you as a quitter, Ruby had said today.

And her mother's answer: *You, of all people . . . you should have.*

But what could her mother have been running away from? And what had kept her away?

The package arrived from Seattle in the late afternoon, while her mother was taking a nap. Ruby knew what it was. She debated with herself for a few moments—after all, she'd purposely chosen never to read her mother's newspaper columns—but the *Caché* article changed things. Now, Ruby needed to know what "Nora Knows Best" had been about.

Quietly, she opened the box and pulled out a manila envelope marked BEST OF. In the living room, she plopped onto the sofa, tucked her feet up underneath her, and withdrew the pile of clippings. The one on top was dated December 1989, from the *Anacortes Bee*.

> *Dear Nora:*
>
> *Do you have any tips for getting red wine out of white silk? At my sister's wedding, I got a little drunk and spilled a glassful on her gown. Now she's not talking to me, and I feel just awful about it.*
>
> *Wedding Dress Blues.*

Nora's answer was short and sweet.

Dear Wedding Dress Blues:

Only your dry cleaner can get the stain out. If it can't be done, you must offer to replace the gown. Because you were drunk, even a little, this is more than an ordinary accident, and your sister deserves a perfect reminder of her special day, a dress she can pass down to her daughter. It may take you a while to save the money, but in the end, you'll feel better. Nothing is more important than family. I'm sure you know that; it's what made you write to me. It's so easy to do the wrong thing in life, don't you think? When we see a clear road to being a better person, we ought to take it.

As Ruby continued to read the columns, she noticed that her mother's mail changed gradually from household-hint questions to earnest, heartfelt questions about life. Ruby had to admit that her mother was good at this. Her answers were concise, wise, and compassionate.

Ruby began to hear her mother in the column. Not the sophisticated, greedy, selfish Nora Bridge, but her *mother,* the woman who'd told Ruby to wear her coat, or brush her teeth, or clean her room.

As she read a column about a sixteen-year-old girl who was having a problem with drugs, Ruby remembered a time from her own life . . .

It had been in that terrible year that Ruby had almost "gone bad." She'd been fourteen, and Lopez Island—and her own family—had seemed hopelessly small and uncool. For a time, skipping school and smoking pot had offered Ruby a better way. She'd even turned away from Dean.

Dad had gone ballistic when Ruby got suspended from school for smoking, but not Nora.

Her mother had picked Ruby up from the principal's office and driven her to the state park at the tip of the island. She'd dragged Ruby down to the secluded patch of beach that overlooked Haro Strait and the distant glitter of downtown Victoria. It had been exactly three in the afternoon, and the gray whales had been migrating past them in a spouting, splashing row. Nora had been wearing her good dress, the one she saved for parent–teacher conferences, but she had plopped down cross-legged on the sand.

Ruby had stood there, waiting to be bawled out, her chin stuck out, her arms crossed.

Instead, Nora had reached into her pocket and pulled out the joint that had been found in Ruby's locker. Amazingly, she had put it in her mouth and lit up, taking a deep toke, then she had held it out to Ruby.

Stunned, Ruby had sat down by her mother and taken the joint. They'd smoked the whole damn thing together, and all the while, neither of them had spoken.

Gradually, night had fallen; across the water, the sparkling white city lights had come on.

Her mother had chosen that minute to say what she'd come to say. "Do you notice anything different about Victoria?"

Ruby had found it difficult to focus. "It looks farther away," she had said, giggling.

"It *is* farther away. That's the thing about drugs. When you use them, everything you want in life is farther away." Nora had turned to her. "How cool is it to do something that anyone with a match can do? Cool is becoming an astronaut . . . or a comedian . . . or a scientist who cures cancer. Lopez Island is exactly what you think it is—a tiny blip on a map. But the world is out there, Ruby, even if you haven't seen it. Don't throw your chances away. We don't get as many of them as we need. Right now you can go anywhere, be anyone, do anything. You can become so damned famous that they'll have a parade for you when you come home for your high-school reunion . . . or you can keep screwing up and failing your classes and you can snip away the ends of your choices until finally you end up with that crowd who hangs out at Zeke's Diner, smoking cigarettes and talking about high-school football games that ended twenty years ago." She had stood up and brushed off her dress, then looked down at Ruby. "It's your choice. Your life. I'm your mother, not your warden."

Ruby remembered that she'd been shaking as she'd stood up. That's how deeply her mother's words had reached. Very softly, she'd said, "I love you, Mom."

That was Ruby's last specific memory of saying those words to her mother . . .

She turned her attention back to the columns. She noticed that this last set was paper-clipped together. The very first sentence pulled her in.

Dear Nora:

Do you ever feel so alone in the world that everything normal looks out of focus? It's as if you're the only black-and-white human being in a technicolor city.

I have married the wrong woman. I knew it when the day came to walk down the aisle. I knew when I lifted the veil and looked down into her eyes. But sometimes you do the right thing for the wrong reasons, and you pray that love will grow.

When it doesn't, a piece of you dies, and day by day, it keeps dying until finally you realize there's nothing of you left.

You tell yourself that only your child matters—the reason you got married in the first place—and you can almost believe it. When you hold your baby in your arms, you finally learn what true love really is.

And yet still you wonder, even as you're holding your daughter's hand or brushing her hair or reading her a bedtime story . . . you wonder if it can really be enough.

I don't know what to do. My wife and I have drifted so terribly far apart. . . . Please, can you help me?

Lost and Lonely.

Dear Lost and Lonely:

My heart goes out to you. I think all of us know how it feels to be lonely, especially within the supposedly warm circle of a family.

I can tell that you're an honorable man, and you obviously know that breaking up a family is the kind of act that irrevocably destroys lives. Believe me, the loneliness you feel within your family is a pale shadow of the torment you'll feel if you walk away.

I pray that if you look hard enough, you will unearth some remnant of the love you once felt for your wife, and that with care, a seed of that emotion can grow again. Seek counseling; talk to professionals and to each other. Take a vacation together. Touch, and not only sexually. Little touches along the way can mean a lot. Get involved in activities—community events, church events, that kind of thing.

Go see a marriage counselor. You don't want to end a marriage and break your children's hearts until and unless there is no possible chance for reconciliation.

Trust me on this.

Nora.

The last item was a handwritten letter; there was no column attached to it. Obviously, it had been submitted for publication and rejected. Yet Nora had saved it.

Dear Nora:

My daughter—my precious baby girl—was killed by a drunk driver this year. I understand tragedy now; its taste, its texture . . . the imprint it leaves on you.

I find that I can't talk to people anymore, not even my wife, who needs me more than ever. I see her, sitting on the end of the bed, her hair unwashed, her eyes rimmed in red, and I can't reach out to her, can't offer comfort. If left alone, I'm certain I could go through the rest of my life without ever speaking again.

I want to gather my belongings, put them in a shopping cart, and disappear into the faceless crowd of vagrants in Pioneer Square. But I

*haven't the strength even for that. So I sit in my house, seeing the
endless reminders of what I once had . . . and I ask myself why I
bother to breathe at all . . .*

Lost and Lonely.

Across the top of that letter, someone had written: *FedEx the
attached letter to this man's return address immediately.* Paper-clipped to
the letter was a photocopy of a handwritten note.

Dear Lost and Lonely:

*I will not waste time with the pretty words we wrap around grief.
You are in danger; you are not so far gone that you don't know this.
I am going to do what I have never done before—what I imagine I'll
never do again.*

*You will come and talk to me. I will not take no for an answer.
Your letter mentioned Pioneer Square; I see that your return address
is in Laurelhurst.*

*My secretary at the newspaper will be expecting your call tomor-
row and she will set up an appointment. Please, please, do not disap-
point me. I know how life can wound even the strongest heart, and
sometimes all it takes to save us is the touch of a single stranger's
hand.*

Reach out for me . . . I'll be there.

It was signed *Nora.*

Ruby's hands were trembling. No wonder these readers loved her
mother. She carefully put the columns and letters back in the manila
folder and left the whole package on the kitchen table for her
mother to find, then she went upstairs.

She hadn't even realized that she was going to call Caroline until
she'd picked up the phone. But it made sense. Ruby felt unsteady . . .
and Caroline had always been her solid ground.

Caro answered on the third ring. "Hello?"

Ruby couldn't help noticing how tired her sister sounded. "Hey, sis. You sound like you need a nap."

Caroline laughed. "I always need a nap. Of course, what I do that makes me so darned tired is a complete mystery."

"What *do* you do all day?"

"Only a single woman would ask that question of a mother. So, what's going on up there? How are you and Mom doing?"

"She's not who I thought she was," Ruby admitted softly.

"How could she be? You haven't spoken to her since *Moonlighting* was on television."

"I know, I know . . . but it's more than that. Like, did you know she was seeing a shrink when she was married to Dad . . . or that she took Valium in nineteen eighty-five?"

"Wow," Caroline said. "I wonder if her doctor told her to leave Dad?"

"Why would he do that?"

Caroline laughed softly. "That's what they do, Ruby. They tell unhappy women to find happiness. If I had a buck for every time my therapist told me to leave Jere, I'd live on Hunt's Point."

"You see a shrink, too?"

"Come on, Ruby. It's like getting a manicure. Good grooming for the mind."

"But I thought you and Mr. Quarterback had a perfect life."

"We have our problems, just like anyone else, but I'd rather talk about—aah! Darn it, Jenny! That's not okay. I gotta run, Ruby. Your niece just poured a cup of grape juice on her brother's head."

Before Ruby could answer, Caroline hung up.

Everything was ready.

Dean knocked on Eric's door, heard the muffled "Come in," and went inside.

Eric was sitting up in bed, reading a dog-eared paperback copy of

Richard Bach's book *Illusions.* When he saw Dean, he smiled. "Hey, bro. It's almost dinnertime. Where have you been?" He reached for the cup on his bedside tray. His thin fingers trembled; he groaned tiredly and gave up.

Dean hurried to the bed and grabbed the cup, carefully placing it in Eric's quavering hand. He guided the straw to his brother's mouth.

Eric sipped slowly, swallowed. Dean helped him replace the cup on the tray, then Eric turned his head, let it settle into the pile of pillows. "Thanks, I was dying of thirst." He grinned. "No mention of death was intentional."

Dean wanted to smile; honestly, he did. But all he could think about was his big brother, up here all alone, thirsty and too weak to reach for his glass of water. He crossed his arms and stared out the window. He didn't dare make eye contact with Eric. He needed just a minute to collect himself. "I've been working on something," he said.

"A surprise?"

Dean looked down at his brother then and saw a glimpse of the old Eric—the young Eric—and his throat tightened even more. It was all he could do to nod. Slowly, he lowered the metal bed rail. When it clanged into place, he said, "Are you up for a little trip?"

"Are you kidding? I'm so sick of this bed I could cry. Hell, I *do* cry . . . all the time."

Dean leaned forward, scooped his brother into his arms and lifted him up from the bed.

God, he weighed nothing at all.

It was like holding a fragile child; only it was his brother. His strong, outspoken big brother, who'd once led the island football team in touchdown passes . . .

Dean shut the memories off. If he remembered who Eric used to be—now, while this frail, hollowed man was in his arms—he would stumble and fall.

He carried his brother downstairs and through the house, past Lottie in the kitchen, who waved, her eyes overbright . . . across the manicured green lawn and down the bank to the beach. On the slanted, wooden dock, he'd already set up an oversize Adirondack chair and piled pillows onto it.

"The *Wind Lass*," Eric said softly.

Dean carefully placed his brother into the chair, then tucked the cashmere blanket tightly around his thin body.

It was nearing sunset. The sky was low enough to touch. The last rays of the setting sun turned everything pink—the waves, the clouds, the pebbled beach that curled protectively along the fish-hook shape of the shoreline. The sailboat was still in bad shape, but at least she was clean.

Dean sat down beside Eric. Stretching out his legs, he leaned back against one of the wooden pilings. "I still have some more work to do on her. Jeff Brein, down at the Crow's Nest, is repairing the sail, and it should be done tomorrow. Wendy Johnson is cleaning the cushions. I thought . . . maybe if we could take her out . . ." Dean let the sentence trail off. He didn't know quite how to sculpt his amorphous hope into something as ordinary as words.

"We could remember how it used to be," Eric said. "How *we* used to be."

Of course Eric had understood. "Yeah."

Eric drew the blanket tighter against his chin. "So, what's it like, being the favored son?"

"Lonely."

Eric sighed and leaned back into the pillows. "Remember when she loved me? When I was a star athlete with awesome grades and a promising future. I was her trophy boy."

Dean remembered. Their mother had adored Eric, her dark-haired angel, she called him. The only time Mom and Dad came to the island was football season. Every homecoming game, Mom had dressed in her best "casual" clothes and gone to the game, where she cheered on her quarterback son. When the season ended, they were gone again.

Eric had lived in the warm glow of his parents' affection for so long, he'd mistaken pride for love, but when he'd told them about Charles, he'd learned the depth of his naïveté. Mother hadn't spoken to him since.

So it had been Dean, the younger, less perfect son, who'd taken over the family business. It had never been something he wanted to do, but family expectations—especially in a wealthy family—were a sticky web. "I remember," he said quietly.

"I heard the phone ring last night about eleven o'clock," Eric said.

Dean looked away; eye contact was impossible. "Yeah. Some phone company rep who—"

"Don't bother, bro. It was her, wasn't it?"

"Yeah."

"Still in Athens?"

"Florence. Mother had the nerve to tell me that the shopping was great." She'd also said, *Come on over, Dean—we've got plenty of room at the villa.* As if it didn't matter at all that her elder son lay dying.

Eric's gaze was pathetically hopeful as he turned to Dean. "Are they coming to see me?"

There was no point in lying. "No."

"Did you tell them this is it? I'm not going to be around much longer?"

Dean reached out, touched his brother's hand. It surprised both of them, that sudden bit of intimacy. "I'm sorry."

Eric released a thready sigh. "What good is an agonizing death by cancer if your own family won't weep by your bedside?"

"I'm here," Dean said softly. "You're not alone."

Tears came to Eric's eyes. "I know, baby brother. I know . . ."

Dean swallowed hard. "You can't let her get to you."

Eric closed his eyes. "Someday she'll be sorry. It'll be too late, though." By the end of the sentence, his words were garbled and he was asleep.

Dean leaned closer. Carefully, he tugged up the blanket, tucked it beneath his brother's chin.

Eric blinked awake and smiled sleepily. "Tell me about your life."

"There's not much to tell. I work."

"Very funny. I get the San Francisco newspapers, you know—just to read about you and the folks. You seem to be quite the bachelor-about-town. If I didn't know better, I'd say you were a man who had everything."

Dean wanted to laugh and say, *I do; I do have everything a man could want,* but it was a lie, and he'd never been able to lie to his brother. And more than that, Dean wanted to talk to Eric the way he once had. Brother to brother, from the heart. "There's something . . . missing in my life. I don't know what it is."

"Do you like your job?"

Dean was surprised by the question. No one had ever asked him that, and he'd never bothered to ask himself. Still, the answer came quickly. "No."

"Are you in love with anyone?"

"No. It's been a long time since I was in love."

"And you can't figure out what's *missing* in your life? Come on, Dino. The question isn't, what's missing? The question is, what the hell *is* your life?" Eric yawned and closed his eyes again. Already he was tiring. "God, I wanted you to be happy all these years . . . " He fell asleep for a second, then blinked awake. "Remember Camp Orkila?" he said suddenly. "I was thinking about that yesterday, about the first time we went up there."

"When we met Ruby." Dean found an honest smile inside of him, drew it out. "She climbed up into that big tree by the beach, remember? She said arts and crafts were for babies and she was a big girl."

"She wouldn't come down until you asked her to."

"Yeah. That was the beginning, wasn't it? We'd never seen a real family before . . ." Dean let the words string out, find one another, and connect. Like threads, he wove them together, sewed a quilt from the strands of their life, and tucked it around his brother's thin body.

Chapter Twelve

Nora woke up groggy from her nap. She lay in bed for a minute, listening to the gentle, whooshing sound of the sea through her open window. It was almost nighttime; she'd been asleep for hours.

Eric.

She pulled the phone onto her lap and dialed the number.

She spoke to Lottie for a few minutes, then waited patiently for Eric to come on the line.

"Nora? Well, it's about damn time."

She laughed. God, it felt good to smile, even better to hear his voice. He sounded almost like his old self. "I've had an . . . interesting last few days. I'm on Summer Island. Caroline is letting me relax here for a while."

"Ah, the lifestyles of the rich and famous. I suppose it's tough to make time for a dear old friend who is facing the Grim Reaper with quiet dignity." He laughed at his own joke, but the laughter dwindled into a cough.

Nora closed her eyes, trying to picture him as he'd been only a few years ago . . . like on the afternoon his team had won the league championships and the kids had poured Gatorade on his head and chanted his name . . .

"Nora? Did you lapse into a coma?"

"I'm here." She made an instant decision: she wouldn't tell him about the scandal. He didn't need to worry about her. But she had to tell him *something*—she couldn't just show up at his house in a wheelchair. "I had an accident and wound up in Bayview."

"Oh, my God, are you okay?"

"For a fifty-year-old woman who drove into a tree, I'm great. And you told me that Mercedes was a waste of money—ha! It saved my life. I came out of it with a broken leg and a sprained wrist. Nothing to worry about. But that's why I haven't been to see you."

"There's something you're not telling me."

She forced a laugh. "Your intuition is wrong this time."

"Nora?" He said her name with infinite tenderness, and in it, she heard the gentle, chiding reminder of all they'd been through together. For the first time since this mess had begun, she felt truly cared for. "No, really, I—" She pinched the bridge of her nose and concentrated on taking shallow breaths.

"Nora. You know you can talk to me about anything."

"You don't need to hear about my troubles."

"Who was it who sat by me in the hospital every night while Charlie was dying? Who was it who held my hand at the gravesite . . . who was there when I started chemotherapy?"

Nora swallowed hard. "Me."

"So, talk."

All the emotions she'd bottled up in the past few days came spilling out. She didn't cry; she was almost preternaturally calm, in fact. But as she spoke, it felt as if the very fabric of her soul was ripping. "The *Tattler* just published naked pictures of me in bed with a man."

"Jesus . . ." His voice was a whisper.

"That's not even the worst of it." Amazingly, she laughed. "I was actually *posing* with this guy. And fortunately for me, the photos were dated—proving that I was married to Rand at the time they were taken. The press is crucifying me. Apparently people are crawling out of the woodwork to call me a hypocrite."

"That's why you're at the summer house? You're hiding out?"

"My career is over. I couldn't get a job counseling toddlers about potty training."

"Come on, this is *America*. Celebrities screw up all the time. It just makes us love them more. Jack Nicholson beats up a car with a baseball bat . . . and we give him another Oscar. Hugh Grant shows us not only moral flexibility but outright *stupidity,* and after a quick apology on Leno, he's in a movie with Julia Roberts. So, you flashed your ass. Big deal. It's not like the photographs showed you giving a blow job to a drug dealer. Hold your head up, cry when you admit your mistake, and beg for a second chance. Your fans will love you more for being one of them. Human."

"That's why I love you, Eric. The glass is always half full. Honest to God, if you were my son I'd be so proud." She heard a sound—a clearing of his throat—and she knew. She could have slapped herself for her insensitivity. "You called your mother."

"She's in Europe. The shopping is great." He sighed, made a sound that was nearly a groan. "She hasn't called me. But it's only been a couple of days."

A couple of days since she found out her son had cancer, and she hadn't found time to call. The woman should be shot. "How about if I come to see you tomorrow? Between the wheelchair and the hospital bed, we'll look like a scene from *Cuckoo's Nest*."

"That'd be great. And you won't believe who's here."

Nora laughed. "Believe me, you won't believe who is *here,* either."

"Dean—"

"Ruby—"

They spoke at the same time.

Nora was the first to recover. "Dean is on the island?"

"He came up to see me."

"I knew he'd come if you called. How is it between you two?"

"Awkward. A little unsure. We're like best friends from high school who meet at the twenty-year reunion and don't quite know what to say. But we'll find our way back. And Ruby?"

"Angry. Truthfully, she hates me."

"But she's there. That means something. Remember, there's a thin line between love and hate."

"Thank you, Yoda." She paused. "I had to tell her about your cancer."

"That's okay. Hell, I don't care who knows anymore." She could hear the smile in Eric's voice. "Hey, do you know what happened between Dean and Ruby? He won't talk about it."

"She won't, either."

"I was at Princeton when they broke up, but it must have been bad. Dean went all the way to boarding school to get away from her. But it's interesting that neither of them ever married."

"Are you thinking what I'm thinking?"

"How do we get them together?"

Nora grinned. It felt great to talk about something besides Eric's illness or her own scandal. And this made her feel like a *mother* for the first time in years. "Carefully, my boy. Very carefully."

By the time Nora hung up, her ankle was throbbing; the pain was only marginally worse than the itching that came with it. She wheeled into the bathroom, washed her face and brushed her teeth, then left the room.

"Ruby?" she called out. There was no answer.

She was halfway into the kitchen when she saw the package on the table.

Slowly, she wheeled closer.

It had been opened.

No wonder Ruby was hiding.

With a sigh, she pulled the slim box onto her lap and went into the living room, where she settled herself onto the sofa, plopping her foot on a pillow on the coffee table. All thoughts of Ruby and Dean and true love vanished.

Her fingers were shaking as she opened the manila envelope marked NEW LETTERS and pulled out the stack of mail. On the top was a small, wrinkled, stationery-size envelope postmarked GREAT FALLS, MONTANA. She carefully opened it, unfolded the letter, and began to read.

> *Nora:*
>
> *I can't bring myself to write "Dear" anymore. I've written to you a dozen times over the last few years. Twice you have published my letters, and once you wrote me a private letter, saying that you hoped things were getting better.*
>
> *You can't imagine what that meant to me. I was drowning in a bad marriage, and you were always there.*
>
> *Can you imagine how it feels to know the kind of person I've been taking advice from?*
>
> *I looked up to you. Believed in you. My husband only broke my heart. You have broken my spirit.*
>
> *If only you had been honest, I might have continued to admire you.*
>
> *Now, I see that you're just another hack celebrity selling a product you don't use.*
>
> *Don't bother answering this letter, or even printing it in Nora Knows Best. I don't care about your opinion, and I certainly won't be reading your columns anymore. I don't suppose I'm alone in that decision. If I want to read fiction, I'll go to the library. You have no right to offer anyone advice on anything anymore.*
>
> *May God forgive you, Nora Bridge. Your fans will not.*

Nora folded the letter and slid it back into the envelope. She needed something to get her mind off of this. She reached for the television remote, not surprised at all to see that Caroline had upgraded the television here at the summer house. With small kids in this media age, it was probably essential.

She pressed the "on" button—and heard her own name being spoken.

It was *The Sarah Purcell Show*—one of those talkfests where women came together to chat. The coffee klatch of the new millennium.

Nora wanted to change the channel or look away, but she was like a fish caught on the hook of her own name.

On-screen, a heavyset woman was standing in the audience. Sarah was beside her, holding a microphone to the woman's mouth. "I *trusted* Nora Bridge," the lady said. "Now, I feel like an idiot."

Another woman in a nearby row stood up. "How could you be stupid enough to trust a celebrity? They all lie and cheat to get ahead. That's how public life is."

The heavyset woman flushed. She looked ready to cry. "I didn't think she was like those other ones . . ."

Sarah took the microphone back. "That brings up a good point, Dr. Harrison," she said, speaking to the gentleman sitting on the stage. "People are angry at Nora Bridge because she lied to them, but is it really a lie? Do you have to tell people *everything* about your life, just because you're in the public eye?"

The doctor smiled coolly for the camera. "Certainly a public figure has a right to his or her secrets . . . unless and until those secrets become germane. In this case, Nora had no right to hold herself out as an expert on love and family and commitments. But of course, it's ludicrous for people to trust her anyway . . . an uneducated woman whose only claim to fame is a daily newspaper column. Trust should be reserved for professionals who are trained to help people."

Sarah stopped. "Now, wait a minute, Doctor. I don't think education—"

"Nora Bridge pretended to have answers, but no one bothered to wonder where those answers came from. Hopefully, Americans have learned that it takes more than an open microphone to solve people's problems. It takes education, and empathy, and integrity—areas in which Ms. Bridge is sorely lacking."

"And she's a coward," someone said from the crowd. "I mean . . . where is she? She owes us—"

Nora snapped off the television.

She couldn't seem to move, not even to wheel herself out of the room. A tremor was spreading through her, chilling her from the inside out, and her throat was so tight it was hard to breathe.

"Nora?"

She froze, her heart pounding. She hadn't even heard footsteps on the stairs.

God, she didn't want her daughter to see her like this . . .

Ruby came into the room, walked slowly around the wheelchair, then sat down on the leather chair across from Nora. "Did you sleep well?"

Nora stared down at her own hands, and thought, Oh, please, just go away . . . don't talk to me now. . . . "Yes," she managed, "thank you."

"I read your columns," Ruby said when the silence had gone on too long.

"Really?" It was a tiny word, barely spoken.

"You're good at it."

Nora's relief was so profound, she gasped. Only *I love you* could have meant more to her in that moment. And yet even as the relief buoyed her, it dragged her down again, too, reminded her of all that she'd lost this week.

"Thank you," she said softly. Finally, she looked up, and found Ruby watching her through narrowed eyes.

"I take it you read a few of your new letters," Ruby said, leaning forward, resting her elbows on her knees. She seemed to see it all—the shaking hands, the television remote that had been thrown onto the floor.

Nora wanted to say something casual and flip, to show how meaningless a few ugly letters were, but she couldn't. "They hate me now."

"They're strangers. They don't even know you. They can't love you or hate you, not really." Ruby flashed a smile. "Leave the big, ugly emotions to your family."

Who also hated her.

That only made it worse. "What family?" Nora moaned quietly. "Really, Ruby . . . what family have I left myself?"

Ruby looked at her for a long minute, then said, "After I read your columns, you know what I remembered?"

Nora wiped her eyes. "What?"

"When I was twelve years old—seventh grade—and my class elected me to run the first tolo. Remember? It was a big deal on Lopez, a dance where the girls asked the boys. Mr. Lundberg, down at the hardware store, said it meant that the world was going to hell in a leaky rowboat."

Nora sniffled again. "Yeah . . . I remember that."

"I wanted the local newspaper to cover the event. You were the only one who didn't laugh at me." Ruby smiled. "I watched you charm that fat old editor from the *Island Times*. I remember being surprised by how easily you got him to agree to what you wanted . . . what I wanted."

Nora remembered that day for the first time in years. "The minute I walked into that cheesy, airless office, I loved it. The smell of the paper, the clacking of typewriters. I envied the reporters, with their ink-stained fingertips, and for the first time in my life, I felt as if I *belonged* somewhere. I'd always known I had words banging around in my chest, but I'd never known what to do with them." She looked up.

Ruby's gaze was solemn. "I realized . . . later . . . that I'd shown you the way out of our lives."

Nora took a deep breath. "I didn't leave my family for a career, Ruby. That had nothing to do with my decision. Less than nothing."

"Yeah, right."

"Ah, Ruby," she said, "you want answers, but you don't even know what the questions are. You have to look at the beginning of a thing, not the end. For me, leaving your dad started before I met him."

"I don't understand."

Nora wanted to ask her daughter if all this talking would actually lead them anywhere, or if it was just a way to pass the hours before they each moved on. A part of her—the cowardly part—wanted to change the subject, maybe talk about Dean or Eric, but she wouldn't let herself take the easy way. She and Ruby were finally approaching something that mattered.

She stared out the window. Night was falling, drizzling dark syrup down the evergreen trees. "My dad was an alcoholic. When he was sober, he was almost human, but when he was drunk—which was most of the time—he was pit-bull mean. It was a secret I learned to keep from everyone. It's what children of alcoholics do. They keep secrets. Hell, it took me fifteen years of therapy to even say the word *alcoholic.*"

Ruby's mouth fell open a little. "Huh? You never told us that."

"On a farm like ours, the neighbors couldn't hear a woman's scream. Or a young girl's. And you learn fast that it doesn't help to cry out . . . to reach out. Instead, you try to get smaller and smaller, hoping that if you can become tiny enough, and still enough, he'll pass you by."

"He abused you?"

Such a thin word, *abuse.* "He didn't do the worst thing a father can do to his daughter, but he . . . molded me. I grew up trying to be invisible, flinching all the time. I don't think I stood up straight until I left your father." She leaned forward, making direct eye contact with her daughter. "For years, I thought that if I didn't talk about my dad, he'd float out of my life . . . out of my nightmares. I thought I could forget him."

Ruby drew in a sharp breath. "Did it work?"

Nora knew her daughter was making the connection: *I'd forgotten you.* "No. All it did was give him more power . . . and turn me into a woman who couldn't imagine being loved."

"Because your own father didn't love you."

"Not unlike how a girl would feel if her own mother abandoned her." Nora wouldn't let herself look away. "Did you ever fall in love . . . after Dean?"

"I lived with a guy—Max Bloom—for almost five years."

"Did you love him?"

"I . . . wanted to."

"Did he love you?"

Ruby got to her feet and went to the bookcase, where she started thumbing through their old record collection. "I think he did. In the beginning."

"How did it end between you?"

Ruby shrugged. "I came home from work one day and he'd moved out. He took everything from the kitchen except our coffeemaker. In the bathroom, he left a razor full of his hair and an almost empty bottle of Prell, but no towels."

Nora longed to empathize with her daughter, tell her how much she understood that kind of pain, but that was the easy way—understanding. What mattered now, in this moment when they were actually *talking,* was not Nora's understanding. It was Ruby herself. Like Nora, Ruby liked to run away from her problems, and sometimes she ran so far and so fast that she never bothered to really look at why she'd left. "Did you ever tell him you loved him?"

"Almost. Practically."

"Ah."

Ruby frowned at her. "What does that mean—'ah'?"

"Did he say he loved you?"

"Yeah, but Max was like that. He told the checker at Safeway he loved her."

Nora could see that she'd have to be more direct. "Let me ask you this, Ruby. How long do you think it takes to fall in love?"

Ruby sighed raggedly. "So your point is this: I never really loved Max, so why did I cry when he left me?"

"No. You lived and slept with a man for almost five years and never told him you loved him, even after he'd said those precious words to you. The question isn't why he left. It's why he stayed so long."

Ruby's mouth dropped open. "Oh, my *God*. I never thought about it like that." She looked helplessly at Nora.

"I told your father I loved him the first time we made love. I'd never said the words before, not to anyone. It wasn't the sort of thing my family did. I'd been hoarding *I love you*'s all my life. And do you know when Rand told me he loved me?"

"When?"

"Never. I waited for it like a child waits for Christmas morning. Every time I said it, I waited, and every second of his silence was a little death."

Ruby closed her eyes and shook her head. "No more. Please . . ."

"I wanted to raise you to be strong and sure of yourself, and instead I turned you into me. I made you afraid to love and certain you'd be left behind. I was a bad mother and you paid the price. I'm so, so sorry for that."

"You weren't a bad mother," Ruby said quietly, "until you left."

Nora was pathetically grateful for that. "Thank you."

She knew she was following a dangerous path, sitting here, falling in love with her daughter all over again . . . but she couldn't help herself. "I still remember the little girl who cried every time a baby bird fell out of its nest."

"That girl has been gone a long time."

"You'll find her again," Nora said softly, "probably about the same time you fall in love. And when it's real, Ruby, you'll know it . . . and you'll stop being afraid."

———

After dinner, Ruby stayed in the bathtub until the water turned cold.

The world—her world—had changed, but she couldn't put her finger on precisely how. It was like walking into a perfectly decorated room and knowing instinctively that somewhere a picture was crooked.

She climbed out of the clawfoot tub and stood on the fuzzy pink bath mat, dripping. By the time she dried off and slipped into a pair of sweats and an oversized UCLA Bruins sweatshirt, she could smell dinner cooking.

She finger-combed her hair and lay down on the bed with her yellow pad open in front of her.

Today I talked to my mother. This is a remarkably ordinary sentence for a truly revolutionary act.

I talked to her. She talked to me. By the end of it, we had both wept, although not, I'm sure, for the same reasons.

What I don't know is where we go from here. How can I walk downstairs and pretend that nothing has changed? And yet, it was simply a conversation, words passed back and forth between women who are strangers to each other even though they share a past. I want to believe I'm wrong in feeling that things are different now.

Why then did I cry? Why did I look at her and feel like a child again and think—even for a moment—"What if?"

Chapter Thirteen

Dean carried the breakfast tray up to his brother's bedroom. It wasn't much—a glass of juice, a soft-boiled egg, and a piece of wheat toast. He knew Eric wouldn't eat more than a few small bites, but it made life seem normal, this offering of food.

When Dean stepped into the room, he found his brother already awake, sitting up in bed.

"Heya, Dino," Eric said.

Dean set the tray down, helped his brother sit up higher in the bed, then carefully placed the tray across Eric's lap.

"I'll bet this smells great," Eric said as Dean went to the window and flipped the curtains open.

Dean opened the casement window just enough to let in the sound of the sea. When he turned back around, he noticed how wan and wasted his brother looked this morning. The shadows beneath his eyes were as dark as bruises. He seemed to have grown sicker since yesterday. "Bad night?"

Eric nodded. His head lolled back into the pillows, as if the pretense of eating breakfast had exhausted him. "I can't seem to sleep anymore, which is pretty damned ironic since it's all I do. The pain cocktail knocks me out but it's not the same as a good night's sleep." He smiled tiredly. "It's funny the things you miss. I don't dream anymore."

Dean pulled his chair up to the bed and sat down.

"I wanted to talk to you last night, but I couldn't seem to stay focused."

Dean reached out and held his brother's cold, thin hand.

Eric turned to him, smiling. "I always thought we'd come back to this house as old men. I pictured us sitting on the porch. We'd have white hair by then . . . or maybe only I would have hair, and you'd be bald as Grandpa. We'd play Chinese checkers and watch your kids run up and down the dock, looking for shrimp."

Dean let himself be carried away by the dream. "They'd have nets . . . just like we used to."

Eric's eyes fluttered shut. "I wonder whatever happened to those nets we bought every year? You and Ruby used to play down on that dock for hours . . ."

Dean swallowed hard. He thought about changing the subject, but suddenly he wanted to remember her, to reminisce with someone who'd known her. "Sometimes when I close my eyes at night, I hear her laughing, yelling at me to hurry up. She was always running off ahead."

"I thought I'd be the best man at your wedding. It's crazy, isn't it, you and Ruby were sixteen years old, but I thought it was true love."

"I thought so, too."

Eric looked at him. "And now?"

Dean wanted to smile, pretend it was just a silly question between grown men about something that had happened long ago and didn't matter. But what was the point? He knew now how precious this time with Eric was. It was obvious that it was running out, leaking away like the color in his brother's cheeks. "Now I know it was."

"She's on Summer Island."

Dean frowned; it took a moment for the full impact of those words to hit him. "Ruby's at the summer house?"

Eric grinned. "Yep."

Dean leaned back. "What . . . with her husband and kids?"

"She's never been married, baby brother. I wonder why that is?"

Dean stood up and strode toward the window. He stared through the glass, trying to see Summer Island through the trees. His heart was beating so fast he felt faint. *Ruby is here.*

"Go see her," Eric said softly.

Dean changed into a pair of Levi's and a T-shirt. At the front door, he slipped on his boat shoes and grabbed his ten-speed from its resting place beneath the eaves. There was no doubt that in this week of June, with the sun shining brightly on the islands, the ferry lines would be endless. Bikes always got on first.

He pedaled down the short, winding hill to the dock and got lucky. A boat was loading. He got right on.

He didn't go up top. Instead, he stood with his bike at the bow of the boat, barely noticing the cars streaming into lines behind him.

On Summer Island, he didn't even wave to Sister Helen as he bicycled past. By the time he swooped onto the Bridges' heavily shaded driveway, he was sweating and out of breath. At the top of the yard, he jumped off the bike and let it clatter to the ground.

Then he stopped. For the first time, he wondered what in the hell he was doing, running toward his first love as if eleven years hadn't passed, as if he'd seen her yesterday . . .

But they'd been apart for all of their adulthood; he had no way of knowing whether she'd thought of him at all.

Their last day together came at him in a rush of images and phrases.

The sky had been robin's-egg blue. Strangely, he remembered looking up, seeing the white trail from a passing jet. He'd been about to point it out to Ruby, to start their familiar "if I were on that plane, where would I be going?" daydream.

But when he'd turned to her, he'd seen what he should have noticed before.

She'd been crying.

That was not so unusual, of course; those were the days when Ruby had cried all the time.

The difference was, this time, she wouldn't let him get near her. He couldn't remember precisely what he'd said, how he'd tried uselessly to comfort her. What he did recall was how she finally stilled, and the sight of Ruby, his Ruby, looking pale and cold had scared him.

I had sex with a boy last night. She'd said it without preamble, as if she'd wanted to wound him with her confession.

He had pulled the whole, sordid story out of her, one painful syllable at a time, and when she was finished, he knew all the facts, but they hadn't added up to a whole truth he could understand.

If he'd been older, more sexually experienced, he would have known the question to ask, the only one that mattered: Why? But he'd been seventeen and a virgin himself. All he'd cared about was the promise he and Ruby had made . . . to wait for each other until marriage.

Anger and hurt had overwhelmed him. She'd lied to him, and she hadn't loved him as much as he'd loved her. He'd felt foolish and used. He'd waited desperately for her to throw herself at his feet, to beg for forgiveness, but she'd just stood there, close enough to touch and yet so far away he couldn't see her clearly. Or maybe it was his tears that were blurring the world, turning her into a girl he'd never seen before.

Go ahead, she'd said, staring dully up at him. *Go. It's over.*

He'd had to leave fast—before she could see that he was crying. He'd turned away from her and run back to his bike. He'd pedaled hard, trying to outdistance the pain, but it had raged inside of him, thumping with every beat of his heart. Everywhere he'd looked, he'd seen her . . . in the shade of Miss McGinty's oak tree, where he'd read Shakespeare's sonnets to Ruby the previous week . . . in the tree-lined darkness of the state park's driveway, where they'd once set up their lemonade stand. And finally, on his parents' land, where he'd kissed her for the first time.

At home, he'd picked up the phone and called his mother. Within hours, he'd been on a seaplane, heading for Seattle. By the next day, he'd been on his way to boarding school back east.

Whatever should have been said or done between them had been lost.

Dean released his breath in a steady, even stream. There was no turning back now.

He walked down the path and stepped up onto the porch. After another quick breath, he knocked.

And she answered.

The minute he saw her, he understood what had been missing from his life. It was hokey, he knew, and sentimental and sappy, but that didn't make it any less true. What he'd been longing for, without even realizing it, had been that elusive, magical mixture of friendship and passion that he'd only ever found with her.

"Ruby," he whispered. It actually hurt to say her name. She was so beautiful that for a second he couldn't breathe.

"Dean," she said, her eyes widening.

He didn't know what to say. He felt like a seventeen-year-old kid again, tongue-tied in front of the prom queen. He was trying like hell to appear casual, but it was difficult. He was sweating suddenly and his throat was painfully dry. All he could think was, *Ruby's home,* and she was standing in front of him and he didn't want to say the wrong thing, but he couldn't imagine what the right thing was. He'd dreamed of seeing her for so long, but now . . . the moment felt spun from sugar, so fragile a soft breeze could shatter it. "I . . . uh . . . I came home to see Eric . . . you probably heard about that."

"How is he?" Her voice was barely audible.

"Not good."

She closed her eyes for a second, then looked up at him again.

"I'm here with my mother. She had a car accident and I'm taking care of her."

"*You?*" It had slipped out, an intimate observation from a man who'd once known the girl. He was instantly afraid he'd offended her.

A smile hitched one side of her mouth. "I know. I should call Ripley's Believe It or Not."

"So, you've forgiven her, then."

Sadness darkened her eyes. "Forgiveness doesn't matter, does it, Dean? When a thing is done, it's done. You can't unring a bell." She smiled, but it wasn't the smile he remembered, the one that crinkled her whole face and sparkled in her eyes. She seemed to be waiting for him to say something, but he couldn't think fast enough, and as usual, she didn't wait long. "Well, it was good seeing you again. Nora is in my old room. Say hello before you leave. She'd hate to miss you."

And with that, she walked past him and headed down to the beach.

Ruby thought she was going to be sick. That was why she'd left Dean so quickly. She couldn't stand there, making polite conversation, not when it felt as if carbonated water had replaced her blood.

She ran down the path toward the beach and sat down on her favorite moss-covered rock, just as she'd done a thousand times in her life.

"Ruby?"

She heard her name, spoken softly in the voice that had filled her dreams since adolescence, and she froze. Her heart picked up a wild, thumping beat. She hadn't heard his footsteps, hadn't prepared to see him again so quickly.

"Can I sit with you?"

She tried not to remember all the hours they'd spent here, huddled out on this rock, staring first out to sea, then gradually at each other. She sidled to the right—it had always been her side.

Dean sat down beside her.

She felt his thigh along hers, and she ached to scoot closer . . . to lay her hand on his the way she'd done so many times before. But she'd lost that right. In her angry, confused youth, she'd thrown it away.

She had always known that she still carried a torch for Dean, but obviously she hadn't understood what that meant. It was more than fond memories or adolescent longings. A torch was hot; it would sear your flesh if you weren't careful.

"This brings back memories," he said softly.

She didn't mean to turn to him, but she couldn't help herself. She wanted to say something witty, but when she gazed into his blue eyes, she was sixteen again. Except he had become a man. Lines bracketed his mouth and crow's-feet fanned out from the corners of his eyes. If it were possible, he was even more handsome now.

She felt a rush of shame. If only she'd worn better clothes today than torn black shorts and a ragged T-shirt, or cut her hair recently. He was probably disgusted that she'd let herself get so . . . ugly.

She reached deep inside for a casual voice. "It's good to see you again," she said, staring back out at the sea. "I hear from Caro that you're a corporate bigwig now."

"It doesn't mean much."

"Spoken like a rich man." She tried to smile. "So, how's life treated you?" God, she wished he'd take the reins of this awkward conversation and ride away . . .

"I saw your act once. At the Comedy Store."

She turned to him, and immediately regretted it. She was close enough to see the green flecks in his blue eyes. She remembered suddenly how his eyes used to seem to change color, to take on the hue of the sea or the sky. "Really?"

"I thought you were funny as hell."

Her smile softened into the real thing. "Really?"

"I was going to talk to you after the show, but there were so many people around you. A man . . ."

"Max." She felt the sting of that missed opportunity, and wondered how often that happened in life. Chances lost and won on a turn of fate so small they couldn't be seen by the naked eye. "We broke up a while ago. And what about you? Are you married?" The moment she asked the question, she flinched, feeling completely exposed. If she could have sucked it back into her mouth, she would have.

"No. Never."

She felt a sudden euphoria, then it fell away, left her even more confused. He could ruin her with a word, this boy she'd loved who'd become a man she didn't know. She'd loved him so much, and yet she'd broken his heart. She still barely knew why. "That summer . . . I found out from Lottie that you'd moved away," she said, her voice unsteady.

"I couldn't face you," he answered, looking at her. "You didn't just hurt me, Ruby. You ruined me."

"I know." She almost reached for him then, placed her hand on his thigh as if she had every right to touch him. And the stinging realization that she *couldn't* touch him, that she didn't even know him, brought her up short.

She lurched to her feet, terrified that if he looked at her again, she would burst into tears. "I have to get back to Nora."

Slowly, he got to his feet and reached for her.

She stumbled back so fast she almost fell over the bank. His hand dropped back to his side, and she had a sudden, overwhelming fear that he wouldn't try to touch her again.

She could see the disappointment in his eyes. "Time is precious," he said. "If I didn't know that before this week, I know it now. So I'm just going to say it: I missed you."

She couldn't imagine what to say next, how to answer. She had missed him, too—missed him so much—and it hurt to know that she would go on missing him until she was an old woman. A more bendable, trusting person could have changed the future in this very moment, but Ruby couldn't imagine that kind of strength.

He waited, and the silence stretched out between them. Then, slowly, he turned and walked away.

Chapter Fourteen

Nora sat on the porch. She could see Dean and Ruby sitting out on that old rock of theirs.

Ruby was the first to stand. Slowly, Dean followed. They stood frozen, close enough to kiss.

Then Dean turned and headed back up toward the house, leaving Ruby behind. He strode up the path, saw Nora on the porch, and came toward her. At the railing he stopped, hung his arms over the wisteria-covered edge, and smiled tiredly. "Hey, Miz Bridge."

She smiled. "Call me Nora. It's good to see you again, Dean. I'm glad you finally made it back to the island."

"It's good to see you, too." He looked at her, and in his eyes, she saw pain. "Thank you, Nora," he said softly. "You're everything to him."

She nodded, knowing she didn't need to say anything. Everything that mattered had passed between them in silence.

Dean turned back, stared down at the beach. Nora knew that they both wanted to talk about Ruby, but neither of them knew what to say. Finally, he pulled away from the porch. "Will you guys come over on Saturday? I've got the *Wind Lass* working. I'm going to take Eric sailing."

"That would be great."

Dean shot a last, lingering look at Ruby, then walked away.

Nora waited, knowing that Ruby wouldn't stay down there for long. Sure enough, a few minutes later, she headed up the path. When she saw Nora on the porch, she paused.

Nora noticed that her daughter's eyes were red. A thin tracing of tears streaked her cheeks.

Nora's heart went out to her. "Come," she said, "sit with me."

Ruby looked torn. She probably couldn't decide which was worse—being alone right now or being with Nora. Finally, she walked up onto the porch, hitched her butt up onto the railing.

Nora longed to touch her daughter, to simply lay a hand on Ruby's head the way she used to. But such intimacy was impossible between them now. The only way she could touch her daughter was with words, with memories. "You know what I was remembering just now? The winter I was pregnant with you. A freak weather pattern moved through the islands."

Ruby looked up. "Yeah?"

"The snow came earlier that year than anyone could remember. Just after Thanksgiving. At first people tried to drive, but by evening, there were more cars in the ditches than on the roads, and we all gave up. By nightfall, the clouds were gone, and we'd never seen such a starry sky." She smiled at the memory. "Your dad and I were on the porch when we heard the laughter. We put on every piece of winter clothing we owned and followed the sound, walking through snow that came up to our knees. I remember having the strangest feeling that I could *see* our words; they seemed to be written in the steam of our breath. The snow didn't crunch beneath our boots. It sort of . . . sighed. We followed the laughter all the way to the McGintys' place. That ugly old swamp on their property—remember it?—well, it had frozen solid. Every kid on the island was there, skating or sliding or inner-tubing. I never knew how it was that everyone knew to be there at just that moment. . . . At midnight, stars started falling. Hundreds of them. The next day on the news, they had all kinds of scientific explanations for it, but we believed it was magic."

Nora closed her eyes, and for a moment, she could almost smell the newly fallen snow, almost feel that stinging cold on her cheeks. "After that, for almost a month, things on the island went a little crazy. Roses bloomed on prickly bushes that had been brown and dead for weeks. Rain fell from cloudless skies. But what I remember most of all were the sunsets. From then until the new year came and chased the magic away, the night sky was always red. We called it the ruby season."

Ruby said softly, "Is that where my name came from?"

"Your dad and I used to sit out here, wrapped in blankets, and watch that ruby sky. We never talked about naming you after it, but when you came, we knew. You'd be our Ruby. Our own bit of magic."

Ruby smiled. "Thanks."

Nora looked at her and paused. "Dean invited us to go sailing on Saturday."

"What will I say to Eric?"

"Oh, Ruby," she said gently, "you start with hello."

Ruby barely slept that night. At first, she tried to tell herself it was the heat. Even with the windows open, summer had always been sweltering on the second floor.

I missed you.

If there was one thing Ruby knew, it was that she hurt people, and she didn't want to hurt Dean again. He deserved a woman who could return his love as fully and freely as he gave it. That was the one thing she'd known even as a teenager.

Finally, at about three-thirty, she went out onto the balcony and sat in the chair her grandfather had made. In the dark before the rising sun, she tried to pull peace from the familiar sounds and smells. The whoosh of the waves . . . the hoot of a barn owl, not too far away . . . the scent of her grandmother's roses, climbing up trellises on the side of the house.

Write. That'll get your mind off everything.

She reached for the pad beside her. Then she stopped. Frowning, she drew her hand back.

For the first time, she considered the impact of her article. She'd agreed to write it because she'd *wanted* to hurt her mother, to strike back for all the pain she'd suffered as a young girl.

But she wasn't a child anymore.

Before, she hadn't wanted to know why Nora left them. Or maybe she'd been so damned certain that she'd seen everything that mattered.

But marriages broke up for *reasons;* women like her mother didn't just up and leave their husbands on a sunny summer's day.

Ruby had glimpsed moments in the past days, images that didn't fit with the picture she'd drawn of her mother. And there was the "best of" file she'd read. The first "Nora Knows Best" column appeared months after her mother had left . . . and in a cheesy local newspaper that couldn't have paid her more than gas money.

It didn't fit, and that bothered Ruby.

She closed her eyes . . . and remembered a cold, crisp October day that smelled of ripening apples and dying black leaves. Dad had been in the living room, sitting in that leather chair of his, drinking and smoking cigarettes he'd rolled himself. The whole house had smelled of smoke. Caroline had been gone on a field trip to the Museum of Flight in Seattle and they'd missed the ferry back. Ruby had been in the bedroom, reading *Misery* by Stephen King. "Groovy Kind of Love" was on the turntable . . .

There was a knock at the door. Ruby sat up in bed, waiting to hear her dad's footsteps, and when he went past her open door, she recognized the stumbling drunkenness of his gait. Please, she thought, don't let it be one of my friends . . .

She heard him say, "Nora," in a voice that was too loud, belligerent.

Ruby froze; then she heard the scratching whine of the record player's needle being scraped across vinyl. Everything went quiet. Chair springs creaked.

Ruby slipped out of bed and crept to the door of her room, pushing it farther open.

Dad was in his chair, Mom was kneeling in front of him.

"Rand," Mom said quietly, "we need to talk."

He stared down at her, his hair was too long, and dirty. "It's too late for talking."

Mom reached for him; he lurched to his feet, swaying unsteadily above her.

Ruby couldn't stand it another minute, seeing her father's pain in such sharp relief. "Get out," she yelled, surprised at the strength in her voice.

Mom got to her feet, turned around. "Oh, Ruby," she said, holding her arms out.

As Mom came toward her, Ruby saw the changes in her mother, the gray pallor in her cheeks . . . the weight she'd lost . . . the way her hands, always so strong and sure, were blue-veined and trembling as she reached out.

Ruby sprang backward. "G-go away. We don't want you anymore."

Mom stopped; her hands fell uselessly to her sides. "Don't say that, honey." She gazed at Ruby. "There are things you don't understand. You're so young . . ."

Ruby ignored her mother's tears. It was easy; she'd cried so many of them herself they'd lost their currency. "I understand how it feels to be left behind, as if you were . . . nothing." Her traitorous voice broke, and the sudden rawness of her pain made it difficult to breathe. Ruby fisted her hands and drew in a deep, shuddering breath. "Go away, Mother. No one here loves you anymore."

Mom glanced back at Dad, who'd slumped into his chair again. He was holding his head in his hands.

Ruby wanted to put her arms around him and tell him she loved him, just as she'd done so often in the past few months, but she didn't have the heart for it now. It was all she could do to keep from wailing. She stepped back into her bedroom and slammed the door shut.

She didn't know how long she stood there, perfectly still, her hands balled into cold fists, but after a while, she heard footsteps crossing the kitchen, then the quiet opening and closing of the front door. Outside, a car engine started; tires crunched through gravel. And quiet fell once again, broken only by the sound of a grown man crying . . .

Ruby lurched to her feet, and found herself unsteady. She couldn't have *forgotten* that day . . . she must have blocked it out, buried it beneath the cold, hard stones of denial.

The world, once so firm, felt as if it had given way beneath her.

Things you don't understand.

Even then, her mother had had a story to tell . . . but no one had wanted to hear it.

Now Ruby was ready. She wanted to learn what had happened more than a decade earlier, under her own roof, within her own family.

And if her mother wouldn't answer those questions, there was always an alternative.

She would ask her father.

PART TWO

"We shall not cease from exploration
And the end of all our exploring
Will be to arrive where we started
And know the place for the first time."

T. S. ELIOT, FROM "LITTLE GIDDING"

Chapter Fifteen

It had been easy to get out of the house. Ruby had simply left a note—*Gone to Dad's*—on the kitchen table.

Now she was in the minivan, driving up the tree-lined road that led away from the Lopez Island ferry dock.

She was a fourth-generation islander, and at this moment, seeing all the new houses and bed-and-breakfasts that had sprouted on Lopez, the full impact of that heritage hit her. She had *roots* here, a past that grew deep into the rich black island soil. Lopez had grown up, and she didn't like the changes. She couldn't help wondering if there were still places where grass grew up to a young girl's knees and apple trees blossomed by the side of the road, where wild brown rabbits came out beneath a full moon and munched their way through summer gardens.

Her great-great-grandfather had come to this remote part of the world from a dreary, industrialized section of England. He'd brought his beautiful, black-eyed Irish wife and seventeen dollars, and together they'd homesteaded two hundred acres on Lopez. His brother had come along a few years later and staked his own claim on Summer Island. Both had become successful apple and sheep farmers.

Now, more than one hundred years later, there were only ten acres on Lopez that belonged to her father. The house on Summer Island had been willed to Ruby and Caroline; their grandparents had feared that their son would lose this land, one acre at a time. And they'd been right.

Randall Bridge now lived on what had once been the farm's

highest point, a rounded thumbprint of land that stuck out high above the bay.

He was an island man, through and through. He'd grown up on this tiny, floating world and he'd raised his children here. He had a closet full of plaid flannel shirts for winter and locally made tourist T-shirts for summer.

He lived on a financial shoestring, from one fishing season to the next. Money had always been tight and "next summer" was always going to change things. He made it through the lean months doing local boat repairs. Most years, it was the repairs—not the fishing— that kept food on the table and paid the steadily rising property taxes.

Ruby came to the crest of the hill and had to slam on the brakes to avoid hitting a trio of deer. A doe and her two spotted fawns stood in the middle of the road, their ears pricked forward. Suddenly they leapt over the ditch and disappeared into the tall, golden grass.

She eased forward again, going more slowly now. She'd forgotten how it was to share the road with animals. In Los Angeles, there had been a different kind of wildlife on the freeways.

She turned off the main road. A gravel road wound through acres of apple trees, their limbs propped up by slanted, graying slats of wood.

At last, she was home. The yellow clapboard house, built in the late twenties, sat wedged between two huge willow trees. The original house—a squat, broken-down log cabin with a moss-furred roof—could still be seen amid the tumbling blackberry brambles at the edge of the property.

She parked alongside her dad's battered Ford truck, got out of the car, and stood there, looking around. It was exactly as she remembered. She walked down the gravel path, past the now empty rabbit hutches she'd built with her dad, toward the back porch. The yard was still a riot of runaway weeds and untended flowers. Shasta daisies grew in huge, hip-high mounds, drawing every bee on the place. A tattered screen door hung slanted, a set of screws missing.

She paused on the porch, steeling herself for the sight of her dad's new family, walking as they did across the floorboards of his old one.

She knew she'd be entering another woman's house . . . a woman she barely knew, who was less than ten years older than Ruby herself . . . seeing a baby brother for the first time. A baby who had no idea that his father had started over in his life, had left his other children stranded in the gray hinterlands of a broken family.

Taking a deep breath, she knocked on the door and waited. When there was no answer, she eased the screen door open and stepped into the kitchen.

The changes were everywhere.

Frilly pink gingham curtains. Lacy white tablecloths. Walls papered in a creamy white pattern with cabbage roses twining on prickly vines.

If she'd needed evidence that Dad had gone on with his life (and she hadn't), it was right here. Their old life had been painted over.

"Dad?" she said, not surprised to find that her voice was weak. She stepped past the table—the chairs had been painted a vibrant green—and poked her head into the living room.

He was there, kneeling in front of the small black woodstove, loading logs into the fire. When he looked up and saw her, his eyes widened in surprise, then a great smile swept across his lined face. "I don't believe it. . . . You're here." He clanged the stove's door shut and got to his feet.

Moving toward her, he started to hold his arms out, then he paused, uncertain. At the last minute, he pulled her into an awkward hug. "Caroline told me you were home. I wondered if you'd come to see me."

She clung to him, fighting a sudden urge to cry. He smelled of wood smoke and varnish and salt air.

"Of course I'd come," she said shakily, drawing back. Although both of them knew it was a half-truth, a wished-for belief. She hadn't even called him, and the realization of her own selfishness tasted black and bitter.

He touched her cheek. His rough, callused skin reminded her of hours spent sanding boat decks at the marina, a girl and her dad, huddled together in the dying red sunlight, saying nothing that mattered. "I missed you," he said.

"I missed you, too." It was true. She had missed him, every day and all the time. Now, standing here, seeing in his eyes how much he loved her, she wished she'd been more forgiving when he remarried, more accepting of his new life.

It was the sort of thought that winged through Ruby's mind all the time, regrets, hoped-for improvements; in the end, she never changed. She said whatever popped into her head and hurt whoever hurt her first. She couldn't seem to help it.

She collected grudges and heartaches the way she'd once collected Barbies, never sharing, never abandoning. Her dad, in the end, had hurt Ruby deeply; it was the sort of thing she had no idea how to overcome. It was always between them, a sliver embedded just below the skin.

She glanced uneasily up the stairs, wondering where Marilyn was. "I don't want to intrude—"

"Mari took Ethan off island for a doctor's appointment." He grinned. "And don't even *pretend* you aren't happy about that."

She smiled sheepishly. "Well . . . I wanted to see the kid. My brother," she added, when she saw the way he was looking at her. She winced, wishing she'd said it right the first time.

"Don't worry about it." But he turned away quickly and headed back into the living room. She knew she'd hurt his feelings. He sat down on the threadbare floral sofa, cocked one leg over his knee. "How's it going between you and your mom?"

She flopped down onto the big overstuffed chair near the fire. "Picture Laverne and Shirley on crack."

"I don't see any visible bruising. I have to admit, I was shocked when Caro told me you'd volunteered to take care of Nora. Shocked and proud."

Ruby ached suddenly for what had been lost between them, and the hell of it was, they hadn't fought or argued. When he'd found Marilyn, he'd simply drifted away from his daughters. He'd stopped calling as much.

. "I meant to come visit you this week," he said, giving her that *you-know-how-it-is* smile of his. The one that always reminded you that he had other things—other people—on his mind.

She refused to be stung by his laid-back attitude. "So, how is the fishing this season?"

Something passed through his eyes, so quickly it would have been easy to overlook. But Ruby saw it. "Dad? What is it? What's wrong?"

"Last summer was terrible. I might . . . have to sell off another chunk of land."

"Oh, Dad . . ." Ruby remembered the last time they'd had this talk. It had been the year after her mother left, when her father hadn't fished all season. Then there had been forty acres left. They'd sold the last waterfront piece. She'd wanted desperately to help, but all she'd had was her berry-picking money. "How much do you need?"

"Three thousand. Don't worry about it. Let's talk about—"

"I could lend you the money."

"You?"

She reached for her purse and pulled out her checkbook. Over her father's protests, she wrote out a check and set it on the table. "There," she said, grinning. "It's done."

"I can't take that, Ruby."

But they both knew he *would* take it. "It means a lot to me to be able to help you."

Slowly, he said, "Okay." Then softly, "Thank you."

An unfamiliar silence settled between them, broken only by the popping of the fire. She wondered if he was thinking about his father; Grandpa Bridge had been deeply disappointed in his only son's lack of ambition. He wouldn't have been proud of Rand at a moment like this.

Suddenly Dad stood up. "Come on, let's take a walk."

She followed him into the bright sunshine. As they'd done a thousand times, they strolled down the gravel path to the marina, where a few fishing boats bobbed along the docks, their green nets wound on huge drums.

Dad headed to his slip—8A—where the *Captain Hook* bobbed lazily against the dock. He climbed aboard, then turned around and helped Ruby on.

He tossed her a tangle of new white line. "Splice that, would you? Ned and I are heading out tomorrow. I told him I'd have everything ready."

Ruby sat cross-legged on the boat's aft deck and brought the slithering heap of rope onto her lap. She had a moment's hesitation, when her mind couldn't access the memory, but then her fingers started moving.

She worked the rope, twined the triple strands into a new, stronger whole and began building the eye. "Nora isn't quite what I expected," she said, trying to sound casual.

"That's hardly surprising."

Ruby experienced a momentary lapse in courage. *Shut up,* she thought, *don't ask.* She drew in a deep breath and looked at her father. "What happened between you two?"

He looked up sharply, eyeing her, then he got to his feet and walked past her to the stern. Every footfall upset the balance and made a soft, creaking sound. All at once, he turned back to face her, but she had the weird sensation that he wasn't really seeing her. He seemed . . . frozen, or trapped maybe, and she wondered what images were running through his mind. "Dad?"

Now she felt as if he were seeing too much of her. Beyond the skin and the hair, to the very bones. Maybe even deeper. "Are you in for the long haul this time, Ruby?"

"What do you mean?"

"Ah, Rube . . ." He sighed. "You have a way of moving on. I've never seen anyone who could shut herself off so easily from the people around her."

"It isn't easy."

He smiled grimly. "You made it look easy. You went off to California and started a new life without any of us . . . but after a while, it was *our* fault, Caroline's and mine. We didn't call enough . . . or not on the right days . . . or we didn't say the right things when we did call. And you moved farther and farther away. You didn't come to my wedding or even call when your brother was born or come to see Caroline when she suffered through that terrible labor. But somehow that was our fault, too. We abandoned *you*. Now, you want to stir up an old pot. Will you be here tomorrow or next month or next Christmas to see what comes of it?"

Ruby wanted to say he was *wrong*. But she couldn't. "I don't know, Dad." It was all she could manage now; a quiet, simple honesty.

He stared down at her for a long minute, then dropped the rope. "Follow me," he said at the same time he jumped off the boat and headed up the rickety dock.

He was walking so fast that Ruby had to run to catch up. They hurried down the docks and up the hill. He pushed through the screen door so fast it almost banged Ruby in the face. He didn't seem to notice.

Ruby stumbled over the threshold. "Jesus, Dad—"

When she looked up, she lost the sentence.

Her father was standing at the kitchen table with a bottle of tequila. He thumped it down hard, then yanked out a chair and sat down.

It was a move that brought back *way* too many memories. She was surprised by the depth of her reaction. The sight of him holding a bottle of booze shook her to the core. She grabbed the ladderback of the chair. "I thought you'd quit drinking."

"I did."

"You're scaring me."

"Honey, I haven't begun to scare you. Sit down, snap on your seat belt, and lock your seat in the upright position."

Ruby pulled the chair out and perched nervously on its edge. Her foot started tapping so hard it sounded like gunfire.

Her dad looked . . . different. She couldn't have put her finger on exactly how, but the man sitting across from her, with the graying hair and well-worn sweater with its threadbare elbows, wasn't the man she'd expected.

This man, hunched over, staring at a full bottle of Cuervo Gold, looked as if he hadn't smiled in years. He looked up suddenly. "I love you. I want you to remember that."

She heard the tender underbelly of his voice, saw the emotion in his eyes, and it reminded her of exactly how far apart they'd drifted. "I could never forget that."

"I don't know. You're good at forgetting the people who love you. The story starts in nineteen sixty-seven, just a few years before the whole damn world exploded. I was at the University of Washington; I'd just finished my senior year, and I was certain I'd get drafted into the NFL. So certain I never bothered to get a degree. I barely studied. Hell, they paid someone to take tests for me. Things were crazy back then. The world was off its axis. Everyone I knew had been bent or mangled by it.

"And then I met Nora. She was scrawny and scared and looked like she hadn't slept in a week. Still, she was the most beautiful girl I'd ever seen. She believed absolutely that I'd play pro football . . ." Dad slumped forward a little, thumped his elbows on the table. "But it didn't happen. No one called. I walked around in a daze; I couldn't believe it. I had no backup plan, no second choice. Then my draft number came up. I probably could have gotten out of it—said they needed me to run the farm—but I hated this island and I couldn't imagine how I'd survive here." He sighed and leaned back. "But I wanted someone to wait for me, to write me letters. So I went back to Nora, my pretty little waitress at Beth's Diner in Greenlake, and I asked her to marry me."

Ruby frowned. She'd heard this story a thousand times in her childhood and this was definitely not the way it went. "You didn't love her?"

"Not when I married her. No, that's not true. I'd just loved other women more. Anyway, we got married, spent a wonderful honeymoon at Lake Quinalt Lodge, and I shipped out. Your mom moved into this house with my folks. By the end of the first week, they were both in love with her. She was the daughter my parents never had, and she loved this land in a way I never could.

"Her letters kept me alive over there. It's funny. I fell in love with your mother when she wasn't even on the same continent. I meant to *stay* in love with her, but I didn't come home the same cocky, confident kid who'd left. Vietnam . . . war . . . it did something to us." He smiled sadly. "Or maybe not. Maybe the bad seeds were always in me, and war gave them a dark place in which to grow. Anyway, I turned . . . cynical and hard. Your mom tried so hard to put me back together, and for a few years, we were happy. Caroline was born, then you . . ."

Ruby had this bizarre sensation that her whole existence had turned into sand and was streaming through her fingers.

"When I came home, your mom and I moved into the house on Summer. I went to work at the feed store on Orcas. Everyone thought I was a failure. 'So much promise wasted,' they whispered to my dad over drinks at Herb's Tavern. God, I hated my life." He looked up suddenly. "I didn't mean for it to happen."

Ruby swallowed convulsively, as if something bitter was backing up in her throat. "Don't say—"

"I slept with other women."

"No."

"Your mom didn't know at first. I was careful—at least as careful as a drowning man can be. I was drinking a lot by then—God knows *that* didn't help—and I knew when she started to suspect. But she always gave me the benefit of the doubt."

"Oh, God," Ruby whispered.

"Finally, that summer, someone told her the truth. She confronted me. Unfortunately, I was drunk at the time. I said . . . things . . . it was ugly. The next day, she left."

Ruby felt as if she were drowning, or falling, and she was desperate for something to cling to. "Oh, my *God,*" she said again. It was too much; she felt as if she might explode from trying to hold it all inside her.

He leaned toward her, reached for her across the table.

She got up so fast her chair skidded out from underneath her.

He pulled back and slowly got to his feet. "We've all been carrying this baggage for too long. Some of us have tried to go on." He looked at her. "And some of us have refused to. But all of us are hurting. I'm your father; she's your mother—whatever she's done or hasn't done, or said or hasn't said—she's a part of you and you're a part of her. Don't you see that you can't be whole without her?"

Ruby's past seemed to be crumbling around her. There was nothing solid to hold on to, no single thing to point to and say *There, that's my truth.* "I'm leaving."

He smiled sadly. "Of course you are."

"Call Nora. Tell her I'm going to Caroline's. I'll be home . . . whenever."

"I love you, Ruby," he said. "Please don't forget that."

She knew he was waiting for her to say the words back to him, but she couldn't do it.

Chapter Sixteen

Ruby had never been to her sister's house, but the address was imprinted on her brain. Caroline was the only person on earth who regularly received a Christmas card from Ruby. It was simply required. Ruby had long ago discovered that it wasn't worth the eleven months of sarcastic jabs. Better to mail off a damn card.

The traffic was stop-and-go as she exited Interstate 5 and crept toward the sprawling suburb of Redmond.

Not so many years earlier, this had been the sticks; hundreds of acres of unspoiled farmland nestled between two rivers. Now it was MicrosoftLand, the *über* suburbia of the geek set. The developments had tried to keep the rural flavor—lots were big; subdivisions had names like Evergreen Valley and Rainshadow Vista, and trees were preserved at all cost. Unfortunately, the houses all looked disturbingly similar. Stepford in a coat of Ralph Lauren paint.

Ruby checked the handy rental car map and turned down Emerald Lane. One big, brick-faced house followed another, each built to the edge of its lot. New landscaping gave the neighborhood an unsettled look.

At last she found it: 12712 Emerald Lane.

She drove up the stamped blue concrete driveway and parked next to a silver Mercedes station wagon, then grabbed her purse from the passenger seat and headed up the path to a pair of oak doors trimmed in beaded brass.

She knocked. From inside came a rustle of movement, then a muffled "Just a minute."

Suddenly the door sprang open and Caroline stood there, looking flawless at one o'clock in the afternoon in a pair of ice-blue linen pants and a matching boat-neck cashmere sweater.

"Ruby!" Caroline pulled Ruby into her arms, holding her tightly.

Ruby closed her eyes; for the first time in hours, she was able to draw a decent breath.

Finally, Caro drew back. "I'm so glad you came."

"I didn't have a chance to go shopping. I meant to get the kids something—"

"Forget about that." Caroline yanked Ruby into the house.

Of course, it was perfect. Uncluttered and flawlessly decorated. Not a thing was out of place.

It didn't look as if a child had ever *been* in here let alone lived here.

They passed through a pristine kitchen, all gleaming metallic surfaces and black granite countertops. Here was the first hint of the family. Pictures covered the Sub-Zero refrigerator. Above the double sinks, a bay window held on to a view of rolling, green lawn. A golf course.

Caro led her through the formal dining room, where Grandma's silver tea service glittered on a massive oak sideboard, and into the living room. Walls painted in a lovely faux marble finish dropped down to a wide-planked oak floor. Two wing chairs, upholstered in an elegant brandy-colored silk weave, flanked a gold-and-bronze tapestried sofa. A pair of crystal lamps sat on gilded rosewood end tables, pouring golden light onto the plush antique Chinese rug.

"Where are the kids?"

Caroline brought a finger to her lips and said harshly, "*Sshh*. We don't want to wake them up."

"Could I tiptoe upstairs and just—"

"Trust me on this. You can see them when they wake up."

Ruby got a glimpse of something—someone—behind Caro's perfect, smiling face, but it was there and gone so fast, it left no imprint behind.

She felt a little prickle of unease. Nothing was ever wrong with Caroline. She was the most balanced, well-adjusted person Ruby had ever known. Even during that horrible summer, Caro had moved along on an even keel, accepting what Ruby never would, smiling, forgetting, going on . . .

And yet now, impossibly, Caroline looked unhappy. "Something's going on with you," Ruby said, "what is it?"

Caro sat like a parakeet on the edge of the chair. Her perfectly manicured hands were clasped so tightly together the skin had gone pale. A Julia Roberts smile flashed across her serene face. "It's nothing, really. Just a bad week. The kids have been acting up. It's nothing."

Ruby couldn't put her finger on it, exactly, but *something* was wrong here. Suddenly she knew. "You're having an affair!"

This time there was no mistaking the genuineness of Caro's smile. It showed how false the others had been. "Since Fred was born, I'd rather hit myself in the head with a jackhammer than have sex."

"Maybe that's your problem. I try to have sex at least twice a week—sometimes even with someone else."

Caro laughed. "Oh, Ruby . . . God, I missed you . . ." She sounded normal now.

"I missed you, too."

"So," Caro said, leaning back now. "What brought you racing to my door?"

"What makes you think I raced?"

Caro gave her "the look." "Nice outfit. I haven't seen so much black since Jenny went to the Halloween party as a licorice whip."

"Good point." They both knew that Ruby usually dressed defensively for Caro. It was easier that way.

"So what is it? You left Mom strapped to the wheelchair and ran screaming out of the house." Caro grinned at her own black humor. "Or maybe you left her at a rest area a few miles back and now she's thumbing it."

Ruby couldn't even smile. "I went to Dad's house this morning."

"Yeah, so?"

She had no idea how to put a pretty spin on such ugliness, so she just said it. "When Nora left . . . Dad was having an affair."

Caroline sat back. "Oh, *that*."

"You *knew*?"

"Everyone on the island knew."

"Not me."

Caroline's smile was soft and tender. "You didn't want to know."

Ruby had trouble finding her voice. "She's not who I thought she was, Caro. We're trapped in that house together, and whether I like it or not, I'm getting to know her. We . . . talk."

"*You're* getting to know her?" Something passed through Caroline's eyes at that. If Ruby hadn't known better, she would have called it envy. Suddenly Caro walked out of the room. A few minutes later, she returned with two glasses of wine and a pack of cigarettes.

Ruby laughed. "*Smoking*—you're kidding, right? A cig in your hand would be like—"

"No jokes, Ruby. Please."

Ruby saw how fragile her sister looked. "Point the way to cancer. That doesn't count—it wasn't funny."

Caro opened the French doors and led Ruby to a seat at an umbrellaed table. The golf course stretched alongside the flowered yard, dipped to a valley, and rose on the other side to a row of houses remarkably similar to this one.

Caroline pulled a cigarette from the pack and lit up.

Ruby followed suit. She hadn't smoked in years, and she had to admit, the novelty of it was fun.

Her sister took a drag, exhaled, and stared out across the green. A stream of smoke clouded her face. "I've been talking to Mom for years, meeting her now and then for lunch, calling her on Sunday mornings, being the daughter she expects, and we're polite strangers. And *you*—" She shot Ruby a narrowed gaze. "You, who treats her like Typhoid Mary, she talks to."

An awkward silence fell between them, and Ruby couldn't think of how to step over it. "We're stuck together."

Caroline took a drag and exhaled slowly, staring out at the green lawn. "That's not it. What's she like?"

"The worst part is, she's smarter than I am. She keeps making me remember who she used to be. Who *we* used to be. And you know, it hurts. When I was on the ferry this morning, before Dad dropped his A-bomb, I was thinking about our visits to the county fair. How we used to walk through the midway with her, eating cotton candy, tossing pennies at ugly china dishes, and I . . . missed her."

"I know how that feels."

Ruby noticed that her sister's hands were trembling. "Have you forgiven her?" she asked. "I mean, *really*?"

Caro looked up. "I tried to forget it, you know? Most of the time, I do, too. It's like it happened to another family, not mine."

"So, you haven't forgiven her any more than I have. You're just nicer about it."

Caroline tried to smile, though there was a bleakness in her eyes that was unsettling. "Your honesty is a gift, Rube, even if it hurts people. You're . . . real. I can't seem to—"

A scream blared through the open window behind them.

Ruby jumped. "Good God. Has someone been shot?"

Caroline deflated. Her shoulders caved downward, and the color seemed to seep out of her cheeks. "The princess is up."

Ruby moved closer to her sister. "Are you okay, Caro?"

The smile was too fleeting to be real. "I'll be fine," she said, and Ruby saw that her sister was pretending again. She got up from her seat and walked woodenly back into the house.

Ruby followed her.

"AAAGH . . ." This time there were two screams.

A jack-in-the-box came crashing and jangling down the stairs and skidded across the kitchen floor.

"Go," Caro said with a tired smile. "Save yourself."

A naked Barbie doll cartwheeled down the stairs and thumped into the table leg.

The screams were getting louder. Ruby fought the urge to cover her ears. "Let's go upstairs. I want to at least *see* my niece and nephew."

"Not when Jenny's in this kind of a mood. Trust me."

Another toy came crashing down the stairs, followed by a shrieking cry. "MO-MMY NOW!"

Caroline turned to her. "Please? Another time?"

"Well . . . next week I'm going to come down here and baby-sit. You and Jere can go out dancing or something."

"Dancing." Caroline smiled wistfully. "That would be nice."

Ruby remembered suddenly that she wouldn't be here next week. She'd be back in California on *The Sarah Purcell Show,* telling the world about her mother. Suddenly she felt sick.

"You'd better get going. The ferry lines are hell this time of day."

Ruby checked her watch. "Shit. You're right."

Caroline looped an arm around Ruby, drew her close, and guided her toward the door. There she paused. "I'm sorry you had to find out about Dad, but maybe it'll help. We're human, Ruby. All of us. Just human."

Ruby hugged her sister, holding her so tightly that neither of them could breathe. "I love you, Caro."

"I love you, too, Rubik's Cube. Now, get going."

Ruby drew back. She had the strange thought that if she said anything except good-bye, Caro would simply shatter.

So good-bye was all she said.

Nora sat at the kitchen table, staring down at the package of letters. Earlier, she'd spoken to Eric, but afterward, the silence had tackled her again.

Idly, she rubbed her throbbing wrist. She'd spent an hour in the morning practicing with her crutches, and she was improving. She could go short distances. By the end of the week, she hoped to be out of the damned chair completely.

But the practice hadn't fulfilled all of its purpose. She couldn't clear her mind completely. The letters were always there.

She'd tried giving herself a little pep talk. They were just words, she told herself, scribblings on paper, and they were from *strangers.* Certainly she could find the strength to pick up a pen and fashion some kind of response. A good-bye and a thanks-for-the-good-times, at the very least.

Not true. Every letter she'd attempted began the same: *Dear readers.*

Sometimes she came up with a sad, pathetic beginning—*I'm more sorry than you can know. . . .* or *How can I begin to say what's in my heart. . . .* or *By now you all know who I really am.*

But there was never a second sentence. And if all that wasn't bad enough, she was worried about Ruby.

Her gaze landed on the note she'd found sitting on the kitchen table. *Dear Nora—Gone to see Dad.*

It looked innocuous enough, but appearances were often deceiving. Ruby wasn't coming back.

It was Nora's own fault. She'd pushed her daughter too hard in the past few days, and that was dangerous. Ruby *always* shoved back; she had from infancy. Unlike Caroline, who smiled coolly and held your hand and stepped aside when reality got too close.

Nora had recognized her mistake the second she saw the good-bye note. Her daughter had had enough.

She slumped forward, dropping her head onto her crossed arms. A good cry would probably help, but she couldn't find even that easy road to relief. She was wrung dry.

Then she heard a car drive up . . . footsteps on the porch . . .

The door opened, and Rand stepped into the kitchen.

Nora understood instantly: Ruby had sent her father to deliver the bad news.

"Hey, Randall," she said, pulling her casted leg off the second chair. "Have a seat."

He glanced around. "I've got a better idea."

Before he'd even finished the sentence, he'd crossed the room and scooped her into his arms. She made a garbled, whooping sound of surprise and put her arms around his neck, hanging on. "What the—"

"Just hang on."

She clung to him as he carried her over the threshold and out onto the porch. There, he pulled an old mohair blanket off of the rocker and wedged it under his arm. He walked down the steps, across the shaggy lawn, out to the edge of the bank.

Beneath a huge madrona tree, he laid the blanket over the rocky ground, then gingerly set her down. Her bare toes stuck out from the end of her cast, and he leaned over and tucked the fringed end of the blanket around her foot.

He sat down beside her, propped up on his elbows, and stretched out his long legs.

"Still can't stand to be inside on a sunny day?" she said.

"Some things never change." He turned to her, his face solemn. "I'm sorry, Nora."

"About what?"

His gaze shifted to a point just beyond her left shoulder. "I should have said it a long time ago."

She drew in a breath. Time seemed to hang suspended between them. She felt the hot summer sunlight on her face, smelled the familiar fragrance of the sea at low tide.

He looked at her finally, and in his eyes, she saw the sad reflection of their life together. "I'm sorry," he said again, knowing that this time she understood.

"Oh" was all she could say.

He leaned closer, touched her face with a gentleness that sapped her strength. "It was *my* fault. All mine. We both know that. I was young and stupid and cocky. I didn't know how special we were."

Nora was surprised by how easy it was suddenly for her to smile. She'd spent twenty years loving this man, eleven more vaguely missing him, and yet now, with him beside her on an old blanket that held their youth in its rough weave, she finally felt at peace. Maybe that was all she'd needed, all these years. Just those few, simple words.

She laid her hand against his, and a peacefulness settled around her, as if everything in their lives had led to this moment. He was her youth, she realized sadly, a youth that was neither well spent nor quite misspent. Just . . . spent. In his eyes, and his alone, was the woman she'd once been. "We were both at fault, Rand. We tried. We just didn't make it."

He leaned closer. She thought for a breathless moment that he was going to kiss her. He wanted to—she could see the desire in his eyes. But at the last second, he drew back, gave her a smile so soft and tender it was better than a kiss. "When I look back—and believe me, I try not to—you know what I remember?"

"What?"

"That day you came back. Jesus . . ." He closed his eyes. "I should have dropped to my knees and begged you to stay. In my heart, I knew it was what I wanted, but I'd heard about you and that guy, and all I could think of was *me*. How would it look if I took you back after that?" He laughed, a bitter, harsh sound. "*Me*, worrying about that, after the way I'd treated you. It makes me sick. And I paid for it, Nora. For eight long years, I went to sleep every night alone. And I missed you."

Nora wanted to weep at what they'd thrown away. "You should have called. I was alone, too." She paused, then said, "It's too bad."

"Yeah."

She reached out, brushed the hair from his eyes in a gesture as natural to her as breathing. "But you've gone on now. Married. I'm happy for that." She realized how true it was. Those few small words—*I'm sorry*—had released her, turned Rand into what he truly was: her first love. Her great love, perhaps, but there would be another one for her someday. She smiled and arched one eyebrow. "And are you being a good boy, Randall?"

He laughed, easy with her now. "Even a stupid dog doesn't get hit by the same bus twice."

"Good. You deserve to be happy."

"So do you."

She flinched, unable to help it. "You screwed around on your wife. I abandoned my children. It's not the same thing."

He gazed at her. She saw the heavy lines around his mouth and eyes, grooves worn by years in the sun and wind. "I told Ruby the truth."

"About what?"

"*The* truth. About us."

Nora felt sick. "That was a foolish thing to do."

"I thought you'd be pleased. It's something I should have done a long time ago."

"Perhaps, but when you didn't—when I didn't—we buried that little piece of family history. You shouldn't have dug it up. It won't make a difference now."

"You deserved it, Nora," he said. "After all these years, you deserved it."

"Oh, Rand. She believed in you. This will break her heart."

"You know what I learned from us, Nora?" He touched her face, smiled tenuously. "Love doesn't die. Not real love. And that's what Ruby's going to discover. She's always loved you. I just gave her a reason to admit it."

Nora couldn't help thinking that, for a grown man, he was incredibly naive.

Chapter Seventeen

After two hours of waiting in the line for the ferry with two hundred eager tourists and a few beleaguered locals, Ruby remembered why she'd been so eager to move off island. Timing your life around a state-operated transportation system was miserable.

The last thing she needed was time to think. The conversation with Caroline repeated relentlessly through her mind. Even when she turned on the minivan's cheesy radio, she heard the singers' voices moaning the words *Everyone knew.*

"Except me," she said bitterly.

She still couldn't get over that.

Finally, the ferry pulled in—late, as usual—and she drove aboard, following the orange-vested woman's directions to a spot at the very back of the lane. As the ferry pulled out, she adjusted her seat to a more comfortable position and closed her eyes. Maybe sleep would help.

Everyone knew.

She opened her eyes and stared up at the van's puffy, velourlike ceiling. She still felt shaky, as if the foundation of her life had turned to warm Jell-O and was slowly letting her sink.

I slept with other women.

It changed everything.

Didn't it?

That was the sheer hell of it. Ruby couldn't hold the ramifications of the day in her hands and study them.

One thing she knew: her novelization of the past, with Dad cast as hero and her mother as villain, wouldn't work anymore.

The world wasn't as she'd thought it was. Perhaps she was late in making that elemental and yet monumental discovery. She felt as if she'd been a child all these years, walking through a land that she alone had devised.

And now something was changing inside of her, growing. It was nothing as cliché or readily definable as her heart. Rather, it was the bones themselves; they were shifting, pressing against her sinew and muscles, and deep down inside, there was a new ache.

She reached under the seat and pulled out the pen and legal pad she'd packed in the morning. After only a moment's hesitation, she started to write.

I was sixteen years old when my mother left us. It was an ordinary June day; the sun rode high in a robin's-egg-blue sky. It's funny the things you remember. The Sound was as flat and calm as a brand-new cookie sheet, and a gaggle of baby geese were learning to swim on the McGuffins' pond.

We were an average family. My father, Rand, was an islander through and through, a commercial fisherman who repaired boats in the off season. He went bowling with his friends every Saturday night and helped us girls with our math and science homework. He wore plaid flannel shirts in the winter and Lacoste golf shirts in the summer. It never occurred to any of us, or to me anyway, that he was anything less than the perfect father.

There was no yelling in our family, no raging arguments, no nights where my sister and I lay in our side-by-side twin beds and worried fever-ishly that our parents would divorce.

After we'd all gone our separate ways, I often looked back on those quiet years. I was obsessive in my search for an inciting incident, a moment where I could say, Aha! There it is, the beginning of the end.

But I never found one. Until now.

Today, my parents pulled back the curtain, and the Great Oz—my dad—was revealed to be an ordinary man.

I didn't know that then, of course. All I knew was that on a beautiful day, my mother dragged a suitcase into the living room.

"I'm leaving. Is anyone coming with me?"

That's what she said to my sister and me. I heard my father in the kitchen. He dropped a glass into the sink, and the shatter sounded like bones breaking.

That was the day I learned the concept of before and after. Her leaving sliced through our family with the bloody precision of a surgeon's scalpel.

At the time, we assumed it was temporary. A vacation getaway that should have been with "the girls," only my mother had no girlfriends. Maybe all kids think things like that.

It's hard to say when my feelings about my mother changed from guilt to anger to disgust to hatred, but that was the arc of it.

I saw what her absence did to my father. In the span of a few short days, he became hardly recognizable. He drank, he smoked, he spent the day in his pajamas. He ate only when Caroline or I cooked for him. He let the marina business go to hell and by the next spring, he had to sell land to pay the taxes and keep food on the table.

I formed an image of my mother that summer. From the hard stone of everything that happened, I carved the image of a woman and called it mother. For all these years, I've kept it on my bedside table; it was no less real for being visible only in my own mind. The statue was a collection of hard edges—selfishness, lies, and abandonment.

But now I know the truth: My father was unfaithful to my mother.

Unfaithful. A cold, detached word that gives no hint of the heat involved in passion. He wore a wedding ring and fucked women other than the one he'd sworn to love, honor, and protect.

That says it better for me. The vulgarity of the sentence matches the obscenity of the act.

I know it changes everything, but I can't seem to follow where it leads. My childhood, I thought naively, was mine alone, those memories painted in vibrant oil strokes on the canvas of my years. Now, it seems that Barbra Streisand was right. Memories are watercolor, and a heavy rain can wash them away.

My father is not the man I thought he was.

Even as I look down on this sentence I have just written, I see the childishness of it, but I can't think of another way to say it. I don't know how to look at him now, this father who has proven to be a stranger.

My mother didn't leave him—and us—for fame and fortune, but simply because she was human, and the man she loved had broken her heart.

I know how it feels when someone you love stops loving you back. It's a kind of mini-death that breaks something inside of you.

This knowing, this understanding . . . it should make me want to forgive my mother, shouldn't it?

I think I'm afraid to love her, even the tiniest bit. The hurt she caused me is so deep that my bones have grown around it. I wonder perhaps who I am without it—

Before she could finish her sentence, the ferry honked its horn. They were docking on Lopez. Ruby looked up. She knew that as soon as it had unloaded a few cars, it would turn to Orcas Island. Summer was the last stop before the boat turned back to the mainland.

Ruby made a snap decision. She didn't want to see her mother yet. They would have to talk about this new information, and Ruby wasn't ready.

She started the car and pulled out of line, speeding down the empty lane. Ferry workers shouted at her, waving their hands. No doubt they thought she was a tourist, getting off on the wrong island. She didn't care. She sped forward, bumped over the ramp, and drove off.

The Sloan house was only a few blocks from the ferry terminal. It was a big, gingerbread-cute Victorian mansion placed on a breathtaking promontory overlooking the bay.

She pulled the minivan into the driveway and parked. It was twilight now; a purple haze fell across the garden, still impeccably tended. A newly painted white picket fence kept everything neatly contained. Just the way Mrs. Sloan liked it, although she probably hadn't set foot on this island in years.

Ruby walked up the crushed seashell pathway that led to the front door. There she paused, gathered her courage, and knocked.

Lottie opened the door. She looked just as Ruby remembered her—puffy cheeks, eyes that disappeared when she smiled. "Ruby Elizabeth!" she said, clapping her plump hands together. "Lordy, it's good to see you."

Ruby grinned. "Hello, Lottie. It's been a long time."

"Not so long that you can't give me a hug, you upstart." She reached out and grabbed Ruby, pulling her against her ample breast. Ruby noticed that Lottie still smelled of the lemon hard candies she kept tucked in her apron pockets.

Ruby drew back, trying to maintain her smile when she said, "I came to see Eric."

"He's upstairs. Dean had to fly to Seattle—something about business."

Ruby was relieved. Now that she was here, she wasn't ready to talk to Dean, either. She glanced past Lottie, into the living room. "Can I go up?"

"Why, I'd beat you with a stick if you didn't. I'll make you some tea if—"

"No, thanks. I'm fine."

"Ah. Run along with you, then." As Ruby passed her, Lottie reached out, touched her shoulder. "Don't be afraid, Ruby. He's still our boy."

Ruby took a deep breath and released it, then slowly mounted the stairs. At the upper landing, she turned toward Eric's old room. The door was closed. She gave it the tiniest push to open it. "Eric?"

"Ruby? Is that you?"

She heard how weak his voice was, how different from the melodious baritone of old, and she swallowed hard. "It's me, buddy." She pushed past the door and walked into his room.

Only sheer willpower kept her from gasping. He looked thin and tired. His beautiful black hair was practically gone, there was only the barest film of it left. Bruise-dark shadows circled his eyes; his cheekbones stood out in pathetic relief above the pale, sunken flesh.

He gave her a smile that broke her heart. "I must be dead if Ruby Bridge is back on the island."

"I'm home," she said, looking away quickly so he couldn't see her shock. She strode over to the window and opened the curtains—anything to get her composure back.

"It's okay, Ruby," he said softly, "I know how I look."

She turned back around. "I missed you, Eric," she said, meaning it, hating herself once again for how easily she'd been able to leave this place, these people.

"It feels like old times with you here," he said, pushing a button and maneuvering his bed to a more upright position.

She smiled. "Yeah. All we need is—"

He reached into the bedside drawer and held out a fat joint. He gave her that same tilted, crooked-toothed grin she remembered so well. "Cancer makes pot easy to come by." He brought the joint to his lips and lit it.

Ruby laughed. "So, you've been getting all our old friends high, huh?"

He took a toke and handed it to her. When he finally exhaled, he said, "There are no old friends around here. Not for me, anyway."

Ruby took a hit. The smoke scalded her throat and made her cough. She handed the joint back to him. "I haven't smoked pot in years."

"That's good news. So, how's the comedy biz?"

She took a smaller drag this time, breathed in, held the smoke in her lungs, then released it. After that, they passed it back and forth. "I'm not funny enough to make it big."

"You're a riot. You always cracked me up."

"Thanks, but that's like being the prettiest girl in Paducah. It doesn't make you Miss America. The funniest girl on Lopez Island isn't going to knock 'em dead on *Leno*. Sad truth."

"Are you giving up on it?"

"I guess so. I think I'll try my hand at writing." She giggled. "Get it—try my *hand* at writing."

Eric laughed with her. "It's not like you can try your foot," he said between bursts of laughter. They both knew it wasn't funny, but just now, with the sweet smell of pot clouded between them, it seemed hilarious. "What kind of book will you write?"

"Well, it won't be on the joys of sex."

"And it won't be on fashion."

Ruby shot him a look. "Very funny. I have my mother to rag about my appearance, if you don't mind. Hey! That's what I'll write about. Dear Old Mom."

Eric laughed more quietly this time. Snuffing the joint out, he leaned back on his elbows. "Somebody *should* do a book on her. She's a saint."

"I must be so high I've lost my hearing. I thought you said she was a saint."

He turned to her. "She is."

His face seemed to loom in front of her, two sizes too big. His pale blue eyes were watery, rimmed in nearly invisible strands of red. His full, almost feminine lips were colorless. And suddenly she couldn't pretend, couldn't make small talk. "How are you, Eric . . . really?"

"It's what the docs call end stage." He smiled weakly. "Funny, they come up with a euphemism for every step of the illness, but then, when you really need a little lip gloss to cover everything, they call it end stage. As if you need another reminder that you're dying."

Ruby brushed the fine, limp strands of hair from his face. "I should have stayed in better touch with you. What happened between Dean and me, I shouldn't have let that extend to you, too."

"You broke his heart," Eric said softly.

"All of our hearts got broken that year, I guess, and the king's horsemen couldn't put us back together."

He touched her cheek. "What your mother did . . . it was really fucked. But you're not sixteen anymore. You ought to be able to see things more clearly."

"Like what?"

"Come on, Ruby. The whole island knew your dad was screwing other women. Don't you think that makes just a little bit of difference?"

So it was true: Everyone did know. "Caroline and I didn't do anything and she left us, too."

There it was, the thing she still couldn't get past.

"I've gotten to know your mom pretty well in the past few years, and let me tell you, she's great. I'd give *anything* to have a mom like her."

"Jet-set Lady had troubles with your lifestyle, I take it?"

"No. No trouble. When I told my mother I was gay, she said she never wanted to see me again."

"How long did that last?"

"She's not like your mom. When my mom said 'Get out of my house,' she meant it. I haven't seen her since."

"Even now?"

"Even now."

"God . . . I'm sorry," she said, knowing how utterly inadequate the words were.

"You know who got me through those tough times . . . when I first realized I was gay and my parents disowned me?"

"Dean?"

"Your mother. She had just moved her 'Nora Knows Best' column to the *Seattle Times*. I wrote to her, anonymously at first. She wrote back, praising my bravery, telling me to keep my chin up, that my mom was sure to come around. It gave me hope. But after a few more years, I knew she was wrong. My mom had drawn her line in the sand. She wouldn't have a faggot son. Period." He grabbed his wallet from the top of the bedside table. Opening it, he withdrew an often-folded piece of paper and carefully unfolded it. "Here. Read this."

Ruby took the piece of paper from him. It was yellowed from age and veined with tiny fold lines. A brown stain blotched the upper-right corner. She focused on the small, neat lettering. It took her a moment to recognize the handwriting. Her mother's.

Dear Eric,

I can't express the depth of my sympathy for your pain. That you would choose to share it with me is an honor I do not take lightly.

For me, you will always be Eric, the rope swing king. When I close my eyes, I see you hanging monkeylike from that old rope at Anderson Lake, yelling Bonsai! as you let go. I see a boy who came by our house when I was sick, who sat on the porch crushing mint in a bowl to spice up my tea. I remember a sixth-grade boy, his face reddened by new pimples, his voice sliding down the scale, who was never afraid to hold Mrs. Bridge's hand as they walked down the school corridor.

This is who you are, Eric. Whom you choose to love is a part of you, but not the biggest part. You are still that boy who couldn't bear to eat anything that had once had parents. I hope and pray that someday your mother will wake up and remember the very special boy she gave birth to. I hope she will look up then, and smile at the man he has become.

But if she does not, please, please don't let it tear your heart apart. Some people simply can't find it in themselves to bend, to accept. If this terrible thing happens, Eric, you must go on. There's no other word for it. Life is full of people who are different, broken, hurting, who simply put one foot in front of the other and keep moving.

It is your mother I fear for. You will grow up and fall in love, and find yourself. When I come to visit you, and we are both old, we will sit on your porch and laugh about the golden days that almost killed us. But not so your mother. If she continues on this path, it will eat her up from the inside. She will find that certain pains are endless.

So, forgive her. It is the only way to lighten this ache in your heart. Forgive her and love her and go on.

I love you, Eric Sloan. You and your brother are the sons I never had, and had I given birth to you, I would have been proud of who you've become.

XXOO

Nora

Ruby folded the letter back into a small triangle that fit in his wallet. "That's a beautiful letter. I can see why you carry it around."

"It saved me. Literally. It took some work—lots of work—but I forgave my mom, and when I did that, my chest stopped hurting all the time."

"I don't know how you could forgive her. What she did—"

"Was human, that's all."

"What about now?"

He sighed, pushed a hand through his hair. "It's harder now. I realize how precious time is. I want just one moment with her to tell her I love her. To hear—" His voice broke, dropped to a whisper. "To hear her say she loves me."

Ruby turned to him, touched his face.

He smiled, pressed his hand on top of hers. "Forgive your mother, Ruby."

"I'm afraid," she said, using the words she rarely allowed herself to speak aloud.

He let go of her arm. "*Christ.* Time is short, don't you understand that? We bump along, blindly assuming we have forever to do things, say things . . . but we don't. You can feel perfectly fine, and go to your annual checkup on a sunny Wednesday afternoon, and discover that your time's up. Game over."

She looked down at him. "How do you forgive someone?"

He smiled tenderly. "You just . . . let go. Unclench."

"If I let go . . . I'm afraid I'll fall."

"There's nothing wrong with falling." He kissed the tips of his own fingers, then pressed the kiss to her cheek. "I love you, Ruby. Don't forget that."

"Never," she whispered. "Never."

When Ruby finally got home, it was past midnight. She crept past her mother's closed bedroom door and went upstairs. Crawling into bed, she reached for her pad of paper and began to write.

One of my best friends from childhood is dying. I stood at his bedside today and talked to him as if life were normal, and yet all the while, I couldn't breathe.

Until a few hours ago, I had not seen him in more than a decade, and in all that time, I had barely thought of him.

Barely remembered him.

This boy, now a man, who had walked hand in hand with me through childhood, I had forgotten. I kept the Saint Christopher's medal he gave me for my thirteenth birthday, but the boy, I lost.

Maybe he never noticed or cared. We did, after all, go on with our separate lives as childhood friends tend to do, but now I see the sadness in that ordinary course of things. I walked away too easily; I didn't think enough about what—and who—I left behind. Now, I can't think about anything else.

I left a boy with black hair and a booming, heartfelt laugh, and I returned to a man so thin I was afraid to touch him for fear that I would see my own bones through his papery flesh.

And this dying man welcomed me home as if I'd never left. Did he know, I wonder, how much it hurt me to look in his watery eyes and see the reflection of my own emptiness? My own lack.

I want to gather the broken pieces of my heart together, pull them into my lap, and study them. Maybe then I could find the hole, the missing piece, that allows me to forget those I love.

I am tired of my solitary life, weary to the bone. I have been running for years, so fast and hard, I am breathless. And here, at the end of it, I see that I've gone nowhere at all.

I want my mother. Isn't that amazing? I would—if I could—go to her now, walk into the circle of her arms and say, "Eric is dying and I can't imagine living in a world without him."

How would that feel? I wonder. Letting her comfort and soothe me? When I close my eyes, I can imagine it, but when I waken, all I see are the doors closed between us. And the ache that is spreading through my chest hurts more and more.

I recognize what it is now, this pain that has been a part of me for so many years.

It is longing, pure and simple. I miss my mom.

Chapter Eighteen

The next morning was one of those perfect June days that convinced out-of-towners to buy land in the San Juan Islands.

Ruby woke late, which wasn't surprising, given that she'd tossed and turned all night.

She knew, of course, that she and Nora would have to talk about her father's confession. Hopefully, they could put it off for a while—like, until Britney Spears's boobs started to sag.

She pushed the covers back and stumbled out of bed. A shower made her feel almost human, and she stayed in it until the water turned lukewarm. Even then, she was reluctant to get out. At least in the shower, she had a purpose.

She stepped out of the shower and stood, dripping, on the fuzzy pink patch of carpet. The old pipes pinged and clanged as water gurgled down the drain.

Through the mist, she saw herself in the mirror. She swiped the moisture away and stared at a blurry reflection of her face.

She experienced one of those rare moments when, for a split second, you see yourself through a stranger's eyes. Her hair was too short, and raggedly cut, as if that stupid, gum-chewing, purple-haired girl at the beauty school had used pinking shears instead of scissors. What in God's name had made Ruby choose to dye it Elvira Mistress-of-the-Night black?

It made her skin look vampire-pale in comparison.

No wonder she'd been unable to attract a decent guy. Laura Palmer looked better in *Twin Peaks*—and she'd washed up dead on the shore.

Ruby realized she'd been *trying* to make herself unattractive. The truth of that realization was so stunning she literally watched her mouth drop open.

All that mascara, the black eyeliner, the haircut and color . . . all of it was a camouflage.

She dropped her makeup bag in the metal trash can. It hit with a satisfying clang. No more heroin-chic makeup or refugee clothing. Hell, she'd even quit dying her hair and find out what color it really was. Her last memory was of a nice, ordinary chestnut brown.

The decision made her feel better. She went into her bedroom, dressed in jeans and a jade-green V-neck T-shirt, and then hurried downstairs.

Nora was standing by the counter, leaning on her crutches. The *plop-drip-plop* of the coffeemaker filled the kitchen with steady sound. She looked up as Ruby entered the room.

An almost comical look of surprise crossed her face. "You look . . . beautiful." Immediately, she flushed. "I'm sorry. I shouldn't have sounded surprised."

"It's okay. I guess I didn't look so great with all that makeup on."

"I'm not touching *that* one with a ten-foot pole."

Ruby laughed, and it felt good. "I need a haircut. Badly. Is there still a beauty salon in Friday Harbor?"

"I used to cut your hair."

Ruby hadn't remembered until that moment, but suddenly it came rushing back: Sunday evenings in the kitchen, a dishrag pinned around her neck with a clothespin, the soothing *clip-clip-clip* of the scissors, Dad's steady turning of the newspaper pages in the living room. Ruby stood there a moment, strangely uncertain of what to do. She had a nagging sense that if she said the right thing now—in this heartbeat of time which felt steeped in sudden possibility—she could change things. She felt vulnerable suddenly, a child wearing her emotions like a kindergarten name tag. "Could you cut it again?"

"Of course. Get the towel, and a clothespin. The scissors should be here . . ." Nora reached for her crutches and limped toward the utility drawer, where the scissors had always been kept.

Ruby was momentarily nonplussed, though she wasn't sure why.

It seemed as if Nora were as eager as Ruby to avoid a breakfast conversation.

"Get the stool from the laundry room and take it outside. It's such a pretty morning."

Ruby gathered up the necessary supplies and carried everything outside. She set the stool on a nice flat patch of grass overlooking the bay and sat down on it.

She heard Nora coming toward her. *Thump-step-thump-step.* Down the porch steps and across the grass, her mother moved awkwardly, a woman clearly afraid of stepping into a hole and twisting her good ankle.

"Are you sure about this?" Ruby asked, watching her. "I'm suddenly hearing you say *oops!* behind me, and I wind up with one of those horrible asymmetrical cuts from when I was in grade school."

Nora moved around behind Ruby. "Remember your sophomore year? You didn't use hairspray—you used boat lacquer. I was scared to death I'd accidentally pat your head and shatter my wrist." Laughing, she wrapped the towel around Ruby's neck and pinned it in place, then began running her fingers through Ruby's still-damp hair.

Ruby released her breath in a sigh. It wasn't until she heard the sound—air hissing through her teeth—that she realized what she was feeling.

Longing, again.

"I'm just going to give it some shape, okay?"

Ruby blinked, came stumbling out of the past. "Yeah," she said. Her voice was barely audible. She cleared her throat and said again, louder, "Okay."

"Sit up straight. Quit fidgeting."

The steady *snip-snip-snip* of the scissors seemed to hypnotize Ruby, that and the comforting familiarity of her mother's touch.

Nora touched Ruby's chin, tenderly forcing her to look straight ahead. *Snip-snip-snip.* "Eric called me last night. He said you'd visited him."

Ruby closed her eyes. "I'm not ready to talk about Eric," she said quietly.

"Okay. Why don't you tell me about your life in Hollywood?"

Ruby's first thought was: *the article.* "There's not much to say. It's like living on the third floor of hell. I don't want to talk about that, either."

Nora paused; the scissors stilled. "I don't mean to pry. I just wonder who you have become."

"Oh." It wasn't something she thought much about—who she was. She usually concerned herself with who she wanted to be. Better to look ahead than behind, and all that. "I don't know."

"I remember when Doc Morane first put you in my arms." Nora paused in her cutting. "From the very beginning, you were fire and ice. You'd scream for what you wanted, but a hurt animal could reduce you to tears. You were walking by eight months and talking by two. And boy, did you have a lot to say. It was like living with a Chatty Cathy doll who could pull her own string. You never shut up."

Ruby realized suddenly that she *missed* herself, missed who she used to be. In forgetting her mother, she'd misplaced herself. "What was I like?"

"You wanted a tattoo at twelve—the infinity symbol, I believe. You never pierced your ears, because everyone else *did.* You wanted to go to an ashram the summer you turned thirteen. You were afraid of the dark for a long, long time, and whenever there was a windstorm, I rolled closer to your dad in bed, because I knew you'd come bolting into our room and crawl into bed with us." Nora turned to her, gently pushing the wet hair out of Ruby's eyes. "Is every part of that girl gone?"

Ruby felt shaky suddenly, uncertain. "I never got my ears pierced."

"Thank you."

"For what?"

"It would break my heart to think that you had changed so much." She reached out, touched Ruby's cheek in a fleeting, tender caress. "You could always light up a room like no one I've ever known. Remember that day we went to the island newspaper to get them to cover the eighth-grade dance?" She smiled. "I sat there, watching you make your argument, and thought, She could run the country, this girl of mine. I was so damned proud of you."

Ruby swallowed hard.

Nora went back to cutting Ruby's hair. A few minutes later, she said, "Ah, there we are. All done." She stepped aside and handed Ruby a mirror.

Ruby looked at her reflection, captured as it was in the silvered oval. She looked young again. A woman with most of her life ahead of her, instead of a bitter, struggling comic who'd left her youth sitting on barstools. "It looks great," she said, turning to her mother.

Their eyes met, locked. Understanding passed between them, quick as an electric shock.

"I went to see Dad yesterday."

"I know. He came to see me."

Ruby should have guessed. "We have to talk about it."

Nora sighed. It was a sound like the slow leaking of air from a punctured tire. "Yes." She bent down and retrieved her crutches. "I don't know about you, but I'll need a cup of coffee for this . . . and a chair. I'll *definitely* need to sit down." Without waiting, she hobbled toward the porch.

Ruby put the stool away, then grabbed two cups of coffee and went out onto the porch. Nora was seated on the loveseat; Ruby chose the rocker.

Nora took a cup of coffee from her. "Thanks."

"Dad told me he'd been unfaithful to you," Ruby said it in a rush.

"What else?"

"Does anything else matter?"

Nora frowned. "Of course other things matter."

Ruby didn't know what to say to that. "He sort of blamed it on Vietnam . . . well . . . maybe not. I wasn't sure what he blamed it on. He said the war changed him, but I got the feeling he thought he would have fooled around anyway."

Nora leaned back in her chair. "I loved your dad from the moment I first saw him, but we were young, and we got married for childish reasons. I wanted a family and a place where I could feel safe. He wanted . . ." She smiled. "I'm still not sure what he wanted. A woman to come home to, maybe. A woman who thought he was perfect. For a while we were an ideal couple. We both thought he was God."

"It was easy to see him that way. He acted so . . . loving and nice."

"Don't judge him too harshly, Ruby. His infidelity was only part of what broke us up. It was just as much my fault."

"Did you screw other men, too?"

"No, but I loved him too much, and that can be as bad as not loving someone enough. I needed so much reassurance and love, I sucked him dry. No man can fill up all the dark places in a woman's soul. I knew he'd be unfaithful sooner or later. I think I made him crazy with my questions and my suspicions."

Ruby didn't understand. "You *knew* he'd be unfaithful? How?"

"You said you lived with a man. Max was his name, right?"

Ruby nodded. "Yeah. But what—"

"Was he faithful?"

"No. Well . . . for a while, maybe."

"Did you expect him to be?"

"Of course." Ruby said it quickly. Too quickly. Then she sighed and sat back. "No. I didn't expect him to want only me."

"Of course not. If a girl's mother doesn't love her enough to stick around, why should a man?" Nora gazed at her; the smile she gave

Ruby was sad. "That's the gift my father gave me, the one I passed on to you."

"Jesus," Ruby said softly. Her mother was right. Ruby had spent a lifetime being so afraid of heartbreak that she hadn't let herself be loved. That's why she'd stayed with Max all those years. She knew she'd never fall in love with him, and her heart would be safe. All that loneliness . . . because she couldn't believe in being loved.

Ruby walked toward the railing and stared out at the Sound. She couldn't figure out what she was feeling . . . or what she should be feeling. "I remembered the day you came back." She heard her mother's sharp intake of breath and waited for an answer. When none came, she turned around.

Nora was sitting there, hunched over, as if waiting for a blow. "I don't like thinking about that day."

"I'm sorry . . . Mom," Ruby said quietly. "I said some horrible things to you."

Her mother looked up sharply. Tears filled her eyes. "You called me *Mom*." She stood up, hobbled toward Ruby. "Don't you dare feel guilty over what you said to me. You were a child, and I'd broken your heart."

"Why did you come home that day?"

"I missed you girls so much. But when I saw what I'd done to you, I was ashamed. You looked at me the way I'd once looked at my father. It . . . broke me."

Ruby couldn't avoid the question any longer. "Okay, so I know why you left Dad, but why did you stay away?"

Nora gazed at her steadily. "The leaving . . . the staying away . . . to you, these were the beginning of the story. To me, it was deep into the middle . . ."

Nora took a deep breath and dove in. The waters of the past were as cold as she'd expected, even in the heat of this gorgeous summer morning. "Everyone thought Rand and I were the perfect couple." She curled her hands around the porcelain of her coffee cup and let it warm her. "I was young then, and I cared about appearances more than substance. Living with an alcoholic will do that to you. You grow up hiding, flinching, protecting the very man you should expose. You make sure that none of the ugliness that goes on inside your house ever spills into the streets. That was a lesson my mother taught me before I was old enough to brush my teeth. Pretend and smile . . . and cry behind closed doors. I suspected your dad of having affairs long before I got hard proof." She glanced at Ruby. "No pun intended."

Ruby almost spit up her coffee. "How can you make a joke about it?"

"What is it they say about comedy—it only hurts when you laugh?" She smiled and went on. "It . . . hurt me to suspect him, but that wasn't the worst of it. The worst was his drinking. He started drinking after dinner—on the nights he came home. You girls probably didn't even notice. A few beers, a scotch and soda here and there. By ten o'clock he was wobbly, and by eleven he was stumbling drunk. And he got . . . mean. All his insecurities—you remember how hard Grandpa was on him—and his disappointments came tumbling out, and everything was my fault. Every time he yelled at me, I heard my dad's voice, and though Rand never hit me, I started expecting it, flinching away from him, and that only made him madder. How could I think he'd *hit* me, he'd scream, stomping out of the house." She looked up at Ruby. "So, you see, I was at least half of the problem. I couldn't separate my past from my present, and the harder I tried, the more the two braided together. I was terrified I'd become like my mother—a woman who never spoke more than two words at a time and died too young. But I was handling everything okay until Emmaline Fergusson told me about Shirley Comstock—"

"My soccer coach?"

Nora nodded. "You remember how much your dad suddenly started liking soccer?"

Ruby gasped. "He didn't . . . not with my coach."

"It's a small island," Nora said ruefully, "there weren't a lot of women to choose from. I told myself it didn't matter. I was his *wife,* and there was honor in that. But he started drinking more and coming home less, and I fell apart.

"It started with insomnia. I simply stopped sleeping. Then the panic attacks hit. I got a prescription for Valium, but it didn't help enough. I would lie awake at night with my heart pounding and sweat pouring off me. Every time I picked you up from soccer, I went home and threw up. Finally, I started to black out. I'd wake up lying on the kitchen floor, and I couldn't remember huge chunks of my day."

"Jesus," Ruby said softly. "Did you tell Dad?"

Nora gave a shaky smile. "Of course not. I thought I was losing my mind. All I had to hold on to was the pretense of a marriage. You and Caro were the center of a world that kept shrinking around me."

Nora looked up, wondering if it was possible to make a single twenty-seven-year-old woman understand how stifling marriage and motherhood could sometimes be. "I couldn't handle it all— your dad's drinking, his screwing around, my insomnia, my sense of being overwhelmed and trapped. It was a combustible mix. And then . . ."

Nora closed her eyes. The day she'd worked so hard to keep at bay welled up inside her. It had been a gorgeous early summer day, not unlike today. She'd gone to the soccer field early to drop off cookies . . . and she'd seen them. Rand and Shirley, kissing, right out in the open as if they had every right. "I took too many sleeping pills. I don't remember if I meant to or if it was an accident, but when I woke up in the hospital, I knew that if I didn't do something quickly, I was going to die. I don't know if you can understand that kind of depression; its debilitating, overwhelming. So, I held my breath, packed my bag, and ran. I only meant to stay away for a few days, maybe a week. I thought I'd come here, stay a few days, get some rest, and be healthy."

"And?"

Nora drew in a deep breath. She wanted to look up, but she couldn't. Instead, she stared down at the cup in her hands. "And I met Vince Corell."

"The guy who sold the pictures to the *Tattler.*"

"He was a photographer, taking pictures of the islands for a calendar. Or so he said; I didn't care about that. All that mattered was the way he looked at me. He told me I was the most beautiful woman in the world. By then, your father and I hadn't been intimate in a long time, and I *wasn't* beautiful. I was rail-thin and I trembled all the time. When Vince touched me . . . I let him. We had a wonderful week together—photographs and all. For the first time, I found someone I could talk to about my dreams—and once I'd said them aloud, I couldn't go back to the way I'd been living. And then . . . he was gone.

"I was devastated. I knew your father would have heard about what I'd done; Vince and I made no secret of our relationship. Maybe I even *wanted* Rand to find out. I don't know, but when the affair was over, and I realized I'd thrown my marriage away and lost my girls, I took too many sleeping pills again. This time it was serious. I ended up in a mental institution in Everett."

"How long were you there?" Ruby's voice was whisper soft.

"Three months."

"*What?*"

"Time wasn't real there. In those days, in that place, they were still doing electric shock therapy. We all lined up at eight forty-five in the morning for medications. After a week, I'd forgotten most of the outside world. It was Dr. Allbright who saved me. He came every day and talked to me . . . just talked until I could breathe again. I worked so hard to get better, so I could come home. But when I did . . ."

"Oh, God," Ruby said softly. "That was the day."

Nora felt tears sting her eyes and it surprised her. She thought she'd spent all her tears for that day long ago. "It's not your fault," she said, and she meant it.

"But Dad should have let you come home. After what he'd done to you—"

"I didn't ask Rand to take me back," Nora answered. "I was too screwed up to take care of my children, and I knew it. I didn't want my marriage back. I wanted . . . me. It's a horrible thing to say, a horrible thing to have done. But it's the only truth I can give you." She longed to reach out, to take her daughter into her arms, but she was afraid. They were moving toward each other now, stepping over the hurts that had accumulated like boulders on the road between them. "The world is full of regrets and times where you think *if only*. We have to move past that. Your dad was angry and arrogant. I was frightened and fragile. You were heartbroken. And on that one day, we came together, and we hurt each other. Mistakes," she said. "Just ordinary human mistakes. But I want you to know this, Ruby, and it's the only part that matters. I never stopped loving you or thinking about you. I never stopped missing you."

Ruby stared at her a long time. Then, softly, she said, "I believe you."

And Nora knew the healing had finally begun.

Chapter Nineteen

Ruby retreated to her bedroom.

I'd wake up, lying on the kitchen floor, with huge chunks of my day gone. I don't know if you can understand that kind of depression.

Mom must have been so afraid, so alone . . .

Ruby knew how it felt. It was the worst, she knew, in the middle of a long, dark night, when the man you lived with was in bed beside you. If he smelled of another woman's perfume, that handspan between you could feel like the North Atlantic.

She opened the nightstand drawer and pulled out her legal pad. She'd learned that it calmed her to write down her thoughts, and God knew she needed to relax.

She sat down on the bed and drew her knees up, angling the pad against her thighs, and began to write.

I'd always believed that the truth of a person was easily spotted, a line drawn in dark ink on white paper. Now, I wonder. Maybe the truth of who we are lies hidden in all those shades of gray that everyone talks about.

My mother was in a mental institution. This is her newest revelation. One of them, anyway; in truth, there have been too many to count.

Tonight, Mom painted a portrait of our family, and through her eyes I saw people I'd never imagined—a drunken, unfaithful husband and a depressed, overwhelmingly unhappy wife.

How is it that I saw none of this? Are children so sublimely oblivious to their own world?

She was right to hide this truth from me. Even now, I wish I didn't know it.

Sometimes, knowing where we come from hurts more than we can stand.

The phone rang.

Ruby was startled by the sound. Tossing the pad aside, she leaned over and answered. "Hello?"

"Ruby?"

It was Caroline's voice, soft and thready. Ruby immediately felt the hairs on the back of her neck stand up. "What's wrong?"

"Wrong? Nothing. Can't a girl just call her little sister?"

Ruby leaned back against the headboard. Caro sounded better now; still, that feeling of wrongness lingered. "Of course. You just sounded . . ."

"What?"

"I don't know. Tired."

Caro laughed. "I have two small children and a cat that pukes up ten thousand hairballs a day. I'm *always* tired."

"Is it really like that, Caro? Does motherhood suck something out of you?"

Caroline was quiet for a minute. "I used to dream of going to Paris. Now I just want privacy when I use the toilet."

"Jesus, Caro. How come we never talk about things like that?"

"There's nothing to say."

Ruby tried to sculpt an amorphous realization into words. "That's not true. When we talk on the phone, it's always about me. My career. My worthless excuse for a boyfriend. My thoughts on comedy. It's always about me."

"I like to live vicariously."

Ruby knew that was a lie. The truth was, Ruby had always been selfish. She didn't form relationships; she collected photographs of people and then cropped away the edges of anything that didn't fit with what she wanted to see. But those edges mattered. "Are you happy, Caro?"

"Happy? Of course I'm—" Caro started to cry.

The soft, heartbreaking sound tore at Ruby's heart. "Caro?"

"Sorry. Bad day in suburbia."

"Just one?"

"I can't talk about this now."

"What's wrong with our family that we can't talk about anything that matters?"

"Talking doesn't change things. Believe me. It's better to just go on."

"I used to think that, but I'm learning so much up here—"

"Ruby!" It was Mom's voice. She must be standing at the bottom of the stairs, yelling up.

Ruby held the phone to her chest. "I'll be right down. Hey, Caro," she said, coming back to the line. "Why don't you come up here? Spend the night."

"Oh, I can't. The kids—"

"Leave them with the stud muffin. It's not like you're stapled to the house."

Caroline's laughter was sharp. "Actually, that's exactly what it's like."

"She's not who we thought, Caro," she said softly, realizing that she'd said the words before, but without truly knowing their power. "She's the . . . gatekeeper of our memories. Who we are. You should come."

Caroline paused, drew in a breath. "I'm afraid."

Ruby understood. She wouldn't have a week ago, but now she did. "You won't break." She halted, thinking. It was important that she phrase it well, that she pass on something of what she'd learned about this family of theirs. "You think you have to hold it all in, and if you let any of it go, you'll shatter into tiny pieces and you won't know who you are. But it doesn't work that way. It's more like . . .

opening your eyes in a room you'd expected to be dark. You can *see* things, and it makes you feel stronger." She laughed. "God, I sound like Obi-Wan on heroin."

"Jeez, Rube," Caroline said, sniffling a little. "My baby sister has finally grown up."

"And only a moment before menopause. But then, I've always been gifted. Top of my class, don't forget."

"There were ten people in your class."

"And three of them flunked out. Come on, Caro, come up and visit us. Run on the beach with me like we used to . . . slam tequila and dance with me. Let's see—finally—who we are."

"RUBY! Can you hear me?"

It was Mom's voice again. This time she was yelling at the top of her lungs.

Ruby accepted defeat. "I gotta go. I love you, big sis."

"You sound like the big sister now," Caroline answered, "and I'm proud of you, Rube. And jealous. God . . . Bye."

Ruby hung up, then hurried downstairs. "Good God, is there a fire in the—"

She skidded to a stop in the kitchen.

Dean was standing there, holding a bouquet of Shasta daisies wrapped in tinfoil.

"Oh," Ruby said, feeling heat climb into her face.

Mom stood beside the table, grinning. "You have a visitor," she said in a perfect sorority-housemother voice.

Ruby took stock of herself: She hadn't brushed her teeth yet and she was still in her pajamas—an old Megadeath T-shirt and fuzzy pink kneesocks. If she were lucky—and she couldn't be—the oak floorboards would simply open up and swallow her.

Dean stepped forward and handed her the flowers. "Do you still like daisies?"

She nodded.

He closed the gap between them. "We need to talk." His voice dropped; its quiet timbre matched the soft pleading in his eyes. "Please."

The way he said it made her shiver. "Okay."

They stood there, staring at each other. Finally, Mom thumped toward them and gently tugged the flowers out of Ruby's hand.

"I'll put them in water," she said.

Ruby turned to her. It felt as if she'd just stumbled into a weird Bradys-gone-wild episode. Then she realized that moms were *supposed* to say things like that.

"Thanks, Mom." Ruby turned to Dean. "So, where are we going?"

He grinned. "Just wear a bathing suit under your clothes. Oh . . . and tennis shoes. I'll meet you outside." He gave her another quick smile, then kissed her mother on the cheek and headed outside.

Ruby could hear his footsteps crunching through the gravel behind the house. She looked at her mother. "Did you organize this?"

"Of course not."

"This is not a good idea."

"Ruby Elizabeth Bridge, you don't have the sense God gave a banana slug. Now get upstairs and get dressed. If you're too damned scared to go out with your first love, then try remembering that he used to be your best friend, too."

She couldn't think of anything brilliant to say, so she left the room. Upstairs, she stood in front of her opened suitcase, staring down at the clothing she'd brought.

A bathing suit. Yeah, right.

Had she noticed when she packed that everything was black? Or did she always dress this way? Every T-shirt said something— MEGADEATH, UCLA BRUINS, PLANET HOLLYWOOD. Her personal favorite was a white T-shirt with a cartoon drawing of a plumber bent over a broken toilet. His low-slung pants revealed a huge part of his ass. The punch line was: *Say no to crack.*

Hardly the right choice for a visit with your first love . . .

Finally, at the very bottom of the suitcase, she found a plain, peach-colored tank top and a pair of frayed cutoffs.

She didn't bother with socks, just brushed her teeth, slicked her hair back (thank God Mom had cut it), grabbed her sunglasses, and raced back downstairs.

Her mother was sitting at the kitchen table, doing a crossword puzzle and sipping tea as if this were an ordinary morning. "Have a nice time," she said, not looking up.

"Bye." Ruby went outside. The first thing she noticed was the sweet scent of the roses and the salty tang of the sea. Baking kelp and hot rocks gave the air a faintly scorched, metallic smell.

She headed down the porch and skipped around to the side of the house.

There stood Dean, just outside the picket fence, with a bicycle on either side of him.

She stopped. "You've obviously confused me with a woman who likes to sweat."

He handed her a bike helmet. It was pink and had a Barbie decal on the forehead. She crossed her arms. "That is definitely not gonna happen."

He smiled. "Too old to ride a bike, Rube? Or too out of shape?"

Damn him. He *knew* she couldn't refuse a challenge. She grabbed the handlebars and yanked the bike around. "I haven't ridden a bike since . . ." She stumbled over the memories. "In a long time."

His smile faded. He was remembering it, too, the day she'd asked him out for a bike ride . . . and broken his heart.

She stared at him for a minute more, trying to read his mind. It was closed to her. "Okay," she said at last. "Lead on."

He jumped on his bike and pedaled on ahead of her. She wanted to watch him, maybe ride alongside, but frankly, she was terrified that she was going to do a face-plant on the gravel driveway and end up as a medical episode on the Discovery channel.

He turned at the end of the driveway and headed uphill.

Ruby tried to keep up. By the top of the street, her pores had turned into geysers. Her vision was blurred by sweat; she could have been pedaling underwater for all she could see.

And it was hot.

Really, really hot.

She would have complained—was, in fact, *dying* to complain—but there wasn't enough breath in her lungs to form the word *stop,* let alone, *you asshole.*

Just when she felt her heart start to stutter, they turned a corner.

Levinger Hill.

They were flying now, racing side by side down the long, two-lane road. Golden pastures studded with apple trees rushed past them.

Dean leaned back, held his arms out . . .

And Ruby sailed into the past. They were fourteen again, that summer they learned to ride without using their hands, when every scraped knee was a badge of courage . . . when they'd whooshed down this very hill, arms outflung, together, the radio strapped to the handlebars blaring out Starship's "Nothing's Gonna Stop Us Now."

The hill slowed down into a long, even S curve, then wound into the entrance of Trout Lake State Park.

Ruby should have known he'd bring her here. "No fair, Dino," she said softly, wondering if he even heard her.

He heard. "What's that they say about love and war?"

"Which one is this?"

"That's up to you. Come on, race you to the park." Without waiting for an answer, he pedaled away from her, down the long, winding, tree-lined street.

It was dark on this road, even on this hot summer morning. Shadows fell across the thin layer of pavement in serrated strips. The air was cold.

She sped up to Dean, then pulled ahead. She heard him laughing quietly behind her, and she knew they were both thinking of the girl she'd been—the one who couldn't stand to lose at anything, even a popcorn dare like "race you to the park."

The road curled around a huge Douglas fir tree and spilled out into the sunshine. Ruby jumped off her bike and set it against the wooden bike rack. There was no need to lock it.

She heard Dean's bike land against the rack with a clatter, but she was already walking toward the lake. She had forgotten how beautiful it was here. The heart-shaped sapphire-blue lake was surrounded by lush green trees and rimmed in granite. A ribbon of water cascaded over the "giant's lip"—a flat, jutting rock at the top of the cliffs—and splashed onto the placid surface of the lake.

There were children everywhere, locals and tourists, playing on the grass, shrieking, swimming along the shore.

Dean came up beside her. "Are you up for a climb?"

She laughed. "I'm an *adult* now. Waterfall Trail is for mountain goats and kids who are desperate to smoke pot or get laid."

"*I* can make it," he said, letting the challenge in his words hang there.

She sighed. "Lead on."

Side by side, not talking, they walked around to the western side of the lake, wound through the horde of picnickers, Frisbee-catching dogs, and screaming children. When they reached the heavy fringe of trees, they left the people behind. Gradually, the sound of human voices faded away. The gurgling, splashing sound of falling water grew louder and louder.

Once again, Ruby was sweating.

The trail was rocky and narrow. It corkscrewed straight up through the trees, salal, and blackberries (which scratched her exposed arms and legs, thank you very much).

Finally, they reached the top. The giant's lip.

It was a slab of gray granite as big as a swimming pool and as flat as a quarter. A thick green moss furred the stone; dainty yellow wild-flowers grew impossibly from the moss. A stream of water no wider than the length of a man's arm flowed across the rock in a groove worn long ago, then spilled over the edge and fell twenty feet to the lake below.

Ruby stepped into the clearing and saw the picnic basket. It was sitting on a familiar red-and-black plaid blanket.

Dean touched her shoulder. "Come on." He led her to the blan-ket, which he'd carefully spread out on a spot where the moss was several inches thick.

They sat down. He reached into the basket, pulled out a thermos, and poured two glasses of lemonade.

Ruby drank hers greedily. When she was finished, she set the glass aside and leaned back on her elbows. The hot sun beat down on her cheeks. "We used to come up here all the time."

"This is where you first told me you were going to be a comedian."

"Really?" She smiled. "I don't remember that."

"You said you wanted to be famous."

"I still do. And you wanted to be a prize-winning photogra-pher." She didn't look at him. It was better to stay separate and talk about the past, as if they were just two old high-school friends who'd bumped into each other. "That's a long way from junior executive."

"Yeah . . . but I still wish for it. If I could, I'd throw everything away and start over. Money sure as hell doesn't make you happy."

It bothered her to think of him as unhappy. "Spoken like a man whose family business is on the Fortune Five Hundred."

He laughed softly. "Yeah, I guess."

A quiet settled in between them, and she was vaguely afraid of what he would say, so she said, "I saw Eric yesterday."

"He told me. It really meant a lot to him."

Ruby wishboned her arms behind her head. A single, gauzy cloud drifted above the trees. "I wish I'd stayed in better touch with him."

"You?" Dean laughed bitterly. "I'm his brother and I hadn't seen him in years."

That surprised Ruby. She rolled onto her side and faced Dean, but he didn't look at her. "You guys were always so close."

"Things change, don't they?"

"What happened?"

He stared up at the sky. "I seem to have a problem with really knowing the people I love. I get blindsided."

"You're talking about his being gay?"

Finally, he looked at her. "That's part of what I'm talking about."

She understood, and knew that it was time. For more than ten years, she'd sworn to herself that if she ever got the chance with Dean, she would say the thing that mattered. "I'm sorry, Dean," she said. "I didn't want to hurt you."

He rolled onto his side, facing her. "You didn't want to hurt me? Jesus, Ruby, you were my whole world."

"I knew that. I just . . . couldn't be someone's world then."

"I tried to take care of you after your mom left, but it was hard. You were constantly picking a fight with me. But I kept telling myself it would be okay, that you'd get past it and come back to me. And I kept loving you."

Ruby didn't know how to explain it to him. How could she? She'd only barely begun to understand it herself. "You believed in something I didn't. Every time I closed my eyes at night, I dreamed about you leaving me. In my nightmares, I heard your voice, but I could never find you. I couldn't stand waiting for you to stop loving me. To leave me."

"What made you so damned sure I would leave you?"

"Come on, Dean . . . we were kids, but we weren't stupid. I knew you'd go off to some college I couldn't afford and forget about me."

Their faces were close together, and if she'd let herself, she could have lost her way in the blue sea of his eyes. "So, you dumped me before I had a chance to dump you."

She smiled sadly. "Pretty much. Now, let's change the subject. This is old news, and we both know it doesn't matter anymore. Tell me about your life. How is it to be a jet-setting superbachelor?"

"What if I said I still love you?"

Ruby gasped. "Don't say that . . . please—"

He took her face in his hands, gently forced her to look up at him. "Did you stop loving me, Ruby?"

She felt the soft exhalation of his breath against her lips. A second later, she heard his question. She wanted to say *Of course; we were just kids,* but when she opened her mouth to answer, the only sound she made was a quiet sigh that tasted of surrender.

His lips brushed against her, and it was a sensation at once familiar and new. She melted against him, moaning his name as his hand curled around the back of her neck.

It was the kind of kiss they'd never shared before. The kind of achingly lonely kiss a pair of teenagers couldn't imagine, the kiss of two adults who'd been alone for too long and knew that God had given them this moment, and that it was a gift too precious to ignore. And for a few brief, heart-stopping seconds, their past faded like a photograph left in the hot sun.

When he drew back, she opened her eyes and saw the missing years drawn in lines on his face. Sun . . . time . . . heartache . . . they had all left imprints on his skin.

"I've waited a long time for a second chance with you, Ruby."

If he said he loved her, she would believe him, and she would love him back. She closed her eyes, battling a wave of helplessness. She wished desperately to have grown up, to have been profoundly changed by all that she'd seen and learned in the past days. But it wasn't that easy.

Her fear of abandonment was so deep it had calcified in her bones. She couldn't get past it. She'd discovered a long time ago why the poets called it *falling* in love. It was a plunging, eye-watering descent, and she'd lost her ability to believe that anyone would catch her.

She pushed him away. "I can't do this. It's too much . . . too fast. You've always wanted too much from me."

"Damn it, Ruby," he said, and she heard the disappointment in his voice. "Have you grown up at all?"

"I won't hurt you again," she said.

He touched her face. "Ah, Rube . . . just looking at you hurts me."

She had never felt so alone. When he'd kissed her, she'd glimpsed a world she'd never imagined. A world where passion was part of love, but not the biggest part. Where a kiss from the right man, at the right time, could make a grown woman weep. "I can't give you what you want. It's not in me."

He brushed the hair away from her eyes, let his fingertips linger at her temple. "You ran me off when I was a boy. I'm not seventeen anymore, and we both know, this thing between us isn't over. I don't think it ever was."

Chapter Twenty

Dean followed Ruby back down the trail. Though they didn't talk, the forest was alive with sounds. Birds squawked and chirped in the trees overhead, squirrels chattered, water splashed.

At the park, he tossed the picnic basket—still filled with a lunch unpacked and uneaten—in the trash can. Curling the heavy blanket around his shoulders, he climbed tiredly onto his bike.

When they reached the summer house, he pulled off to the side of the road and got off his bike.

Ruby stopped a few feet ahead, then set her kickstand and turned to him, frowning. "I guess this is where I say good-bye."

He heard the crack in her voice and it gave him hope. Ruby could push him away from now until forever, and he would still know the truth. He could see it in her eyes, hear it in her tremulous voice. He'd felt it in her kiss. "For now."

"It was just a kiss," she said. "Don't turn it into *Gone with the Wind*."

He took a step toward her. "You must have confused me with one of your Hollywood idiot-boys."

She wanted to move backward; he could tell. "Wh-what do you mean?"

Now he was close enough to touch her, to kiss her, but he stood perfectly still. "I know you, Ruby. You can pretend all you want, but that kiss meant something. Tonight we'll both lie in bed and think about it."

Ruby flushed. "You knew a teenager a decade ago. That doesn't mean you know *me*."

He smiled. It was so precisely the sort of thing she would have said at sixteen. "You might have built a wall around your heart, but you haven't exchanged it. Somewhere, deep inside, you're still the girl I fell in love with." At last he touched her cheek, a fleeting caress.

He wanted to do more, to pull her into his arms, hold her close and whisper, *I love you,* but he knew he couldn't push her that far. Not yet.

"For years after you were gone, I thought I saw you," he said quietly. "Every time I rounded a corner or came up to a stoplight or got off an airplane, I'd think for a split second, *There she is.* I'd run up to the person, tap her shoulder, and find myself smiling awkwardly at a stranger. I still walk on the right side of the sidewalk, because you like the left."

Her mouth trembled. "I'm afraid."

"The girl I knew wasn't afraid of anything—"

"That girl's been gone for years."

"Isn't there some part of her left?"

She stood there a long time, staring up at him, then finally she turned away.

He knew she wasn't going to answer. "Okay," he said with a sigh. "I'll concede this round." He climbed onto his bike and started to go.

"Wait."

He stumbled off his bike so fast he almost fell. It clattered to the ground as he spun back to face her. The way she was looking at him reminded him of when she was nine years old and she fell out of the oak tree on Finnegans' farm . . . or when she was twelve and broke her arm skateboarding down Front Street.

She took a step closer and looked up at him. He couldn't be certain, but she looked ready to cry. "You sound so sure."

He smiled. "You taught me love, Ruby. Every time you held my hand when I was scared, or came to one of my ball games or left a note in my locker, I learned a little more about it. Maybe when we were kids, I took that for granted, but I'm not a kid anymore. I've spent a lot of years alone and every date I went on only proved again how special we were."

"My parents were special," she said slowly. "You and Eric were special."

"So, your point is, love dies."

"An ugly, painful death."

It saddened him, knowing how her heart, once so open and pure, had been trampled by the very people who should have protected it. "Okay. Love hurts. I can't deny that. But what about loneliness?"

"I'm not lonely."

"Liar."

She stepped away from him. Without a backward look or a wave or anything, she jumped on her bike and rode away.

"Go ahead," he called after her. "Run away. You can only go so far."

Ruby knew her mother would be waiting for her. She'd probably be sitting at the kitchen table, or in the rocker on the porch, pretending to be occupied by some small task. Maybe knitting; she'd always loved to knit.

Ruby stopped pedaling. The bike slowed down, rattling and bumping over the uneven road. When she reached the minivan, she dumped the bike at the side of the gardening shed and headed down to the house. The gate creaked loudly at her touch.

She stepped into the kitchen and found her mother at the stove, stirring something in an old iron pot. She was wearing her old apron—the one that said A WOMAN'S PLACE IS IN THE HOUSE . . . AND THE SENATE.

"Ruby," she said, looking up in surprise. "I didn't expect you back so soon." She glanced at the door, now closed behind Ruby. "Where's Dino?"

Ruby stood there. God help her, she couldn't talk. The kitchen smelled of pot roast, slow-cooking all day with baby carrots and oven-browned potatoes. A cookie sheet sat on the counter. On it, homemade biscuits were rising. And unless Ruby missed her guess, that was vanilla custard Mom was stirring.

She'd made Ruby's all-time favorite dinner.

Just then, Ruby didn't know which hurt more—the effort her mother had made to please her, or the fact that Dean wasn't here to share it. All she knew was that if she didn't get out of this room soon, she was going to burst into tears.

"Dean went home," she said.

A frown darted across her mother's face. She turned off the burner, carefully placed the wooden spoon across the top of the pot, and grabbed her crutches, then limped toward Ruby. *Step-thump-step-thump.* The uneven footsteps matched the beat of Ruby's heart. "What happened?"

"I don't know. I guess we started something we couldn't finish. Or maybe we finished something we'd started a long time ago." She shrugged and looked away.

"This won't be like Max," her mother said.

"I love Dean," Ruby admitted. "But that's not enough. It wouldn't last, anyway."

"Love is nothing without faith."

"I lost that faith a long time ago."

"Of course you did. And you're right to blame your dad and me for it, but that doesn't matter anymore—whose fault it is. What matters is *you.* Can you let yourself jump without a net? Because that's what love is, what faith is. You're looking for a guarantee, and those come with auto parts. Not love."

"Yeah, right. Love put you in a mental institution."

Mom laughed. "I think it makes lunatics of us all."

It felt good to talk to her mother this way. As friends. It was something Ruby had never even imagined.

It was true; love made everybody crazy. All those years Ruby had spent angry with her mother, sending back presents unopened and refusing all contact—it wasn't because she'd felt betrayed.

Those years, those feelings and actions, had been about . . . longing. Simple longing.

She'd *missed* her mother so much that the only way she'd been able to go on in the world was to pretend she was alone.

I'm not alone anymore.

That one sentence, once thought, formed a road that led Ruby to herself. She didn't say it aloud. Instinctively, she knew that if she spoke, her voice would be a child's, full of awe and bewilderment. And she would cry.

I can't write the article.

"I've got to go upstairs," she said suddenly, seeing the surprise on her mother's face. Ruby didn't care. She ran upstairs and went to the phone, dialing Val's number.

Maudeen answered on the second ring. "Lightner and Associates, may I help you?"

"Hi, Maudeen," Ruby said, sitting on the bed, drawing her knees up. "It's Ruby Bridge. Is the Great Oz in?"

Maudeen laughed. "He and Julian went to a premiere in New York. He'll be back on Monday, and he's calling in for messages."

"Okay. Tell him I won't be delivering my article."

"You mean it's going to be late?"

"I'm not going to turn it in at all."

"Oh, my. You'd better give me your address and phone number again. He'll want to talk to you."

Ruby gave out the information, then hung up. She hadn't even realized that she was reaching for her writing pad, but there it was, sitting on her lap. It was time now to finish what she'd begun. Slowly, she began to write.

I have just called my agent. When he calls back, I will tell him that I can't turn in this article. I never thought about what it meant to write an exposé on my own mother.

Can you believe I was so blind? I took the money that was given to me—my thirty pieces of silver—and I spent it like a teenager would, on a fast car and expensive clothes.

But I didn't think.

I dreamed. I imagined. I saw myself on Letterman and Leno, a witty, charming guest plugging her own skyrocketing career. I never noticed that I'd be standing on my mother's broken back to reach the microphone.

My dreams, as usual, were all about me.

Now, I see the people around me, and I know what the price of my selfish actions will be.

As I write, I am reminded of that passage from the Bible—the one that is read at every wedding: "When I was a child, I spake as a child, I understood as a child, I thought as a child."

Now, I understand as an adult. Maybe for the first time in my life. This article would break my mother's heart, and perhaps even worse, her spirit. That didn't matter to me a week ago; in fact, I wanted to hurt her then.

My only excuse: then I was a child.

I can't do it anymore; not to her and not to me. For the first time, I have drawn back the dark curtain of anger and seen the bright day beyond.

I can be my mother's daughter again.

Even as I write that sentence, I feel its powerful seduction. I can't fully express to you—strangers—how it feels to be motherless. The ache . . . the longing.

She is the keeper of my past. She knows the secret moments that have formed me, and even with all that I have done to her, I can feel that still she is able to love me.

Will anyone else ever love me so unconditionally?

I doubt it.

I can't give that up. Caché will have to find someone else to betray Nora Bridge. I am going home.

Ruby felt better now. Her decision was down in print, formed and solid in bright blue letters.

She would not turn in the article.

———

In Friday Harbor, the marina was a hive of activity; boats coming in and going out, kids racing along the cement docks, nets in hand, boaters bringing groceries down to their moored boats in creaky wooden carts.

This town was the center of the American section of this archipelago. For more than one hundred years, islanders had come to this port for groceries, boat repairs, and companionship. The town was an enchanting mix of old, decrepit buildings and newer ones, built with a reverence for the past in mind. It was a place where pedestrians and bikers were as liable to be in the middle of Main Street as an automobile, and the honk of a car horn was almost never heard. Like all of the islands, San Juan had learned long ago to depend on the tourist trade. The downtown area was an eclectic mix of art galleries, souvenir shops, gift emporiums, and restaurants—with prices that forced the locals to drive off island for their daily needs, and encouraged the Californian tourists to buy two of everything.

Dean walked aimlessly up and down the streets. Today had depressed the hell out of him, and he knew it shouldn't have. Nothing had ever been easy with Ruby. Love would be the most difficult of all.

He came to a camera shop and went inside. On a whim, he bought a kick-ass camera and enough film to record the tearing down of the Berlin Wall. Finally, he heard the ferry's horn, and knew it was time to get down to the dock. He jumped on his bike and raced downhill. He was late, so he followed the last car onto the boat.

On Lopez, he stopped by the grocery store and bought a few things, then pedaled home as fast as he could. By the time he reached the house, the sun was just beginning to set. In the kitchen, Lottie was busy chopping up vegetables for stir-fry. He gave her a quick wave hello and hurried up to Eric's room.

"Hey, bro," Eric said, smiling tiredly, sitting up. "How was your bike ride?"

Dean went to him. "Guess what I bought?" He opened the small blue insulated bag and withdrew a melting Popsicle.

Eric's eyes widened. "A Rainbow Rocket. I didn't think they still made them."

Dean unwrapped the soggy white wrapper and handed his brother the dripping, multicolored Popsicle. He had to help Eric hold it—his hands were weak and unresponsive—but the smile on Eric's face was straight from the old days.

Eric closed his eyes and made groaning sounds of pleasure as he licked the Popsicle. When he finished, he set the gooey stick on the bedside tray and sighed. The bed whirred to a more upright position. "That was great," he said, leaning deeper into the pillows. He slowly turned his head. "I'd forgotten how much I loved those things."

"I remembered," Dean said. "I've been remembering a lot of things lately."

"Like?"

"Remember the fort we made inside that dead log on Mrs. Nutter's land? When she discovered us, she chased us all the way down her driveway with a broom—"

"Screaming that we were rich-kid hooligans."

"She threatened to call our parents—"

"And we told her Mom was in Barbados and the call would cost her a fortune." Eric's laughter faded into a hacking cough, then disappeared altogether.

"There's something else, too," Dean said. He went to his own bedroom, then returned with a comic book.

Eric blinked up at him. "My missing *Batman*. The only issue I ever lost."

Dean smiled. "You didn't lose it. Your little brother was mad at you one day for not sharing your Wacky Wallwalker, and he took your *Batman*. He could never figure out how to give it back."

Smiling, Eric took the comic, thumbed through it. "I always knew you took it. Shithead."

"Do you want me to read it to you?"

Eric set it on his lap. "Ah . . . I guess not. I'm too tired. Just talk to me."

Dean leaned over the bed rail and gazed down at his brother. "I went to see Ruby today."

"And?"

"Let's just say the door hit me in the ass on the way out."

Eric laughed. "That's our Ruby. Never gives an inch. Did you tell her you loved her?"

"I asked her what she would say if I did."

Eric rolled his eyes. "How Cary Grant of you. It's hard to sweep a girl off her feet with a line like that."

"How would you know?"

"Girl. Boy. It's all the same, kiddo. Romance. And frankly, you'd better get a move on. I want to be around for your happily-ever-after."

"I know, I know. You're dying."

"Damn right, I am. So, when is round two?"

Dean sighed. "I don't know. I'll need to stock up on defensive weapons. Maybe something will happen tomorrow, when we all go sailing."

"You *do* love her, though?"

"I don't think I ever stopped loving her. I wanted to, I tried to, but she was always in my dreams, the girl I measured every other woman against. But that doesn't mean she still loves me. Or that, if she did love me, she'd believe in it."

"Don't let her push you away again."

"It's not that easy. I can't do all the work. I *won't* do all the work. If she wants a future, she's gonna have to put out a little effort."

"Well, I hope it works out fast. I wanted to be the best man at your wedding."

"You will be." Dean struggled to keep his voice even. Their eyes met, and in his brother's gaze, he saw the sad truth. They both knew it was dream-spinning, this conversation of theirs. Eric would not be putting on a tuxedo and standing in shiny shoes beside Dean at the altar.

"I'm glad you came home, Dino. I couldn't have done this without you."

Home. The simple, complex word found purchase in his heart. He'd known it would be hard to stand by and watch his brother die, but until this moment, he hadn't realized that it would end. This goodbye, strung out as it was over the briefest of time spans, was all that was left to them, and Dean would have to cling to these memories in the dark days that were sure to follow.

If Ruby did miraculously admit to loving Dean, who would he tell? Who would laugh at him and say, *You must have done something to piss God off if He chose Ruby as your one true love.*

There were so many things left to say between him and Eric, but how—where—did you begin? How could you experience a lifetime in a few short days? And what about the things that floated past them, accidentally unsaid? What if Dean ended up moving through a colorless, Eric-less world in which he couldn't think of anything except what should have been said?

"Don't," Eric said.

Dean blinked, realizing he'd been silent too long. Tears stung his eyes. He tried to casually wipe them away. "Don't what?"

"You're imagining the world without me."

"I don't know how to get through this."

Eric reached out. His pale, blue-veined hand covered Dean's and pressed firmly. "When I start feeling overwhelmed, I go back in time instead of ahead. I remember how we used to play red rover at Camp Orkila. Or how you used to sit cross-legged in your room, with your eyes closed, trying to levitate your toys when Lottie made you clean your room." He smiled tiredly and closed his eyes, and Dean could see that he was losing his brother to sleep once again. "I remember the first time I saw Charlie. He was making a sandwich at the college lunch hangout. Mostly, I just remember what I've had and not what I'm leaving behind."

Dean's throat was so tight he couldn't answer.

"The best part is you." Eric's voice was barely above a whisper now. His words were starting to sound garbled, as if he were more than half asleep. "Since you're back, I dream again. It's nice . . ."

"Dream," Dean said softly, placing his brother's limp hand on top of the blanket, then stroking his warm forehead. "Dream of who you would have been, and who you were. The bravest, smartest, best brother a kid ever had."

After dinner, Nora went out to the porch and sat in her favorite rocking chair. In this magical hour, poised between day and night, the sky was the soft hue of a girl's ballet slipper.

The screen door squeaked open and banged shut. "I brought you some tea," Ruby said, stepping into the porchlight's glow. "Constant Comment with cream and sugar, right?"

"Thanks," Nora said. "Join me."

Ruby sat down in the rocker. Leaning back, she crossed her legs at the ankle and rested her feet on the small, frosted glass table beside the loveseat. "I've been thinking."

"There's aspirin in the bathroom cabinet."

"Very funny. It didn't give me a headache. It gave me . . . a heartache."

Nora turned to her.

"I think I was easy to leave."

"Don't say that. You were an innocent victim."

"I'm tired of that answer." Ruby smiled, but it was a sad, curving of the lips that lasted no time at all. "I was a bitch to Dean after you left."

"That's understandable."

"I know. I had every right to be a bitch. I was lost and in pain. But was he supposed to love me when I wasn't lovable, when I wouldn't let him get close? I expected love from him when I gave none, and then I fucked another guy just to see if Dean would love me no matter what. Big surprise: He didn't." She leaned forward again, rested her forearms on her thighs, and studied Nora. "And I was worse to you. All those years, you sent letters and gifts and left phone messages. I knew you cared about me. I knew you were sorry, and I was *proud* of hurting you. I thought it was the least you deserved. So, don't disagree with me when I say that I have been the architect of some of my own pain."

Nora smiled. "We all are. Growing up is when we finally understand that. Remember those strawberry hard candies that used to show up in your Easter basket every year?"

"Yes."

"That's you, Ruby. You've built a hard shell to protect your soft heart. Only it doesn't work. I know you don't have faith in love, and I know I made you that way, but it's a half life, kiddo. Maybe you see that now. Without love, the loneliness just goes on and on."

Ruby looked down at her clasped hands. "I was lonely when I lived with Max."

"Of course you were. You didn't love him."

"I wanted to. Maybe I could have if I'd let myself."

"I don't think love is like that. It just . . . strikes. Like lightning."

"And fries you to a crisp."

"And turns your hair white."

"And stops your heart."

Nora's smile faded. "You should give Dean a chance. Stick around a while longer, see what happens. Unless you need to get back to your career . . ."

"What career?" The moment she said it, Ruby looked up sharply, as if she hadn't meant to say that.

"What do you mean?"

"I'm not funny."

The words seemed to take something away from Ruby; she looked young and vulnerable.

Nora didn't know how to respond. Did her daughter want honesty, empathy, or contradiction?

There was no way to know. All Nora could do was speak to the girl she'd once known. That girl, the young Ruby, had been honest to a fault and able to look life square in the eye.

"We both know you *are* funny. You've always had a great sense of humor. But are you funny enough, and often enough, to make a living at it? Have you taken classes, analyzed people like Robin Williams and Richard Pryor and Jerry Seinfeld? Do you know *how* they make their material sound funny?"

Ruby looked stunned. "You sound like my agent. He's always trying to get me to take classes. At least, he used to. He's kind of given up on me now."

"Why didn't you take his advice?"

"I thought it was about talent." The word seemed to make her uncomfortable. She gave Nora a little half smile as if to acknowledge it.

"Most things take more discipline than talent." Nora studied her daughter. "Is your material funny?"

"Most of the time. It's my delivery that sucks. And I'm not comfortable onstage."

Nora smiled. She couldn't help remembering—

"Mom? You're spacing out on me."

"I'm sorry. I heard your act once. One of my readers sent me a tape of it."

Ruby turned pale. "Really?"

"I have to admit it hurt like hell. You compared me to a rabbit— soft and pretty on the outside, and capable of eating her young." She laughed. "Anyway, I thought your stuff was funny, and I wasn't surprised by that. I always thought you'd be a writer."

"Really?"

"Your stories were wonderful. You had a way of looking at the world that amazed me."

Ruby swallowed hard. "I like writing. I . . . think I'm good at it. Lately, I've been thinking about writing a book."

"You should give it a try."

Ruby bit her lower lip, worrying it, and Nora knew she'd overstepped. "I'm sorry. I didn't mean to suggest—"

"It's okay, Mom. It's just that I almost did write something, but it was too personal. About us, our family. I didn't want to hurt . . . anyone."

Ruby looked heartbreakingly young and earnest right then. "Sometimes people get hurt, Ruby. It's never something you should seek out, or do on purpose, but you can't live a life that hurts no one. If you try, you'll end up touching no one."

"I wouldn't want to hurt you," Ruby said quietly.

Before Nora could respond, she heard the sound of a car driving up. It parked, and the engine fell silent. A door slammed shut.

Ruby glanced toward the garden. "Are we expecting someone?"

"No."

Footsteps rattled on gravel. A rusty gate creaked open and clattered shut.

Someone thumped up the sagging porch steps and walked into the light.

Chapter Twenty-one

Nora stared up at her elder daughter in shock. "Caroline?" she whispered, setting her tea down on the table beside her.

"I don't *believe* it!" Ruby ran across the porch and pulled her sister into a fierce hug.

Nora drank in the sight of it, her girls, back together on Summer Island. In the old days, she would have joined them, thrown her arms around both girls for a "family hug." But now a lifetime's worth of poor choices left her on the outside, looking at her own daughters through a pane of glass as thick as a child's broken heart.

Nora got awkwardly to her feet and limped forward. "Hey, Caro. It's good to see you."

Caroline drew back from Ruby's embrace. "Hello, Mother." Her smile seemed forced; it wasn't surprising. Even as a child, she'd been able to smile when her heart was breaking.

"This is *great*," Ruby said. "My big sis is home for a slumber party. We haven't done that since Miranda Moore's birthday party."

In the soft, orange light, Nora studied her elder daughter. Caroline was flawlessly dressed in a pair of creased white linen pants and a rose-colored silk blouse with ruffles that fell around her thin wrists. Not a strand of silvery-blond hair was out of place, not a fleck of mascara marred the pale flesh beneath her eyes. Nora had the feeling it wouldn't dare.

And yet, in all that perfection, there was a strange undercurrent of fragility. As if she were hiding some tiny, hairline crack. Her gray eyes seemed suffused with a silent sadness.

Nora wondered suddenly what had brought Caroline here. It was unlike her daughter to do anything spontaneously—she planned her grocery-shopping days and marked them down on a planner. An unannounced trip to the island was startlingly out of character.

Ruby peered past her sister's shoulder. "Where are the kids?"

"I left them with Jere's mom for the night." She glanced nervously at Nora. "It's just me. I hope that's okay. I know I should have called."

"Are you *kidding*? I begged you to come," Ruby said, laughing.

Ruby looped an arm around her sister's narrow shoulders. The two women moved into the house, their heads tilted together.

As she limped along behind them, Nora heard Ruby say softly, "Is everything okay at home?" but Caroline's answer was too hushed to be overheard.

Nora felt like a third wheel. She stopped at the kitchen table and cleared her throat. "Maybe I should leave you two alone for a while. You know, for a sisterly chat."

Caro and Ruby were almost to the living room. Together they turned around.

It was Ruby who spoke. "That's what got us into this pathetic mess, don't you think?"

"I just thought—"

"I know what you thought," Ruby said with a tenderness that squeezed Nora's heart.

Caroline moved forward, her left arm clamped tightly down on her designer overnight bag, her heels clacking on the hardwood floor. Nora could see her daughter's fear; it was close to the surface now.

Poor Caro. She actually thought it was possible—if you were careful—to skate on ice too thin to hold your weight.

"So," Caro said, offering a quick smile that didn't reach her eyes, "would you like to see the newest photos of your grandchildren?"

"We could start there," Nora said, knowing it wasn't her line. She was supposed to be desperately thankful for even the pretense of normalcy. "But if we really want to get to know each other, it will take more than pictures."

Caroline paled—if that were possible—then went on seamlessly. "Good." She unzipped her bag and took out two flat photo albums. "Let's go sit in the living room," she said, already moving. She went to the sofa and sat down, her knees pressed demurely together, her fingers splayed on top of the albums on her lap.

Ruby rushed over and sat beside her.

Nora ignored her crutches and hopped on one foot after her daughters. She sat down beside Caroline.

Caroline glanced down at the album. Her long, manicured fingers stroked the tooled leather.

Nora noticed that those hands, so perfectly cared for and heavy with gold and diamond jewelry, were trembling.

Slowly, Caroline opened the book. The first photograph was an eight-by-ten color shot of her wedding. In it, Caroline stood tall and stiffly erect (not nearly as thin as she was now), sheathed in an elegant, beaded-silk off-the-shoulder gown. Jere was beside her, breathtakingly handsome in a black Prada tuxedo.

"Sorry," Caro said quickly, "the new photos are in the back." She started to turn the page.

Nora boldly laid her hand on top of Caroline's. "Wait."

Who gives this woman to be married to this man?

When the priest had asked that special question, it had been Rand alone who'd answered. *I do.* Nora had been in the back of the church, doing her best not to weep. It should have been: *We do; her mother and I.*

But Nora had given up that precious moment.

She had been there for Caroline's wedding, but she hadn't *been* there. Caroline had invited her, placed her at a close-yet-distant table, one reserved for special guests, but not family. Nora had known that she was a detail to her daughter on that day, no more or less important than the floral arrangements. And Nora, lost in the desert of her own guilt, had thanked God for even that. She'd gone through the receiving line and kissed her elder daughter's cheek, whispered "Best wishes," and moved on. There were endless questions she hadn't allowed herself to even ask then, but now, as she stared at the beautiful photograph of her daughter, Nora couldn't remain detached.

Who had acted as Caroline's mother on that day? Who had sewn the last-minute beads on Caro's dress . . . or taken her shopping for ridiculously expensive lingerie that she would never wear again . . . who had held her, one last time, as an unmarried young woman and whispered, *I love you?*

Nora drew her hand back. She heard the sound of a turning page and forced her eyes open again.

Ruby laughed, pointing to a shot of the whole wedding party. "I want you to know, I never wore that dress again."

"Yeah, and you never came home again, either," Caroline shot back.

Ruby's smile faded. "I meant to."

Caroline smiled sadly. "Words that could be our family motto."

She quickly turned another page. "This is our honeymoon. We went to Kauai."

Nora noticed that Caroline's fingers were trembling again. She kept gently touching the photographs.

"You look so happy," Nora said softly.

Caroline turned, and Nora saw the sadness stamped on her daughter's face. "We were."

And Nora knew. "Oh, Caro . . ."

"Enough honeymoon shots," Ruby said loudly. "Where are the kids?"

Caroline turned back to the album, flipped through a few more sand-and-surf photographs, and came to a stop.

This one was in a hospital room festooned with balloons and flower bouquets. Caroline was in bed, wearing a frilly white nightgown and an exhausted smile. For once, her hair was a mess. She held a tiny baby in her arms; the red-faced infant was wrapped in a pink blanket.

Here, at last, was a genuine smile, the kind that shone like sunlight.

Nora should have seen that smile in person, but she hadn't. Oh, she'd visited Caroline in the hospital, of course. She had come, bearing an armload of expensive gifts. She'd talked to her daughter, commiserated about labor, then commented on how pretty the baby was . . . and then she'd left. Even then, with the miracle of a new generation between them, they hadn't really talked.

Nora hadn't been there when Caroline realized how terrifying motherhood was. Who had said to her, *It's okay, Caro; God made you for this?*

No one.

Nora clamped a hand over her mouth, but it was too late. A small, noise escaped. She felt the tears burn her eyes and streak down her cheek. She tried to hold her breath but it broke into little gasps.

"Mom?" Caroline said, looking at her.

Nora couldn't meet her daughter's gaze. "I'm sorry . . ." She meant to add *for crying,* but the apology cracked in half.

Caroline was quiet.

Nora didn't realize that her daughter was crying until a tear splashed onto the album, landed in a gray blotch beside a picture of Jenny in a bassinet.

Nora reached out, placed her hand on Caroline's cold, still fingers. "I'm so sorry," she whispered again.

Caroline bent her head. A curtain of hair fell forward, hid her face. "That was the day I missed you most." She laughed unevenly. "Jere's mom was a take-charge kind of gal. She whipped in and packed me up and sent me on my way with a list of instructions." Another tear fell. "I remember the first night. Jenny was in a bed beside me. I kept reaching out for her, touching her little fingers, stroking her little cheek. I dreamed you were standing beside my bed, telling me it would be okay, not to be afraid." She turned, looked at Nora through mascara-ruined eyes. "But I always woke up alone."

Nora swallowed hard. "Oh, Caroline . . ."

"I tried to remember that prayer you used to say when I was scared at night. I know it was stupid, but I just kept thinking that everything would be fine if I could only remember those words."

"'Starlight, star bright, protect this baby girl against the night.'" Nora smiled uncertainly. "Caro, there aren't enough words in this galaxy to say how sorry I am for what I did to you and Ruby."

Caroline leaned toward her and let Nora take her in her arms.

Nora's heart cracked open like an egg. She was crying so hard she started to hiccup. When Nora drew back, she saw Ruby, sitting on Caroline's other side. Her face was pale, her lips drawn into a thin line. Only her eyes revealed emotion; they were shimmering with unshed tears.

Ruby stood up. "We need to drink."

Caroline wiped her eyes self-consciously and frowned. "I don't drink."

"Since when? At the junior prom, you—"

"It's a dozen lovely memories like that one that keep me sober. In college, Jere used to call me E.D. for easy drunk. Two drinks and I start thinking strip-and-go-naked is a perfect game."

"E.D? E.D.? Oh, this is too good. I'm twenty-seven years old and I haven't gotten drunk with my sister since before it was legal. Tonight we're changing all that."

Nora laughed. "The last time I drank, I drove into a tree."

"Don't worry—I won't let you drive," Ruby promised.

Caroline laughed. "Okay. One drink. *One.*"

Ruby did a little cha-cha-cha toward the kitchen, then threw back her head and said, "Margaritas!" Before Nora had figured out how to start another conversation with Caroline, Ruby was back, dancing into the living room with glasses that could have doubled as Easter baskets.

Nora took her drink, then laughed out loud when Ruby went to the record player, picked an album, and put it on.

We will . . . we will . . . rock you blared through the old speakers. Ruby had the volume so high the windows rattled and knickknacks seemed to dance spasmodically across the mantel.

Ruby took a laughing gulp of her drink, wiped her mouth with the back of her hand, and slammed the drink down onto the coffee table. Then she snapped a hand toward Caroline. "Come on, Miss America, dance with Hollywood's worst comic."

Caroline frowned. "That's not true."

"Dance with me."

Shaking her head, Caroline grabbed Ruby's hand and let herself be pulled into a twirl.

Nora cautiously sipped her cocktail and leaned forward, mesmerized by the interplay between her daughters. They were standing side by side, both sweaty from dancing, and they looked so happy and carefree it actually hurt Nora's heart. These were the adult versions of the girls Nora had borne, the women she'd imagined her daughters would have become if their mother had never left.

The girls danced and drank and laughed together, bumping hips and holding hands, until Caroline held up her hands and said breathlessly, "No more, Ruby. I'm getting dizzy."

"Ha! You're not dizzy enough, that's your problem," and with that proclamation, she handed her sister her margarita. "Bottoms up."

Caroline wiped the damp hair off her face. It looked for a moment as if she were going to decline.

"Oh, what the hell." Caroline drank the rest of her margarita without stopping, then held out the empty glass. "Another one, please."

"Yee ha!" Ruby danced into the kitchen and started up the blender.

On the stereo, the next album dropped down, clicked on top of the first one. With a whining screech, the arm moved to the beginning and lowered.

It was an old album by the Eurythmics. *Sweet dreams are made of these* pulsed through the speakers.

Caroline stumbled unsteadily to one side and held her hand out. "Dance with me, Mom."

Mom. It was the first time Caroline had called her that in years.

"If I step on your foot, I'll break every bone."

Caroline laughed. "Don't worry, I'm anesthetized." The last word came out hopelessly mangled, and Caroline laughed again. "Drunk," she said sternly, *"drunk."*

Nora grabbed her fallen crutch and limped over to Caroline. She slipped one arm around her daughter's tiny (too tiny; frighteningly tiny) waist and used the crutch for support.

Caroline pressed her hands against Nora's shoulders. Slowly, they began to sway from side to side.

"This is the last song they played at the senior prom. I had them play it at my wedding, remember?"

Nora nodded. She was going to say something impersonal, but then she noticed the way Caroline was looking at her. "Do you want to talk about it?" she asked gently, tightening her hold on Caro's fragile waist.

"Talk about what?"

Nora couldn't help herself. She stopped dancing and released Caroline's hand, then touched her daughter's cheek. "Your marriage."

Caroline's beautiful face crumpled. Her mouth quavered as she released a heavy sigh. "Oh, Mom . . . I wouldn't know where to start."

"There's no—"

Ruby spun into the room, singing, "Margaritas for the señoras." She saw Nora and Caro standing there, and she stopped in her tracks. "Jesus, I leave you two for five minutes and the waterworks start again."

Nora shot her a pleading look. "Ruby, please."

Ruby frowned. "Caro? What is it?"

Caroline took an unsteady step backward. She looked from Nora to Ruby and back to Nora. She was weeping silently, and it was a heart-wrenching sight. It was the way a woman wept in the middle of a dark night with her husband beside her in bed and her children sleeping down the hall.

"I wasn't going to tell you," Caro said to both of them in a breathy, broken voice.

Ruby stepped toward her, hand outstretched.

"Don't touch me!" Caro said. At the shrill desperation in her voice, she laughed. "I'll fall apart if you touch me, and I'm so god-damn sick of falling apart I could scream."

Caroline sank slowly to her knees on the floor. Ruby sat down beside her, and Nora followed awkwardly, landing on her fallen crutch.

Caroline took a big gulp of her margarita, then looked up. Her eyes were dry now, but somehow that only made her look more wounded. A little girl looking out through a woman's disillusioned eyes, wondering how she'd stumbled into such heartache.

"Are you sleeping?" Nora asked.

Caroline looked shocked. "No."

"Eating?"

"No."

"Medications?"

"No."

Nora nodded. "Well, that's a good thing." She held Caroline's hand. "Have you and Jere talked about this?"

Caroline shook her head. "I can't tell him. We're always going in different directions. I feel like a single parent most of the time. And I'm lonely. God, I'm so damned lonely sometimes I can't stand it."

"You haven't even *talked* to him about it?" Ruby said, leaning toward her sister.

Caroline turned to her. "You don't know what it's like, Ruby. You can say anything to anyone. It's harder for me."

"Yeah, but—"

Nora touched Ruby's thigh. "She doesn't need that now, Ruby. There's a time for the real world and consequences, Caroline knows that. This is a time for letting her know that whatever happens, we'll always be there for her." Nora gazed lovingly at Caroline. "I know what you're going through, believe me. You're at that place where your own life overwhelms you and you can't see a way to break free. And you're suffocating."

Caroline drew in a gulping, hiccuping breath. Her eyes rounded. "How did you know that?"

Nora touched her cheek. "I know" was all she said for now. There would be more to come, she knew, but now they had to lay all the cards on the table. "Is Jere seeing another woman?"

Caroline made a desperate, moaning sound. Tears rolled down her cheeks. "Everyone always said Jere was just like Daddy. I guess I should have been afraid." She sniffled and wiped her eyes. "I'm going to leave him, though."

"Do you love him?" Nora asked gently.

Caroline went pale. Her lower lip trembled; the hands in her lap tightened into a bloodless knot. "So much . . ."

Nora's heart felt as if it were breaking. Here was another legacy of her motherhood: she'd taught her children that marriages were disposable.

"Let me tell you what it's like, this decision you think you've made," she said to Caroline. "When you leave a man you love, you feel like your heart is splitting in half. You lie in your lonely bed and you miss him, you drink your coffee in the morning and you miss him, you get a haircut and all you can think is that no one will notice but you. And you go on with a broken heart, you go on." She took a deep, unsteady breath. "But that's not the worst of it. The worst is what you do to your children. You tell yourself it's okay; divorces happen all the time and your children will get over it. Maybe that's true if the love is really gone from your marriage. But if you still love him, and you leave him without trying to save your family, you will . . . break. You don't just cry in the middle of the night, you cry forever, all the time, until your insides are so dry there are no tears left, and then you learn what real pain is."

Nora knew that what she was saying wasn't true for all marriages, all divorces. But she was certain that Caroline hadn't tried hard enough, not yet, not if she loved Jere. She closed her eyes, trying to think of Caroline . . . but then she was thinking about her own life, her own mistakes, and before she knew it, she was talking again. "You walk around and get dressed and maybe you even find a career that makes you rich and famous. You think that was what you wanted all along, but you find out it doesn't matter. You don't know how to feel anymore. You're dead. Somewhere, your daughters are growing up without you. . . . You know that somewhere they're out there, holding someone else's hand, crying on someone else's shoulder. And every single day, you live with what you did to them. Don't make my mistake," Nora said fiercely. "*Fight*. Fight for your love and your family. In the end, it's all there is, Caroline. All there is."

Caroline didn't look up as she whispered, "What if I lose him anyway?"

"Ah, Caro," Nora said, stroking her daughter's hair, "what if you find him again?"

Chapter Twenty-two

Ruby felt as if someone were pounding a drum inside her head. Though she was exhausted, she couldn't sleep. She'd tried turning the light on, hoping Caroline would wake up, but no such luck. Her sister had obviously lapsed into a tequila coma.

After their evening of margaritas and tears, she and Caro had finally stumbled up to bed. They'd lain in the darkness for hours, talking, laughing; sometimes they'd even cried. They'd said all the things they'd gathered up in the years between then and now, but finally, Caroline had fallen asleep.

Ruby closed her eyes and pictured Mom as she'd been a few hours earlier . . . sitting on the dirty rag rug like a kindergartner, with her casted leg sprawled out to the side, a half-finished margarita beside her thigh. In profile, with the firelight haloing her face, she'd looked like an angel carved from the purest ivory.

She had been talking quietly to Caroline.

They'd held hands, Mom and Caro, and whispered about marriage, about how it wasn't what you expected. Their two voices had blended into a music that Ruby couldn't quite comprehend. At first, she'd felt left out, a child eavesdropping at her parents' closed bedroom door.

She had been right there, sitting beside them, and yet she'd felt isolated and alone. Unconnected. Never in her life had Ruby felt such an intense sense of her own shortcomings.

She'd been unable to join in the conversation because she'd never made a commitment to another human being; she'd never tried to love someone through good times and bad. In fact, she'd purposely chosen men she *couldn't* love. In that way, her heart had always seemed safe. And always, it had been empty.

She'd had the realization before, but this time it struck deep.

Caroline and Mom had been talking about love and loss, and most of all, commitment; about how love was more than an emotion. In the end, Mom had said, sometimes love was a choice. Like the tide, it could ebb and flow, and there were slack-tide times when a woman had nothing to believe in except a memory, nothing to cling to except the choice she'd made a long time ago.

Mom had looked at Caroline and said softly, "I let the bad times overwhelm me, and I ran. It wasn't until I'd gone too far to turn back that I remembered how much I loved your father, and by then it was too late. For all these years, I've been left wondering, 'What if?'"

What if?

Ruby closed her eyes. The darkness pressed in on her. She heard the whispering of the sea through the open window.

Do you believe in second chances?

Dean's question came back to her, filled her longing.

"I do," she said out loud, hoping that tomorrow, when they went sailing, she would find the courage to say the same words to Dean.

Before tonight, it would have seemed impossible to expose her heart so openly, so boldly. To admit she wanted to love and be loved. But tonight, life seemed different.

As if anything were possible.

The next morning, Nora woke feeling refreshed and rejuvenated. Almost young again. She thanked God that she'd sipped a single margarita all night.

She pushed back the coverlet and limped into the bathroom. When she was finished with her morning routine, she dressed quickly in a pair of khaki walking shorts and a white linen shirt.

In the living room, she saw the relics of last night's blowout—three glasses, each with at least an inch of slime-green liquid in the bottom; an ashtray filled with the cigarettes Caroline had furtively smoked; a pile of discarded record albums.

For the first time this summer, the house looked lived in. This was a mess made by Nora and her daughters, and she'd waited a lifetime to see it.

She put a pot of coffee on, then limped upstairs. The bedroom door was closed. She pushed it open. Caroline and Ruby were still sleeping.

In sleep, they looked young and vulnerable, and at the sight of them, she remembered her own nights in this room, nights she'd slept in this bed with her husband, more often than not with two small, warm bodies tucked in between them.

And now those babies were women full grown, sleeping together in the bed that had once held their parents. Caroline slept curled in a ball, her body pressed close to the mattress's edge. Ruby, on the other hand, lay spread-eagle, her arms and legs flung out above the bedding.

Nora walked to the bed. Slowly, she reached down and caressed Ruby's pink, sleep-lined cheek. Her skin was soft, so soft . . .

"Wake up, sleepyheads."

Ruby groaned and blinked awake, smacking her lips together as if she could still taste the last margarita. "Hi, Mom."

Caro blinked awake beside her, stretching her arms. She saw Nora and tried to sit up. Halfway there, she groaned and flopped backward. "Oh, my God, my head is swollen."

Ruby didn't look a whole lot better, but at least she could sit upright. "Obviously E.D. here should have done a little alcohol training before last night." She squeezed her eyes shut and rubbed her temples. "Do we have any aspirin?"

"Aspirin?" Caroline moaned. "That's an over-the-counter medication. I have prescription-level pain." She scooted slowly to a seated position, and slumped against Ruby. "I'm never listening to you again. Oh, shit, I'm gonna puke."

Ruby slipped an arm around her sister. "Aim at Mom. She looks way too happy this morning."

Ruby's laughter rang out, and Nora felt a sharp tug of nostalgia. *My girls,* she thought. Suddenly it seemed like only yesterday they'd begged for Disco Barbies for Christmas.

Nora clapped her hands. "Get a move on, girls. We're going sailing today with Dean and Eric—remember, Ruby? Lottie has dinner planned for us around seven."

Caroline turned green. "Sailing?" She rolled out of Ruby's arms and dropped onto the floor, landing on all fours. She crouched there a minute, breathing shallowly, then she crawled toward the bathroom. At the door, she grabbed onto the knob and hauled herself upright. She turned and gave Ruby a pained smile. "First in the shower!"

"Shit." Ruby sagged forward, buried her face in her hands. "Don't use all the hot water."

Nora smiled. "It's like old times around here."

Ruby angled a look at her, gave her a pathetically sloppy smile. "I don't remember tequila in grade school, or all of us dancing to 'Footloose,' singing at the tops of our lungs, but . . . yeah."

"'You and Me Against the World,'" Nora said, her smile fading at the suddenness of the memory. "That was our song."

"I remember."

Nora wanted to move toward her, but she remained still. Last night, Caro had come back to Nora completely, but even in the midst of their laughter-and-sob-fest, Ruby had held herself back. "Well, I'm going to start breakfast and pack us a light lunch. Dean's supposed to bring the boat around eleven." She waited for Ruby to say something, but when the silence stretched out, Nora turned and headed downstairs, thumping down each step.

She was halfway down when she heard a car drive up. A quick

glance at her watch told her it was nine-thirty. Not dawn, certainly, but pretty early for the local islanders to be visiting.

Nora tried to hurry down the stairs, but with her cast, it was difficult. She felt like Quasimodo hurrying down the bell tower.

She made it into the kitchen just as a rattling knock struck the front door. She finger-combed her hair and opened the door.

Standing on her porch was one of the best-looking young men she'd ever seen. He had the kind of beauty that made old women long for youth. Though she hadn't seen him since the wedding, she'd recognize her son-in-law anywhere.

"Hi, Jeremy," she said, smiling.

He looked surprised. "Nora?"

"I guess it's a shock to realize you have a mother-in-law." She took a step backward, motioning for him to come inside.

He smiled tiredly. "Given my other shocks in the past twenty-four hours, that's nothing."

Nora nodded, unsure of how to respond. "Caroline is upstairs. She's not feeling real well."

He looked instantly concerned. "Is something wrong? Is that why she left?"

"Tequila. That's what's wrong."

He relaxed, even grinned. "So, you met Ed."

"It wasn't a pretty sight. Can I get you a cup of coffee?"

"That would be great. I missed the final ferry last night, so I slept in my car on the dock. My body feels like it's been canned."

Nora went into the kitchen and poured him a cup of coffee. "Cream? Sugar?"

"Yeah, thanks."

She returned with the coffee, and handed him a cup.

"Thanks." He glanced toward the stairs. "Is she awake?"

The look he gave Nora was so utterly helpless that she said, "I'll get her. You wait here."

"I'm here."

Nora and Jere both spun around. Caroline stood in the living room. She was wearing the same silk and linen clothes from last night, only now they were wrinkled beyond recognition. Her hair was a tangled mess. Flecks of caked mascara turned her eyes into twin bruises. "Hi, Jere," she said softly. "I heard your voice."

Ruby came stumbling down the stairs and rammed into her sister. "Sorry, Caro, I—" She saw Jeremy and stopped. Her laughter dwindled into an uncomfortable silence.

Jere walked over to Caroline. "Care?"

The tenderness in his voice told Nora all she needed to know. There might be trouble between Caro and Jere—maybe big trouble—but underneath all that there was love, and with love, they had a chance.

"You shouldn't have come," Caro said, crossing her arms. She took a step backward, and Nora knew her daughter was afraid of getting too close to this man she loved so deeply.

"No," he said softly, "you shouldn't have left. Not without talking to me first. Can you imagine how—" His voice cracked. "—how I felt when I got your letter?"

"I thought—"

"Your *letter*, Care. All these years and you leave me a *letter* that says you'll be back when you feel like it?"

Caro looked up at him. "I thought you'd be glad I left, and I couldn't stand to see that."

"You thought." He sighed, ran a hand through his hair. "Come home," he whispered. "Mom's watching the kids for the rest of the weekend."

Caroline smiled. "She'll be bleeding from her ears before tomorrow morning."

"That's *her* problem. We need some time alone."

"Okay." Caroline turned and went upstairs. She came down a minute later with her overnight bag. She enfolded Ruby in a fierce hug, whispering something that Nora couldn't hear, and then both girls laughed.

Finally, Caroline walked across the kitchen to Nora. "Thanks," she said quietly.

"Oh, honey, I've waited a lifetime for last night."

Caroline's eyes were bright. "I won't miss you anymore."

"No way. You can't get rid of me now. I love you, Caro."

"And I love you, Mom." Nora pulled her daughter into her arms and held her tightly, then slowly released her.

Jeremy took the overnight bag from his wife, then held on to her hand. Together, they left the house.

Ruby and Nora followed them as far as the porch, watching as the gray Mercedes followed the white Range Rover out of the driveway.

"She's gone," Ruby said.

"She'll be back." Nora stared out at the beautiful blue sky and choppy green sea. It was going to be a great day for sailing; no clouds, a little breeze shivering through the trees, sunlight on the water.

Ruby sidled up to Nora, stood so close their shoulders were touching. "I'm sorry, Mom."

Nora turned. "For what?"

Ruby looked different somehow. Serious. "For all the presents I sent back and all the years I stayed away. But mostly I'm sorry for being so damned unforgiving."

Nora wasn't sure how it happened—who moved first—but suddenly they were clinging to each other, laughing and crying at the same time.

At exactly eleven, a boat horn blared. A loud *ah-oo-gah, ah-oo-gah.* The *Wind Lass* pulled up to the dock.

Ruby glanced down at the water, watching Dean tie the boat down. "They're here." There was a strand of worry in her voice.

Nora understood. "Are you afraid to see Dean?"

Ruby nodded.

Nora laid a hand against Ruby's cheek. "You could travel the world and you wouldn't find a better man than Dean Sloan."

"He's not the problem. I am."

"Your whole life has been tangled up with Dean. When someone pinched him, you got a welt in the same place. He's a part of you, Ruby, like it or not. Being afraid of him is like being afraid of your own arm. Just let go. Have fun. Let yourself remember the good times, not only the bad."

Ruby looked up at her. "I want that, Mom. I want it so much . . ."

The sailboat honked its horn again.

"Grab the picnic basket," Nora said, pointing to the pile of supplies on the kitchen table.

Within minutes, they were headed down the path to the beach. Nora moved as fast as her crutches would allow.

The sailboat was tied down. Dean was on the bow, holding the two ropes that held the boat against the dock. "Welcome aboard."

Nora handed her crutches to Ruby and stepped carefully onto the boat, trying to ensure that her cast didn't leave a mark on the teak decking. When her balance was steady, she took her crutches and tossed them onto the settee belowdecks. Limping awkwardly, she sidled around the giant silver wheel and sat down beside Eric. A pillow rested behind his stocking-capped head and a thick woolen Navajo blanket covered his body. Although he was smiling, he looked terribly pale and weak. The shadows were purple beneath his eyes. His lips were chapped and colorless.

Nora was shocked by his appearance. He looked so much worse than the last time she'd seen him. It wasn't Eric; this gaunt, too-fragile man was a whittled-down version of him, perhaps, but when she looked into his huge, sad eyes, she saw the spirit that cancer couldn't touch. With exquisite gentleness, she curled an arm around him and drew him close.

He rested his head against her shoulder, shivering a little. "You feel good," he murmured.

Dean started the engine. Ruby untied the boat and jumped aboard; they motored out of the bay, and when they passed the tip of the island, Dean rigged up the mainsail.

The boat immediately heeled starboard and caught a gust of wind, slicing through the water.

Eric pressed his face into the wind, smiling brightly.

Nora tilted her head against his and stared out at the lush, green islands. Ruby was up on the bow of the boat, standing in the wind. Nora didn't have to see her daughter's face to know that she was grinning.

Dean hurried belowdecks. When he came back up, Robert Palmer's "Addicted to Love" blared through the speakers.

On the bow, Ruby moved her hips to the beat. Nora imagined that she was singing—off key—at the top of her lungs.

There was a pause between songs, and the silence seemed endless and perfect, a moment trapped in a time that was somehow both then and now: Dean at the wheel, Eric and Nora sitting on the aft deck, Ruby poised at the bow, always eager to see where they were going.

Nora felt the hot sun on her cheeks and heard the loose flapping of the ties against the mast.

"I'm glad you're here," Eric said.

She smiled at him. "Where else could I be? You and Dean and Ruby . . . you're the best parts of my life. I'll always remember my dark-haired boy. Every time I turned around, you were there, grinning up at me, saying, 'What are we gonna do next, Miz Bridge?' It seems like only yesterday you were sitting at my kitchen table with your banged-up elbows on the pink placemat. God, the time goes so fast . . ."

"Too fast." Eric's gaze was steady.

Nora's throat closed up, but she refused to let him see her cry. Gently, she touched his face.

Eric turned away; she could tell that he was collecting himself again, distancing himself from the truth they'd dared to touch upon.

He looked at Ruby, standing on the bow, then at Dean. They were the full boat-length apart, each trying not to get caught staring at the other. "You think they'll figure it out?"

"I hope so. They need each other."

"Take care of him for me," Eric said in a throaty voice, wiping his eyes with the edge of the blanket. "I thought I'd always be there for him . . . my baby brother."

"You will be."

Eric laughed and wiped his eyes. "God, we're out sailing and we look like we just watched *Brian's Song.*"

Nora laughed and wiped her eyes.

A swift breeze rose suddenly, filling the canvas sail with a *tharump-ing* noise. The boat keeled over and cut through the sunlit, glistening water.

Dean looked down at his brother. "Do you want to take the wheel?"

Eric's face lit up. "Oh, yeah."

Dean slipped an arm around his brother's frail body and helped him hobble toward the big, silver wheel. Eric took hold; Dean stood behind and beside him, resting a hand on his brother's shoulder, to keep him steady.

Wind-tears streaked across Eric's temples, his thinning hair flapped against the sides of his face, his T-shirt billowed against his sunken chest.

"Orcas!" Ruby said suddenly, pointing starboard.

At first, Nora didn't see anything. She stood up and tented a hand across her eyes.

She saw the first black fin rise slowly, slowly from the water. Then there were six of them—black fins moving through the sea like the upended teeth of a comb, impossibly close together.

"I'm the queen of the world!" Eric yelled, flinging his arms out. He laughed out loud, and for the first time in weeks, it was *his* laughter, not the weak, watered-down version that cancer had left him with.

Nora knew that when she looked back on Eric's life, and the ugliness of the past few weeks and months seemed overwhelming, she would picture him now. Standing tall, squinting into the sun, laughing.

And she would remember her boy. Her Eric.

Chapter Twenty-three

It was early evening by the time they got back to the house. Lottie served them a delicious dinner of Dungeness crabs, Caesar salad, and French bread. She'd laughed as she set the meal on the table, saying that she hadn't figured too much had changed over the years—the Sloans and the Bridges loved crab, but were too softhearted to boil one.

Even though they'd eaten a big lunch on the boat, they'd descended on dinner like *Survivor* contestants. Eric had even managed to eat a few tender, buttery bites.

While "the girls" washed and dried the dishes, Dean had carried Eric up to bed. Finally, Nora and Ruby went upstairs, and they all stood around Eric's bed, talking softly until he fell asleep.

Now, the three of them were back on the *Wind Lass*, headed for Summer Island. The trip, being undertaken at night, without radar, took twice the usual amount of time. And still Ruby hadn't found the courage to hand Dean her heart.

All day she'd waited for The Moment, the one when she could turn to him and touch his arm and say she wasn't afraid anymore. But every time she'd started for him, she'd seized up. The shale of old habits collected beneath her feet and made it dangerous to move.

There had always been a roadblock between them, something Ruby couldn't climb over—a crowd of people (okay, so Eric and Mom weren't *really* a crowd, but when you were eating crow, one extraneous witness was too many), a set of chores, a whooshing wind.

So Ruby had waited. And waited.

She was still waiting when the *Wind Lass* glided up to the Bridges'
dock.

"Get the lines, Ruby," Dean yelled.

She grabbed the lines and jumped onto the dock, tying the boat
down. She was still figure-eighting the line around the midship cleat
when she saw her mother step down onto the dock.

"Thanks, Dean," she heard her mother say. She felt, rather than
saw, Mom turn toward her. "Ruby? Honey, I'll need some help up
to the house. The bank is slippery."

Ruby shot a glance to the boat; it was all shadows up close, strips
of white and gray that bobbed up and down. She couldn't see a flash
of Dean's blond hair. He was probably down below. What if he left
before she could get back?

"Ruby?"

She dropped the excess coil of line and headed toward her
mother. Mom turned and waved. "Bye, Dean. Thanks for a
great day."

And there he was, standing beside the wheel. She could make out
his golden hair and yellow sweater, and even a flash of white teeth as
he smiled, but that was all. "Bye," he said in a subdued voice.

"Uh . . . If you need help leaving—you know, untying or something—I could come right back down," Ruby said.

There was a moment's pause before he answered. She wished she
could see his face. "I can always use help."

Ruby felt a rush of relief. She tightened her hold on her mother's
shoulders, and together they walked up the slightly angled bank and
across the lawn.

At the front door, Mom smiled. "Go ahead. And Ruby?"

Ruby reached down for the afghan on the rocker and slung it
around her shoulders. It was getting chilly out here. "Yeah?"

"He loves you."

"That would be a miracle. I've done everything but stab him in
the eye."

Mom grinned. "All love is a miracle. Now, go to him. Don't be afraid. And try not to be your usual obnoxious self."

Ruby couldn't help laughing. "Thanks, Mom."

As she hurried across the yard, a cloud scudded across the sky and revealed a nearly full moon. It lit up the sky, tinged the world in eerie blue.

At the edge of the bank, Ruby paused, tightening the blanket around her shoulders. She knew what she needed to do, but knowing didn't grant her courage. She was afraid that she'd taken too long to grow up and had lost her chance.

He was standing at the end of the dock, with his back to her. She moved soundlessly down the bank and stepped onto the dock. Her footsteps were indistinguishable from the ordinary creaks and moans of old wood. "I remember when we used to jump off of that dock at high tide," she said softly. "Only Washington kids would swim in that water."

He spun around.

Ruby moved toward him.

She was afraid suddenly to speak. She wanted to simply put her arms around him and kiss him until she couldn't think, couldn't move, couldn't remember everything that was between them. But she couldn't do it. For once, she had to do the right thing. She owed Dean a few words—small, simple words—and she couldn't be too cowardly to speak.

She couldn't turn back now.

The silence between them felt loaded, dangerous. In it, she heard the slap of the waves on the pilings below.

She closed the last, small space between them and took hold of his left hand, caressing his fingers. Then, slowly, she drew her hand away. "I remember the first time you kissed me. I got so dizzy, I couldn't breathe. I was glad we were sitting down, because I would have fallen. But I fell anyway, didn't I? I fell in love with my best friend. When most kids were planning how to sneak out of their parents' house on a Saturday night, you and I were dreaming about our wedding . . . the children we would have." She swallowed hard and smiled. "When we were fifteen, you said we'd live in a penthouse on Central Park . . . that we'd honeymoon in Paris. When we were seven, you promised that someday we'd own a boat as big as a ferry, with a bathtub in the master stateroom, and that Elvis would sing at our wedding." She gave him a smile. "The dreams of children playing at adulthood. We should have known we were in trouble when Elvis died."

Dean closed his eyes for a moment, only that, and she wondered if it hurt him to hear the old dreams. "Yeah," he said woodenly, "we were young."

"I tried to forget those things we said, but mostly, I tried to forget how it felt when you kissed me," she said. "I kept telling myself it was a crush . . . that I'd grow up and go on and feel that way again. But I didn't." She heard the rawness in her voice, the desperate tenor of hope, and she knew he heard it, too. She was exposed now, vulnerable.

"You never fell in love again?"

"How could I . . . when I never fell out of love the first time?"

"Say it."

She stepped closer and tilted her face up to his. "I love you, Dean Sloan."

He didn't respond for a heartbeat, just stared down at her. Then he pulled her into his arms and kissed her the way she'd always dreamed of being kissed. And suddenly she wanted more. More . . .

She fumbled with his T-shirt, shoved it over his head, and let her fingers explore the coarse, wiry hair on his chest. She touched him everywhere, moved her hands across the hardness of his shoulders, down the small of his back, down into his underwear.

He yanked the afghan down, letting it puddle on the dock around their feet. With a groan, he slipped his hands beneath her shirt, scooping it off her, and tossed it away. She kicked it aside and grappled with the buttons on her cutoffs.

Naked, kissing, groping, they knelt on the blanket, smoothed it out, then collapsed on top of it, laughing at the awkwardness of their movements.

Ruby heard the hiss of paper ripping. She blinked, feeling drugged by the intensity of her desire, and saw that he was opening a small foil packet.

It stunned her. "You *planned* this?"

He gave her a crooked, boyish grin. "Let's just say I prayed for it."

And he was laughing again, kissing her, and she couldn't think. Her body was on fire. His hands were everywhere—her breasts, her nipples, between her legs—stroking, rubbing, pulling. His mouth followed the path of his magical fingers, and when he leaned over her and took a nipple in his searching mouth, she gave in to sex in a way she never had before. She relinquished control over her body and let him bring her to the throbbing, desperate edge of pain. Finally, she couldn't stand it anymore; her whole body was aching, needing . . .

"Please," she moaned beneath his touch, "now . . ."

He flipped onto his back and pulled her on top of him, entering her with a thrust. His hands were on her bottom, holding her against his grinding hips, teaching her to match his movements.

She threw her head back and closed her eyes.

He arched forward, capturing her nipple in his mouth, and she cried out. Her release was so intense it felt as if she were breaking apart. "Oh, God," she said, breathing heavily, feeling his own climax inside her.

She collapsed on top of him, buried her face in his sweaty chest.

He held on to her tightly, as if he expected her to pull away, and stroked her damp back.

"Oh, my God," she whispered, finally rolling off of him. She remained tucked against him, one leg thrown across his thighs.

"We should have done that a long time ago."

"Believe me, it wouldn't have been as good." She sighed, flopping back, staring up at the moonlit sky.

So simple. It had always been like this between them. Just a touch, a gentle brushing of his skin against hers, and she'd known a kind of peace that could be found nowhere else. She rolled onto her side and stared down at him. "Let's live together."

He gave her a strange look. "In Hollyweird?"

"God, no." It was an instinctive answer. She hadn't even thought about it, but as she heard her voice, she knew it was true. She didn't want to live there anymore. "I could live in San Francisco."

He laughed. "No, thanks." He reached up, touched her hair. "We've had those lives, Ruby. I don't know about you, but I don't want to go back to anything that came before. I want to start over. And I'm *not* going to live with you."

"Oh." She tried to sound casual, as if he hadn't just stomped on her heart.

"We're getting married, Ruby Elizabeth. No more excuses or running away or lost time. We are *going* to get married. My vote is that we move back here and try like hell to find out what we want to do with the rest of our lives. I'm going to give photography a try; it's what I've always wanted to do. Most importantly, we're going to promise to grow old together. And we're going to do it. We'll sit on our own porch until we're blind and hairless and I can't remember what the hell my own name is. And the last thing you're going to feel in this world is me kissing you good night."

"We'll have children," she said, dreaming of it for the very first time.

"At least two, so they'll each have a best friend."

"And our son. We'll name him Eric . . ."

Ruby would have slept on the dock all night, wrapped in Dean's arms and that old blanket, but he'd wanted to get back to Eric, and so they'd kissed—and kissed and kissed—good-bye.

Then she helped Dean untie the boat and walked up to the top of the bank to watch him leave. Moonlight shimmered on all the white surfaces of the boat, turned everything silvery blue. He started the engine; the boat pulled away from the dock. The *chug-chug-chug* of the motor broke the silence of the night.

Moment by moment, he lost coloring. It started with the tip of the mast; it turned black suddenly, then the rest of the boat followed. In the last slice of moonlight, a dark hand lifted, raised, waved good-bye. Though Dean couldn't see her, he knew somehow that Ruby was still there, watching him leave.

It was what she'd always done.

She stood there until the boat disappeared into the choppy silver-tipped sea, then turned and went to the house.

The kitchen light was on, and Mom's bedroom door was closed.

Ruby walked—okay, skipped—over to the closed door. There was no doubt in her mind that her mother would want to be wakened. After all, it wasn't every day your daughter got engaged.

She was just about to knock when the phone rang.

She ran for the kitchen and answered the phone on the second ring, hoping it wasn't about Eric. "Hello?"

"Ruby—where in the goddamn hell have you been? I've been calling all night. And what kind of podunk, backwater, double-wide house doesn't have an answering machine?"

Ruby immediately relaxed. "Val?" She glanced at the clock. It was one in the morning. "Can we have this discussion in the morning? I—"

His voice was muffled. "Yeah, another Stoly martini, babe . . . three olives. Sorry, Ruby. Anyway, what is this *shit* about you not turning in the article? Tell me Maudeen wasn't listening well."

"Oh, that. I'm not going to deliver, that's all."

"That's all. That's *all*? Look comedy princess, this isn't some low-rent vanity-press publisher we're talking about. This is *Caché* magazine. They've reserved the space in the issue, printed the cover—with *your* picture on it, I might add—and leaked the story." He paused; she heard the exhalation of smoke into the receiver.

"And I've gotten some interest in you from the networks; NBC wants to talk to you about writing a pilot."

"A . . . pilot? My own sitcom?" Ruby felt sick. That had always been a pie-in-the-sky dream of hers. Every comedian dreamed about her own show.

"Yeah, your own sitcom. So, no dicking around. You're supposed to deliver the article tomorrow. I FedExed your plane tickets yesterday. They're probably on your front door now. You're scheduled for *Sarah Purcell* on Monday morning."

"I can't do it, Val." Ruby closed her eyes. In that minute, she could *feel* the warm imprint of her mother's hand on her head, the gentleness of that touch. Panic rushed through her.

Val drew in a deep breath, then exhaled slowly. "Christ. I knew you were a pain in the ass, but I promised them you were professional. I gave them my word, Ruby."

"I am a professional." Even to her own ears, her voice sounded small. Afraid.

"Professionals don't take money from national magazines and then break the contract. Can you pay them back?"

Ruby flinched, thinking of the Porsche in her parking spot, the designer dress in her closet, the money she gave her dad. "If they'll give me some time—" *Like, twenty years.*

"It doesn't work that way. The only chance of getting out of this deal is to pay them back, and even then they have to agree. And baby doll, they won't."

"You mean they can *force* me—"

Val laughed. "Where have you been living . . . Potatoville, USA? This is big business. You can't just change your mind. Is it written?"

She hated the weakness that made her answer. "Yes."

"And the problem is . . ."

Ruby felt like crying. "I like her." She swallowed thickly. "No. I love her."

Val was quiet for a moment, then he said, "I'm sorry, Ruby."

His concern was harder to take than the yelling. "I am, too," she answered dully.

"You'll be on the plane then, right? I'll have Bertram pick you up."

Ruby hung up the phone in a daze. She wandered out onto the porch, found the FedEx envelope. Inside, there was a first-class ticket and a short itinerary. They were taking her to Spago to celebrate after the taping of *Sarah Purcell* . . .

A week ago that would have thrilled her.

She walked dully past her mother's door. At the last minute, she stopped, pressed her fingertips to the wood.

"I'm sorry," Ruby breathed. But she knew those two little words wouldn't be enough. Not nearly enough.

With a sigh, she turned and went upstairs. She flopped onto the bed and tried to sleep, but she couldn't keep her eyes closed. At last, she flicked on the light and reached for her pad of paper.

I just got off the phone with my agent.

The joke is on me, it seems. I can't get out of this deal. I have to deliver the article as promised or some corporate Mr. Big will sue me until I bleed.

And I will lose my mother, this woman whom I've waited and longed for all of my life, whom I've alternately deified and vilified. Whatever we could have become will be gone. And this time it will be all my fault. The whole world will see the bankruptcy of my soul.

I finally learned that life is not made up of BIG moments and sudden epiphanies, but rather of tiny bits of time, some so small they pass by unnoticed.

All this I can see now . . . and it is too late.

Monday, I will appear on The Sarah Purcell Show, *and after that, what I see will matter only to me. My mother won't care.*

But I want to say this—for the record, although I'm aware it comes too late and at too great a price—I love my mother.

I love my mother.

Ruby released her hold on the pen. It rolled away from her, plopped over the edge of the bed and onto the floor, where it landed with a little click.

It was too much, all of this, and on the day she'd finally believed in a happy-ever-after future for herself. She couldn't write anymore, couldn't think.

"I love you, Mom," she whispered, staring up at the spidery crack in the ceiling.

Chapter Twenty-four

Nora sat at the kitchen table, reading a fifteen-year-old newspaper that she'd found in the broom closet and sipping a cup of lukewarm coffee. The front-page story was an outraged report that Washington State officials had set off underwater firecrackers to scare away sea lions at the Ballard Locks. The sea lions were eating the salmon and the steelhead. Beside that story was a smaller column—complete with photograph. President Reagan's dog had received a tonsillectomy.

Mostly, she was waiting for Ruby to come downstairs. Nora had tried to wait up for her daughter the previous night, but at about twelve-thirty, she'd given up. It had to be a good sign that Ruby hadn't come home early.

At least, that's what Nora told herself.

She was about to turn the page when the phone rang. Ignoring the crutches leaning against the wall, she hobbled to the counter and answered. "Hello?"

"It's me. Dee."

Nora sagged against the cold, pebbled surface of the refrigerator. "Hi, Dee. What excellent news do you have for me today?"

"You're not going to like it."

"That's hardly surprising."

"I just got off the phone with Tom Adams. He called me at *home.* On *Sunday,* to tell me to tell you that if you didn't get those blankety-blank columns on his blankety-blank desk by Wednesday morning, he was going to slap a ten-million-dollar lawsuit on you. He said the paperwork was already done on it, he was just giving you a last chance." She made a little coughing sound. "He said he was going to sue everybody you'd ever worked with—including me."

"He can't do that," Nora said, though, of course, she had no idea whether or not he could.

"Are you sure?" Dee sounded scared.

"I'll talk to Tom myself," Nora answered, before Dee could really get going.

"Oh, thank God."

"What else is going on there? Is the brouhaha dying down?"

"No," and to her credit, Dee sounded miserable about it. "Your housekeeper went on *Larry King Live* last night and said . . . terrible things about you."

"*Adele* said bad things about me?"

"A woman named Barb Heinneman said you'd commissioned an expensive stained-glass window from her and never paid for it. And your hair lady—Carla—she said you were a lousy tipper."

"Oh, for God's sake, what does that have—"

"The *Tattler* reported that guy in the pictures wasn't your first . . . affair. They're saying that you and your husband had an 'open' marriage and you both slept with tons of other people. And sometimes . . ." Dee's voice dropped to a conspiratorial whisper. "You did it in groups. Like in that movie, *Eyes Wide Shut*. That's what they wrote, anyway."

Nora's head was spinning. Honest to God, a part of her felt like laughing, it was that ridiculous. *Eyes Wide Shut? Group sex?* For the first time since this whole mess began, she started to get mad. She'd made mistakes—big ones, bad ones—but this . . .

This, she didn't deserve. As she'd heard in a movie once—this shit she wouldn't eat. They were trying to make her out to be some kind of whore. "Is that it? Or am I carrying some space alien's mutant child, too?"

Dee laughed nervously. "That's mostly it. Except . . ."

"Yes?" Nora drew the word out, gave it at least three syllables.

"There was a thing in Liz Smith's column this week, one of those gossipy hints she loves to make—you know the ones. It sorta made it sound as if someone was writing a tell-all story about you. An ugly one."

"That's hardly—"

"It's supposed to be by someone close to you."

Nora released her breath in a sigh. She wasn't surprised; she'd expected this, and yet still it hurt. "I see."

"And your housekeeper said you ripped up parking tickets and threw away jury summonses. Some guy on the city council said they were going to launch an investigation."

That was it. "Good-bye, Dee," Nora said, uncertain as to whether her assistant was still talking or not. She hung up the phone and wrenched the cupboard doors open.

There they were: the cheap, yellow crockery plates she'd bought at a garage sale a lifetime ago. She picked one up, felt the heft of it in her hand. And hesitated. There was no point in making a mess—

Launch an investigation.

She wound her arm back and threw the plate. It went flying through the air and smacked the wall by the arch, shattering.

Like Eyes Wide Shut *. . . group sex.*

She threw another one. It hit with a satisfying smack.

Open marriage . . . lousy tipper.

Another plate flew.

There were bits and pieces of china everywhere now; dents in the walls, scratches in the paint. Nora was breathing heavily. And smiling.

She should have tried this years ago. It actually helped. She reached for another plate.

Ten-million-dollar lawsuit.

And sent it sailing across the room.

Just then, Ruby came running downstairs. "What in the he—" She ducked, flung a protective hand across her face. The plate brushed past her head and hit the wall. When the pieces clattered to the floor, she hesitantly looked up. "Jesus, Mom . . . if you don't like the plates, buy a new set."

Nora sank to her knees on the hard, cold floor. She laughed until tears leaked out of her eyes . . . and then she was crying.

She buried her face in her hands, ashamed to let her daughter see her like this, but she couldn't seem to stop . . .

It was too much for her suddenly, all of it—Eric's illness, her career, her ruined reputation.

She felt lonely, and old. A woman who'd traded everything in her life for a treasured gold coin, and found that in a heavy rain, the gold had washed off, leaving an ordinary bit of copper in her hand.

She looked up at Ruby, saw her daughter through a blurry curtain of tears.

"Mom?" Ruby knelt in front of her. "Are you okay?"

"Do I look okay?"

"In that Courtney Love, presurgery, after-concert sort of way." She reached out, pushed a damp strand of hair out of Nora's eyes. "What happened?"

"A lady is suing me for fraudulent advice. And someone close to me—apparently a friend—is writing an ugly tell-all about my life. Oh, and don't be surprised when you hear that your dad and I engaged in group sex." She tried to smile; it was a dismal failure. "But don't you worry, I can get through this. I've been through worse. It's just a midlife tantrum. The only thing that matters is how much I love you."

Ruby jerked back, let her hand drop into her lap. "Oh, man . . ." she whispered.

Nora climbed awkwardly to her feet and hobbled to the kitchen table. She slumped onto a chair, plopped her casted foot on another one.

It occurred to her then, as she watched her daughter, who still knelt on the floor with her head bowed, that there was no silence

more cruel and empty than the one that followed that simple decla-
ration: "I love you."

She'd spent a childhood waiting to hear those words from her
father, then an eternity waiting to hear them from her husband.

Now, it seemed, she was destined to wait again. And she'd thought
things were going so well with Ruby . . .

"Would you like some coffee?" she said, pushing the newspaper
aside. Her voice was calm and even, as if it were completely ordinary
for them to be here together, amid a smattering of broken yellow
china.

Ruby looked up at her. "Don't."

Nora saw that her daughter was crying; it confused her. "What is
it, Rube?"

"Don't pretend you didn't say it. Please."

Nora had no idea how to respond. Ruby got up, turned, and went
upstairs.

Nora heard each footfall on the steps. She couldn't seem to draw a
steady breath. *What in the world just happened?*

Then she heard the steps again; Ruby was coming back downstairs. She walked into the kitchen, carrying a suitcase in one hand
and a tablet of paper in the other.

Nora's hand flew to her mouth. "I'm sorry. I thought we'd gotten
to the point where I could say that to you."

Ruby dropped the suitcase. It landed with a *thunk* that shook the
thin windowpanes.

"Ruby, honey . . ." The endearment slipped out on a current of
longing and regret.

"It was never about forgetting or forgiving," Ruby said slowly.
Tears welled in her dark eyes, bled down her cheeks. "It took me so
long to figure that out. And now it's too late."

Nora frowned. "I don't understand—"

"I love you."

Ruby's voice was so soft Nora thought at first she'd imagined the words, drawn them up from her own subconscious and given them the substance of sound.

"You love me?" Nora dared to whisper.

Ruby stood there, a little unsteady. "Just try . . . to remember that, okay?"

"How could I possibly—"

Ruby slapped a yellow pad of paper on the kitchen table. "I spent all of last night making you a copy of this."

Nora barely glanced at it; she was too busy watching Ruby. "What is it?"

Ruby backed up, stepped alongside her suitcase. "Read it," she said dully.

With a little shrug, Nora pulled the table close. "I might need my glasses . . ." She peered down at the paper, squinting.

In the interest of full disclosure, I must tell you that I was paid to write this article. Paid handsomely, as they say in the kind of restaurants where a person like me can't afford to order a dinner salad. Enough so that I could trade in my beat-up Volkswagen Bug for a slightly less beat-up Porsche.

I should also tell you that I dislike my mother. No, that's not true. I dislike the snotty salesclerk who works the night shift at my local video store.

I hate my mother.

Nora looked up sharply.

Ruby was crying now, so hard her cheeks were bright pink and her shoulders were trembling. "It's an article for *C-Caché* magazine."

Nora drew in a sharp, gasping breath. She knew it was all in her eyes—the stinging betrayal, the aching sadness . . . and yes, the anger. "How could you?"

Ruby clamped a hand over her mouth, grabbed the suitcase, and ran out of the house.

As if from a great, unbreachable distance, Nora heard the car start up and speed away, sputtering through loose gravel.

It was quiet once more.

Nora tried not to look at the yellow pages, with their scrawled blue words marching across the even lines, but she couldn't help herself. Those horrible, hateful words leapt out at her.

I hate my mother.

She took a deep, deep breath, then looked down again. Her hands were shaking as she lifted the pad and began to read.

The story of us starts a dozen years ago, in a place few of you have ever seen: the San Juan Islands up in Washington State.

It was only a few sentences later that Nora began to cry.

Ruby made it all the way to the end of the driveway, then she slammed on the brakes.

She was running away again, but there was nowhere to hide on this one, no way past except through. She'd done a terrible, selfish thing, and she owed more to her mother than an empty house.

She put the minivan in reverse and backed down the driveway. Parking, she walked down the path, through the fragrant garden, and out to the edge of the bank. She would have gone to sit on her favorite rock, but her mother couldn't get there on crutches.

She *wanted* to be seen. When Mom finished the article, she would undoubtedly head for the porch; it was her favorite place. Then she would see her daughter, sitting out on the edge of the property.

She sat down on the grass. It was a beautiful summer's day. The islands were an endless mosaic of color—blue, blue sky, green forested land, silver, choppy sea.

She lay back on the grass and closed her eyes. The air smelled sweetly of grass and salt, of her childhood.

She knew she would remember this day for the rest of her life, and probably at the oddest times—when she was elbow-deep in sudsy water, washing the dinner dishes. In the shower, with the sweet, citrusy scent of her mother's favorite shampoo all around her, or holding the babies she prayed someday to have. At times like that, she would remember this moment, and all the others that had led up to it. In a very real way, this would be the beginning of her adult life; everything that grew afterward would be planted in the soil of what she and her mother said to each other right here.

She wondered if she would ever get over her shame, or if she would carry it with her always, the way she'd once been weighed down by anger.

Now Ruby would be the one sending gifts across the miles, leaving phone messages on machines, waiting, forever waiting, for an answer . . .

"Hey, Rube."

Ruby opened her eyes and saw her mother standing beside her. She was leaning awkwardly forward on her crutches. The sun haloed her auburn hair in brightness.

Ruby jackknifed up. "Mom," she whispered, finding that her throat was too tight to say anything more.

"I'm glad you came back. You can't get away from me so easily on an island, I guess."

Mom tossed the crutches aside and knelt slowly onto the grass, then sort of fell sideways into a sitting position. She set the article on her lap and stared down at it. The curled edges fluttered in the soft breeze. "I read every word you wrote about me, and I have to admit, it broke my heart."

Ruby wanted to curl up and die. She considered how far they'd come, she and her mom, the winding, shaded road that had taken them from then to now, and she ached for what her selfishness had wrought. If not for the article, Ruby would be laughing right now, telling her mother about the night before. Maybe they would have talked about ridiculous, girly things like wedding rings and brides-maids and flower arrangements.

"I'm so ashamed," she said. "I knew those words would hurt you. In the beginning, that's what I wanted to do."

"And now?"

"I would give anything to take it all back."

Nora smiled sadly. "The truth always hurts, Ruby. It's a law of nature, like gravity." She glanced out at the Sound. "When I read your article, I saw myself. That doesn't seem like much, but I've spent a lifetime running away from who I am and where I came from. I never trusted anyone enough to be myself. When I started my advice column, I knew people wouldn't like *me,* so I made up Nora Bridge, a woman they could trust and admire, and then I tried to live up to that creation. But how could I? The mistakes I'd made—the woman I really was—kept me on the outside all the time, looking in at my own life." She looked at Ruby again. "But I trusted you."

Ruby squeezed her eyes shut. "I know."

"I was right to trust you, Ruby. I knew it when I finished reading. You listened and you wrote, and when it was over, you'd revealed *me.* From the girl who hid under the stairs, to the woman who hid behind the metal bars of a mental institution, to the woman who hid behind a microphone." She smiled. "To this woman, who isn't hiding now. You made me see *me.*"

"I know I gave away all your secrets, but I'm not going to publish the article. I won't do that to you."

"Oh, yes you are."

Ruby wasn't surprised that her mother didn't believe her. "I'm making you a promise. I won't deliver it."

Nora leaned forward, took Ruby's hands in hers, and held them tightly. "I *want* you to publish this article. It's a beautiful, powerful portrait of who we are, and it shows who we can be, both of us. It shows how love can go wrong, and how it can find its way back to the beginning if you believe in it. What you wrote . . . it isn't a betrayal, Ruby. Maybe it started out that way, but why shouldn't it have? We had a long, long road to walk. And at the end of it, what I saw was how much you love me."

Ruby swallowed hard. "I do love you, Mom. And I'm so sor—"

"Sshh, no more of that. We're family. We're going to trample all over each other's feelings now and again. That's the way it's supposed to be." Nora's eyes were bright with unshed tears. "And now, we're going to go inside and call your agent. I'm appearing on *Sarah Purcell* with you."

"No way. They'll eat you alive."

"Let 'em. I'll be holding my daughter's hand for strength. They can't hurt me any more, Ruby. And I'm itching to fight back."

Ruby stared at her mother in awe. She was doing it again, changing before Ruby's eyes. She had a sudden glimpse of yet another woman altogether. "You're amazing."

Nora laughed. "It took you long enough to notice."

Chapter Twenty-five

I had my fifteen minutes of fame, and amazingly, when the clock struck the quarter hour, I was still famous. My mother and I had become, it seems, symbols that the world wasn't on such a fast and ugly track, after all. It makes sense, when you think about it. We live in a time when the evening news is laden with one depressing story after another.

Sadly, none of it surprises us anymore. We sit in our living rooms, on our plush sofas that a decade's affluence has allowed us to purchase, and we shake our heads at the stories. Sometimes—boldly—we turn off the news or change the channel. What we rarely do is ask why. Who has declared that murder is more newsworthy than the heartwarming story of an elderly woman who delivers Meals-on-Wheels to local AIDS sufferers?

But, as Dennis Miller says, I'm off on a rant. It's just that I have seen firsthand that celebrity is not the utopia I'd imagined, and it has made me question my interpretations of the world around me. Famous people have more money . . . and less freedom; they have more choices . . . and less honesty. Everything is a trade-off. And when we let the media choose our heroes for us, we are lost already.

What Mom and I discovered was that we are not as isolated—any of us—as we believe. People want good news as well as bad, and they loved the story of my redemption. Girl hates mother . . . girl learns to love mother . . . girl gives up career to keep from breaking her mother's heart.

People loved it. They loved me.

But most of all, they loved my mother. They heard the story of her whole life, laid out before them like a novel, and they cheered at what she had overcome. She became something more than a celebrity . . . she became one of them. An ordinary woman, and surprisingly, it made her more famous and more beloved.

I listen to her on the radio now, and I hear the responses. Every now and then she gets an angry caller, who labels her a hypocrite and a loser for abandoning her children.

The old Nora Bridge, I think, would have fallen apart at such a personal and accurate attack. No more. Now, she listens and agrees, and then goes on, talking about the gift of mistakes and the miracle of family. She hopes that people will learn from her bad choices. And she wraps that spell around them, the one only she can spin, and by the end of the show, her listeners are reaching for tissues and thinking about how to find their way back to their own families. The smart ones are reaching for the telephone.

There's no substitute for talking to the people you love. Thinking about them, dreaming about them, wishing things were different . . . all of these are the beginning. But someone has to make the first move.

I guess that's one of the things I learned this summer, but it's not the most important; it's not the thing I will hold close and pass on to my own daughter when the time is right. The truths I gathered on Summer Island were so easy; they were lying right there on the grass. I should have tripped over them. I would have, if only I'd opened my eyes.

As mothers and daughters, we are connected with one another. My mother is in the bones of my spine, keeping me straight and true. She is in my blood, making sure it runs rich and strong. She is in the beating of my heart.

I cannot now imagine a life without her.

I know how precious time is. I learned this from my friend, Eric. Sometimes, when I close my eyes, I see him as he once was, laughing, standing at the bow of his sailboat, looking forward to the rest of his life. I hear his voice in the wind, I feel his touch in the rain, and I remember . . .

Life is short. And I know that when Eric loses his battle with cancer, I will find the missing of him unbearable. I will reach for the phone then and call my mother, and her voice will bring me back to myself.

A daughter without her mother is a woman broken. It is a loss that turns to arthritis and settles deep in her bones. This I know now.

I left Los Angeles as a hard, bitter, cynical young woman with a huge chip on her shoulder. On Summer Island, I became complete. And it was all so easy. I see that now.

I went in search of my mother's life, and found my own.

"Do you think they'll be coming home soon?"

Dean didn't need to ask who Eric was talking about. In the three days since Nora and Ruby had left, he and Eric had speculated end-lessly about their return. Dean knew that Eric often forgot their conversations on the subject. Sometimes, they would end one dis-cussion and moments later Eric would ask the familiar question again. *Do you think they'll be coming home soon?*

"They'll be here any day," Dean answered. Although he always answered similarly, he wasn't so sure, and the uncertainty was killing him. It was Nora who called every night to talk to Eric; Ruby was always off somewhere, doing publicity or "taking a meeting." She'd talked to them only once, and although she'd said all the right words to Dean, he'd felt a distance blossoming between them.

She was famous now. It was what she'd always wanted, even as a little girl; she'd dreamed of being loved by strangers. He couldn't blame her for enjoying every minute of her newfound celebrity, and he couldn't help wondering if there would still be a place in her life for him.

Eric coughed.

Dean turned away from the window. For a split second, the sight of his brother shocked him. The past few days had been like that. Eric's decline had come so suddenly that sometimes, from moment to moment, Dean was caught off guard. Eric was so hollow, so shrunken; smiles were becoming rare. He seemed exhausted by the simple act of breathing, and the medications didn't stave off the pain for long.

"Can we go outside?" Eric asked. "I can see what a beautiful day it is."

"Sure." Dean ran outside and prepared everything. He set up a wooden lounge chair in the shade of an old madrona tree, placed it so that his brother could see all the way to the beach. Then he went back upstairs and bundled Eric in heavy blankets and carried him outside.

It was like carrying a small child; he weighed nothing at all.

Dean gently placed his brother on the chair. Eric settled back, sinking into the mound of pillows. He closed his eyes. "Man, that sun feels good on my face."

Dean looked at his brother, whose face was tilted up to catch the sunlight. What he saw wasn't a thin, balding young man huddled in a multicolored blanket . . . what he saw was courage, distilled to its purest essence.

"I'll be right back." He ran into the house and got his camera, loaded it with black-and-white film, and hurried back out into the yard. He started snapping pictures.

Eric's eyes fluttered open. It took him a minute to focus, a few more to comprehend the silvery box Dean was using. Finally, he gasped and held up a weak, spotted hand. "Oh, God, Dino . . . no photos. I look like shit on a lounge chair." He turned his head away.

Dean eased the camera from his eye and went to his brother, kneeling down. "Come on, you put Tom Cruise to shame."

Eric turned to him. "I used to be a fine specimen of a man," he said, smiling crookedly. "And you wait until I look like something out of *Alien* to take my picture."

Dean stroked his brother's damp forehead. He could tell that Eric was tiring already. "I missed those years, pal. I don't want to miss these. I'll need . . . pictures of you."

Eric groaned. "Shit." He brought a hand up, rubbed his eyes. "You know what I see when I look through this lens? I see a hero."

Slowly Eric opened his eyes and smiled. "I'm ready for my close-up, Mr. DeMille."

Dean finished the roll of film, then tossed the camera onto the picnic table, and lay down in the grass beside his brother.

"Do you think they'll be home soon?"

"Any day now." Dean rolled onto his side and looked up at his brother. "Ruby's famous now. Remember we saw her on *Entertainment Tonight* yesterday? It's what she always wanted."

"Yeah, well, I used to want to be an astronaut. Then I took a ride on some vomit-comet at the state fair."

"I think Ruby needed to be famous."

Eric scooted onto his side, groaning a little at the movement. He stared down at Dean. "You think *fame* is what she wanted?"

"I've seen the media up close. I dated a supermodel a few years back. It can be a pretty wild thing, everybody loving you."

"That's not love."

"Yeah," Dean said, but he didn't feel the truth of it in his bones.

"I know what love is, pal. She'll come back to you, and if she doesn't, she's too stupid to live."

Dean came up to a sit. This was the one subject they'd steered clear of, the thing Dean had never been able to ask and Eric had been too cautious to mention. But it had always been between them. At first, it had been the size of a boulder; now, it was a pebble. But always, it was there, nagging, waiting to be released. "What was it like between you and Charlie?"

Eric made a little sound of surprise. "You sure you want to go there?"

"Yeah."

A slow, heartbreakingly earnest smile transformed Eric's face, made him look almost young again. "I looked at Charlie and saw my future." He grinned. "Not that this seemed like a good thing at the time, mind you. I mean, I knew I was supposed to see my future on a body that held a uterus. I didn't want to be gay. I knew how hard it would be . . . that it would mean giving up the American Dream—kids, a house in the suburbs, my own family. It tore me up inside."

Dean had never thought about that, about what it really meant to be gay. To have to choose between who you were and who the world thought you should be. "Jesus . . . I'm sorry."

"I wanted to talk to you about it, but you were sixteen years old. And I was afraid you'd hate me. So I kept silent. Finally, what I felt for Charlie was more important than everything else. I loved him so much . . . and when he died, a huge part of me went with him. I wouldn't have made it without Nora. She was always there with me . . ." He closed his eyes. His breathing made a fluttering sound. Then suddenly he woke up, angled forward. "Where did I leave my eraser?"

Dean touched his brother's forearm. "It's on the kitchen table. I'll bring it to you."

"Oh." Eric immediately calmed down and sank back into the pillows. "Do you think they'll be here soon?"

Dean stroked Eric's forehead. "Any day now." When he heard his brother's breathing even out into sleep, Dean lay back in the grass and closed his own eyes. The hot sun felt good on his face, and if he tried really hard, he could almost pretend that this was an ordinary summer's day from long ago. That he and Eric were exhausted, sleeping on the beach after a day spent swimming in the cove . . .

He woke when a car drove up. "Hey, Lottie," he called out, waving sleepily. He didn't bother to get up. It felt so good to lie here with his eyes closed.

"Is that any way to greet your newly famous, still ringless fiancée?"

Dean's eyes snapped open. Ruby was standing beside him, arms akimbo, blocking out the sun's rays. He scrambled to his feet and swept her into his arms, giving her the kisses he'd been counting since she left.

She drew back, laughing. "Jeez, I'm going to have to make a point to leave *lots* in our marriage. Coming home is great." Taking his hand, she bent down to Eric, who was still sleeping. "Hey, Eric," she said softly.

Eric blinked up at her. "Hi Sally."

She frowned at Dean.

"He's getting pretty bad," he whispered. "Keeps forgetting where he is."

Ruby sagged against him. Dean anchored her in place with an arm around her waist. "We watched you and Nora on *The Sarah Purcell Show*. You were great."

Ruby grinned. "It was fun. In a reporters-following-you-into-the-bathroom-stall sort of way. Being famous is harsh. I turned down the sitcom offers."

"Really?"

"I took a book deal. A novel this time. I figured it was something I could do up here."

"Hey, guys!" Nora shouted, waving. She came beside them, limping on her brand-new walking cast. She touched Dean's shoulder. "How's Eric?"

Dean shook his head, mouthed *Not good*.

Eric's eyes opened again, focused. "Nora? Is that you?"

She knelt beside him. If she was shocked by how bad he looked, she showed no signs of it. "I'm here, Eric." She held his hand. "I'm here."

"I knew you'd be here any minute. Have you seen my eraser? I think Sally hid it."

"No, honey, I haven't seen it." Her voice was throaty. "But do you know what day it is?"

Eric looked at her. "Monday?"

"It's the Fourth of July."

"Are we gonna have our party?"

"Of course."

"With sparklers?" He smiled sleepily.

"You go ahead and sleep for a minute. I'll get your brother to start the barbecue."

"Dean's shitty at barbecuing. He drops everything onto the coals. You always let me cook the fish."

She stroked his forehead. "I know. Maybe you could supervise."

"Yeah." He grinned up at Dean. "Just take the meat off *before* it bursts into flames."

Nora leaned forward and kissed Eric's cheek. By the time she got to her feet, he was asleep again. When she turned around, Dean saw the moisture in her eyes. He reached for her hand, held it. The three of them stood there, holding hands in the middle of the yard for a long, long time. No one spoke.

Finally, Ruby said, "Let's get this party rolling."

Dean gave Nora a last, heartfelt look. "Thanks," he said softly. June hadn't yet rounded the bend into July, but this party was exactly what Eric needed.

While Nora and Ruby set the groceries and supplies out on the picnic table, Dean went upstairs and turned on the stereo. Music had always been a big part of their celebrations. He stuck the old-fashioned black speakers in the open window, pointing them toward the yard. Then he found the local golden-oldies station (none of them needed to be reminded now of the passing of time), and cranked the volume. For this one night, he would do his best to turn the clock back a dozen years.

As if in answer, the first song to blare through the speakers was Dire Straits' "Money for Nothing."

By the time he got back outside, Nora and Ruby had everything ready. The corn on the cob had been shucked and wrapped in tinfoil; the store-bought macaroni salad was in a pottery bowl and ready to be served; and the salmon was seasoned and layered in slices of Walla Walla Sweet onions and lemons.

The music changed. Now it was "Crazy for You" by Madonna . . .

Dean looped an arm around Ruby's shoulder and drew her close. They moved in time to the music. "God, this brings back memories."

She pulled him away from the picnic table. "Dance with me."

He took her in his arms and danced back in time. If he'd closed his eyes, he would have seen the high-school gymnasium, decorated in glitter and tinfoil and tissue paper. He would have seen Ruby, wearing an ice-blue polyester dress with braided spaghetti straps, with her long hair flowing down her back.

Only he didn't close his eyes, didn't look back. From now on, he only wanted to look ahead.

When the music changed again, to Shaun Cassidy's "Da Do Ron," Nora limped out and started dancing with them. On the lounge chair, Eric was doing his best to clap along to the song.

They spent the rest of the day laughing, it seemed. They talked, they reminisced about the old days and spun dreams about the days to come. They ate dinner off paper plates balanced on their laps. Eric even managed a few bites of salmon. And when the darkness finally came to their party, they lit up the sparklers and shot off the fireworks.

Ruby stood at the bank, with her back to the Sound, and wrote RUBY LOVES DEAN in glittering white bursts of light. Beside her, Nora wrote I LOVE MY GIRLS and SUMMER ISLAND FOREVER. They were both grinning as they waved at Dean and Eric.

Eric turned his head. When their gazes met, Dean felt a clutch of fear. His brother looked hopelessly old and tired. "I love you, baby brother."

The world spiraled down to the two of them, sitting in this darkened yard. A silence swept in, snuffing out the music and the sound of the women's laughter. The sudden quiet felt endless, dark, and dangerous.

"I love you, too, Eric."

"No funeral. I want you guys to have a party, something like this, like the old days. Then throw my ashes off the *Wind Lass.* Maybe under the bridge at Deception Pass."

Dean couldn't imagine that, standing on the boat, watching gray ashes float on the surface of the choppy green sea, thinking about a pair of blue eyes that would never look at him again . . .

Eric's breathing grew labored. He closed his eyes. "I can't find the practice roster."

"I'll get it for you."

Eric opened his eyes. He didn't seem able to focus. "Get Mom, would you? I need to talk to her."

Dean froze.

"She's here, isn't she?"

Dean nodded quickly, wiping the tears from his eyes. "Of course she's here."

Eric smiled and leaned back into the pillows. "I knew she'd come."

"I'll go get her." It seemed to take Dean an hour to cross the small patch of lawn. As he walked, the sounds came back to him—the music, the laughter, the waves on the beach. "That's What Friends Are For" was playing on the radio.

"Come on, Dino." Ruby laughed, reaching for him. "You haven't written my name yet."

Dean couldn't hold out his hand. He felt as if he were unraveling, and the slightest movement could ruin him. "He's asking for Mom."

Nora immediately covered her mouth with her hand. A small gasp escaped anyway.

Ruby dropped her sparkler. It shot sparks up from the grass, and she carefully stomped it out with her foot.

In utter silence, the three of them walked toward Eric. Dean could hear everything now, down to the crushing of the grass beneath their shoes.

Ruby was the first to kneel beside Eric. She stared down at him, and Dean could see the tears in her eyes.

Eric smiled up at her. "You're unclenched . . ."

Dean frowned at the garbled words; amazingly, Ruby seemed to understand. "I am," she said softly, leaning down to kiss his cheek.

"You take care of my brother."

"I will."

Eric sighed and closed his eyes again. Dean moved in close to Ruby, took her hand and squeezed it.

"Oh, God," she whispered, and he knew she was wondering how she would possibly get past this. How would any of them?

Eric fell asleep for a few minutes, then opened his eyes, blinking hard. "Mom?" He looked around. There was an edge of panic to his voice. "Mom?"

Dean clung to Ruby's hand. The feel of her was a lifeline, the only thing that kept him steady.

Nora lowered herself to the chair, sitting on the edge beside him. "I'm here, honey. I'm right here."

Eric stared up at her, his eyes glassy and unfocused. "Dino came home . . . to me. I knew you would, too. I knew you wouldn't stay away. Where's Dad?"

Nora stroked his forehead. "Of course I came home. I'm sorry it took me so long."

Eric let out a long, slow sigh. Then he smiled, and for a split second, his eyes were clear. "Take care of Dino for me. He's going to need you now."

Nora swallowed hard. "Your dad and I will watch over him," she said in a throaty voice.

"Thanks . . . Nora. You were always my mom." Eric smiled and closed his eyes. A moment later, he whispered *Charlie, is that you?*

And he was gone.

Epilogue

December

The chapel on Summer Island was a narrow, pitch-roofed, clapboard building set on the crest of a small rise. Even now, in the middle of a cold, gray winter, the building was cloaked in glossy green ivy. Ropey brown clematis vines framed the double doors; in a few short months, they would again produce a riot of green leaves and purple blossoms.

"I still can't believe you wouldn't let me fill the church with flowers."

Ruby laughed at her mother. They were standing in the tiny gravel parking lot adjacent to the church, waiting for the ferry to dock.

"Thank you, Martha Stewart, for that wedding-fashion update. This is exactly how we wanted it. There's only one decoration that matters to me."

"It's the dead of winter. You know there's no heat in the chapel." Nora crossed her arms. Her elegant green St. John knit suit set off the flawless ivory of her skin. There wasn't a breath of wind to upset her carefully arranged hair. Unfortunately, it was about thirty degrees out here—unusually cold for Christmas week.

To her credit, Nora tried to smile. "I wanted to plan this day for you. Make it perfect in every way."

Ruby's smile was soft and understanding. "No, Mom. You wanted to plan it for you."

"And that's my right, damn it." A quick smile tugged at her mouth. "Maybe Jenny will do it right?"

"That's a fight I'd pay to see—you and Caroline battling for control

315

over Jenny's big day. You'd probably settle on a small service at the Vatican."

Nora laughed and moved closer. "I love you, Ruby," she said softly, then, "Oh, damn, I'm crying already."

Ruby started to say something, but the ferry honked its horn.

Within minutes, three cars drove up, parked side by side. The doors opened, and the rest of the gang appeared.

Caroline, looking as cool and elegant as a water flower, was in pale ice-blue silk. Beside her, Jere brought up the kids. They all belonged in a Ralph Lauren ad.

Caroline hugged Ruby fiercely, then drew back. Her eyes were full of tears as she smiled. "My baby sister in—" She frowned. "What are you wearing?"

Ruby posed. What had once been her dress of shame had become her wedding gown. "Isn't it great?"

Caroline's narrowed gaze swept her from head to foot, noticed the plunging neckline and the ankle-to-crotch slit up the side. "You didn't find that in *Modern Bride*."

"It's Versace."

Caroline grinned. "It certainly is. You look gorgeous." Jere came up beside his wife and took her hand. "Hey, Ruby," he said, settling Freddie on his hip. "You look great."

Ruby grinned. "I could get used to this."

Then Rand was there, wearing an elegant black tuxedo. Marilyn was beside him, holding their son. Lottie was there, too, wearing her frilly "town" dress and a big straw hat. The only concession she'd made to winter was a pair of oversized black snow boots.

Rand kissed Ruby, whispering, "Heya, Hollywood, you look like a princess," before he drew back.

"Hey, Dad." Ruby looked up at Marilyn, who stood back from the crowd. Ruby gave her a bright smile. "Hi, Marilyn—it's good to have you here. How's that beautiful baby brother of mine?"

Marilyn broke into a smile and moved forward. "He's great. You look fabulous."

After that, they all started talking at once, their voices climbing over one another.

Then another car roared into the parking lot. Dean stepped out of the car and slammed the door shut. In his black Armani tux, he was so handsome that, for a moment, Ruby couldn't breathe. He walked up to her and gave her a smile so slow and seductive that she felt heat climb into her face.

Gently, he took her hands in his. "Are we ready to do this thing?"

I've been ready all my life, she wanted to answer, but her heart was so full, she could only nod.

"Then let's go."

Together, they went into the church. Inside, an aisle separated two short rows of rough-hewn benches. The altar was a plain wooden trestle table that held two thick white beeswax candles. Their flickering flames released the sweet scent of hand-dried lavender. A gold silk scarf decorated with a single red cross draped the width of the table. In the corner stood a small noble fir that sparkled with white Christmas lights.

The family found their seats and crowded in. Jere whipped out a video recorder and started filming.

Dean walked down the aisle alone and took his place at the altar.

"Are you ready?"

Ruby heard her father's voice and turned slightly. He came up beside her, offered his arm. She knew her smile was a little shaky, and that it was okay. She slipped her arm through his and let him guide her down the aisle.

At the altar, he stopped, then leaned down and kissed her cheek. "I love you, Hollywood," he whispered.

Her emotions teetered on the edge of control. It was all she could do to nod as he stepped back, leaving her standing beside Dean.

Directly in front of them, on the altar, was a big photograph, framed in ornate, gilded wood. The only decoration that mattered.

Eric.

In it, he was about fifteen years old and standing on the bow of the *Wind Lass,* half-turned back to face the camera. His smile was pure Eric.

Dean stared at the picture. He sighed, and she knew he was remembering. She slipped her hand in his and squeezed tightly, whispering, "He's here."

"I know," he answered, holding her hand tightly. "I know."

Father Magowan smiled at them. Sister Helen gave Ruby a quick wink, then waddled over to the organ and sat down.

"Dearly beloved, we are gathered here to celebrate the union of this man and this woman in holy matrimony." His rich, melodious voice filled the small chapel.

Finally, he came to "Who gives this woman to be wed?"

It was the only thing Ruby had requested of this service, that question, and when she turned around and saw her mom and dad standing together, she knew she'd done the right thing. It was a vision that would stay in her heart forever.

Rand looked down at Nora, who was weeping openly. He slipped his arm around her and drew her close. "We do," he said proudly, "her mother and I."

Caroline was crying now, too, and Ruby saw the way Jere moved closer to her, sliding his arm around her waist.

Ruby turned back to Dean, gazed up into his shining blue eyes . . . and forgot everyone else. The service kept going, words thrown into a silence broken only by the soft organ music.

". . . You may kiss the bride."

Dean stared down at her, his eyes moist. "I've waited a lifetime for this," he said softly. "I'll always love you, Ruby."

She saw it all in his eyes: her past, her present, her future. She saw tow-headed children playing in the cold, cold waters of Puget

Sound . . . and Christmas dinners with lots of chairs at the table . . . she even saw them when they were old, their hair gone white and their eyesight dimmed, and she knew she'd never forget this moment.

"That's good," she said, grinning up at him, tasting the salty moisture of her own tears. She knew she was ruining the makeover her mother had paid for, but she didn't care.

He leaned down and kissed her.

Behind them, the family clapped and cheered and laughed out loud.

Suddenly Elvis—in full beaded white jumpsuit—pushed through the doors. The King ran a hand through his pompadour, gave a sneering little half smile, and burst into song.

He was all shook up.

About the Author

Kristin Hannah lives in a small town in the Pacific Northwest with her husband and son.

FIC   Hannah, Kristin.
HAN
             Summer Island.

                        33910021916821
$21.00   03/12/2001

DATE			

001700   9766024